A KIM BRADY MYSTERY

DECEIVED BY ORNAMENT

A NOVEL BY

EDWARD J. LEAHY

Black Rose Writing | Texas

ISBN: 978-1-68433-907-5
PUBLISHED BY BLACK ROSE WRITING
www.blackrosewriting.com

Printed in the United States of America
Suggested Retail Price (SRP) $21.95

Deceived by Ornament is printed in Baskerville

*As a planet-friendly publisher, Black Rose Writing does its best to eliminate unnecessary waste to reduce paper usage and energy costs, while never compromising the reading experience. As a result, the final word count vs. page count may not meet common expectations.

PRAISE FOR

DECEIVED
BY
ORNAMENT

"A tough woman detective, a group of anti-immigrant terrorists, and the politics of policing come together for a thrilling ride in Edward J. Leahy's *Deceived by Ornament*. Unforgettable characters, all too believable situations, and unforeseen plot twists make Leahy's second novel a gripping page turner. Bravo."

–S. Lee Manning,
award-winning author of *TROJAN HORSE* and *NERVE ATTACK*

"Played out on a teeming urban canvas where New York City is its own unique character, this twisting, high-octane thriller keeps raising the stakes. Authentic, gritty, and compelling without ever losing the human touch, Edward J. Leahy is the real deal."
–Debbie Babitt, author of *SAVING GRACE.*

"With this *Detective Kim Brady series*, Edward Leahy has distinguished himself as one of the best police procedural authors in the business today."
–A.J. McCarthy, award-winning mystery suspense author

"So may the outward shows be least themselves: the world is still deceived with ornament. In law, what plea so tainted and corrupt, but, being seasoned with a gracious voice, obscures the show of evil?"
—Bassanio in *The Merchant of Venice*, Act 3, Scene 2

DECEIVED
BY
ORNAMENT

CHAPTER ONE

Friday, March 16th

On her fifteenth birthday, what should have been her *quinceañera*, Amara Delgado flushed her pills, determined to end the nightmare that had been her life for more than a year. But with nightfall, she was back on the street, seeking the right moment to run.

An elevated train thundered into the station overhead. The roar was worse now that she'd stopped taking the pills. Maybe *Papi* was wrong, and they should have stayed in Mexico. She hated this place, Brooklyn. She peered up and down Livonia Avenue, but business was slow, and she saw no johns. The other girls waited, staring with vacant eyes.

Lights blazed in the church on the corner. After the train pulled out, strains of a hymn familiar from home reached her. *Pescador de Hombres.* It was time to seek other shores.

A black car approached. Icy gusts bit into her exposed thighs—the cheap, ultra-short sheath dress provided no protection. Blade always said chilly weather made for better business because the girls were eager for heated cars.

The passenger-side window slid down, the well-dressed driver's hungry eyes devouring her. A repeat customer. "Hey, *Señorita.*" He waved a wad of bills. "The usual?"

From the church, voices rose in unison. *"Señor, me has mirado a los ojos."*

The driver shoved the passenger door open. One last glance along Livonia Avenue. A police officer stood with the man who sometimes argued with Blade. Perhaps God had sent an angel for her.

The john's grin vanished. *"Señorita? Si?"*

She couldn't run now. Roscoe, one of Blade's goons, was watching. But the echoes of the hymn pulled at her soul.

She got into the car. The john pulled into an alley between two vacant storefronts. "Fifty, right?" He laid three bills on the dashboard.

She nodded, trembling. The twitching of her eyelid that had begun in the afternoon grew worse. "Thank you." Back home, tourists had often taken pity on the poor girl selling trinkets, slipping her an extra dollar.

Where was Roscoe? How far could she run before he caught her?

The john pulled her close, but a loud scream startled them both, and he released her. "What the fuck was that?"

Maybe it was the angel crying out.

Another scream. She yanked the door open and ran out of the alley, a stumbling dash in her stiletto heels. Roscoe was looking the other way. He was heavy and couldn't run fast. Might she have a chance?

She ran toward the warm glow of the church. The singing had stopped. The police officer she'd seen jogged across the street, toward her side. *Papi* had warned *turistas* exploring alone, "If there's a policeman approaching you, and there are bandits across the street, cross over because your chances are better with the bandits."

Roscoe shouted and broke into a lumbering run. She kicked off her cumbersome shoes and ran barefoot, as she had back home. Please God, no broken glass.

The policeman stopped in the street and stared at her as another train rumbled overhead.

No choice, now. She grabbed his arm. "Please, help me." His sleeve was wet and red.

He shoved her away. "Get away from me, you BB whore." He pulled away from her and ran up Livonia, his pants leg also spattered with red.

Roscoe was getting closer. "You fucking bitch. Get the fuck back to work or I'll cut your heart out."

She rushed up the steps of the church and yanked the door open.

The church was empty.

Except for the priest.

CHAPTER TWO

Saturday, March 17th

"The city is still reeling from the mayor's sudden resignation this past Monday for unspecified health reasons. A spokesperson yesterday refused to confirm or deny reports that the mayor had entered Sloan-Kettering Hospital for treatment of advanced stage cancer. Sabrina Dunn, the Public Advocate and now the acting mayor, announced that a special election would be held in early June to choose someone to finish the last three years of the mayor's term. She added that she will be a candidate in that election."

***

Detective Kim Brady, third generation NYPD, turned away from the television mounted on the wall and resumed tapping away at her laptop, finishing her report on a case she and her group at the department's Internal Affairs Bureau had closed. Her immediate superior, Lieutenant Steve Colangelo, appeared at her shoulder. "In my office, now, please." He turned away without another word.

She followed him to the cramped office. It wasn't even nine o'clock, yet.

His tone turned conversational. "Fine work on the Bronx operation."

"Thanks. I'm writing it up." A ring of police officers had been running a protection racket on drug dealers. She was glad to have the case over and done with, as it had dredged up memories of Dad's misdeeds in the department, memories she'd thought she'd laid to rest.

"Hear about the murder of Mariano Avila in East New York last night?"

She'd seen the headlines. "A community activist, wasn't he?"

Colangelo picked up a printout with his signature coffee stains in one corner. "A lawyer who mostly served the immigrant community. People there idolized him. He was stabbed to death right outside his Livonia Avenue office."

"Livonia and what?" she asked.

"Smallwood," Colangelo replied.

The Seventy-Fourth precinct. Seven-Four in police parlance.

"Your old stomping grounds," he added.

"No, I was in the Seven-Three." Her rookie post of duty. Foot patrols in Brownsville. Hallways reeking of stale urine; crack vials everywhere. "Who called it in?"

Colangelo remained pleasant. "I meant Brooklyn North. There was an anonymous call to 911 that someone was being attacked. And an eyewitness, an underage hooker who's also undocumented, described the killer as a police officer."

"Could she have called 911?"

"No. The caller was male."

It hit her. "The killer was in uniform?"

"That's what the girl said."

"Had to be an impostor." She thought for another moment. "Unless it was an argument gone bad." A little more thought. "But a stabbing? Anything from the Medical Examiner, yet?"

Colangelo stifled a laugh.

Her inner alarm rang out a warning. "What?"

"Nothing. It's good to see you eager to get started. Whether it was a Member of Service or an impostor, it's an Internal Affairs case, now, because IAB handles both. Since it's a homicide, Captain Forrest wants you to lead the investigation."

"I'm not the senior detective in the unit." But her pulse was already quickening. IAB had drafted her just as her career in Homicide was taking off, following a mass murder that became known as the Cove Shooting case. With thirteen months to go on her mandatory two-year tour, she wasn't thinking about what came next.

"You may not be senior, but you have by far the most experience with homicides. You've also worked well with other commands. We'll need that here." He handed her the printout. "We got an undocumented Mexican immigrant—so, there's potential Immigration involvement—who's also an underage hooker. Cue the Special Victims Unit; SVU can be territorial. I'll be straight. This shapes up as a hornet's nest, so don't be afraid to ask for extra help when you need it. Okay?"

Her pulse didn't slow. The Cove case, the mass shooting that had earned her a transfer from Manhattan South Homicide to Internal Affairs, had looked impossible, too. "Okay. Who am I partnering with?"

"Work with entire unit, including our most recent addition. Officer David Cadman starts today. Deploy them as you see fit, but keep Cadman involved. They sent him with the highest recommendations."

Oh, shit. That meant he had a rabbi, someone highly enough placed in the department to circumvent the usual procedures, looking out for him. It was exactly the kind of maneuver that departmental procedures regarding Internal Affairs were designed to prevent. "Got it. Who did Brooklyn North Homicide put on the case?"

"Abe Stewart. He's the one who called it in to us." Colangelo waved to someone outside his office. "Cadman's here."

A tall guy with brown hair and a fair complexion entered, wearing a gray wool jacket and cobalt blue tie. Colangelo made the introductions. "The media hasn't discovered the killer was in uniform, but they will. Gotta move fast."

Kim was already planning next steps. "I need to talk to the girl, Lieutenant."

"She's staying in the rectory at Blessed Mother Church, across the street from Avila's office," Colangelo said. "The pastor's name is Fr. Joseph Lynch."

Cadman snickered. "Shacked up with a priest? That'll make a great headline."

Her first negative vibe. "Okay, the girl's undocumented, so I'll need to take someone fluent in Spanish to translate."

Colangelo turned to Cadman. "Dave, you're fluent in Spanish, aren't you?"

"Yes, sir."

Kim had already learned the hard way, back in Manhattan South Homicide, that being the lead detective meant leading. But she didn't need to piss off Colangelo this early in the case. "I want to make sure we're sensitive to this girl's situation."

"Understood," Cadman replied with an eager nod.

She turned back to Colangelo. "After we interview the girl, we'll check with the Crime Scene Unit and the lawyer's office. Across the street from the church, right?"

"Correct." Colangelo repeated the name for Cadman's benefit.

"Thanks, Lieu. I'll also check in at Brooklyn North Homicide with Abe Stewart."

"That's a lot of day ahead of you," Colangelo replied. He was almost smirking.

"Yes, it is. We'd better head out now. When the others come in, could you please get someone started checking cases in the Seven-Four; see if anyone used Avila for their lawyer. Then, after we talk to the girl, we'll see what we can find at Avila's office."

CHAPTER THREE

Fr. Joseph Francis Xavier Lynch tried to mask his increasing worry when he saw Amara in the living room with deep circles under her eyes and a pallid complexion. "My dear, didn't you sleep well?"

She held her arms crossed against her abdomen and shook her head. Dressed in the nondescript yoga pants and loose-fitting sweatshirt the rectory's housekeeper had dug up for her, she looked forlorn and lost. For a moment, a wave of shivering overwhelmed her.

"Are you sick?" he asked.

"I think so."

He tried to place his palm on Amara's forehead, but she backed away. "I just want to check for a fever. No one will hurt you. That's a promise."

For an agonizing moment, she only stared. Then she edged a little closer. After the briefest touch of his hand to her forehead, she pulled back and returned to her defensive posture.

He tried a reassuring smile. "You're cool to the touch. No fever." The doorbell rang. He let the housekeeper answer it.

"Amara," he asked, "were you taking any drugs before you ran away?"

"*Si.* But I don't know what."

"How did this happen to you?" He hoped he wasn't being too abrupt. "How did you get here?"

"When we came here from Mexico, men loaded us into a truck. Very long trip with stops only to…" She appeared lost.

He gestured for her to continue.

She blushed. "Go in bushes. After a long time, the truck stopped. They pulled me out with other girls my age. Blade took me, said I was going to school. But we get here, and…" She stopped as pain engulfed her.

He knew better than to touch her again, so he waited for it to pass. "Go on, Amara."

"He made me do sinful things. Under the el. For money."

Fr. Lynch shuddered, recalling his arrival at his new parish four years earlier. He'd come by subway and had descended the stairs from the elevated subway stop in early evening. A prostitute not much older than Amara had approached him, her eyes glazed. Her pimp had steered her away.

He'd later learned the pimp was Blade Morales.

Amara burst into tears. "God must hate me…"

"No, Amara. God hates no one. He loves all His children. Also, He knows it's your love for Him and desire to lead a moral life that drove you to run away. And where did you turn? You came to His house. I promised you last night that I would protect you in His name, and I meant it."

She stared at him, her face stained with tears, as if desperate to believe him. He smiled and nodded. She hesitated, then relaxed her arms, dropping them from their protective self-embrace. She folded her hands in prayer. "*Señor mío, Jesucristo, Dios y hombre verdadero…*" The Spanish Act of Contrition.

When she finished, he pronounced absolution and gave her his blessing. Not that she had sinned, but she needed assurance that God forgave her.

A shrill voice sounded from the rectory's center hall. "I have to talk to him now, Ms. Westwood."

A moment later, a petite woman with chestnut brown hair and brown eyes that Fr. Lynch thought lovely when they weren't blazing with anger, as they were now, burst in. "Have you heard about Mariano? Do you realize what this means?" She stopped and stared at Amara. "Who's this?"

Amara shrank back.

Fr. Lynch grinned, as much to ease Amara's fears as to ease the tension. "Julie Campbell, social worker, please meet Amara Delgado, refugee."

The housekeeper, Ms. Westwood, was right behind. "I tried to tell her to wait, but Miss Julie, she don't want to listen."

"So I gathered." Julie Campbell, social worker, had been among the first to greet him when he'd arrived at the parish with its decrepit church. He'd been on the roof of the church making repairs, and she'd mistaken him for a workman. Their relationship was often stormy, but they knew they needed each other to help the community.

Fr. Lynch now held up a hand to forestall the social worker's protest. "Always the model of decorum and tact. I suggest that you and I go into my office for a quiet discussion while Ms. Westwood prepares a light breakfast for our guest." He gestured toward the housekeeper.

Julie's eyes narrowed to fierce slits, but she remained silent as she followed him to the office on the other side of the center hall. He closed the door behind him and sat behind his desk.

Julie flopped into a visitor's chair. "What the hell is going on?"

"She ran into the church last night as I was closing up after Stations of the Cross, trying to escape the clutches of a pimp named Blade Morales."

"She's a hooker? I thought you said she was a refugee." Her scowl grew deeper. "Or perhaps she's a refugee who became a hooker."

He glanced out the window, from which he could see the church and the elevated line beyond. He repeated what Amara had told him. "Last night she escaped Morales' clutches and sought the church's protection. She may have seen Mariano's killer."

"So, you knew he was dead."

"Yes. And the police understand about Amara. A detective talked to us last night, and I explained to him, as I am telling you now, that Amara is under the church's protection."

Julie jumped up from her seat. "You don't get it. She's on the cops' radar, so it's a race to see who gets to her first: Special Victims Unit or Immigration and Customs Enforcement. Hmmm. SVU or ICE? What do you think? If you let me do an intake, now, I might locate a place to settle her."

He scoffed. "Where? With a foster family? Please."

"Being in the care of a responsible city agency with all its available resources is better than living as a house guest in a parish that's on the diocese's short list for closure. It'll keep her from being deported as an orphan because this city prohibits undocumented aliens from being turned over to the feds. She's lucky New York is a Sanctuary city."

"An interesting choice of words," he replied. "She came here seeking sanctuary, the kind the church was granting centuries before this city existed. I'm sure your agency doesn't have a Sanctuary Acknowledgment Form, and the police department doesn't have a Sanctuary Notification Form, or a Notice of Request for Sanctuary—with a separate schedule for each appropriate sect, please include the PIC, the Parish Identification Code."

"Not funny."

He turned serious. "No, it isn't. Any waltz through officialdom, however well-intentioned, would terrify an adolescent who's endured Amara's experiences. So, spare us the manuals, code books, policies and procedures—just once, forget checking Westlaw—and let's find a workable solution."

"There's no legal basis for Sanctuary in American law. I could get a court order..."

"Bzzzt. Wrong answer. Even if you did, she'd refuse to go with you. What then? Take her at gunpoint? Not recommended for establishing a trusting relationship."

Julie sank back into her seat. "You can be a major hard-ass, can't you?"

"Only when provoked."

That pulled her up short, and she lapsed into deep thought. "Have you noticed anything alarming about her? She looked kind of strung out to me."

He described her complaints of stomach pain, fatigue, and difficulty sleeping.

"That bastard has her hooked on something." She spat the words. "Those are all symptoms of withdrawal."

He recalled Amara in her flimsy dress. "I didn't see any needle marks."

She shook her head. "Not heroin. I'd guess pills." She stood and started pacing in the tiny office. "Okay, you win, we'll do it your way for now. But if she doesn't get some medical help fast, she's in for a week or more of absolute hell, pain that will have her begging to go back to that piece of sh—garbage."

He grinned at her mid-word correction.

She ignored the grin. "I'm establishing a file for her and arranging for a doctor to visit her here, and that's final."

"Won't that start some kind of clock ticking?"

"Let me worry about that."

He extended a hand. "Congratulations, Ms. Campbell. Once again, we have started down the road of cooperation."

She took it. "Yeah, well, for the record, I don't believe for a minute that this will work, and I'll give you a load of... trouble... when it goes bad. Think she knows what she was on?"

"She doesn't. I asked." He led her back to the dining room, where Amara was forcing down some oatmeal at Ms. Westwood's urging. "Miss Julie will bring a doctor for you. But she needs some information, first. You can trust her as you trust me. She and I are working together to protect you."

Julie crouched next to her, making eye contact while giving her space. "When you were with Blade, did he have you taking any pills?"

At first, the girl only stared. But then she nodded. "One small white one each morning, and a kind of long red one twice a day. He said they were so I wouldn't get pregnant."

"The white one probably was. The red capsules sound like barbiturates. When did you stop?"

"Yesterday morning. I always felt... I don't know... fuzzy. Sometimes, I almost liked it. Nothing seemed so terrible. But over the past month, I became afraid."

Julie nodded and stood. "Thank you, Amara."

"All right, my dear. That's all for now. Please rest a while." Fr. Lynch led Julie back to his office.

Julie waited until he closed the door. "She couldn't have taken downers for a year and not become addicted. It can be worse than withdrawal from heroin. She needs to get into a rehab program, but she needs to be examined by a doctor immediately. I have a doctor friend who serves this area. I'll get her here as soon as possible. If she examines her and says that this arrangement poses an undue risk for her, then I expect you to do things my way."

CHAPTER FOUR

Kim took the Manhattan Bridge, turning onto Flatbush Avenue, passing a stone's throw from the apartment she shared with her husband, Jake Dudek, on Monroe Place. At the Barclay Center, she turned left onto Atlantic. The lights were timed to keep traffic flowing toward Manhattan, slowing their progress.

"I get the sense you're not happy about me being partnered with you," Cadman said.

"The department doesn't assign officers to Internal Affairs; IAB selects them. Department policy. And IAB only selects rookies if they've exhibited excellence in certain uncommon skills at the Academy. You graduated last June and were the top marksman in your class. After serving a brief tour in the One-Oh-Seven they posted you to IAB." She cast a sidelong glance at him while stopped at a light and tried not to smirk at his stunned expression. "I only had five minutes to check. Care to further enlighten me?"

"I also excelled in martial arts and did rather well in investigative technique."

"How about the law?" The light turned green.

"I held my own."

Red flag. "What are the six exceptions to the requirement for a search warrant?"

He scowled. "Hey, what is this?" A temper. Another red flag.

"I need to be confident you've learned this stuff, cold. You get one of those exceptions wrong and evidence gets tossed. A criminal walks. Our focus in IAB is on dirty cops, and they know their rights. Tomorrow morning, I want you to rattle off those six exceptions as easily as your name. I need to trust you."

"Okay."

She changed the tone. "The One-Oh-Seven. Fresh Meadows, Queens. Easy duty?"

He shrugged. "Lots of noise complaints about drunken college kids, some burglaries. Car thefts. The occasional rape. Rookie cops don't choose their postings, correct?"

"And, after nine months, you got assigned to IAB. The usual departmental requirement is eighteen months of service before you can transfer anywhere."

He squirmed in his seat a little. "IAB isn't voluntary. I got assigned."

"What did you do at the One-Oh-Seven to rate it?" When he didn't answer after three blocks, she continued. "Okay, so it's obvious that someone well placed in the department is looking out for you. But your rabbi—whoever it is—didn't do you any favors by getting you assigned to Fresh Meadows instead of East New York or South Jamaica. Because wherever you go in this department, you must prove yourself every day."

He stewed in silence before replying, "You looking to ditch me?"

"Stop acting like a wounded adolescent. The lieu—Lieutenant Colangelo—wants me to train you up, so that's what I'm doing." She turned onto Livonia Avenue for four blocks, then turned onto Smallwood Avenue and pulled into the parking lot, up to the rectory.

A heavyset West Indian woman answered the door. Kim displayed her badge. "May we speak with Fr. Lynch, please?"

The woman waved them in and directed them to a small office off the center hall. A few moments later, a priest with the map of Ireland on his face appeared.

"I'm Fr. Lynch," he said. Kim was almost surprised he didn't speak with a brogue. "I assume you're here about the murder of Mariano Avila?"

"That's correct. We understand a young woman staying with you may have seen something. We need to speak with her."

His face curled into a deep frown. "I'm sorry, Detective, but she's in a very fragile state. I'm afraid..."

"She spoke to another detective last night, correct?" Kim asked. "We just need to clarify some things."

"I understand. But she's experiencing withdrawal symptoms. A doctor is coming today. I doubt she'd be of much help."

"Is she comatose?" Kim asked.

"No," the priest replied. "But she's shaking and suffering from severe abdominal cramps. And, as an undocumented immigrant, she's terrified of any authority figure."

Two sharp knocks on the door. A petite woman with chestnut brown hair poked her head in. "Sorry to disturb you, but the doctor won't be here until later this afternoon."

Fr. Lynch waved her in. "Julie Campbell, social worker, this is Detective Brady and Officer Cadman."

Kim stood. "I will ask both of you to please not discuss any aspect of this investigation with anyone. I need to talk to the girl now."

"She's in no condition to endure an interrogation," Julie said.

Kim smiled. "Interview. We're on her side, Ms. Campbell. We want to see the girl get straight, with luck even find her family, and we want to catch Mariano Avila's killer. Do either of you object?"

"No," Fr. Lynch replied. "Our concern is with the methods you may use. I've assured Amara that we will not turn her over to the police. Since she comes from Mexico, police terrify her. I've also promised her she can stay here for as long as she likes."

Time for a reality check. "You will be able to keep your first promise, Father. We won't take her into custody unless she's in danger. You won't be able to keep the second one for long. We're a city of laws, and there are departments that handle these cases."

Ms. Campbell glanced at the priest with an expression that looked like, "I told you so."

Kim continued. "But I'll honor your promise for as long as possible. I need a detailed description of our suspect. If you and Ms. Campbell stay, may I please speak with her?"

Fr. Lynch led them to the dining room.

The girl was sitting at the table, a deck of cards in front of her. The eights, nines and tens were face-up on a small pile to the side.

"I asked her to teach me a card game," the priest said. "We started a short while before you arrived. I'm afraid I'm not much on card games."

Kim kneeled in front of her. "Amara, my name is Kim. I'm with the police department. This is David. You're not in any danger."

Amara gave a tight nod but said nothing.

Kim pointed to the cards. "I see you've made it a Spanish deck."

Another tight nod.

"What game were you teaching Father?" Kim asked.

After a moment's hesitation, Amara replied, "Conquian."

"I know that game." Kim turned to the priest. "It's very similar to our rummy."

Amara's eyes brightened.

"Would you like to play a hand with me?" Kim asked.

Amara picked up the deck. But her hands were shaking too much for her to shuffle.

Kim held out her hand. "I'll deal, if you like."

Amara placed the cards in Kim's outstretched hand without touching her.

Cadman rolled his eyes. "Um, do we really have time for this?"

Kim's gaze never left Amara. "I love this game. Ten cards each, right?"

The girl nodded, and Kim dealt, picking her cards up and sorting them. "The idea is to form groups of three or four cards of the same rank, like fives, or a straight of three to eight cards of the same suit in rank order. Since there are no eights, nines, or tens in the deck, jacks follow sevens. Aces are low, never high. You lay down, or meld, your groups as you form them. Whoever melds eleven cards first wins the hand."

Amara turned up the jack of hearts and immediately laid two other jacks next to it.

Kim turned up a three of diamonds and left it there, even though she already had a three. "You can't simply pick up a discarded card and hold it for later. Either you can meld with it or you must leave it there."

Cadman started pacing.

Kim turned to him. "Please sit down."

"We have a lot to do, today."

"And we'll get to it." She turned to Amara. "Your turn."

The girl dropped a card as she reached for the three Kim had turned face up. Kim smiled at her. Amara slid it over toward her prior meld and laid the four, five, and six of diamonds next to it.

After several more turns, Amara laid down another four-card sequence and won the hand, flashing a shy grin at Kim. They played two more hands. Amara won them both.

"Talk now?" Kim asked. When Amara nodded, Kim picked up the cards, gave them a brief shuffle, and put them aside. "I realize you're suffering, but can you describe the man you saw last night?"

Amara nodded. "He was fat. He wore a police uniform with stripes." She gestured toward her upper arm. "Here."

"What stripes?" Kim asked. "Like this?" With her finger, she traced an upside-down V. Amara nodded. "How many?"

"Three."

"*Gracias*. Was he as tall as Fr. Lynch?" Amara shook her head. Kim gestured for Cadman to stand. "Can you show me how tall he was? Compared to Officer Cadman?"

Amara walked over to Cadman, holding her hand at his chin. She doubled over and staggered back to the sofa.

Kim waited until Amara straightened up. "Just a few more questions." The girl nodded. "Was he carrying a gun?"

"I didn't see one. Not even when he pushed me away."

Kim's attention snagged on the additional detail. "He pushed you?"

"Yes. I ran to him. For help. He told me to get away from him and pushed me away. He spattered a little blood on my dress."

Whoa. "What blood?"

"He had blood on his sleeve, and some on his pants leg. He pushed me away and some of it got on me."

Kim turned to Fr. Lynch. "Do you still have the dress?"

"My housekeeper may have thrown it out. It was this awful, cheap..."

"It's evidence, Father. If you still have it, I need it, now." She turned to Cadman. "There are some evidence bags in the car."

Cadman and the priest left together. The priest was back first, the housekeeper's howls audible in the background, holding a flimsy red sheath dress with multiple bloodstains.

"Have you washed this?" she asked. Fr. Lynch shook his head. She had Cadman bag it. "Amara, what else can you tell me about him?"

"Black hair, big nose, thick lips."

"What did he say when he yelled at you?" Kim asked.

"He called me a 'BB whore' and said to get away from him."

"Did you see which direction he walked after he pushed you?" A direction would help.

"I was desperate to reach the church. I only saw him walk away." Then she added, "Past the church."

He'd gone east on Livonia Avenue.

CHAPTER FIVE

Outside the rectory, Kim put in a call to the Sketch Artist Unit and arranged for the artist whose work she most respected, Sheila Gregg, to see Amara at one o'clock the following afternoon. Selling Fr. Lynch on it wouldn't be easy. But she'd worry about that later.

They crossed Livonia to the gravel parking lot marked off by yellow police tape. Two officers from the Brooklyn Crime Scene Unit were standing guard. Cadman, walking a few steps ahead of Kim, was stepping over the tape when one officer, a sergeant, called out, "Where the hell you think you're going, Junior?"

Kim pulled Cadman back. "He's with me."

The sergeant laughed. "Kim Brady, the erstwhile Queen Bee of the Seven-Three. They got you playing nursemaid to cadets, now?"

"Good morning, Sergeant Vitello." She introduced Cadman. "He joined our unit this morning. CSU has you watch-dogging crime scenes on weekends, now?"

"Bad luck, I guess."

She laughed at that. She'd bet money he'd volunteered. Phil Vitello, his black hair now flecked with gray but still as dedicated as they came, had a nose for a hot case. She turned serious. "So, what can you tell me?"

Phil looked Cadman up and down. "Pay attention, Junior. Gruesome crime scene last night, Kim. A few bloody footprints, men's size eight, leading out of the alley suggest the killer crossed Livonia at an eastward angle. The killer stabbed the lawyer in the neck, causing him to bleed out like a stuck pig. He landed on his left, facing down. That side of his jacket absorbed a lot of blood because of pooling. You can see how it drenched all the gravel in this area."

Why not push her luck? "Find the weapon?"

Phil shook his head. "Not for lack of trying. Did a complete sweep of the area. No dice."

Kim pointed to additional blood spatter further to the left. "What's that from? Avila get a piece of his attacker?" If so, the DNA evidence might give them a leg up.

But Phil shook his head. "We grabbed some gravel, but I doubt it. When we got here, Avila was flat on his back."

Cadman's head snapped up. "But you said..."

Phil grinned at him. "Nice to see you're paying attention, Junior. He landed and bled out. Then the killer flipped him over and slashed him in the chest. The slash wounds on the chest didn't bleed at all. Tank must have been empty by then."

"Is there any way the killer would have been able to avoid getting spattered while he flipped Avila?" Kim asked.

"Only if he got someone else to do it. And there are only two sets of footprints in this alley, one of them Avila's, size ten, and the bloody ones, the attacker's, size eight."

Small feet. And Amara had described a man of about five-eight. Phil broke into a grin as he studied her. "You already have something, don't you?" He dropped his voice so the other CSU officer wouldn't hear. "I wondered why they involved Internal Affairs."

Welcome news. Abe Stewart had kept quiet about Amara's description. "Your ears only. A witness saw someone in a police uniform leaving the scene." But the slashing of the chest bothered her. "If he'd bled out, he was already dead. Why waste time flipping him? And getting soaked with his blood?"

Phil shrugged. "That's why the department has smart folks like you on the payroll."

"Notice anything unusual about the slashing on the chest?"

"I got a quick look. It didn't strike me as important. We look at what, how, and when."

The who and why were up to her. "Who did the ME's office assign?"

"Dr. Lloyd Shelton," Phil said. "You'd already moved on to Manhattan South when he started. I'll have him call you."

"Did anyone else respond?"

"Two plain-clothes guys from the Seven-Four got there first. Ron Coburn and Frank Tyler." Phil said it with disdain. He answered her questioning look by adding, "Tweedle-dum and tweedle-dumber. Abe can tell you more about them than I can."

CHAPTER SIX

Kim and Cadman entered the cramped waiting room of Mariano Avila's law office, the walls lined with folding chairs, with posters in English and Spanish urging the readers to learn their rights. A woman in her late thirties, her black hair tied back in a tight bun, dressed in slacks and a pink wool sweater, was clattering away at a computer keyboard. Half-dried tears streaked her cheeks.

Kim introduced herself, and Cadman. "I'm very sorry for your loss."

The woman stopped her work and stood. "I'm Aida Velez, Mr. Avila's assistant. Thank you. You wouldn't understand how devastating this is to our community."

"I've spoken to Fr. Lynch at the rectory, and a social worker named Julie Campbell. I understand this community loved Mr. Avila and considered him their leader. Was his practice limited to immigration and criminal law?"

Aida nodded. "He did anything anyone needed, but those were the primary areas."

"Did he have any enemies?" Kim asked.

"Not possible. Everyone loved him."

"There were never any threats or hate mail? Zero unhappy clients?"

"No, not even Eduardo Ortega."

"Who's he?" Ortega might have been more unhappy than he'd let on.

22

"Someone who was being investigated by Immigration. Mr. Avila said he had a solid case, even with things as they've been recently. But then the police suspected him of murder, and he returned to his country. ICE is a dirty word around here. He feared he'd never get a fair trial. But he didn't blame Mr. Avila."

ICE was Immigration and Customs Enforcement. "Do you remember who from the police department worked on the murder case?" Kim asked as casually as she could.

"There was someone from the precinct. A sergeant. I don't remember his name. About four months ago, he came and asked for Mr. Ortega's immigration file. Mr. Avila refused, as any attorney would. The sergeant was furious and said Mr. Avila was allowing a felon to escape."

"Do you remember what he looked like?"

Aida frowned. "Average height. On the heavy side. Brown hair. That's all I remember about him."

Kim needed another question so that wouldn't be the last thing they talked about. "Who else works here?"

"Two interns from New York Law School. I'm the receptionist, secretary and paralegal, combined."

Kim remembered the footprints. "Do you have video surveillance of the alley?"

"Yes, but it hasn't been working since Thursday night," Aida said.

"Do you have the tape from Thursday?"

Aida nodded. "It's a flash drive. I'll get it for you."

While they waited, Cadman whispered, "You want the video of the night before the murder?"

"I want to see if it caught whoever disabled the system." When Aida returned and gave her the flash drive, Kim asked for a list of Avila's cases, and Aida gave her a printout. Kim scanned it, but nothing jumped out at her. "Who will handle all these cases, now? What happens to you and the staff?"

"There's an attorney, Evelyn Burke, who has an office downtown, on Livingston Street. She often worked with Mr. Avila on criminal cases. She'll be taking all of Mr. Avila's open cases. We all work for her, now. She wants to maintain this office because she wants to help this community."

"May I use your fax machine?" Kim faxed the list to Detective Cordell Washington, a member of her unit at IAB, and asked him to check the status on each, including Ortega's. "Thank you for your help, Ms. Velez. I may return with additional questions. In the meantime, please don't repeat any part of our conversation to anyone."

Phil Vitello approached her as they left the office. "I spoke to Dr. Shelton. He'll have something for you tomorrow afternoon."

"Thanks, Phil." She stared along Livonia as they waited for the light, noting several businesses along the south side. Did any of them have video surveillance? No time to check, now.

They stopped for a red light at the corner of Bushwick and DeKalb Avenues. Cord Washington's response came in by text. *Only open criminal case is Ortega's. Suspect in the murder last October of one Joey Simmons.*

Did they ever arrest him? The light changed, and she made the turn and stopped at Evergreen.

Nope. Suspect has fled the jurisdiction. No outstanding warrants on him. But the lead detective on the case is Bob Nolan.

The former Narcotics detective who'd known and admired Dad, and whom she'd once accused of interfering with her investigation of the Cove Shooting. But she'd been wrong.

Nolan had transferred out of Narcotics to Brooklyn North Homicide after cooperating with IAB.

Their paths were crossing again. She wondered how he'd feel about that.

CHAPTER SEVEN

"Where did you learn that card game?" Cadman had been quiet since they'd left Avila's office.

"My first tour of duty, the Seven-Three in Brownsville. I had a lot of cases in which I needed information from people who had serious problems. Card games allowed them to relax and gained me their trust. I didn't need your peevish behavior back there."

"Sorry, but I know there's a lot of pressure to solve this case."

"That's not your worry, it's mine. The most important thing about a tough case is to get it right, so please do what I tell you. I need that girl to trust us."

Patrol Borough Brooklyn North—PBBN for short—stood near the corner of Wilson and DeKalb Avenues. The corner building sported a tall, round tower with a roof resembling a battlement, earning PBBN's headquarters the nickname, "the Castle." A television was on as they entered. Acting mayor Sabrina Dunn was eulogizing Mariano Avila.

Kim approached the desk sergeant. "I'm looking for Detective Stewart."

"He's lunching at Millie's." He looked her up and down. "Millie's Cuban Café, two blocks west on Wilson."

The lunchtime crowd at Millie's was large, but mostly takeout, as there were only a few tables, and only one with two men wearing jackets and ties. As Kim approached, Bob Nolan stood and said, "Hello, Kim. I suspected we might see each other today." He looked a little worse for wear; he could be off the wagon again. At least this time it wasn't because of her.

She took his hand. "Good to see you, Bob." Still couldn't read his mood.

Abe Stewart stood, too. "Good to meet you, Kim. Bob said IAB would send you. Pull up a chair and join us. Help yourself to some *croquetas* and some *tostones*."

"Nice to meet you." She introduced Cadman, and they both sat. "You guys investigated the crime scene?"

"I did, Bob didn't," Abe said. "My regular partner had to leave early with severe abdominal pain. Turned out he had a hot appendix. I asked for Bob this morning."

Interesting. "Great. Who arrived before you?"

"Two detectives from the Seven-Four..."

"Coburn and Tyler? They were there before the uniforms?"

"Tweedle-dum and Tweedle-dumber?" Cadman asked with a grin. Kim shot him a glare.

"Same time," Abe replied. "They were in the neighborhood."

"Did they notice the underage hookers working Livonia Avenue?" Cadman asked, serious this time.

Abe scowled at him. "You'd have to ask them. The only underage hooker I saw was the girl at the rectory, and she was pretty fucked up. And who the fuck are you?"

Kim was thinking she might not get through the day without getting violent. "Quiet, Cadman." Back to Abe. "He's new. Have you learned anything else today?"

Abe hesitated. "Would you mind if we stepped outside and spoke in private for a moment?" Once outside, he waited for an ambulance to pass, its siren wailing. "You were Mike Resnick's partner at Manhattan South. He and I go way back. He thinks the sun rises and sets in you, and that's good enough for me. But I'm getting a bad vibe off your sidekick, and I don't like a police officer pretending he's a detective."

She shrugged. "Can't help it. Folks far above my pay grade assigned him to me."

He took a moment to digest that. "We all have our crosses to bear, I guess. My lieu was, ahem, displeased with me going to IAB. His exact words to me were, 'It is what it is, but you don't give them one more fucking thing.' That's off the record. Don't use it against him, because he's a good man who thinks he's doing the right thing. We good on that?"

"We're good. On that. But if I find any..."

"You won't."

She allowed a slight smile. "I'm sure."

"Fair enough. What else do you need?"

This guy reminded her of Mike. "Why did you ask specifically for Bob Nolan as a replacement?"

"I meant, what else do you need regarding Avila's murder?"

Either he was testing her, or he was being territorial. "What can you tell me about the Joey Simmons case?" She kept her voice neutral. "Avila had a client named Ortega who was a suspect."

Abe's expression curled into a deep scowl. "A cluster-fuck from the word go. The two precinct detectives on the case were Coburn and Tyler. First on the scene."

"That's some coincidence."

Abe snorted. "Yeah. I wasn't on the Simmons case."

"I understand Bob Nolan was."

Abe pulled out a cigarette and lit it. "Not at first. Larry Grant was assigned. He was a close friend, a veteran cop in lousy health, and he deserved better on his last case than dealing with those two assholes. They only focused on Ortega and never looked at anyone else." He grew irritated. "When Ortega fled the jurisdiction, they yelled their heads off about him being the guy, and Larry looked like the fuck-up. He dropped his papers, said farewell, and moved out east. A week later, he collapsed and died. Turned out he was full of cancer inside."

"I'm sorry, Abe. That was a lousy end."

He exhaled a stream of smoke, turning away from her for a moment so she wouldn't catch it in the face. "Bob was assigned to take over, but the case had already gone cold. He had nothing to work with. He didn't look so good, either. That's why I asked for him on this case."

She'd passed Abe's test.

Back at the table, Bob was staring into his coffee cup with disgust; Cadman was staring at the line of takeout customers, looking like he'd rather be elsewhere. She'd deal with him later. "Bob, do you have any idea why Coburn and Tyler would've been so keen on Ortega for the Simmons murder?"

"He was an illegal immigrant, and Simmons had ratted him out to ICE."

She had to admit, that sounded like a motive. Except… "But who told Ortega? And how did Simmons discover Ortega was illegal?"

Bob gestured toward the door. "May we?" Once outside, he continued. "I asked those questions and received bullshit answers. I reported the situation to my lieu and suggested we had a problem. He told me to let the case go cold."

"Why couldn't you tell me that inside?"

"Because your partner, the Eagle Scout, asked me if I gave a shit about teenage hookers."

She studied him. "Bob, are you okay? Since coming here, I mean?"

He shrugged. "I'm glad I'm out of Narcotics, like your dad when he got out. But at least he got some respect after he moved. Here… Well, fuck it."

She looked at him in alarm.

"No, Kim, I'm not back on the sauce. Still going to the meetings. And Abe asking for me was a major solid. But please muzzle your sidekick. He pisses me off."

"I can't imagine why." Back inside, she said, "Abe, I'm recommending IAB attach you and Bob to our unit for this investigation. Last night, did you notice any businesses along Livonia with surveillance cameras?"

"I didn't check," Abe said, "but we'll take a run over there this afternoon and check it out."

CHAPTER EIGHT

"What was that back there?" Kim asked as they walked back to the car. "Your fixation on the hookers was irrelevant, inflammatory, and a total distraction."

Cadman turned snippy. "Sorry. But doesn't it bother you that high school girls are being pimped under the noses of the Seven-Four?"

She unlocked the car. "There are many things that bother me, but I don't allow them to derail an investigation. I feel sorry for the girl, too, and I'll do whatever I can to protect and help her, but right now we have only one job—to figure out whether this murderer was a real cop or an impostor, and in either case to run him to ground. And as lead detective on this case, I'll decide what steps we take and what questions we ask. Am I clear?"

"Yeah." He slumped down in the seat as far as the shoulder strap and seat belt would stretch. Pouting.

She called Fr. Lynch. The doctor had already examined Amara and determined she was addicted to Seconol. She'd prescribed something to wean her off the drug and control the withdrawal symptoms. Kim's request that he and Amara come to One Police Plaza the next day to see a sketch artist resulted in initial resistance, but he agreed in the end.

She pulled up to the Seven-Four station house on the corner of Sutter Avenue and Smallwood. Kim showed her badge to the desk sergeant. "I'm looking for Detectives Coburn and Tyler."

The sergeant's face flashed recognition. "What's the problem?"

"I didn't say there was one," Kim replied. "Are they here?"

The sergeant thought it over, but Kim added, "This isn't a choice, Sergeant. Please point them out to me, now."

All conversation and clattering of keyboards stopped. "Third office on the right, you'll find their lieutenant."

"Thank you."

All eyes locked on Kim and Cadman as they walked back. The lieutenant was in his office, sitting up and leaning forward on his desk, a printout in front of him.

She introduced herself, and then Cadman. "IAB has taken over investigating Mariano Avila's murder." Which he already knew. "Coburn and Tyler arrived first. We need to talk to them." When he only glared at her, she added, "Now, please."

The lieutenant led them outside. "Coburn and Tyler. Room Three." Tyler reminded her of a schoolboy on his way to the principal's office. Coburn looked more like the schoolyard bully. The lieutenant opened the door to a vacant interrogation room. "Now," he said to Kim, "you want to tell me why IAB grabbed this case?"

"A witness saw someone fleeing the scene in a police uniform," Kim replied. She turned to the two detectives. "Please explain how you arrived first."

"We heard the radio run," Coburn said. "We were cruising the neighborhood—on New Lots Avenue—when we heard the call. Since we were so close, we responded."

"Do you always respond to radio runs?" she asked.

Tyler stirred. "We heard it was..."

Coburn cut him off. "The radio run said, 'assault in progress'. We didn't think we should stand on ceremony since we were only a few blocks away."

"When you arrived, did you notice anything out of the ordinary?"

Coburn sneered. "Other than the guy lying there, dead?"

She didn't flinch. "Yeah, other than that."

"Not a thing."

Without missing a beat, Kim said, "So, hookers on Livonia, that's business-as-usual?"

"Wait a second," the lieutenant put in. "You claimed you're investigating the murder."

"We are," she replied. "I'm trying to understand the scene, including the hookers. Detective Coburn," she said before the lieutenant could argue, "did you notice anything unusual about the scene, the body's position or its condition?"

"Nope. Someone had stabbed the guy. He was dead when we got there."

"Did you take his pulse at his neck or his wrist?"

Coburn threw up his hands. "He was lying in enough blood to fill my kid's swimming pool, for Christ's sake."

"So, you didn't take his pulse. Did you talk to any witnesses?"

"We didn't find any."

"Did you look for any?"

The lieutenant broke in. "I don't like your tone, Detective."

She met his glare. "I hope that isn't the sound of obstruction I hear, Lieutenant."

"Are you investigating my unit?"

In her time in IAB, she'd grown used to this. "Should I?"

He turned to Coburn. "Answer the detective's question."

Coburn stared for a moment. "Yeah, we did. There was no one on the street. We canvassed the area, but no one saw anything. Detective Stewart checked out the church across the street but didn't tell us if he found anything."

"And yet someone called 911."

"They didn't leave a name."

She nodded. "Been back to the scene today?"

"We got word this morning that IAB had the case," the lieutenant replied. "I told them to leave it until we received further instructions."

She stood. "Thank you, gentlemen. Other than answering questions we may have, no one from the Seven-Four is to take any action involving this case or to comment on it. We'll be in touch."

CHAPTER NINE

As Kim exited the elevator at the Clark Street subway stop, the lobby of what had once been the Hotel St. George was abuzz with groups of law students heading out to various hot spots in the city. She marveled at their energy when she felt so exhausted. They weren't much younger than she was.

It's not just the years; it's the experience.

Dad had tried to warn her off going to the Academy, but he'd also schooled her at a young age in policing. She was her father's daughter, her grandfather's granddaughter, with a calling to protect and serve. As she turned onto Monroe Place, the light shining from the front windows, illuminating the small magnolia tree in front, reminded her she already had one blessing she'd thought she'd never have, her marriage to Jake Dudek.

She glimpsed him through the window as she mounted the steps. Outside their apartment door, she could hear an announcer on TV. "Harris makes the lay-in off the LeVert pass..." The Brooklyn Nets, his employer, were playing an away game, so he'd only be watching, not working.

"Hi, babe." Jake's fingers were flying over the keys of his laptop. "Can't talk, now." Another burst of typing. "Dinner plate's in the fridge, all you need to do is nuke it."

She leaned down and kissed him on the head.

"I'm standing in, providing stat support for the broadcast team tonight." He shook his head as he listened to a burst of breathless commentary. "Geez, this guy doesn't even add an original thought. Recites what I give him, verbatim."

She kissed him again. "You're the man." The on-screen clock showed under three minutes remaining, so she sat and watched the rest of the quarter.

As the image on screen dissolved into a car commercial, he took her in his arms, but the kiss was brief. "Sorry, I'm digging up factoids to feed the studio guys for halftime." As he resumed his tapping, he said, "Long day today."

She unbuttoned her blouse, eager for a hot shower. "I caught a new case. A murder. East New York."

"The lawyer? How did Internal Affairs get involved?" When she said nothing, he added, "Come on, you can trust me."

Yes, she could. They'd settled that a year ago. "We think the killer either was a cop or was impersonating one."

"Holy shit. A homicide. You haven't had one of those since joining the Internal Affairs Bureau. Got the old juices flowing, didn't it?"

She tried not to smile. "It's a case. That's all." She slipped off the rest of her clothes as the half ended and headed for the shower as he turned back to his laptop.

Halftime was ending by the time she'd showered and changed. He had nuked her dinner and had a place set at the table for her, complete with a glass of wine.

He sat in front of the TV, poised for action, as she ate. "The club is creating a new position reporting to the general manager, providing analytics for decisions on player acquisitions. Better pay, almost total flexibility in hours."

She put her wineglass down. "Do you have a chance for it?"

"I got a strong hint that my application would receive a favorable review. I've been itching to tell you all day. It would mean working from home pretty much whenever I wanted, except for meetings and prepping for the draft or trade deadline. Certain times during the off-season, I'd work crazy hours, but the rest of the time, I'd be there for anything you needed."

An odd phrase. "Anything I needed? Like what?"

He hesitated. "Whatever. I mean, this IAB gig is only for another year, and who knows where they'll send you, then?"

"Colangelo likes me a lot. So does his boss, Captain Forrest. They might offer me another tour."

He turned back to his laptop to tap out a message. "What hours did you work today?"

"Eight to four, plus about three-and-a-half hours of overtime. Why?"

"That's the first time you've logged overtime like that since transferring to IAB."

"It's the second. The first was the perv cop sting last November. And this is a murder case. You remember what they're like."

He relaxed as the broadcast broke for a commercial. "Yes, and I recall what you're like when you're on one. Your eyes are flashing with fire, now. Forget another IAB tour. You want to get back to homicide. If I get this new position, it'll be easier for us in case..." He stopped.

"Yes?"

A shrug. "Anything."

But as she sought his eyes, they turned away. "Look at me, Jake. In case of what?"

He turned sheepish. "In case we ever changed our minds about having children."

"We agreed long ago that we didn't need children, and you know I don't want them. Don't want the... responsibility. God, today on this case, I came across a fifteen-year-old girl who's spent the last year turning tricks for a pimp who's kept her addicted to downers."

He grinned. "I thought this was a murder case."

"It is. She's a witness. She..." Kim shook it off. Not now. "You said 'in case we changed our minds'. Have you changed yours?"

"I was never as opposed to the idea as you were, Kim. You realize I'm agreeable either way. All I meant was that this new job would allow me to be a stay-at-home dad, so there would be no infringement on your career. Isn't that why you objected?"

"There was also the matter of my own shitty upbringing," she said.

"Oh, yeah. That." He kissed her on the cheek. "But if we ever had children, which I accept we won't, we would never be those kinds of parents. I'm confident I wouldn't be, and you sure as hell wouldn't."

"How can you be so sure?"

"Your voice caught when you mentioned that girl."

He hadn't accepted it. Please, don't become a problem.

"On a different note," he said, "my mom called earlier. Easter is two weeks from tomorrow. We're invited for dinner."

Easter already? Early this year. "Um, sure. That'll be..." Her cell buzzed. It was a text from Fr. Lynch. *Amara agreed to go tomorrow, but I'm not sure she'll be too helpful in her current state.*

CHAPTER TEN

Sunday, March 18th

Kim introduced Amara to Sheila Gregg, the police artist whom she considered the best. But Amara froze, and Kim wondered if she might be overwhelmed by this. "Sheila, can you wait a bit before getting started?"

"Sure. I came in today for you."

Kim pulled out a pack of playing cards, from which she'd already extracted the eights, nines, and tens. "Amara, why don't we teach Sheila how to play Conquian?"

The girl's panicked expression softened, and she nodded. Kim taught Sheila the basics and Amara won the first hand.

"Okay," Sheila said, "how about another?"

Amara nodded and Kim dealt for her. Sheila won this one.

"Okay," Kim said. "Ready to get started?"

Amara smiled and agreed.

Sheila took out her pencils and sketch pad. "Your English is quite good. Have you been in this country long?"

Amara shot a wary glance at Fr. Lynch, who nodded encouragement. She hesitated. "I think about a year. They teach English in school in Mexico, but I learned more by working with my parents."

"What did they do?" Sheila laid out her face templates.

"They sold souvenirs at their stand in Playa del Carmen. I learned a lot from talking to American tourists."

"I'll bet you were a very good salesperson."

Amara gave a hint of a smile. "That's what *Papi* said." The smile vanished. "I miss him and *Mami*. And my brother."

"Where are they, now?" Sheila asked.

"My brother was killed in Mexico. That's why *Papi* came here. We rode on a boat. Two days. Then, a few more days on a smelly truck, eating hardly anything. Finally, they pulled us out and told us they were taking us to a school while our parents found jobs."

"Ready to start?" Sheila pointed to her templates.

Amara chose a round face, Roman nose, droopy eyes, short black hair, bushy eyebrows and thick lips. Sheila compiled those choices into a sketch. "What do you remember most about him?"

"The uniform and how he smelled," Amara replied.

Sheila chuckled. "I can't draw a smell..."

"Wait," Kim said. "What kind of smell?"

Amara didn't shrink back. "It was like nail polish remover. I smelled it when he shoved me away." Her description of the uniform fit the department's standard issue.

Kim wanted more. "Did you notice anything on the collar? Metal numbers?"

Amara thought for several moments before shaking her head. "I don't remember anything on the collar itself."

Kim was about to ask what she meant when her cell buzzed. A text from Cord. She excused herself and stepped outside to read it. *Checked Avila's cases. No others connected with the Seven-Four.*

Kim gave Cord the description she'd heard Amara give to Sheila. *Check the profiles of all the sergeants in Brooklyn North and see if you get anything close to a match. Start with the Seven-Four. When Sheila gets the finished sketch back to me, we can narrow the field.*

Cadman emerged from Sheila's office. "Amara started talking about a possible tat on the guy's neck. Sheila tried to get her to describe it, but it sounds like she could only see part of it. She sketched what Amara described."

Sheila came out of the office with her sketch pad. "He told you? Here, look."

Kim stared at the small, curled figure poking out of the left side of the collar of the sketched figure. "Any ideas?"

"Beats the hell out of me," Sheila said. "Possible tat. He might have meant to keep it concealed with the uniform. I included it because she described it. I can remove it."

"No." There were several reasons a cop would want to keep a tat concealed. Some were innocent. Others weren't. "Leave it and we'll see if it leads us anywhere. When can I get a copy?"

"I have to clean it up a bit. I'll scan it and e-mail it to you later this afternoon. Want copies sent to DCPI?"

The Deputy Commissioner of Public Information would get them into the media, which would alert the killer to how much the police knew. And the uniform would be sure to stir up an anti-police shitshow. "Not yet. For now, just me, Cord and Lt. Colangelo." Aware of Cadman's eyes on her, she added, "I'll get copies to the rest of the team, myself."

She returned to Sheila's office to say goodbye and pulled Fr. Lynch aside. "Amara is a material witness. At some point, I'll need to take her into protective custody." She held up a hand to forestall his protest. "Not everyone respects the church, and she won't be safe until she's somewhere more secure. I'd appreciate you and Ms. Campbell developing some options."

He considered it. "She'll be frantic until she's reunited with her family. She's afraid she'll get deported after you've gotten what you need and wind up selling her body on the streets of Mexico City."

Great. First Cadman, and now the priest. She kept her temper. "We'll do everything for her we can."

"A wonderful start would be getting her pimp off the streets," he said. "But I guess that's not your department."

CHAPTER ELEVEN

Kim made the turn from Smallwood Avenue onto Linden Boulevard. "The Medical Examiner's office isn't far. Ever been to one?" Cadman shook his head. "You can wait in the car if you like."

"What, you think I can't take it?"

"I don't know the strength of your stomach. I'm leaving it up to you. And, no, I won't give you any shit if you pass out." She shot him a sly grin.

"Thanks. What about Amara? The priest didn't look happy."

"I'm working on it. In the meantime, tell me the six exceptions to the search warrant requirement."

He took a deep breath. "Incident to lawful arrest, plain view exception, consent given by someone reasonably believed to be authorized to consent, stop and frisk if there's reasonable suspicion, the automobile exception, and when in pursuit."

"Good. Has New York City restricted any of those exceptions?"

"Yeah, the stop and frisk exception. Total bullshit if you ask me."

"No argument. Let's see what Dr. Shelton has for us." She pulled into the circular drive of the Medical Examiner's Office.

Dr. Shelton was well over six feet tall and very thin, younger than Kim had expected. "I finished with Mr. Avila a short while ago. If you'll follow me, I'll show you what I found." He led them to an examining room. Mariano Avila's body was on the table.

Cadman hesitated a moment.

"You can wait outside, if you like," Dr. Shelton said.

"I'm good," he replied.

"Okay." The doctor took command. "No question regarding the cause of death. The killer stabbed him through both the carotid artery and the internal jugular vein, causing him to bleed out quickly. The attacker also twisted and gouged the blade, severing both the artery and the vein. He destroyed the initial stab wound, making it impossible to even guess at the model of knife used."

Cadman paled but forced himself to look.

"How big was the wound?" Kim asked.

"Four centimeters in diameter. But I'd say it's probable the blade was smaller than that. The attacker knew what he was doing."

"Sergeant Vitello mentioned something about slash wounds to the chest?"

Dr. Shelton drew back a sheet covering most of Avila's body. The outline of a triangle was visible. "Nothing like typical slash wounds. These were likely carved. The attacker took his time and was meticulous. On close examination, the points of the triangle are neat, no overlap, the lines are straight and of equal length. His chest wounds didn't bleed at all because of the damage done to the neck. He was already dead."

"Is this, like, a signature?" Cadman asked. "Like a serial killer?"

Kim stared at the triangle. "It's apex down, which strikes me as a message of some sort. Without context, it's impossible to decipher." She studied the wounds a little more. "Doctor, the blade had to be rather thin to make these, correct?"

"Yes. And given the image, I'd say the killer used the point—a well-sharpened point."

She made some entries in her cell's Notes app.

"Anything else I can help you with?" Dr. Shelton asked.

Kim glanced through her notes. "Could you pull a file for me on a case from about five months ago? One Joey Simmons?"

"One of yours?"

"We haven't decided, yet. His murder was the only recent criminal case Avila had been working on. The case remains open, and our file is incomplete. I need the cause of death."

Dr. Shelton sat down at a desktop and logged in. "Simmons? Not one of mine. I'll need permission to access the file."

"You can't just check the cause of death?" Cadman asked.

Kim responded before Shelton could. "It's like the NYPD. They require a need to know." She turned to Shelton. "Use my name and be sure to mention IAB. That always gets their attention. Please text me when you hear."

Back in the car, she said, "You didn't puke or pass out. Congratulations. Let's head back to Hudson Street."

As she pulled out onto the road, her cell rang. She hit the button on the steering wheel to answer on Bluetooth. "Brady. We're on speaker."

Cadman frowned, but she was playing matters close to the vest for now.

It was Cord. "Hey, Kim. I took a run through all the sergeants in Brooklyn and there's one who's kind of close. Guess which precinct."

"The Seven-Four?"

Cord laughed. "And the lady wins the stuffed owl."

"You said the match is 'kind of close'?"

"Yeah. Heavy and a round face. The short, black hair comes close. Droopy eyes? Not really. I don't know what a Roman nose is, but he's got a good size schnoz. Thick lips, kind of. I'll shoot you a secure e-mail with his profile photo and you can see for yourself. But an important additional fact: he was on the scene of the Simmons murder."

She pulled over. "What's his name?"

"Sergeant Peter Warren. I checked the Master Roll Call. He wasn't on duty Friday night, not on duty today. Sorry, Kim. He's on the eight-to-four starting tomorrow."

"Thanks, Cord. You, the lieu, and I should get an e-mail of the sketch later. Please forward copies to the rest of the group, including Cadman." Cadman relaxed. "When you get it, examine the left side of his neck. Sheila thinks it's a tat. See if you can make it out. Also, we saw the body." She repeated what Shelton had said about the knife. "Any idea what kind of knife we're looking for?"

"Gee, Kim, I'm thinking a stiletto?"

"A typical stiletto blade wouldn't be both wide enough to gouge that large a wound in the neck and small enough to conceal it from view."

"A switchblade?" Cord asked.

Possibly. "The initial stab had to be hard and fast. Possibly an assisted-opening knife. Sturdier than a switchblade, wider than a stiletto; can still conceal the blade while allowing it greater opening speed. Some of them have nasty points."

Cord chuckled. "I'll see what I can find that fits the bill in my spare time."

CHAPTER TWELVE

Captain Jeremiah Forrest of the Internal Affairs Bureau had settled into that comfort zone of reading in which the hum of background noise ceased to register when the shrill ringtone of his cell phone yanked him back to reality. "Private" appeared on the screen. Tempted though he was to let the call go to voicemail and return to Anthony Trollope's Nineteenth Century England, he knew he had to take it. "Good evening, Senator."

Raymond Brandt, the state senator for Southwest Brooklyn and Chair of the Senate Committee on Crime and Correction, never minced words. "A pleasant evening, Jeremiah. I'm checking on your protégé."

As if he needed the senator to remind him that having done this favor meant he now "owned" Cadman. "I have him working on the Avila case with Kim Brady. She's mentoring him."

"Why would mentoring him be necessary?"

Forrest hesitated. For a seasoned legislator with both eyes glued to the upcoming special election for mayor and a penchant for "law and order" issues, Brandt could be a very dim bulb. But not that dim. The senator meant to put Forrest on the defensive. A sudden craving struck him for a cigarette, despite having quit years ago at his wife's insistence.

He'd sensed impending danger when the police commissioner had called him out of the blue three weeks earlier to confirm Colangelo had not yet filled the vacancy left by the departure of one of his detectives.

"Senator Brandt has suggested a candidate to fill it. It's up to you whether you accept his suggestion." Except it hadn't been up to him. He was the commissioner's fig leaf.

The senator broke his reverie. "Captain Forrest?"

"Sorry, something distracted me. As I may have mentioned when we first discussed Officer Cadman, he came to us with no experience to speak of. Detective Brady is an experienced, dedicated…"

"Yes, and I understand she learned it all at her father's knee."

"Senator, if you check her record at the Academy…"

"I have. Impressive. But still wild and unpredictable, like her father was. Where does she come off quizzing Cadman on the law, like he's some schoolboy?"

Forrest allowed himself a silent grin. Brady had done that? Good for her. "As I recall, the law—you know, the thing we're supposed to uphold—was an area of weakness for your protégé when he attended the Academy. If she thinks a brief review is necessary, I'm all for it. It's in the boy's best interest." He still hadn't figured out why Brandt was so concerned about a kid like Cadman. He didn't see them in the same room.

"All right," Brandt said at last. "If you say so. He got a raw deal out there in Queens. The veterans treated him like shit."

"He would have been better off doing a tour in one of the city's tougher precincts."

"That was not an option, nor is failure in his current post."

Because if he fails and their arrangement becomes public, Sabrina Dunn will have a field day in the press. He decided not to mention it.

"As I told you when we first spoke, Captain, success for Officer Cadman will also mean success for you. How does Deputy Inspector sound?"

CHAPTER THIRTEEN

Monday, March 19th

The text from Dr. Shelton had kept Kim agitated most of the night: *Meet me at my office at seven tomorrow morning. You need to see this.*

She went alone. Dr. Shelton was waiting when she arrived. "Good morning, Detective." He led her to a consultation room and closed the door behind them. He'd clipped two groups of photos to a display board, one array from the crime scene and the rest from the autopsy. "I'm sorry for all the cloak-and-dagger. But I didn't want anyone to overhear this conversation. I didn't conduct this exam; a colleague of mine did. He's moved on, now. When you mentioned Simmons yesterday, and that the case was still open, it rang a bell. So, I accessed the file."

"Without permission?" Kim liked this soft-spoken professional more with each fresh development. "Doesn't that put you in…"

"Jeopardy? Yes, if you don't back me up when I say you came to me with an urgent request to see the Simmons file."

Aha. He needed her to say she was taking over the Simmons investigation to justify giving her the file, and she needed him to give her the file to justify taking over the investigation. And if she told him she was taking over the case without knowing what was in the file, she'd be taking his place in jeopardy. Then again, he'd already peeked. "The police file on this case does not list a cause of death, and I need to rule out any potential links between the two murders. I need to see the Simmons file."

He pointed to several photos. "They found Simmons at night in a deserted playground on Elton Street under the el line leading into the Livonia Yards." He tapped a photo from the exam. "Note the deep, gouging stab wound on the left side of the neck."

"Similar to Mr. Avila's fatal neck wound."

The doctor shook his head. "Not similar, identical. The wound severed both the carotid artery and the interior jugular vein. The condition of the wound suggested that his attacker twisted the knife to cause maximum damage."

"Would you conclude," she asked as she entered her notes, "that the same attacker made both attacks?"

"There are some subtle differences. Simmons' neck wound is about an inch longer, and at the rearmost point, not as deep. It's likely his attacker struck him from behind. If you look at the first crime scene photo, the left side of Mr. Simmons' jacket is soaked with blood. CSU concluded he landed on his left side following the stabbing."

"But in the photo," she said, "he's lying on his back."

"Correct. That's how they found him." He pulled another photo off the display board and handed it to her without comment.

Joey Simmons was lying on his back on a table in the examining room, his chest bared. In the middle of his chest was a triangle, inscribed with precision, apex down, points perfectly formed, all sides equal, but with a line through the middle.

"The same type of cut," Dr. Shelton said, "the same size, shape, and location. The same method of attack. Avila may have been turning when his attacker struck. That would explain the wild blood-spatter patterns at the scene."

"And Avila's attacker's clothing being soaked with blood?" Kim asked.

"Yes. You're chasing the same attacker for both attacks, or two killers using similar knives and identical methods."

Kim studied the photo. "A horizontal line through the middle bisects the triangle on Simmons' chest, made with equal precision."

Interviewing Warren would have to wait. Kim needed to get to Hudson Street and get everything lined up. She texted the latest to Colangelo to give him a heads-up.

CHAPTER FOURTEEN

"Good morning." As soon as Kim entered the unit's office, Detective Martin Stransky, the quietest member of the unit, straightened up, blushing. Officer Marisa Fuentes, the object of his attention, stared at him, eyes wide, and stopped chewing gum long enough to blow a big bubble in Martin's direction. Recruited by IAB straight out of the NYPD Academy, she was now twenty-three but still looked like a teenager. She'd taken up chewing bubble gum on the sting Kim had mentioned to Jake. Marisa had posed as a fifteen-year-old to catch a cop who'd been stalking young girls online.

Kim broke into a grin, glad that Marisa had at last returned Martin's interest. "Come on, Martin. It's not like no one knows."

The enormous bubble shrank without a sound.

Cord popped up from his workstation. At six-foot-four, he was a dominant presence. "I told him, either be totally cool on the job or put it up on the scoreboard at Yankee Stadium. Ain't no middle ground in this department."

Kim had been watching them for almost a year. Stransky had already shown his interest when Kim moved to IAB. After a half dozen sting operations, Kim saw the toughness underneath the cute exterior. Marisa had a brilliant future in the department.

Cadman sauntered in, checking his reflection in the door's window to the hallway.

"Is this the rookie?" Martin asked.

A nice attempt to change the subject. Kim made the introductions. Nothing more than polite nods all around, even from Marisa. Exactly what she'd expected.

Cadman looked put out but focused on Marisa, ignoring the others. "Great to meet you."

She said nothing, popping her latest bubble with a look of annoyance.

"The lieu told us you're in charge, Kim." Cord glared at Cadman. "Looks like you got your work cut out for you."

"Yeah, looks like a bitch of a case." No need to make it any worse than it already was. "Or rather, cases."

As if on cue, Colangelo emerged from his office and waved them into the conference room. "I've notified Brooklyn North Homicide that IAB is reopening the Simmons case. We're assuming the same guy did both Simmons and Avila?"

Kim could still see the triangles. "Not assuming. It's a strong possibility."

Colangelo studied her for a moment. "What's bothering you?"

She'd been stewing ever since her talk with Dr. Shelton. "Avila's was a plain triangle, but Simmons' had a line through it. Done with precision. That's a deliberate difference."

"You think Avila was a copycat?" Cord asked. "Or possibly revenge for Simmons?"

Kim pondered it before answering. "If so, whoever killed him would have needed the details of Simmons' death. The press never reported the stab to the neck or the triangle, just as they haven't reported it with Avila. All they said was 'death by stabbing'. So, not a copycat, but it's possible different attackers with similar training and working in concert."

"What if Avila's killer was a cop?" Colangelo's face turned sour at the thought, but this was part of what IAB did. "He could have known."

Kim thought about it. "There was nothing in the case file, so he'd have to be with the Seven-Four. When do we get Stewart and Nolan?"

"I spoke to their lieu a little while ago. He was pissed." Colangelo shrugged. "Another Christmas card I won't be getting. They'll report here this afternoon."

Good. Reinforcements coming in. "Let's try analyzing backwards from the crime scene. Where did the killer come from? Where did he go afterward? After his encounter with Amara, it appears he headed east on Livonia along the north side."

"I'm working on getting the Transit video for you," Cord said. "It might take another day or two."

"Abe Stewart said he and Nolan would check the businesses along Livonia to see if any of them have their own security video," Kim added.

Cadman spoke up. "Do you have a guess whether he came by car or subway?"

God, he could be annoying. "No guessing. Focus on our facts. The killer waited for Avila, not knowing when he'd appear, or when a subway or bus might be available for escape. He'd have wanted to clear out in a hurry, undetected. That suggests a car, parked on Livonia or right off it."

"What about that sergeant at the Seven-Four? Warren?" Cord asked. "If Avila's murder was revenge, he'd be the guy."

Kim studied Sheila's sketch based on Amara's description. The eyes suggested a lack of regard for the law or any kind of authority, the bushy brows accented a kind of inner anger, and the turn of the mouth appeared surly. Funny how Sheila could capture that in a sketch. She'd compared it to the photo of Sergeant Peter Warren. The face shape and hair were identical to the sketch. But Warren's eyes were different, warmer. His brows were neater, lips thinner, and his nose wasn't so imposing. It was a friendly face. No tattoo visible. "Warren's not our guy. Let's drop the revenge angle, at least for now."

"You still want to talk to him?" Colangelo asked.

"Yes. He was on the scene for Simmons, and he may have been the sergeant who confronted Avila."

"I reached out to Hal Adams last night," Cord said. "His group coordinates all NYPD joint operations with the FBI. I sent him the sketch. He called me this morning. He's got something on the tat."

That was fast. "Okay. Cadman, check Joey Simmons for priors. Anything from a summons for pissing in public to a major felony, I want all details of the incident."

Another pout. "I thought maybe you'd want Marisa to do that."

"If I wanted Marisa to do it, I'd have asked her. Just do what I tell you. In the meantime, Lieutenant, we should contact Brooklyn SVU and see if they can arrange for a sweep of Livonia for the rest of the girls. We can bag Blade Morales and see how he fits into all of this."

"Proceed," Colangelo replied.

"Marisa," Kim said, "I'd appreciate it if you could handle that."

Fuentes stood and saluted. "Yes, ma'am."

"Lieutenant," Kim continued, "now that we've taken on the Simmons case, we should pull Coburn and Tyler in for a formal interview."

His eyebrows shot skyward. "You wouldn't rather low-key it at the Seven-Four?"

"No. Something about these guys reeks. I want them scared and defensive."

"You think they're involved?" Cord asked.

"I couldn't say for certain. For the moment, it's important to hear whatever they have to say about the Simmons case."

"I'll pull them in this afternoon." Colangelo looked over his notes. "Anything else?"

"Yes," Kim said. "We need display boards for everything we have so far on each case, noting everything that's connected. If Simmons had any priors, include them. We'll add details as they emerge."

"Use this conference room." Colangelo gestured at the two wall-mounted marker boards.

"Also, Cord, please check the Simmons case file access history." Kim made some notes in her app.

"Sure, although I thought you might want me to join you with Hal Adams."

Martin spoke up for the first time. "I've worked with the FBI before. I might save us some steps."

Cord took no offense. "I'm cool."

Kim stood. "Okay, Martin. Let's go."

CHAPTER FIFTEEN

Kim was taken aback. Hal Adams looked exhausted. His tie hung loose, and he needed a shave. The air in his office at Federal Plaza was stale.

"Geez, Hal," Martin said. "You look like hell. Haven't you slept?"

"No. Thanks to you guys. I must have examined a couple hundred images." He placed an enlarged print of the sketch on his desk. "Judging by the top of the tat, it's a symbol. This tiny hitch, here, tells me it ain't a letter. You wouldn't write it in script, and you wouldn't print such a wide loop. My conclusion, after perusing popular symbols for tats most of the night, is that it's the top of the head of a snake." He clicked the mouse on his desktop, and the enormous screen on the side wall sprang to life. "And not just any snake. He's got an extensive history."

"How extensive?" Kim asked.

"About two hundred and fifty years." Adams tapped the enter key for emphasis and the image of the top of the tat appeared on the screen. "Here's what we have. Now, we'll see where it fits." He clicked on the mouse, and lines traced over the image already on the screen. The lines expanded out until they completed the outline of a coiled snake rising with jaws open and tongue extended. The lines solidified, and the slogan "Don't tread on me" appeared at the bottom. "A favorite of anti-government types everywhere."

Martin shook his head. "Shit!"

"Yeah," Adams said. "You'd expect to find this tattoo on the upper arm. This dude has it on his neck. I'd say it's more than mere expressing an opinion; it's a badge."

"So," Kim said, "we'll need the FBI's help on this."

"I already called Ken Taylor. Martin knows him." He picked up his phone and called a number. "Please join us."

After a loud knock, Taylor entered. Tall, slim, conservatively dressed in a sport jacket and tie with short, light brown hair, he could have been a recruiting poster for the FBI. The tiny flecks of gray in his well-trimmed dark hair lent him an air of experience and authority.

Taylor gestured to the wall screen. "I see you've met our friend. I understand someone with this tattoo is a murder suspect."

"That's right," Kim said, "the murder of a Latino attorney whose specialty was immigration law." She gave him the details. "The eyewitness who gave us the description for that sketch said that he called her a 'BB whore.'"

"'BB' is anti-immigrant slang for 'border bandit'," Taylor said, "so the motive is clear enough. And someone who'd be wearing a tat like this would be certain to fit the bill. I can get you a list of every organization we've seen that uses this as a badge of membership. Most of them are anti-immigrant—well, anti-anything-you-can-think-of. Most of their members are barstool generals or overweight warrior-wannabees who love tromping around the woods in camos, and it's easy to laugh them off. But their numbers are growing and that's no laughing matter. Also, this is a much different attack than what we've seen in the past—they've accomplished it by stealth."

"Meaning?" Kim asked.

"This isn't necessarily a group. Could be a lone wolf, waging his own personal war or nursing a personal grudge. It's possible there is no message behind this attack."

"There were two," Martin said.

"There was no witness to the other one," Kim hastened to add. "But the *modus operandi* was the same. Stabbed in the neck with a triangle carved on the chest. On the lawyer it looked like this." She grabbed a sheet of blank paper from Adams' desk and drew it. "The other one, Simmons, had a line through his."

Adams and Taylor both stared at them, but with no sign of recognition.

"You're positive there was nothing more?" Adams asked.

"If you like, I can forward the ME's photos of the victims," Kim said.

"Uh... no, thanks. I'll take your word."

Kim suppressed a grin. "When can you put together a list?"

"I'll try to get it to you before the end of the day," Taylor replied. "I did some preliminary checking when Hal first alerted me. Here's a list of five websites attracting a lot of local attention, and their URLs."

Kim took the list. "Can we determine where their members are located?"

"We can monitor activity according to IP addresses, and we can often track each IP address to its location. But volume isn't necessarily the key indicator, here. Many groups are small, and there are more of them emerging every day. And, with increasing persistence, they favor action over venting, the kind leading to sensationalist press coverage. Besides working up a list, we'll monitor any mention of 'activities' having a potential connection to your murders. I'll keep you informed of anything we pick up."

She wrote her cell number on her card and gave it to him. "One other thing. The one eyewitness in this case is an undocumented fifteen-year-old whose abductor forced her into prostitution." She repeated Amara's story. "Once SVU runs their sweep, I may get information on her traffickers."

"That would be useful," Taylor replied.

"My goal," she added, "is to reunite the girl with her family, not to deport her family."

"New York's status as a sanctuary city is a matter of public record," Taylor said. "I can't promise you we'll track down her family. But, if you give me a good lead, I'll follow it."

She hated to press the point, but... "I need assurance the FBI won't turn them over to ICE."

"I understand, but once we identify and locate the traffickers, ICE will be all over us. And once they discover your witness is an illegal, they'll be all over your department. I can't stop any of that. What I can do is keep the girl and her family off ICE's radar for as long as possible."

It wasn't very much.

CHAPTER SIXTEEN

Abe Stewart was putting out a cigarette and Bob Nolan tossed an empty coffee cup in a receptacle as Kim and Martin emerged from the elevator at IAB's Hudson Street offices.

"Sorry to keep you guys waiting," she said. "Glad you're here. Coburn and Tyler are coming in today."

"Already here," Cadman said. "They're in Lieutenant Colangelo's office. Here's the access log on the Simmons file. Cord printed it out. Oh, and Simmons had priors. Two years ago, he was arrested for threatening an itinerant construction worker waiting for a contractor to pick him up. No one filed charges. A month later, they arrested him in a similar incident and this time he pled guilty to Menacing-Three, a Class B Misdemeanor. He served a one-month jail sentence. Apparently, he couldn't afford to pay the fine." He preened, as if expecting a compliment.

"So, Joey Simmons had a problem with immigrants." She turned to Martin, who was momentarily distracted. Looking for Marisa, no doubt. "Can you run down those web sites Taylor gave us? Cadman, please give him a hand. Abe, why don't you and Bob join me for this interview?"

Cadman's shoulders sagged.

"Glad to," Abe said, "but it may not do much to secure their cooperation."

"I don't expect them to cooperate. And your presence will save me from playing Telephone."

"Before we go in," Abe said, "we took a run past the scene. At the eastern end of the block on the south side of Livonia is a plain brick building, no signage, coiled barbed wire across the edge of the roof. It also has two video cameras mounted on the exterior wall, with views in both directions. It's a small business doing computer rebuilds. I got video for both cameras for last Friday night."

"Thanks, Abe. Cord will send them to our video analysts. We're keeping them busy this week."

Colangelo was reading reports while Coburn and Tyler sat waiting when Kim walked in. "Sorry about the delay, Lieutenant. Do we have room for two more?" No need to allow them glimpses of the case boards.

"It's cramped," Colangelo replied, "but if you don't mind standing..."

She waved Abe and Bob into the office. "I believe you've both met Detectives Stewart and Nolan. They, of course, know you."

Coburn and Tyler both stiffened.

As she expected. "They're remaining on the Avila case, working with IAB. Since our chat on Saturday, we've learned of another case in which you took part, the murder of Joey Simmons back in November. Can you tell me the cause of death?"

"I don't recall," Coburn said, a little too quickly.

Kim pulled out one of the ME's photos and held it up in front of him. "Can you tell me now, Detective Coburn?"

"Looks like someone stabbed him in the neck."

"Hmm. Looks like that to me, too. Sound familiar?"

"It was four months ago..."

"And you were first on the scene."

"No, we weren't," Tyler said. "Warren was."

"That would be Sergeant Peter Warren, correct?" she asked. Tyler nodded. She pulled out another sheet. "Report from CSU stating that Sergeant Warren and you two all arrived together. Identical murders, severing the same blood vessels, and you two are first on the scene for both. In how many other murder cases have you arrived at a crime scene before the uniforms?"

Coburn squirmed in his seat. "Can't recall any."

"Because uniforms typically respond to radio runs."

"In Simmons' case," Coburn replied, "a civilian saw the dead body while walking through the playground. They called it in as a homicide."

"And you were hanging around the Livonia train yards?"

"I don't remember where we were," Coburn said. "But it wasn't far."

"A mere coincidence. I hate those." It was time to change gears. "The Simmons case file was incomplete. There was no cause of death. Why was that?"

Coburn shrugged. "It was Larry Grant's case."

Colangelo, who'd been sitting back in his chair listening, sat up straight. "He's dead."

Kim never enjoyed giving up the ball to anyone when she had a straight line to the basket, not even to her lieu. "Who finished his file work on the Simmons case?"

Coburn paled at the extra pressure. He nodded toward Bob. "Nolan. Right after Grant dropped his papers."

"And when did Detective Grant retire?" Kim asked.

"December 9th," Tyler said. Coburn shot him a glare but said nothing.

"And Detective Nolan made his last entry in the file on December 27th." Kim pulled out the access log. "Yet, Detective Tyler, you accessed the Simmons file two weeks after Detective Nolan's last entry. Why?"

"What specific charge are you leveling?" Coburn asked.

"This is an inquiry, Detective." Kim's calm demeanor was in sharp contrast to Coburn's agitation. "I'm not making any charge. Yet. I'm asking Detective Tyler—and only Detective Tyler—why he accessed a case file without proper authorization. And I expect him to answer, or there will be charges."

"I wanted to see if he'd written anything about us in the file." Tyler's voice was soft, his manner diffident. "Grant hadn't agreed with us." He turned to Bob. "Neither did you, and you made it clear you were pissed at us."

"What was the basis of the disagreement?" Kim asked.

"A Panamanian illegal named Ortega had murdered Simmons," Tyler continued. "Simmons found out Ortega was illegal and reported him to ICE."

"How did Simmons know Ortega at all?" Kim asked. "Let alone that he was illegal?"

"They were both doin' the same woman," Tyler said, despite Coburn's subtle hand-across-the-throat gesture.

Kim took a step forward. "If you say or do one more thing to interfere with my questions—if you so much as shift in your seat—I'll arrest you here and now for obstruction. Are we clear?"

He nodded and slouched.

She stepped back. "Detective Tyler, what was the woman's name?"

Tyler swallowed hard. "Mercedes. Like the car. I don't remember her last name. She worked in a bodega on Smallwood, a little south of Pitkin. She admitted to Ortega she'd been sleeping with Simmons. Ortega threatened Simmons, and Simmons reported him to ICE. We..." Tyler stopped, unable to go on.

She turned to Coburn. "You have anything to add?"

"It struck us as a powerful motive. Ortega was shacking up with the bitch. Um, girl. She lives near the Livonia train yard. We figure Simmons was going to see her that night and ran into Ortega at the playground."

"Were there any witnesses to the murder?" Kim asked. "The Elton playground faces residential buildings to the west, north, and east."

Coburn and Tyler both shook their heads.

"Did you canvass the area?" Kim asked.

Bob Nolan spoke up. "There's no record in the file of anyone having interviewed potential witnesses that night, so I'd say, no, they didn't."

"We asked around," Coburn said. "No one knew anything. I thought I mentioned that in the file."

"No," Bob replied. "You didn't."

"Did CSU identify forensic evidence at the scene indicating Ortega had been present?" Kim asked. "We found no mention of forensic evidence in the case file, either."

"Not that I remember," Coburn said.

Kim glared at Tyler, who shook his head. "Did either of you speak to anyone who knew Ortega about whether he ever carried a knife? No? Any evidence that he ever carried one?"

"We never got that far," Coburn replied. "He fled the jurisdiction before we could look into it."

"There was no reference to a girlfriend in the case file, either," Kim said. "No contact information. Why not?"

"How the hell should I know? It was Grant's file..."

"Which both you and Detective Tyler accessed several times during the investigation," Kim replied.

Coburn snapped back at her. "When we both had valid reasons to do so."

"Then you both should have been aware of key information missing and added it yourselves." She paused for emphasis. "Unless you removed it."

"We removed nothing," Tyler said.

"Then give me the full name and address of the girlfriend." Kim shoved a notepad in Coburn's face.

"Gentlemen," Colangelo said, "as of now you are both on Administrative Leave while IAB investigates your actions in this case. Check in with this office twice per day and you are not to leave the city."

Coburn shoved the notepad back at Kim and stood. "I don't remember her last name and I don't remember her exact address. And that's the last fucking question we answer without lawyers present." They walked out.

"So, they've lawyered up," Colangelo said. "Is that what you wanted, Kim?"

"Not quite, but they'll stay out of our way while we work. And if they try to insert themselves, we'll hear about it. We need to find that bodega."

CHAPTER SEVENTEEN

She'd taken Nolan with her. When Colangelo had frowned because she wasn't taking Cadman, she rationalized it. "I want to keep Nolan fully involved since Simmons was his case."

The bodega was near the end of a block on which all the storefronts had operating businesses, and the doors and walls were free of graffiti. A petite, attractive woman in her mid-twenties with jet black hair, high cheekbones and deep brown eyes stood at the register. "Can I help you?"

Kim flashed her badge. "Police. I have some questions if you wouldn't mind. Is your name Mercedes?"

The woman nodded. "Mercedes Ruiz. If this is about Joey Simmons, I already talked to the police."

Kim smiled. "I understand. We're investigating another murder, but some additional questions have arisen about Joey Simmons. I understand that you and he were lovers."

"For a brief time."

"How did you meet him?" Kim asked.

"He came in here one day last summer, early July, for a cold drink. As I was making change, he was checking me out. At first, it was creepy, because he was looking at me like I was some exotic object he'd never seen before. But then I realized I might be oversensitive; I'd broken up with someone and was still hurting. He started talking to me, asking me how I liked it around here, how long I'd been here, that kind of thing. He left, but he kept coming back. One day, we had a display of fresh flowers outside, and he bought a bunch and gave them to me."

"That was sweet," Kim said.

"Yeah. And the attention was nice." She gave a rueful smile. "But I should have known."

"What?"

"When he gave me the flowers, he said he'd never met anyone like me, and that I was nicer to him than any other girl he'd ever met. And then he kissed me. On the cheek, like a bashful teenager. He waited until I finished work, and then I invited him to my apartment. I think I was his first, because I had to, um, explain things to him. After that, he always rushed matters."

"So, enter Eduardo Ortega?" Bob asked.

Mercedes blinked. "Excuse me?"

"Is that when you started seeing Ortega?"

Mercedes' smile vanished. "What the fuck?"

Kim reinserted herself. "You were living with Eduardo Ortega when someone murdered Joey Simmons, weren't you?"

"He was staying with me until he could manage a place of his own. So, what?"

Kim forestalled Bob's reply. "Eduardo Ortega wasn't your lover?"

Mercedes jammed her hands onto her hips. "You got that shit from those other cops, didn't you? They were trying to hang Joey's murder on Eduardo, blaming me."

"Just what was your relationship with Eduardo Ortega?" Kim asked.

Mercedes grew fierce. "He's my cousin. We were real close as kids, and, yeah, he liked me that way when we were twelve, until we learned it was a sin. In Panama, he was my protector. So, when he arrived in New York needing somewhere to stay, I insisted he stay with me."

"Did you tell this to the police?" Kim asked.

"No. Eduardo told me not to. They were trying to send him back, and he was afraid they'd send me too. Green card or no green card. When the cops started making it like I was..." She shook her head. "Made me mad."

Kim needed all the answers. "Why had Eduardo come from Panama?"

"He'd been in trouble with someone involved in a gang and got out before it got him killed. Eduardo didn't like Joey—said there was something foul about him—but he didn't kill him. I can prove it; we were together at my aunt's, in her apartment in Brownsville, the night Joey was killed. But Eduardo wouldn't let me say that, either. He was desperate to protect all of us. And any money he made, he gave to me as rent, even though I told him he didn't have to."

"How did he earn money?" Bob asked.

"He worked with builders whenever he could. He'd wait outside for contractors to offer him work. He got paid a few dollars an hour and always gave it to me."

"Was he aware that Simmons had reported him to Immigration?" Kim asked.

"He'd gotten a notice. That's when I had him go see Mr. Avila. But neither of us knew who had ratted on him. You think I'd have tolerated that?"

Kim smiled. "Some might think it would've given you a motive to kill him yourself."

Mercedes looked Kim in the eye. "You're right. It would have if I'd known." She was battling tears. "That motherfucker betrayed my trust."

Kim braced herself. "What do you mean?"

"The first time Joey saw Eduardo here, he got real upset. Totally jealous. He stormed out. Eduardo stopped me from going after him. Said he was no good, that he'd hurt me real bad if I kept on with him. But the next day, Joey came into the store at lunchtime and said he was sorry, that he loved me so much and he couldn't stand me being with someone else. So, I explained Eduardo was my cousin and why he was staying with me, that he'd been living at my place for over six months. Joey promised he'd never tell a soul. He totally fucked Eduardo, even in death."

Kim gestured for her to continue.

"When Eduardo first spoke with him, Mr. Avila didn't think he'd get deported. We didn't learn Joey was the person who'd reported Eduardo to ICE until the cops said so after Joey's death. Mr. Avila explained Eduardo had nothing to fear. But the cops said he'd serve twenty-five years in prison and then they'd deport him, and they'd convict me as an accomplice and deport me, too. So, Eduardo returned home to Panama. He figured chilling things there would be easier than beating a murder charge here."

"But he had an alibi," Bob said. "You just told us."

"Where we come from," Mercedes said, "if the police want you bad enough, they make you look guilty. Where were you decent cops four months ago? It's too late, now. He's already gone. He'll never come back."

Kim pulled out the sketch. "Have you ever seen this man?"

Mercedes gasped. "Yes. Here, in the store. He started coming in last summer, not long after I started seeing Joey. I never knew he was a cop; he was never in uniform. After a while, he stopped."

"After Joey died?"

"No, before. I don't remember how long."

"Did he speak to you?" Bob asked.

Mercedes thought about it. "I believe he bought a pack of cigarettes or something. Nothing more."

Kim pointed to the collar. "Do you remember if he had a tattoo there?"

"Yes. It was a snake."

Kim pulled out the printout Hal Adams had given her. "This snake?"

Mercedes' eyes sprang wide open. "*A Dios mio.*"

CHAPTER EIGHTEEN

Joey Simmons, thirty-two when he died, had lived with his mother in a detached shingled house off Myrtle Avenue in Glendale. The plot was barely wide enough for the house and driveway, which was barely wide enough to accommodate the twelve-year-old Ford Focus parked next to the narrow front steps.

Clara Simmons sagged when Kim showed her badge, and with an air of resignation invited her in. "I don't know what else I can tell you, though. Didn't they catch Joey's killer and deport him?"

"No," Kim replied, "the man left the country before they could charge him."

"I heard they deported him." Mrs. Simmons snorted. "Well, they ought to keep them all out to begin with, and then our boys could stay alive and get suitable jobs."

"Didn't Joey have a job?"

"I suppose, if you call picking up garbage a job."

"He worked for the Sanitation Department?" A city agency file could provide useful information.

"No. He would have had to pass a test. He worked for a carting company over here in Maspeth. Regal Carting. He wanted to be a builder, but he wasn't in a union. And contractors who hire nonunion workers hire illegals, who work for next to nothing. My Joey deserved better. It made him so mad, sometimes."

Kim nodded. "I've read the record of his arrests."

Mrs. Simmons shook her head. "These lowlifes sneak across our border, get on welfare, and take all the jobs. All Joey did was to complain about being treated unfairly, and they sent him to jail. He was never the same after that."

Kim tried not to think of Amara, or her parents. And she refrained from explaining that undocumented aliens could not receive welfare. "Didn't he have any friends he could talk to about it?"

"Oh, sure. There were three boys he'd gone to school with. Rafer Harwood, Jeff Desmond, Cliff Conroy. 'The four horsemen', I used to call them when they were together. But they couldn't do anything about it anymore than he could. So, he picked up his garbage until they fired him. That began his downward spiral. He bickered with his friends. He'd go out at all hours. I never knew where."

"Perhaps he had a girlfriend?" Kim asked as gently as she could.

"No. He was painfully shy with girls. Rafer arranged his date for his senior prom in high school." She shook her head. "Something else he never experienced—falling in love." She was fighting back tears. "Is it true they found him someplace in Brooklyn?"

Kim nodded. "Did his work take him there? Or did he have other friends there?"

"Who knows? He was so secretive after jail. Why didn't they hold that illegal here and put him on trial for killing Joey?" She started sobbing, but soon regained control of herself. "I guess I'm not being much of a help."

Kim patted her arm. "I'm so sorry. I realize this is difficult, so we won't take much more of your time. When did Joey lose his job?"

"Last summer, I think. He never told me; I found out after I lost him. He was so ashamed he left home every morning pretending he had a job. Why?"

"Just trying to piece it all together." Kim had to be careful, here. "There's no evidence Eduardo Ortega killed your son. I'm convinced he didn't."

"Who killed him?" It was a desperate cry.

"That's what I'm investigating. Did Joey have a cell phone?"

"No. I wouldn't let him. He would never have left it alone, or he'd have lost it."

"How about a computer?"

Mrs. Simmons nodded toward a desk. "Yeah. Waste of time. Used to keep it over there. Once I lost Joey, I couldn't stand looking at it. I threw it out."

Kim walked over to the desk. "Did Joey keep any papers or notepads in here?"

A gesture of disgust. "All the time. 'Codes', he called them. And 'passwords'. What did he need codes for? I haven't gone through that top drawer, yet. Too painful."

"May I?" Kim gestured to the desk.

Mrs. Simmons nodded. "Please take it all with you when you leave."

Kim found a tattered legal pad, with haphazardly placed post-it notes covering the top sheet. Underneath were two small note pads and several loose sheets. Kim gathered them, leaving only a few pens and pencils and a stapler behind. Bob stuffed them in an evidence bag.

"Thank you," Mrs. Simmons said. "If only Joey could have met a nice girl like you."

"I'll inform you if I learn anything new on your son's case, Mrs. Simmons." Kim and Bob crossed the street to their car. As she slid into the driver's seat, the bumper sticker on the back of Mrs. Simmons' car caught her eye: "Will the last American to leave New York please remember to take the flag".

No doubt where Mom stood.

CHAPTER NINETEEN

The first thing Kim did when she got back to her desk at Hudson Street was to text Jake and tell him she'd be late.

How late? I figured since I'm off tonight, we could dine out.

Looking to make it up to her after their talk about children? She could almost feel disappointment radiating from the small screen. *I'm sorry. But we might've picked up something valuable. I need to get started on it. I'll be home as soon as I can.*

No worries. That was a relief. *I've got an analytics project to work on. Any chance you'll be home in time for a late supper?*

I'll try. Translation: Order out and enjoy your project.

As she hit "send" she waved Cord and Bob into the conference room. "Abe and Martin are reviewing video over at One-PP."

"Which reminds me," Cord said. "The video from Avila's surveillance camera gave us nothing. One minute, you see the alley, the next, the side of the building."

"So, he checked it out in advance." She shrugged it off. It hadn't been likely.

Colangelo and Marisa joined them. On the side marker board, Cord had listed the known facts and posted a copy of the sketch and copies of the morgue photos of Simmons and Avila.

"It's your show, Kim," Colangelo said.

"Nice layout, Cord. Thanks." Kim opened the Notes app on her phone. "Got a line on a few groups based in the city from Ken Taylor." She paused and wrote them on the empty board, along with what they'd learned of Ortega. "I'm assuming the sergeant who confronted Avila in his office was Warren, whom I will see tomorrow."

"Pull him in here," Colangelo said. "You're losing too much time shuttling to East New York and back."

Kim gestured toward the ME's photos. "The triangles bother me." She drew them both on the board. "The killer carved them with precision, and with identical placement on each victim. Without question, it's a signature." She pointed to the line through the second triangle. "That's the only difference."

"Maybe," Cord said, "he's just fucking with us."

Kim was adamant. "No. That extra stroke was deliberate, like every other aspect of the killings. It has meaning for him."

"Don't get bogged down," Cord said.

"Wait." Marisa strode to the board and, in a vacant spot, drew the two triangles, but this time, the Simmons one first, under which she wrote, "Earth", then the Avila triangle, under which she wrote, "water". She drew a third triangle, apex up with a line through it, which she labeled "air". and a fourth, also apex up but no line, which she labeled, "fire". For the last figure, she drew a circle which she labeled, "spirit". "The five elements of pagan beliefs."

Kim bit her lip to keep from smiling. "So, you're saying the murderer is a Wiccan?"

"Or maybe a druid?" Cord added.

Marisa remained serious. "I couldn't say what he is. But those two symbols are pagan references. You said yourself you thought they were a message or code."

Kim turned serious. "How do you know all this?"

"I took a course in comparative religions at LaGuardia Community. I could explain…"

Colangelo interrupted. "Anything with immediate relevance to the case?"

"Immediate relevance? No."

"Save it until it does. In the meantime, what about the Special Victims Unit?"

"They want to execute the sweep tomorrow night, with me undercover, posing as a runaway." She put a hand on her hip and struck a pose. "Ima make it my way." She blew a small bubble.

"Nobody got authorization from me." Colangelo was adamant about procedure.

Marisa straightened up. "Sorry, Lieu. I only spoke to them a minute before you called us in and had no time to explain. You should have a message pending from Lieutenant Fredricks at SVU. She thought with me involved, you'd want to have our unit there for backup."

He checked his cell. "Yeah, she called."

"And we don't want the Seven-Four involved with this," Kim said.

"Her street people say Blade Morales has grown more brazen in recent months. A runaway teen looking to make it on the street will appeal to him since he's now one girl short." Marisa struck her sassy pose again. "Ima give him more than he can handle."

Colangelo considered it. "Okay. Kim, you'll stick with Fredricks or whoever's senior from SVU on site. Cord will do his 'street guy' thing, providing our own eyes on Marisa. Bob, you'll be available, along with Cadman, Martin and Abe, as additional backup. As soon as we bag these motherfuckers, I want you guys there to interrogate them. Our primary aim is to find out whatever they can give us on the Avila murder, but we also want any info we can turn over to the feds."

"I'd be glad to be out on the street for extra protection," Cadman said.

Marisa popped a bubble and scowled.

"Absolutely not," Kim said. "Just do your job."

"You have no training or experience in undercover work," Colangelo added.

"What about the girls?" Marisa asked. "If their histories match Amara's, SVU will have their hands full."

Kim broke into a grin. "I have some thoughts. Meanwhile, Cord and I will review Simmons' notes and see what we glean from them." But the grin faded as they left the conference room, and the television mounted on the office wall caught her attention. There was no sound, but the images were of people keeping vigil outside Mariano Avila's office. They were placing candles and laying wreaths beyond the police barricades.

"Looks peaceful enough," Cord said.

"For now," Colangelo added with a growl.

Kim gestured toward her desk. "Okay, Cord, let's see what we've got."

CHAPTER TWENTY

Simmons notepad included logins, passwords, cheat codes for video games, and URLs for websites, but no pagan symbols. He had an e-mail account, a Facebook account, and an account with a video game company. Kim checked the Facebook account first.

He hadn't been all that active, only seven friends. Most items in his "news feed" were political, a lot of them anti-immigrant. There were several news items posted about various vigilante groups, almost all of them by Rafer Harwood, Jeff Desmond, and Cliff Conroy. The four horsemen, indeed.

"None of them have profile photos on their pages, and none have ever used Facebook's private messaging feature." Kim punched up the number of Vera Koshkin of the computer tech group at One-PP. "If I give you an IP address, can you follow the trail of breadcrumbs?"

"Of course. Just one?"

"I only have one address." She recalled what Ken Taylor had said. "But I also have three other e-mail addresses."

"Give to me. Is easy, unless accounts are cellphone based. I get back to you tomorrow or next day, *da*?"

"That's fine, Vera. Thanks." Remembering her last session with Coburn and Tyler, about Tyler accessing the Simmons file after Bob had closed the case, she added, "Remember during the Cove Shooting case when we checked an old case file to see if there had been any changes made to it?"

"Was when I realized how much brilliance you have."

"Your brilliance discovered the hacking. I need it on another file, same issue." She provided Simmons' case number.

"Is easy. Will tell you with other information. *Dasvidaniya*."

Cord's head popped up. "You're bringing in Vera Koshkin?"

"Uh huh." Kim tried not to smile.

Cord sat back in his seat and spread his arms apart, palms up. "Oh, Lord, we give thee thanks."

Kim couldn't suppress a laugh. "Geez, you're like a high school kid with a crush on a cheerleader. Why don't you ask her out? The rumors about her being ex-*Politsiya* are nonsense."

"Yeah, but she must get fifty come-ons a week."

Kim was back to typing, checking Harwood, Desmond, and Conroy for priors. "So? You afraid of some competition?"

"No. Yes. I don't know."

"Well, that narrows..." Her smile vanished. "Shit. When they collared Joey Simmons the first time for harassing illegals waiting for pickup for construction jobs, they nabbed Cliff Conroy with him." A few more keystrokes. "And Jeff Desmond."

"Is that the one they let Simmons walk on?"

"Yeah." More keystrokes. "Harwood didn't take part. Or, if he did, he avoided arrest."

"What about the second time, when they convicted Simmons?"

"No. On his own." She returned to the notepad. A notation in the margin caught her eye. "You ever hear of a place called the Eagle?"

Cord shook his head.

She called Ken Taylor and asked him. "I'm thinking it's someplace in Queens. That's where Joey Simmons lived. And his pals."

"Let me dig into it," Taylor replied. "I'll get back to you when I have something."

"Okay. Martin will handle any undercover assignments."

As soon as she dropped the call, her cell buzzed with a text from Martin. *Nothing on any of the Transit videos. We checked all the stations from Pennsylvania Avenue to New Lots.*

He didn't hang around the neighborhood. With luck, the private security video caught him.

CHAPTER TWENTY-ONE

Tuesday, March 20th

As Kim approached the building on Hudson Street, Cadman was standing by a parked red BMW M4 that appeared to be fresh from the showroom, embracing a woman several years older. She wore a knee-length skirt and blazer. Not wanting to intrude, Kim picked up her pace.

But Cadman and the woman separated, and he called Kim over. "It's not what you think, Kim. This is my sister, Loretta."

"Nice to meet you." Kim extended her hand.

Loretta took it, her nails shaped to perfection, clear polish, white tips. "Very nice to meet you. Dave's told me so much about you."

"I'll bet." Kim couldn't suppress the smile.

But Loretta's smile in return was warm. "Oh, I think it's great how you're schooling him, especially the homework. That was always his weakness."

Cadman blushed.

Loretta's skirt and blazer were designer quality. And she wore Christian Laboutin heels. "I have such respect for you. Thanks for looking out for my baby brother." She checked her watch. Longines. "Sorry, must run. Lovely meeting you, Kim." She jumped in the car and drove off.

Cadman shook his head and chuckled.

"So, that's your big sister, huh?"

"She's the only family I've had since our parents died in a car crash when I was thirteen. What's on the agenda this morning?"

"Sergeant Warren is coming in for his interview. So, let's get moving."

***

Sergeant Warren arrived twenty minutes early, leaving Kim barely enough time to review his file. He was a twelve-year veteran. He'd been a sergeant for seven, so he'd taken the sergeant's exam as soon as he was eligible. He'd done patrol tours in the Four-Oh in Mott Haven and the Fifteen in Manhattan and had three commendations in his file. Upon making sergeant, he'd moved to the Seven-Four, where his upward progress ended. He'd taken the lieutenant's test twice, but both times the list had expired with him nowhere near the top.

He came alone, as if he had nothing to hide. Abe, Bob, and Cadman joined them in the conference room. She had Cadman take notes, which she hoped would keep him from asking questions.

"Thank you for coming." Kim jumped right in. "You had met Mariano Avila?"

"Yes."

"And you had occasion to speak with him in his office a few months ago, did you not?"

Warren cast a momentary sidelong glance at Abe Stewart. "Am I a suspect?"

"I'm trying to understand all the events prior to the murder," Kim replied. "Did you speak to him in his office? If so, what about?"

Warren heaved a sigh. "Yes, about a client of his, Eduardo Ortega. Detectives in the Seven-Four liked him for the murder of Joey Simmons." He turned to Bob. "But you guys weren't buying it..."

Kim stopped him. "You mean Brooklyn North Homicide?"

"Yes. The case was all circumstantial evidence. They were looking for a knife, and a jacket that likely had bloodstains on it, but they couldn't get a warrant. The judge didn't buy the motive."

"You mean the jealousy angle?"

Warren shook his head. "Revenge. Simmons had ratted out Ortega to Immigration and Customs Enforcement. They were looking to deport him."

"How did you learn that?" Warren blushed but said nothing. He'd gotten it unofficially. "Who was your source? It's better if you tell us, Sergeant. We're not after petty offenses."

"My... girlfriend. She's on the call-in desk at ICE at Federal Plaza."

Kim shoved a notepad at him. "I'll need her name and contact information."

He wrote a name, phone number, and an address in Canarsie. "If they find out, she'll lose her job."

"So, you never told the judge?" Not that it mattered, but she needed to grasp how it all fit together.

"No. Grant said no judge would buy that without corroborating evidence. ICE wouldn't tell us on the record the informant's name."

"And you thought they'd tell Avila?" Could Warren be that dim?

Warren threw up his hands. "I went to see him to ask him to see his file on Ortega. He refused. Attorney-client privilege."

"I've heard of that. Did you grow angry during the discussion?" Maybe Warren was the guy despite Amara's description.

"Yes. It frustrated me. He was letting a murder suspect get away. But I didn't kill Avila."

Kim pulled out both the Master Roll Call and the Seven-Four's Duty Roster for Friday Night, March 16. "You were not on duty last Friday evening. Is that correct?"

"That's correct. I was on leave all that week."

"And while you were off duty on Friday, did you approach Mr. Avila?"

"No. I wasn't even in the city. My wife and I were at my sister's cottage in the Catskills. My sons stayed with my sister on Long Island."

Kim locked eyes with him. "Odd time of year for the Catskills. What was it that drew you—the vast expanse of leafless trees and arctic mountain winds? Or was it the scarcity of human contact?"

Warren glanced away. "After Ortega got away, I broke it off with my girlfriend and came clean to my wife. I took the week off so we could go away and try to work things out." He met her gaze. "And we did."

Kim made some notes. "When did you first learn of Avila's murder?"

"When I got back to the city Saturday night, I saw it on the TV news. I called the Seven-Four and spoke to the desk officer to find out what had happened. He told me they'd found Avila's body in the alley next to his office, stabbed to death. There'd been an anonymous 911 call."

Kim made some entries in her Notes app. "We will verify your alibi for Friday night with your wife. But I'm confused about why you even approached Ortega's attorney. Normal procedure would be for a detective on the case or an ADA to contact an attorney. Not a sergeant."

"The two precinct detectives on the case complained they were up to their eyeballs in casework, and the DA's office kept telling them they needed solid evidence to make a case. They asked me to go to Avila to nail down the ICE angle. And I tried."

Coburn and Tyler. Kim recalled Phil Vitello's name for them: Tweedle-dum and Tweedle-dumber.

Bob inserted himself into the discussion. "Did they ask you, or did you volunteer?"

"They asked."

"You and they arrived at the Simmons crime scene together, correct?" Kim asked.

"That's right."

"All of you?" Abe asked. "Arrived at the same time?"

Warren's cool slipped a bit. "I didn't log anyone's arrivals, Detective. I got out of our patrol car and they were getting out of their car."

"You didn't see them pull up?" Kim kept her voice soft, but not her glare.

Warren looked away first. "No."

Kim opened another note on her cell. "Your partner that night was Police Officer Isaac Burrows?"

"Yes."

She was missing something. "Who first established that Ortega knew Simmons had ratted him out?"

Warren only stared.

ICE did not reveal its sources. Period. "For the call to ICE to have been a motive for Ortega to kill Simmons, Ortega must have known it was Simmons who reported him. Who did you tell and when?"

"Just Coburn, Tyler and Burrows. I blurted it out at the scene when Burrows checked Simmons' wallet and told me his name. My girlfriend had told me about the call a week before when I'd been at her place. Simmons had tried hitting on her while reporting on Ortega. She found it funny."

Ortega couldn't have known, unless Simmons had told him, personally. "Thank you for coming in. You're not to reveal any part of this conversation to anyone."

CHAPTER TWENTY-TWO

After Warren left, Kim gathered the group in the Conference room and made some additional notes on the board. "Abe, I need you to run down Warren's alibi with his wife, and Ortega's alibi with the aunt. Nail those doors shut. Take Cadman with you since he speaks Spanish and the aunt may not speak fluent English. Also, talk to the girlfriend at ICE; nail down when the Seven-Four knew Simmons ratted out Ortega."

Kim glanced back at the board where Cord had taped a map of Brooklyn and Queens. "I have to interview these three friends of Simmons."

"They've already briefed me on my role for tonight," Cord said. "Nothing for me to do but get into my rent-a-rags, splash on some Eau de Garbage, and I'm set."

Bob raised a hand. "Just a thought. These three bear all the earmarks of white nationalists. Having a person of color present may not promote friendly dialogue."

"No," Kim replied, "but it might prove very useful."

Cord broke into a grin. "I'm game."

"Okay," Kim said. "One other thing. Transit video surveillance came up with nothing. Bob, I need you and Martin to examine the private security video from the business near the scene. Thoroughly. We know the killer proceeded east on Livonia, and those cameras were only a hundred yards east of the scene. They must have caught something. See what you can get."

The group broke up and Marisa approached. "Kim, can we talk privately for a minute?"

Kim waited for the room to empty. "Did you call Fr. Lynch, as I asked?"

Marisa nodded. "And SVU called Julie Campbell."

Cord poked his head in. "You got a visitor, boss-lady." He was grinning ear-to-ear.

Kim patted Marisa on the arm. "You've got tonight to get ready for, and we have to track these guys down."

Marisa passed Vera Koshkin on her way out.

Vera opened a legal-size accordion file and extracted several printouts. She wore no makeup and kept her straight, blond hair tucked behind her ears. There were circles under her eyes.

"Were you at One-PP all night?" Kim asked.

"*Da.* Is how I work. I start, I finish." She gave a tired smile. "Is why I have no boyfriend."

The first page was a list of sites that Joey Simmons frequented. Defend Our Home, a site on Ken Taylor's list, was one he'd visited several times. He'd frequented Facebook, too. Then Kim saw it. "Hot Latinas?"

"*Da*, he browses sites with Latina models. But no porn."

Joey's computer had been in the living room. "I suspect he was terrified his mother would catch him." There were dates listed under each site. "Are these when he browsed each site?"

Vera smiled. "You're a brilliant American lady detective."

He'd started the last week of the previous June. They petered out by mid-July. Kim checked the updated timeline on the board. Simmons had first come into Mercedes Diaz' store in late June. "What else do we have?"

Vera turned the other sheets toward Kim as Cord joined them. Conroy and Desmond were both more active, including porn sites. "Perhaps computers in more private places." Both were persistent visitors to Defend Our Home.

Harwood was the most active. He visited not only Defend Our Home daily but also several national anti-immigration sites. Frequently, he'd returned to a site that described efforts by self-appointed militia groups to monitor and harass "illegals".

"I also get into e-mail accounts," Vera said, handing over another stack of printouts. "E-mail lists from last June onward. On top of the first page is IP address and location of its unit. Also, text of all e-mails within group up to last October. Tell me if you want any others. Is easy."

Kim browsed the first page of each stack. "This is quite helpful, Vera. Thanks."

Vera gave a tired wave of her hand. "Is nothing. Oh, and I checked that case file for you. No deletions and no funny business with changes to master file."

At least they weren't dealing with a self-proclaimed computer whiz, as they had the last time they'd worked together. "Thanks, Vera."

"I go home, now, and sleep."

"Is it true, you don't have a boyfriend?" Kim asked.

"Is not possible. Job comes first, that's my nature. Guys don't understand."

"Guys who are cops understand." Kim tried not to glance at Cord.

Another tired wave. "I'm not a cop. I'm a computer genius."

"You're both," Cord blurted, then shrank back.

Vera tilted her head and grinned at him. "*Dasvidanya*." And she left.

"We can grab someone's e-mails whenever we want?" Cadman was incredulous.

She would lose it before they solved this case. "No, not whenever we want. But tonight, after end-of-tour, you will research the subject and tomorrow, you will tell me why Vera can access these particular e-mails, and under what circumstances she couldn't."

Cord shook his head and muttered under his breath, "Jesus Christ."

Colangelo waved Kim over. "Got a minute?"

Her radar didn't register trouble until he closed the door to his office.

"I was speaking with Lieutenant Fredricks. Her command post tonight will be a van like the one we sometimes use. She knows you'll be with her. You'll be able to maintain radio contact with the rest of our guys, and she'll coordinate the sweep."

"Sounds good." But his demeanor set off alarm bells. "Anything else?"

"Slight change of plans. Cadman is to be in the van with you."

Shit. "Lieutenant, he can only get in the way, there. At least if he's with Abe, Martin, and Bob, they can keep him from doing something stupid. You're the one who said he's not trained for this."

"I'm sure you can keep him in line. So far, your partnership with him seems to work."

"Thank you, but I would prefer to leave him with Abe and..."

Colangelo picked up a printout and stared only at it. "Captain Forrest decided, Kim. I'm sure it will be a monumental success."

As she left Colangelo's office, her attention snagged on the sound of the television tuned to a local news show. "...as pro-immigrant groups, inspired by the vigil remembering Mariano Avila last night in East New York, intend to march tonight from Downtown Brooklyn over the Brooklyn Bridge to City Hall to protest human rights depredations against immigrants."

Cord sidled up to her. "Look at it on the bright side. Maybe it'll draw out the Defend Our Home crowd and everyone can discuss it, nice and peaceful."

CHAPTER TWENTY-THREE

According to Vera's lists, Rafer Harwood's IP address was in Woodside, Queens. Upon checking, Kim found one Harwood listed in that neighborhood, a woman. "I expect Rafer still lives with his mom." It was Kim's third attempt at conversation since leaving Hudson Street. Cord answered with a grunt, as he had the previous two. It was easy to guess why.

"I thought you'd be jumping for joy," she said as they turned onto the lower roadway of the Queensborough Bridge.

"Yeah, right."

At last, progress. "I don't understand why you're angry."

"All that talk about boyfriends. Why did you bring that up, anyway? So she could laugh at me like she did?"

She couldn't laugh now, much as she wanted to. He'd explode. "I didn't bring up boyfriends, she did. And she didn't laugh at you, she flirted. Sort of like the way Marisa blows bubbles to flirt with Martin."

"Yeah? Did you laugh at Jake when you flirted with him? Or did you blow bubbles?"

They came off the bridge into Queens Plaza and made the left onto Northern Boulevard. "I never flirted with Jake. He pursued me. Talking about hoops." Now, they'd been married for almost a year. "I've never tried being a matchmaker, Cord. But if I ever did, I'd try with you and Vera. That's all I'll say."

She made the half-right turn onto Broadway. After half a mile, Cord, staring at the Waze app on his cell, said, "Next right."

Kim made the turn. There was a building on the corner with a brightly lit neon sign, *Iglesias de Dios*, and a Ravidassian temple on the opposite corner.

"Looks like a nice, diverse neighborhood." Cord chuckled. "Harwood must love that." When Kim stopped at a light, he added, "There's a Bangali eatery—must mean from Bangladesh—with a Mexican deli next door. Woodside looks like a pretty cool place."

Harwood lived in a semi-attached brick three-family in desperate need of pointing up. Black wrought-iron grates mottled with rust covered the windows on the first two floors. Doorbell buttons lay between the front doors. Kim pressed the lower one. "I wonder which apartment doesn't get its own front door."

"Who is it?"

"Police," Kim replied. "Does Rafer Harwood live here?"

"What's this about?"

She wasn't about to fence with him through a closed door. "May we come in, Mr. Harwood? We won't take much of your time."

"Give me a minute." A short while later, he answered the door in jeans and a stained gray tee shirt, with a scraggly brown beard that appeared to be more from neglect than a conscious choice. He was very tall, thin as a rail and prematurely bald, with only a fringe of blond hair around the back and sides remaining, accented by shaggy pork chop sideburns. There were no tattoos visible.

Kim flashed her badge. "We're from the NYPD's Quality Assurance Unit. We're following up on the police investigation of the murder of Joey Simmons. I believe he was a friend of yours?"

Harwood regarded her with bloodshot eyes. "Yeah. Some border bandit killed him."

"We have a few questions for you," Cord said. "May we come in?"

Harwood crossed his arms. "No."

"You and Joey go way back, I understand," Cord said.

Harwood glanced up at the detective towering over him and hesitated for a moment. "Yeah. We went through school together. So?"

Kim spoke up. "So, you don't seem all that interested in his death."

Harwood uncrossed his arms with a humorless laugh, placing his hands on his hips. "Let me get this straight. We got millions of illegals fucking up this city—stealing jobs, mooching welfare, dealing drugs, raping and killing, but you cops don't do shit about it. Instead, you come sniffing around about a crime that's already been solved."

"Solved?" Kim asked.

"Yeah. Joey and the illegal were banging the same piece of wetback trash. Joey ratted out the illegal, and the illegal took revenge. You assholes let him get away. Case closed."

Kim remained pleasant. "You mean Joey told the guy he reported him?"

Harwood snorted. "Joey wasn't the sharpest knife in the drawer, and he had a big mouth. I saved his ass enough times to know. But he wasn't stupid enough to tell him."

"Joey agreed with you about illegals?" Cord asked.

"Yeah, he did. You threw him in jail because he dared to speak his thoughts."

"And yet," Cord went on, "he was making it with a Latina."

"Joey didn't always see the full picture. Besides, she was the best he'd ever do. I told him not to go all 'West Side Story' on it, but he wouldn't listen. Now, why don't you two go find a nice doughnut shop?"

Kim remained impassive. "Ever hear the name Mariano Avila?"

"That part of your 'quality assurance'?" Harwood shook his head. "Saw his name on the news. Lawyer got himself killed Friday night. Next, you'll ask me how I feel about that, so I'll save you the trouble. It made my weekend. It's always nice to see a cockroach get killed, but even better when it's one who helps the other cockroaches infest this country. And to answer your next question, I got the news around eleven while having another of several beers at the Eagle Tavern. Arrived at seven, stayed until midnight. Feel free to verify my statement. Ask for Tom, he was tending bar all night." He looked right at Cord and gave a derisive laugh. "You might not feel too welcome there."

Cord started forward, but Kim touched his arm.

Harwood caught it. "That's right, princess. Keep your buck in line. You, on the other hand, might be very welcome, if you wear a short enough skirt and high enough heels."

84

"Have a pleasant day, Mr. Harwood," Kim said.

Cord was smoldering as they got back in the car.

"Violence wouldn't have been a wise course," Kim said.

"You don't think I get that? But I wanted to make him fearful for a minute, fucking coward. I didn't need you making it like you had control over me."

She started the engine. "I couldn't take the chance. I'm not a mind-reader..."

"We've worked together long enough that you should trust me. And why didn't you press him more on Avila."

"He's not the guy Amara saw in the uniform, and it's obvious from their mugshots that neither Conroy nor Desmond are."

"So, why bother with them?"

"Because our little run-in with Harwood made my nose twitch, and we have major gaps of information to fill." Kim made a right turn onto Thirty-Ninth Avenue. "He knew the full official version of who killed Joey and why."

Cord relaxed. "Well, there's a reason it's the official version."

"Except that the department never made it public. Clara Simmons knew nothing about a supposed love triangle, or even about Mercedes Ruiz. And she thought they had deported Ortega for Joey's murder."

Cord nodded. "Selective disclosure."

"Which makes me wonder who made a full disclosure to Rafer Harwood."

CHAPTER TWENTY-FOUR

The interview with Desmond, also living in Woodside, followed the same path as the one with Harwood, so Kim tried a fresh approach with Conroy, whom they'd tracked down in Ridgewood, by Fresh Pond Road. "You and Jeff Desmond were both arrested with Joey two years back."

"Yeah," he replied. "We'd tried finding jobs, but we couldn't get decent pay because illegals work for peanuts."

Clara Simmons had mentioned Joey wanting to be a builder. "So, all three of you worked construction?"

"Well, we tried to," Conroy replied.

"What kind of construction work do you do?" Cord asked.

"Carpentry."

Cord broke into a grin. "Handy with a pining ridge, huh?"

Conroy grinned back. "Yeah. Anyway, Joey got pissed and made a stink about it, so Jeff and I joined him to back him up."

"In East New York?" Kim asked. "That's a long trip to make a stink."

Conroy snorted. "Nah, not so much. The B-20 bus stops at the end of this block."

"What happened when you guys and Joey confronted these other guys?" Cord asked.

"The illegals were all hanging around outside a bodega on the corner of Smallwood and Pitkin, not even trying to hide the fact they were waiting for a truck to pick them up." Conroy shook his head. "When the cops busted us, we made it like the illegals had pushed Joey's buttons, driven him nuts, and he'd just lost it, and they let him go."

"Played with the truth?" Kim asked.

Conroy shook his head. "Joey got pissed as shit like I'd never seen him even before we got to East New York. Don't know why. As soon as he saw them, he started screaming at them, making threats. Nasty stuff. A few of the illegals shouted back. A woman came out of the bodega and yelled at everyone to stop, but as soon as she went inside, it escalated. And then a bunch of cop cars showed up. Everybody else scattered, but we got caught. So, we told the cops the illegals started it, and we got off. Afterward, we told Joey to cool it. But once Joey got hold of something, he couldn't let it go."

Harwood had complained that Joey wasn't too bright. "This excursion to East New York was all Joey's idea? He planned it?"

Conroy hesitated. "I don't remember. Planning wasn't Joey's strength."

"Could he have gotten the idea from someone else?"

Conroy grew more guarded. "I dunno. Maybe. Couldn't say."

"Did he come to you about it?"

Conroy nodded.

"So, what happened with the second arrest?" Cord asked.

Conroy shrank back a little. "A month after we all got busted, Joey went back and started confronting the illegals again. I don't know the details of what happened because we didn't hear nothing about it until we heard they'd arrested him. This time there wasn't nobody to save his ass."

"So, he spent some time at Rikers," Cord said.

"Yeah." Conroy shook his head. "Shit, no way anyone should've thrown him in jail."

"What happened to him?" Kim asked.

Conroy sat back, crossed his arms tightly across his chest, and shook his head. "All I can say is he was way more messed up after his sentence."

Kim leaned forward a little, and Conroy clenched his arms tighter. "Cliff, tell me what you think." But Conroy stared at the floor and said nothing.

"Detective," Cord said, "would you mind waiting for me in the car? I'll only be a minute."

Conroy blanched.

"Sure." She stood and patted Conroy on the shoulder. "Thanks for your help. I'll let myself out." While waiting for Cord, she made additional notes on her cell.

Cordell slid into the passenger seat a few minutes later. "There are certain subjects guys like him could never discuss with any woman, let alone a woman cop."

"So, they assaulted Joey in Rikers?"

"Our boy Cliff can't say for sure," Cord replied, "but he knows Joey was awful jumpy when he got out, and real eager to prove his manliness. Cliff thinks he went chasing after Latinas because he believed they'd consider him a catch."

"And he lucked out catching Mercedes Ruiz on the rebound," Kim replied. "He'd seen her at the bodega. He bedded her, then found out about Ortega, assumed he was a rival, and got rid of him. Hence the tip to ICE." She drove a little further in silence. "Except Mercedes told Joey that Ortega was her cousin, so he knew he wasn't a rival."

She remained quiet until she pulled onto the Expressway, heading for the Midtown Tunnel. "I wonder who told Joey Simmons where the undocumented construction workers hung out."

"I wonder what they would have done if a contractor had come by to offer them work," Cord replied. "The pining ridge thing? I made that up. Ain't no such tool, and Conroy ain't no carpenter."

CHAPTER TWENTY-FIVE

SVU's surveillance van, which looked like a Con Ed truck, had picked up Kim and Cadman at Hudson Street. Lieutenant Lauren Fredricks greeted Kim as she climbed inside. "Good to have you with us." But when Cadman followed, she added, "Who the hell is this?"

Colangelo hadn't given her the word. Wonderful. "This is Officer David Cadman, who's been partnering with me on the Avila case. Lieutenant Colangelo wanted him in the van on this operation."

"What the hell for?" Fredricks turned to Cadman. "No offense, Sonny, but we don't have an inch to spare." She turned back to Kim. "What's his role here, anyway?"

"Backup, along with four other detectives from..."

"Yeah, yeah. Nolan, Stewart, Stransky, and Washington." The van pulled away. "He should've been with them. Too late now. Keep him out from underfoot."

Cadman found a spot in the corner and, to Kim's disgust, pouted.

Fredrick's tone changed as she described the operation. "We have several cars with our people posing as johns who will roll in and engage the girls. Once Marisa busts Morales, your guys can grab his two goons. Don't worry, we've got backup. Everyone gets taken to the Seven-Four. I realize you have objections, but we've got the five girls and the three pimps. The closer the better. I've already spoken to the precinct commander, and he's pledged full cooperation."

Cadman stirred. "Considering that this ring has been flourishing right under his nose…"

Oh, no. Not now. "I'm speaking with the lieutenant, Cadman. Quiet."

The van pulled into position on the corner of Smallwood and Livonia, in front of Blessed Mother Church, at 8:45 PM. Two officers got out wearing Con Ed uniforms, pulled up a utility hole cover, deployed a portable guardrail and set up a light.

The dome on the roof of the van was fitted with two high-definition video cameras, each with its own dedicated monitor in the van. Both cameras could swing three hundred and sixty degrees. Once activated, Camera One focused on their side of Livonia Avenue while Camera Two focused on the opposite side of the street. Cord was wearing a wire and earbud receiver, but Marisa would only wear a wire.

Fredricks grabbed a microphone and had her team check in. Then she gave it to Kim.

"This is IAB Command," Kim said. "Radio check. Crazy Dude, show me you hear me."

On Screen Two, Cord held up a near-empty forty bottle, turned it upside down to empty it, then dropped it. The sound of glass breaking came through the speaker.

"He does that so well," Kim said with a smirk before squeezing the mic button. "Read you loud and clear, Crazy Dude. IAB Backup, check in."

"Read you loud and clear," Abe said. "By the way, both alibis checked out. Got sworn statements to prove it."

Warren didn't murder Avila, and Ortega didn't murder Simmons. Coburn and Tyler could have discovered that in one day. "Thanks, Abe. All team members hold positions until I give the word. IAB Command, out."

Screen One showed five teenage girls at various places under the el, alternating pacing with standing. "Slow night," Fredricks said. "The not-so-subtle traffic checkpoints at Pennsylvania Avenue and Schenck Avenue may have something to do with that. Keeps the real johns out."

"Our girl approaching from the east," one officer outside said over the wire.

At 9:05, right on time, Marisa strutted past the van in a black micro-miniskirt, a flimsy pink top, black fishnet thigh-highs, one of which had a small tear above the knee, and stilettos.

Cadman chuckled. "Wonder what Stransky's thinking right now."

Kim snarled at him. "Not one more word."

The radio crackled. "All hail," Cord said in little more than a whisper. "The sweetest mother of all doth approach."

"All mobile units," Fredricks said into her mic. "Proceed as planned."

On Screen One, Marisa approached the first girl, who pointed hurriedly to the other side of Livonia Avenue. A technician changed the camera's angle to follow her. As she reached the other side, Blade Morales came into view. Camera Two now had the view of Marisa and Blade, while Camera One swiveled back to their side of the street.

Five cars rolled along Livonia, unevenly spaced. The first one stopped about where Marisa had crossed the street. The same young hooker approached and got in the car. It turned down an alley.

On Screen One, the second car rolled up, and a girl got in. On Screen Two, Marisa was now talking with Blade.

"More volume on the audio," Fredricks said.

"Yeah, well, you came to the right place, *Chica*," Blade was saying. "I get you plenty of work, you get free rent, I pay all the bills, and you get an allowance."

"Where's the wire?" Kim asked.

"The pin on her top," Fredricks replied.

"You like that?" Blade asked as he reached down and groped Marisa.

"Ooh, yeah," Marisa replied. "But Ima earn the money, right?"

"Decisions, decisions. Looks like it's getting busy. After every trick, you give the money to Roscoe, Hammer or me, whoever's close. No holding back. You get busted, I bail out your ass. You need help to chill?"

"I'm good."

On Screen One, Mobile Three was pulling into an alley while the remaining girls got into Mobiles Four and Five.

"We got it," Kim said into the mic. "All units, execute."

Cord jumped up, covered in garbage, pointing his piece at Morales. "Police! Freeze!" When one of Blade's goons reached inside his jacket, Cord took aim. "Don't even think about it."

Two SVU detectives rushed in, one grabbing Morales, the other grabbing the goon.

Abe, Bob, and Martin dashed across Smallwood and grabbed the other goon.

A police van burst into the intersection from Smallwood Avenue, lights flashing, and screeched to a halt in the middle of the street. A second van entered from the opposite direction. SVU officers deployed at both ends. Each of the mobile unit uncles brought his girl over to the van at the Smallwood end.

Kim left the van with Cadman and Lieutenant Fredricks.

"Outstanding work, Detective," Fredricks said. She turned to Cadman. "Well done."

He was still pouting. "I didn't do anything."

"Correct."

Cord finished reading Morales his rights as Kim arrived.

Morales struggled against the handcuffs. "What you mean, 'Human Trafficking'?"

"You buy adolescent girls from immigrant smugglers," Kim said, "and then you pimp them on the street. That's the textbook definition." As she spoke, a television news van pulled up on Smallwood Avenue. A second followed closely behind. "We're ready to blare this story across the entire city."

"But," Cord said, "consider the positives. Think how popular it will make you in Rikers. They'll love you for it."

Morales was shaking. "No, you got it all wrong. We weren't..."

"You have the right to remain silent," Kim said, "which I suggest you invoke. We'll talk more at the precinct. And, because we're reasonable, we'll slip you into a car now, before the cameras catch you." She waved a group of the backup cops and the four mobile uncles over. "Please take Mr. Morales and his two associates to the Seven-Four. Make sure they stay separated from the girls."

Kim's cell buzzed. It was Colangelo. "Who the hell leaked our sweep to the media?"

"Fredricks thought it would reassure the community and scare other rings in the city."

Her explanation didn't mollify him. "You should have told me."

"Since you and Fredricks are the same level, I assumed she'd tell you." It was the first time she'd ever lied to Colangelo. Kim had not only been sure Fredricks wouldn't tell him, she'd counted on it. He would have freaked, and Kim couldn't risk losing the pressure that the hint of public exposure would bring to bear on Morales. She also felt less guilty about it than she otherwise might have. It wasn't like he had her back on Cadman. "Lieutenant Fredricks agreed to handle the entire thing. She'll say this was SVU's sting. She'll say nothing about us."

"You'd better hope so," he said with a growl.

She hesitated. As awkward as it was, she needed to clear something else with him right now. "I arranged for a social worker to handle placement of the girls."

"Well, that's good. We can finally place Amara in an appropriate facility."

From awkward to excruciating in an instant. "She's doing well there, Lieu. And she's safe."

No answer.

She sighed. "Besides, I already agreed."

"You don't have the authority to agree. How did Cadman do?"

"He did nothing other than occupy valuable space in the command van and make an inappropriate comment."

"No fuck ups. Good. I'm on my way over."

CHAPTER TWENTY-SIX

The Seven-Four was a madhouse. Kim had known it would be.

Warren was the desk sergeant. "We got Morales in Room One, his goons in Two and Three. The girls are in the holding cell."

Kim was framing her objection to placing the girls in a cell when Colangelo approached. "Fredricks is still with the press. I came to..."

Julie Campbell blew past Warren, stopping when she saw the girls in the holding cell. "What the fuck are they doing behind bars?" Her voice carried over the general commotion.

"We're in cramped quarters here," Warren replied. "We don't have a more spacious place."

"In a cell?" Julie's voice grew shrill. Heads turned throughout the station.

Kim caught Colangelo's stunned expression. "This is Julie Campbell, the social worker I told you about."

"They're under arrest?" Julie turned on Kim. "I'd expect this from them, but you should know better. You asked me to find a place for them, and I did, at Youth Colony in Clinton Hill."

Kim held up a hand. "Ms. Campbell, we put this operation together to put Morales out of business. I'm aware of the circumstances of the girls' involvement. I am also aware, as are you, that the system grinds at its own pace. I want those girls placed in safety as much as you do. They're scared to death. You'll go with them when they go."

"How, by paddy wagon?"

The main door opened. Fr. Lynch walked in with a slim blonde woman in her mid-forties.

"Father Lynch," Julie said. "Evelyn. What are you two doing here?"

The blond woman smiled. "The same thing you are, Julie." She turned to Kim. "Detective Brady? I'm Evelyn Burke. I worked with Mariano Avila on his criminal cases. Where are our wayward young ladies?"

"Locked up," Julie said with a sneer.

Fr. Lynch laughed. "That might have some instructive value. I have the parish van outside, and we can take them as soon as you give us the word."

Julie shook her head. "I should have known."

"Who's with Amara?" Kim asked.

"One detective from SVU, one of your detectives, and your Officer Fuentes," the priest replied. "Ms. Fuentes', ahem, uniform made Amara rather uncomfortable, but she adjusted."

"She was working undercover tonight," Kim said. And Martin was staying close.

"Under very scant cover. It took a bit of convincing for Amara to accept her."

Lieutenant Fredricks came through the front entrance with a dark-haired woman in her fifties, who greeted both Julie and Evelyn. It was getting crowded around the front desk.

"Detective Brady," Fredricks said, "this is Randi Mozlin, ADA with the Brooklyn Special Victims Bureau, Human Trafficking Unit."

"Nice to meet you." Kim took the older woman's hand. "Will you be prosecuting this case?"

"Based on what Lauren's told me, I'd say yes. Why?"

Kim gestured to the door. Once outside, she explained the basics of Morales' operation. "I'm nailing these bastards, but I'm trying to discover where the girls came from. The FBI wants…"

"Lauren told me you're from IAB, previously from Homicide. You're partnering on an SVU sweep of a human trafficking ring. Now, you want information for the FBI. What in God's name is going on?"

"I'm working the Avila murder case. A Member of Service may or may not have taken part, but immigration has some bearing." She nodded toward the entrance. "These dirtbags may have seen something, or they may have taken part. I have to find out."

Randi fished a business card from her purse. She wrote a name and number on the back. "Tomorrow morning, call Rick Conti. He's an ADA in the Criminal Court Division. I'll give him a heads-up. You'll want him assigned when you make an arrest."

Back inside, Randi took command. "Evelyn, I will not charge the girls. I suggest we not even question them tonight. Where are they going to stay?"

"All five girls will stay at Youth Colony," Julie replied. "They can remain there until we find a better situation, or we locate their families. I want to get them settled by midnight, if possible."

Randi turned to Sergeant Warren. "Please release all five girls into the custody of Ms. Campbell at once."

Kim, along with Julie, Evelyn Burke, and Fr. Lynch, followed Warren back to the holding cell. The girls were still pale and shaking. "Okay, girls, here's the deal. You will go now with Fr. Lynch and Miss Julie. Nothing bad will happen to you, I promise. No one will charge you with any crime."

Julie translated, and the girls relaxed. Warren unlocked the cell, and the girls followed Fr. Lynch and Julie out.

Randi stopped Kim before entering Room One, where a police officer stood guard. "Are you sure you don't want to move the sixth girl to be with the others?"

To Kim's annoyance, Cadman was checking his reflection in a pane of glass. "I'm sure. She's safe at the rectory. And she's the one eyewitness we have to the murder." She led Cadman into the interrogation room, where Abe, Bob, and Colangelo were waiting.

Morales tried playing it tough. "What's this shit about human trafficking?"

"Your game is up," Kim said. "You held six underage girls against their wills, feeding them barbiturates and not much else, and pimped them. You have a prior felony, a drug conviction in 2011. So, you're looking at eight to twenty-five years in prison, per girl."

He slumped in his seat. "Get me a lawyer."

Bob glanced up. "And a calculator."

Morales crossed his arms against his chest. "I ain't gonna say shit till a lawyer gets here."

"Suit yourself," Kim replied.

Both of Blade's goons, Ramon "Roscoe" Burton and Alvin "Hammer" Greene, lawyered up as soon as Kim questioned them.

"One of my detectives will take them all down to Central Booking," Lieutenant Fredricks said.

The officer who'd been standing guard outside of Room One walked by. Kim caught the name plate: Burrows. "Excuse me. Officer Burrows? Officer Isaac Burrows?" The Table of Organization for the Seven-Four only had one Burrows listed.

"Yeah?"

A group of uniforms led Blade, Roscoe, and Hammer past the front desk. All three interrogation rooms were free. Kim identified herself. "Can I talk to you for a minute?" She gestured toward the first interrogation room. "Five months ago, you responded to a radio run on a stabbing murder in a playground on Elton, a victim named Joey Simmons?" Burrows nodded. "You partnered that night with Sergeant Warren?"

Another nod.

"What did you notice regarding the victim?" Kim asked. "Anything besides the fatal stab wound?"

"Um... no. Should I have?"

Kim looked him in the eye. "You noticed nothing else unusual about the body?" Burrows shook his head. "What duties did you have here tonight?"

"I was writing up a response to an earlier call. Domestic disturbance on Van Siclen Avenue."

"So why were you loitering outside this room earlier this evening when we were interrogating a prisoner?"

"I saw a prisoner in there alone. Thought it best to monitor him. Thought I was helping."

"Standing guard over a handcuffed prisoner?"

He stared at the floor. "I didn't realize…"

"Did you have any prior knowledge of Mr. Simmons?"

"No." His response was immediate.

Bob knocked once and entered. "You ready to go?"

She glanced back at Burrows. Something wasn't adding up, but she didn't have time to pursue it now.

CHAPTER TWENTY-SEVEN

Captain Forrest checked the caller ID on the first ring and experienced a powerful desire to ignore the call. He was already regretting having ever taken a call from the person on the other end. But he knew if he ducked it now, it would only be worse later. He answered on the third ring. "Good evening, Senator."

"Good evening, Deputy Inspector…"

"Captain." He wasn't taking anything for granted.

"Oh, don't be so modest. I understand tonight's operation went off without a hitch. That so?"

"You mean he already reported to you?"

A hearty chuckle. "No. I don't think he even knows I'm the one looking out for him. But, as a politician of some influence, I have friends among the press corps as well as enemies. I've already received requests for interviews, and I will announce my current opinion to the press in the morning. Don't worry, I won't say anything about the Avila murder investigation. But I'm afraid I'll have some unpleasant comments for the Seventy Fourth precinct."

"I'm sure you won't be alone," Forrest replied.

"I wanted to give you a heads-up because you may get some calls afterward, asking what you intend to do about them. In the meantime, how did your protégé do, tonight?"

"He didn't fuck up." He had a sudden craving for a cigarette.

The long silence spoke volumes of the senator's disapproval. "I would hope we could be more positive about it. I'm hoping he learned something about command."

Forrest was tiring of this game. "He's still learning the basic tenets of police work. You're doing more harm than good by putting him into situations without the experience to deal with them."

Another lengthy silence. "Deputy Inspector…"

"Captain."

"Be careful it doesn't become lieutenant." The senator let the threat sink in. "We often receive assignments for tasks without the requisite resources, and, regardless of whether we like it, we must do our best. I expect the same from you."

"Fine. Then at least do me the courtesy of not making it even more difficult by micromanaging the process." Forrest held his breath.

"All right. To the extent I'm not micromanaged, I will not micromanage you. Anything else you want to get off your chest?"

Further protest was pointless. The senator had stuck him with Cadman.

CHAPTER TWENTY-EIGHT

"What the fuck, Rafe?" Desmond was irate. "I thought the Panamanian killed Joey."

Rafer Harwood took a long swig of beer and surveyed his little kingdom—the three-room apartment on the first floor of the attached three-family his mother owned. She still lived in the second-floor apartment, but never left the house. He arranged for any work needed on the house, and she paid him fifteen hundred a month, plus he lived in the apartment rent-free. Since her stroke, they had put her bank accounts in both her name and his, allowing him to pay the bills and himself, including extras for when fifteen hundred didn't get it done.

Desmond glared at him, like he had the right to demand an answer. Fine. "The Panamanian killed Joey because he reported the Panamanian to ICE so he could make it with his girlfriend. I gotta write it in blood?"

When the fuck were these assholes going to get it through their thick skulls that Rafer T. Harwood was the leader, the mastermind, the only one who had finished college, even if it had taken five years going full time, plus summer sessions.

"Then why was that detective..." Desmond began.

Harwood cut him off. "So, the bitch detective and her 'minority' lap dog sniffed around. Let 'em sniff."

"Yeah," Conroy said. "But all three of us?"

Harwood slammed down his can of beer; some of its contents sloshed onto the old end table. "I told you. Joey's mother told her we were all friends."

"But why was she even asking questions to begin with?" Conroy pressed.

Desmond was still glaring. "Maybe the Panamanian didn't kill Joey."

"My source says he did," Harwood replied. "But they couldn't get a search warrant for his place. Cops are like the media. They hate the truth. Fucks up the cash flow." He grabbed the remote. "Time for the eleven o'clock lies."

The wide-screen TV, a gift from mom she didn't know she'd given, sprang to life. "Police tonight conducted a sweep of an underage prostitution ring on Livonia Avenue in Brooklyn," the anchor said. "The Brooklyn Special Victims Unit took five girls in their early teens into custody and turned them over to the Administration for Children's Services. It appears all the girls had been separated from their families upon arriving in this country. Police arrested three men accused of running the ring, including the alleged ringleader, Ramon Morales, and will charge all three with multiple counts of human trafficking, drug possession and weapons possession."

Conroy blanched. "What?"

Desmond started laughing. "There goes your playground, Cliffy-boy."

"Police say the ring was operating a block from the scene of another recent crime, the murder of Mariano Avila. The sweep's timing raised questions about potential connections between the ring and the murder case. Police would not comment on either investigation."

Conroy was pale. "They arrested the girls?"

"And turned 'em over to ACS," Desmond replied. "Just think, Cliffy. Within the week, the city will pay some 'foster parent' for getting the same action you were paying for."

Conroy jumped to his feet, teeth clenched, face red, fists balled and shaking. Desmond drew back a little.

"Knock it off, both of you," Harwood said. "You wake my mother, and I'll kick both your asses." He'd made such threats often, but never carried them out. Someday these idiots might figure that out. Might need a fresh approach. "So, the cops think this pimp, Morales, knocked off Avila?"

"…An anonymous tip to this station claimed that Avila's attacker was a police officer in uniform."

"No wonder they're so eager to pin it on the pimp." He stood and patted Conroy on the shoulder. "Too bad about your girls, Cliff. There'll be others."

"What if he'd been dipping his stick tonight and got busted with the rest of 'em?" Desmond asked.

Harwood drained the rest of his beer and strode to the fridge to fetch another. Might need to tap Mom for another "loan" this week. "Shit, no. They never bother with the customers. One of the few remnants of civilization we still have. Men have their needs; women have their place." Although the number of women who knew their place was shrinking at an alarming rate.

Desmond shot Conroy a fresh look of disgust. "They'd sure as hell bother with a guy who gets it on with ninth-graders. Face it, Cliffy-boy. You're a pedophile."

Conroy took a threatening step toward his tormentor, and Harwood stepped between them. "Cliff, go sit down. Desmond, shut the fuck up." Desmond was getting ideas above his rank, although he had a point. If Cliff got caught, it would make it much harder for Rafer T. Harwood to accomplish his goals. But recruiting was difficult.

Desmond was still standing, glaring at him.

"Sit down, Jeff," Harwood said in his rarely used fatherly tone. "It's not like Cliff's stalking little American girls coming home from school. Besides, I doubt you'd want anyone to poke around your web-browsing habits. Might not make your mom too proud." He thought about the lingerie catalogs that didn't always remain in the mailbox of the couple on the third floor. "We all have our little hobbies."

Desmond flopped into a chair across the room.

Rafer continued in his TV-dad tone. "We have to keep the long-term goal in sight—bringing this so-called Sanctuary City to heel. We can't allow anything to interfere with that, so we put our own little personal disagreements aside. Got it?"

"Yeah," Desmond replied. "Now, tell me, oh great wise leader, why was the bitch detective asking about both Joey's murder and Avila's?"

"She knows the Panamanian killed Joey, and Avila was the Panamanian's lawyer, who let ICE deport him rather than do twenty-five-to-life. And she knows we're Joey's friends."

"Maybe, but she sounded like she didn't believe the Panamanian did it. So, why is she looking at the two murders together?"

Harwood threw up his hands. "A fucking tactic. She's desperate to pin it on someone else because a cop killed Avila. She's got nothing to go on, so she throws some bullshit around to get us to say something incriminating, which we don't because we had nothing to do with it. Okay?"

Desmond chewed on that for a while. "Guess so."

Harwood sat back as Desmond and Conroy focused on news about the Mets, relieved at the quiet. Because the detective's questions had made him uncomfortable.

CHAPTER TWENTY-NINE

Wednesday, March 21st

As Kim left the apartment at six-fifteen, she caught sight of the stoppered wine bottle still sitting on the dining room table and their two Waterford Crystal wine goblets. The Nets had offered Jake the job of Special Assistant to the General Manager for Analytics.

She'd struggled for words and failed.

The evening had ended in stiff silence with Jake dripping with resentment, and now she was slipping out to avoid facing him before regrouping. The text she'd gotten from Martin Stransky as she entered the apartment last night—*Meet me at One-PP at seven in AM for video party*—had monopolized her attention and she hadn't slept a wink.

Martin was waiting outside the building. "I think we may have something."

"I hope so. Word about Avila's killer having been in uniform is spreading fast."

A few minutes later, they were sitting with a video technician at two twenty-seven-inch monitors, each with the view afforded by one of the two cameras.

"I've synchronized the two tapes," the technician said. "I'll start from eight o'clock the night of the sixteenth at two times speed." Nothing moved, but every few minutes, a car would zip past. The technician paused the video. "Okay, we're now at eight-thirty-seven. Back to normal speed."

For a few moments, there was nothing. Then, a stocky figure in dark blue strode past on the far side of the street. The tech paused the video and zoomed in at a point at which the figure in the image was facing the camera.

"Looks like our guy," Martin said.

Kim did a twenty-second check, first the sketch, then the image on the screen, back and forth. "Not sure. Can we zoom in closer or get more clarity?"

The tech shook his head. "It's a fixed-focus lens, so this is as clear as it gets. I could zoom in further, but that would blur the image."

Sheila Gregg often said that sketches from witness statements were all about impressions. Kim studied the image on the screen. Stocky, which the ill-fitting uniform made worse. The bushy eyebrows and prominent nose. Her gut told her this was the guy. "Is this all you have?"

The tech didn't answer but played the tape at normal speed, and the figure disappeared from the left screen. On the right screen, the image never changed, but a dark Honda Civic appeared on the left screen, heading in the opposite direction. "Bingo." The tech froze the image.

"Same guy," Martin said. "No doubt about it."

Kim had to agree. "He's driving a 2013 or 2014 Civic. Please tell me you caught part of the plate."

The technician burst into an enormous grin. "Let's see." The image inched forward a frame, and he froze it and zoomed in. The license plate was visible. "Lima, Tango, Alpha, one, followed by either a four or a nine, followed by a number I can't make out."

"And he drove right back past the scene," Kim said.

"That's balls," Martin replied. "Think he's flipping us the proverbial bird?"

"Or hiding in plain sight. Any sign of him arriving earlier on the tape?"

"Just this," the tech said. He rewound the tape to a minute after seven. The same figure appeared on the left screen, but on the other side of the street. A few moments later, he appeared on the right screen, his back to the camera. "No sign of the blue Civic."

"So," Kim said, "he approached from the east on Livonia and parked east of the cameras on the westbound side. That's why he crossed the street when he ran from the crime scene."

CHAPTER THIRTY

"Sorry I'm late," Marisa said as she rushed to join the team in the conference room. "Train trouble again. What else is new?"

"Great job last night, Marisa," Colangelo said.

"Yeah." Cadman leered at her. "Totally."

Marisa snapped a bubble while Stransky shot Cadman a dirty look.

"Thanks, everyone." Kim finished making notes on the board. "Back to our case. The killer drove west on Livonia. Any chance of live traffic cams in the area?"

"In East New York?" Abe replied. "A handful of red light and speed cameras along Linden Boulevard and Atlantic Avenue, but nothing else between Cross Bay Boulevard and Kings Highway."

Kim resisted the urge to hurl the marker across the room. Work the problem. "All right, Cord, try to track down that plate." She stared at the board. "Based on the video, he knew where the cameras were and how to avoid them. He scouted this out in advance."

"Then why cross the street when leaving the scene?" Cadman asked.

"The cameras were focused on the sidewalk on the near side of the street. He retraced his steps." She reread the timeline. "Amara said she heard a scream right before she ran away. The killer had to hear it, too, and realized someone had seen him. That might explain why he made such a hash of flipping Avila's body, but not Simmons'."

"Assuming he's the same killer," Colangelo said.

The pagan symbols. "It's the same killer. Once he knew someone saw him, he knew the clock was ticking. Perhaps he thought the witness was watching him. He ran across the street to prevent anyone from getting a better look at him. When he ran into Amara, the police ruse fell apart."

Colangelo cut in. "You're sure he's an imposter? Some cops dislike illegals as well as New York being a Sanctuary City. Don't underestimate how bad it is that word leaked to the press."

And that had been bothering Kim. "I checked the 911 recording. The caller said nothing about the attacker being a cop or being in uniform. So, who leaked it to the press?"

"Jesus," Cord said. "You think it was one of us?"

The memory of having been undermined from within during the Cove Shooting case nagged at her.

Bob nodded toward Cadman. "What about Junior?"

Colangelo held up a hand. "Hold it, folks. Kim, a word in private?" He led her outside and closed the conference room door. "Flashbacks?"

"Not exactly. But the similarities are hard to ignore."

"You think Cadman leaked it? Bob Nolan sure does."

"It would make sense. He gets shoved down our throats the same day we catch this case, along with his dictated role—for which he is utterly unprepared."

"But you don't think he's the guy?"

Deep breath time. "I doubt it. The group dislikes him and so do I. But he's intimidated by the unit and realizes he's in over his head. It's no one in the unit, either. They're a dedicated team. But there is a leak. Maybe it came from the killer, himself, looking to cement the idea that the killer was a cop."

Back in the conference room, Colangelo took command. "Okay, folks. This is a bitch of a case. We don't know where the leak came from, but there's no reason to believe it came from here. We do have some issues, like Coburn and Tyler fucking up the Simmons investigation."

"And two uniforms who keep turning up in connection to both cases," Kim said. "None of them resemble the guy Amara ran into, and he was Avila's killer."

"The lab confirms the blood on her dress was Avila's," Cadman added.

"Nice to see you can read." Martin gestured at the board where Kim had noted that there had been no other blood on the dress or the gravel from the alley but Avila's.

She needed to refocus the meeting. "The killer's uniform had no precinct or command insignia on the collar, and no firearm was visible. The conduct of the four guys from the Seven-Four smells like week-old fish, but at most they might have been providing cover. Abe and Bob, please go back to the computer rebuild place and get their videos for the week before the murder. Maybe they caught our guy before he figured out where the cameras were." She turned to Marisa. "Any information from the girls we took off the street?"

"None of them recognized the guy in the sketch, but they all recognized Conroy's mug shot. He was a regular. He always came alone, except one time he brought someone with him."

"Get a description?" Kim asked.

Marisa shook her head. "Sorry. No one had seen the tat, either."

Cord was getting restless. "Anything for me?"

He'd love this. "Yes. Please see Vera Koshkin and go over those e-mail lists she got. Highlight anything that looks persistent, with particular concern when it's anyone outside their little group. Track their search histories, look for anything recurring that isn't porn. Note visits to any of the sites on Taylor's list, and anything that looks like militia."

"Yes, ma'am." He tried to look cool. He failed.

Her cell pinged. It was a text from Randi Mozlin. *Interview with Morales et al set for eleven at BDC. Can you make it?* At least it wasn't from Jake.

"And what will keep you busy this morning, Detective Brady?" Cord asked.

"I'm interrogating our three dirtbags from last night at the Brooklyn Detention Center."

"Take Cadman with you," Colangelo said.

Cadman sprang to full alert at the mention of his name.

"Okay. Meanwhile, Martin, please ask Taylor if he has any additional information for us." She thought back on her conversation with Harwood. "Mention the Eagle Tavern to him. See if he's come up with anything."

As Kim waited for Cadman at the main door to their offices, the office television blared the latest from *City News*, a local cable news station. On the screen was a still image of a familiar political figure.

"Following the arrest of an alleged human trafficking ring last night in Brooklyn, State Senator Raymond Brandt simultaneously praised and berated the NYPD this morning while speaking with reporters in Albany," the anchor said.

The still image dissolved, replaced by a tape of the senator. "I want to praise the work done last night by the Brooklyn Special Victims Unit. The sting reflected the NYPD at its absolute best. However, I'd be remiss if I failed to point out that this ring was operating with impunity on the doorstep of the Seventy-Fourth Precinct. My committee will keep a keen eye on how the department handles this matter in the coming days."

"Senator," one reporter asked, "are you suggesting that there may have been an element of corruption at work that prevented the ring from being shut down sooner?"

Colangelo sidled up next to Kim to watch.

"I suspect," the senator replied, "that this has much more to do with this administration's refusal to follow proven crime-fighting measures than any departmental corruption."

"You mean the former mayor's refusal to accept the Broken Windows Theory?" the reporter asked.

"I mean everything—from abandoning Stop and Frisk to relentlessly talking down the police, from forgetting Broken Windows to embracing so-called Criminal Justice Reform, including eliminating cash bail, which turns every thief, vandal, and recipient of a city summons into a scofflaw. Ms. Dunn, as public advocate, supported those measures, and as acting mayor is now calling for even more ludicrous 'reform' measures."

Another reporter chimed in. "So, in a precinct where most of the population is nonwhite, you're willing to ignore police corruption, but if it were, say, Bay Ridge, you'd be screaming for Internal Affairs?"

Brandt spluttered. "That's ridiculous. Internal Affairs was present for the sweep, and they have my full support."

Kim turned to Colangelo. "Who the hell told him that, and what's he doing blabbing it to a bunch of reporters?"

Colangelo was livid. "I don't know, Kim. But I'll damned well find out."

One voice carried over the babble of several reporters. "Do you condone a police officer murdering a beloved citizen like Mariano Avila?"

Brandt spluttered before yelling back, "I know for a fact that Mr. Avila's murderer was not a police officer."

CHAPTER THIRTY-ONE

"Tell   aight up," Kim said as she searched for a parking spot near the   Detention Center. "Did Brandt get this position for you?"

    ?" Cadman's surprise appeared to be genuine. "The sena

    ever even met him."

    not what I asked you."

    never met him, how could he get me this position?"

    ack-parked into a tight space. "Don't fuck around with me, We both know someone has greased the skids for you. I asked you   ct question. Yes or no?"

    't know. I've asked no one for any help. And that's the truth."

    you tell anyone about last night's bust? Or about this case?"

    ody. Not even Loretta."

    r sister."

    nan smiled. "Loretta first encouraged me to apply to the A   y. It was something that I'd always dreamed of doing—becoming a   fter our parents died, she dropped out of college and landed a job as   administrative assistant at Emory Equities. She's done very well, t   but she wanted me to follow my dream."

Kim thought back to when she'd met Loretta. A
assistant with designer clothes and shoes and a perfec
must do extremely well.

Randi Mozlin and Detective Julio Espada from SVU
them at the entrance to the detention center.

"I'll set the bar high," Randi said. "You can tell the
Then pump them for what you need."

"We tossed Morales' crib this morning," Espada said
other girls. But we grabbed these." He placed an evic
hands. "Six bottles of Seconol, all prescribed by a Dr. Eps
and filled at three different pharmacies scattered around

Kim thanked him. "So, you have everything you need

"It's your show." Espada turned grave. "But please
girls were only fourteen. The oldest was sixteen."

They saw Morales, first. As they all sat at the small ta
favorite spot, directly across from the accused. She said
glared.

Randi turned to the Legal Aid attorney. "We have yo
six counts of Human Trafficking. Caught him in the act la
least six counts of Prescription Fraud, a federal offens
squeeze Dr. Epstein in Riverdale, I'm confident the
multiply. When we're finished with you, we'll hand you o
for the prescription charges."

Morales lurched in his seat, but his lawyer clamped
shoulder before he could say a word.

"Last Friday night," Kim said, "you lost a fifteen-year-o
girl. She told us all about how you kept her and the other girls c
and pimped them under the el." She held up the evidence bags.
Espada found these at your place."

"I'm not inclined to make a deal with your client," Randi s
serve a hundred and fifty, no possibility of parole. However,
Brady has some questions of her own. Provide satisfactory an
perhaps I'll do something for you."

"Like what?" Morales asked.

"If you can give her everything she needs, you might persu
have you separated from the general population—sex offender

well there. If you can tell her where the girls came from and how they got here, I'm sure Detective Brady will inform the Feds about how helpful you've been."

Morales was crestfallen.

Randi turned to the Legal Aid attorney. "I'm a reasonable woman."

"Okay," Kim said. "Mariano Avila was murdered Friday night, and you'd confronted him, true?"

"Yeah. He threatened to call the cops on us," Morales said. "I told him to mind his own fucking business. I don't think he did, but the cops never bothered us, anyway."

"Why was that?" Kim asked. "Who were you paying?"

"Nobody. Hey, you don't think I'd hand you some dirty cops to get out of this?"

Okay, that made sense. "Did you see anything going on outside Avila's office Friday night?"

He shook his head. "Roscoe guarded that end of the street."

Kim pulled out the sketch. "Have you seen him, either Friday night or any other?"

Morales studied the sketch. "This guy a cop?"

"Just answer the question."

He studied it for several moments. "Didn't see him Friday night. But I seen him around a few times, just never in uniform. He'd check out the girls, but he never looked interested to buy. So, I thought he might be a private detective, looking to catch out some wayward hubby. After a while, he stopped coming around."

"How long ago was that?"

"Started last summer. Stopped after a month."

She laid out the mugshots of Conroy, Desmond, and Simmons. "Ever see any of these guys around?"

He pointed at Conroy. "This guy's a regular. Real hot for the bitch who ran away." He studied Desmond's photo. "Nah, never saw this guy." He turned to the shot of Simmons. "This guy came once with the regular. But he wasn't buying. They got into an argument about it. Got heated. Roscoe had to tell them to chill."

Kim gestured to the sketch. "Was he on Livonia Avenue the night Avila was killed?"

Morales looked helpless. "I didn't see him."

"Okay. Whenever you saw him, did he hang around any particular place?"

"By the stairs to the el station."

Kim recalled the layout of the station. "At Smallwood?"

"Yeah. Ask Roscoe. He always has Smallwood because he's in way better shape than Hammer, and if someone tried to get away by running up the stairs, he'd have a better chance of catching them."

Time to shift gears. "The girls were all smuggled into the country, and you got them from the smugglers. We know this. Who were the smugglers and how did you contact them?"

Morales cocked an eye at his attorney, who sighed and leaned over to whisper in his ear. Morales muttered something under his breath that Kim couldn't catch, and the attorney nodded. "I never knew their names. Epstein handled it. I paid him two grand per girl, and he wrote the prescriptions. Sometimes he used his own name, but most times he used his partner's."

"How did you get started with Epstein?" Kim asked.

"He was a customer. When he first came around, all my girls were runaways. They'd work for me, then they'd leave and go on their own. Epstein came up with keeping 'em wasted so they'd stay put. Sometimes it worked, sometimes it didn't. Then, about a year ago, he told me about a trucker he'd met with some interesting cargo, and how girls who were illegals would be much easier to control."

Kim made notes on her cell. While she did, a text popped up from Jake. *We need to talk. Please call.*

"All right," she said to Morales. "This seems useful. I have to warn you, though, that if anything you've told me turns out to be false..."

"It ain't," Morales said.

"I've urged my client to cooperate," the Legal Aid attorney added.

"I'll pass this information on to the FBI," Kim said. "We'll see where it leads. If it's helpful, I'll recommend the Feds go easy on you for the Prescription Fraud."

"With all due respect," the attorney said, "that's not much considering you're waving a hundred-and-fifty-year sentence at him."

"Tell you what," Randi said. "Let's check back after Epstein's in custody and we've gotten his statement."

Hammer was useless, but Roscoe provided more details on the man in the sketch. "Yeah, I saw him Friday night. The Mexican bitch ran into him when I was chasing her. I saw him a few times recently."

Kim choked down the urge to snap at the reference to Amara. "How recent?"

"The last few weeks. He wasn't interested in the girls. Looked like he was hanging out down near the church. Who knew he was a cop?"

Kim's cell buzzed as they walked out. Her first thought was, "Oh, Jake, please give me a minute."

But it was a text from Colangelo. *Nolan and Stewart responded to a call from their lieu. A body in Clinton Hill, right behind Youth Colony. Looks like it's linked. Check in when you know.*

CHAPTER THIRTY-TWO

Before pulling out for the quick drive to Clinton Hill, Kim texted Jake. *Can't talk now. Promise to call later. Promise.* When Jake had wanted to marry her, she'd feared the future. She wasn't afraid now, just preoccupied.

"So," she said to Cadman, "can you tell me when we can and can't access someone's e-mails?"

"We can access e-mails stored on a server, not a personal computer, if they're at least 180 days old." His demeanor reeked with resentment at being quizzed.

"That's all?"

"Why? Isn't it?"

"Go back and check again. Hint: court case."

She parked in the lot behind Youth Colony. CSU was already there. Phil Vitello waved her over but blocked her path to the body. "It's connected. Same MO. Stabbed in the neck, design carved in the chest. I'm guessing it happened early this morning, but the ME will fix the time of death."

Kim tried to peer around Vitello without him noticing. Skinny jeans. Black ankle boots.

But Cadman had a better angle. "Hey, isn't that the social worker?"

Julie Campbell.

Vitello turned and led them into the area marked off by CSU, avoiding a pool of blood that was already drying at the edges. "Neater than the last one. He didn't drench himself. No bloody footprints, just some spatter to one side. Since the killer stabbed her on the left side, like the others, the spatter pattern shows she was walking toward the building. That truck's remained parked there since last night, so it's possible he hid there, waiting for her. Visitor parking is along here, so she had to walk past this spot."

Kim kneeled beside Julie's body and pulled the front of her jacket away, revealing her torn blouse. She pulled that away, too. There, on her chest was a triangle, apex up with a single line through it.

Air.

Kim punched up Fr. Lynch's number on her cell. "Father, this is Kim Brady. I have terrible news. Someone murdered Julie Campbell this morning in the parking lot behind Youth Colony."

There was a lengthy silence. "Can you keep her body there for a little longer?"

"Guys from the ME's Office are here," Phil said.

Kim greeted them. "I'd like Dr. Shelton to handle this."

"He's on call," one technician replied, "so, no problem."

She turned back to her cell. "I'm afraid that's not possible. The Medical Examiner's Office is already here. Besides which, I don't want you leaving the rectory until I have a detail assigned there." Before he could protest, she added, "Please trust my instincts on this, Father."

"You won't move Amara, will you?" he asked.

"Not yet."

He didn't like it, but it was the best she could do. She needed Amara alive and well, and Amara needed security.

She turned to a technician. "Judging by her neck wound, can you determine the angle of attack?"

"Sorry. That's beyond my level of expertise."

"Cadman, call the lieu and fill him in. Ask him to arrange for a security detail at Blessed Mother Rectory."

But her mind was racing. How did the killer discover the girls' location? They'd only decided the previous night where the girls would stay. At the Seven-Four.

Kim and Cadman entered the facility. Kim flashed her badge and asked to see the Security Director. There were several cameras, and he pulled the previous night's and the morning's flash drives. She checked the sign-in book. Julie signed in at 10:30 and signed out ten minutes after midnight. But the tape showed no one lurking in the interim. They switched to the morning video.

"Stop," Kim said. "Time stamp reads 7:15." A heavy figure in a dark jacket and a dark blue baseball cap with the bill pulled down low slipped behind the van that had been there all night. "Can you rerun that segment, please?" The image zipped backward and then repeated. "What's that he's laying down?"

"Looks like a rake," the security director replied.

"So, today, he's a landscaper," Kim said.

"Can't be. They were here Monday."

The image rolled forward. Periodically, she saw the baseball cap peeking out from behind the van. At 8:17, Julie's car pulled into the lot. It disappeared once it turned into the parking spot, but the guy in the baseball cap appeared and began raking. As she walked toward the building, he again vanished behind the van. Julie drew closer, then stopped and turned. "He must have called out to her." But the van blocked their view of whatever happened afterward. The killer didn't appear again until he was walking out of the lot at the far end.

"Wait a minute," Kim said. "If that's our guy, he's no longer wearing the blue jacket. That's a light gray sweatshirt."

She snatched the two flash drives and dashed out.

The CSU team was still working outside. She flagged down Vitello. "We got him on video. He had on a dark blue jacket when he got here, but he was wearing a gray sweatshirt when he left. And he wasn't carrying anything."

Vitello scratched his head. "We searched the grounds. Found nothing..."

"He didn't toss it in the bushes."

He was already grinning. "There are several storm drains scattered around the lot. What can you tell me to make the job easier?"

"The camera is on a direct line along this last row of cars. He disappeared behind the van and never reappeared until he ducked out the exit."

"That narrows it down. I'll call you if we find anything."

CHAPTER THIRTY-THREE

As Captain Forrest sat in the reception area of Senator Brandt's office, he fumed at being kept waiting. If someone saw him, it wouldn't look good for either of them. After cooling his heels for twenty minutes, longing the entire time for a cigarette, he was finally shown into Brandt's inner sanctum.

"Good morning, Deputy Inspector. Sorry to keep you waiting. It's been…"

"A busy morning. My heart bleeds. And stop the deputy inspector shit. What the hell were you thinking, tipping the press that we took part in SVU's sweep last night?"

"Oh, that. Sorry, it was a slip of the tongue. Although, I don't see the harm…"

"And then blabbing about the imposter? It's bad enough it's already leaked to the press that the killer might have been a cop."

"The public needs to know it wasn't."

"We don't yet know it ourselves, for certain. Your comment sounded like pure cover-up. Sabrina Dunn and most of the press will mount an anti-police offensive strong enough to emasculate the entire department as it confronts mobs of angry protesters."

"They should lock them all up and throw away the key."

"Pure fantasy. Besides, with the new no-bail law, anyone we arrest will be back on the street in no time. I realize you think this will be good for your mayoral hopes, but no one relishes the city in flames."

The senator responded with a harrumph. After a moment, he added, "How's the boy doing?"

"Weak on the law, weak on procedure, weak on deportment. And, from now on, I think it's best not to tell you what he's working on."

"I have other sources. My benefactor needs assurances the boy is gaining experience."

"And your benefactor's name?" Worth a try.

"You don't need to know."

"Then neither does he. And if I lose the promotion, fine with me."

The senator glared at him through an interminable silence. "You realize we could reverse direction."

Forrest hesitated. Brandt had the commissioner's ear. It was unlikely Brandt could get Forrest demoted, but reassignment to some dead-end job wasn't a reach. "I assure you we will keep him involved. I'll provide you as much information as the needs of the investigation allow."

"Spoken like a genuine leader. Let's see if we can get moving on your promotion."

He left Brandt's office and headed for the subway. But first, he stopped at a convenience store for a pack of smokes. In case he felt the need.

CHAPTER THIRTY-FOUR

She needed to call Jake, so she sent Cadman inside as soon as they got back to Hudson Street.

Jake answered on the first ring, his voice soft. "Hey."

"Sorry I couldn't call before now. It's been crazy. I'm sorry."

His voice softened. "I haven't seen you like this since your last homicide case."

She wanted to argue. That had been when she'd been desperate to get a handle on the Cove Shooting, but also afraid for the safety of her witnesses and, most of all, for Jake. She'd wrestled with her fear of marriage. She'd almost lost him. This wasn't anything like that.

And yet it was. She was responsible for the safety of six girls now that Julie was dead, and the safety of the priest who was sheltering one of them. Jake faced a major career decision, but her focus was elsewhere. "I'm sorry."

A soft chuckle. "No need to be sorry. I told you a long time ago, I understand how your job can be for you. To be honest, I love seeing you this committed."

Did he really, or was he trying to convince himself? "But I am sorry about last night. You were excited, and I was someplace else."

"It's okay. Any chance you'll be home at a decent hour tonight? No game, so I'm free."

"I'll do my best. Promise." She dashed inside.

Marisa intercepted her and they stepped into the conference room. "Cadman said something about another symbol?"

Kim brought up the photo she'd taken with her cell.

Marisa pulled out a tattered spiral notebook. "You remember what I told you about the symbols?" She drew a five-pointed star with one continuous line.

"A star?" Kim asked.

"A pentagram. These are basic pagan beliefs. The pentagram represents the elements progressing from the most basic..." At the point on the lower left, she drew the symbol for Earth. "The most solid and the least ethereal. Follow the continuous drawn line to the upper right, and we have the next most basic..." She drew the symbol for water. "Follow the line straight across to the upper left, and we have the more spiritual, ethereal..." She drew the symbol for air. "Now, down to the lower right..." She drew the symbol for fire.

"The opposite of water," Kim noted.

"Correct. And air is the opposite of earth. And completing the pentagram..." She drew a circle. "Spirit, completely ethereal. Five elements, connected by an unbroken line."

Kim took a moment digesting this. "So, what does it mean for us?"

"The killer is progressing up the line of elements. But I can't tell you what the elements represent for him. That would depend on what particular beliefs he was embracing."

Cadman and Colangelo joined them. Martin Stransky and Ken Taylor were right behind.

"The FBI has dispatched a detail to collar Epstein," Colangelo said. "Cord volunteered to ride shotgun."

Wait. She'd asked Cord to work with Vera Koshkin. She decided not to ask about it, yet.

Colangelo gestured to the board. "What's this?"

Marisa had added the names Simmons, Avila, and Campbell in parentheses below each of the first three symbols. "Five symbols, including three attached to events that have already occurred. We're not sure what it means, beyond signaling a progression. The symbols left at each murder follow the exact sequence of symbols around the pentagram. I suspect that whoever is behind this has two more events planned."

"Events?" Colangelo asked. "You mean murders?"

Kim turned to Marisa. "We've been analyzing the murders as a simple progression: first, second, third. But the symbols imply more, don't they?"

Marisa studied them before she answered. "Yes, they suggest progression through a hierarchy, beginning with earth and culminating in spirit. It may have a deeper meaning."

Colangelo snorted in irritation. "Can we turn from this mumbo-jumbo to something a tad more concrete? Ken, what do you have for us?"

"Something's up with this Defend Our Home group," Taylor said. "Based on what we've seen on their site, there is a splinter group that wants to do something drastic. The administrator of the site is James Maitland, who lives over on Staten Island, and he's not cool with the notion at all. He keeps taking down inflammatory posts."

"We might want to send Martin in undercover to the Eagle Tavern," Colangelo said, "where they like to gather. We need eyes and ears on these guys."

"We don't have anything on the Eagle," Ken said, "but the local precinct reports it's growing unpopular in the neighborhood. Outbursts from the patrons have generated an increase in noise complaints."

Okay, ask now. "Vera Koshkin is analyzing the traffic for Defend Our Home, and e-mail traffic of Joey Simmons' group. Cord was working with her. Why was he pulled off?"

"We needed someone there when they busted Epstein," Colangelo said. "He volunteered. Said Vera didn't need him. Didn't he tell you?"

Kim checked her cell. Two missed calls while she was interrogating Morales. The one from Jake she'd seen. The second she'd missed. It was from Cord. "He did, and I missed it, but I wouldn't have been able to discuss it with him if I'd taken it."

Colangelo broke into a grin. "These things will happen."

"So, what's the plan?" She'd deal with Cord later.

"No wire," Ken replied. "We're not recording incriminating statements, yet; we want intel on the place. One guy you interviewed used the Eagle as an alibi. They'll be expecting some police presence, and we can't take a chance that they'd detect a wire. Besides, if they accept Martin as one of them, it gives us the opportunity to send him back. Maybe he wears a wire then."

She doubted they had sufficient time. "The gap between murders one and two was five months; between two and three, five days. Whoever is doing this has gone up tempo."

"You're assuming they're connected," Taylor said.

Kim stabbed the marker board with her finger. "They're connected. I'm all for sending Martin into the Eagle, but not until we've got more intel. Let me see what Vera Koshkin has and what we can glean from it. I'll go over it with Martin and Ken afterward. Let's send Martin in tomorrow night prepared instead of tonight half-prepared. And please have Cord call me the minute they've bagged Epstein."

CHAPTER THIRTY-FIVE

It was shortly after two when Abe's text interrupted Kim's study of the board. *Have seen nothing new. Started viewing at the day before Avila's murder and worked backward from there.*

She recalled Roscoe's information. *Try starting at three weeks prior and working forward.*

Cord walked in.

"So, what happened this morning?" She tried to keep her tone light. "I thought you were so eager to work with her."

"Vera works better alone." Then, he added, "Look, it's no big deal. We got Epstein, and he's singing more tunes than Aaron Neville. He gave up this dude named Juan Caballo who charges families everything they have and brings them by boat to Louisiana, then by truck to the northeast. When they get here, Caballo's guys sell the adults to sweatshops and the kids to pimps, making money at both ends. They often stop at Epstein's because some of them get sick or injured, and Epstein treats them. Feds are already talking about letting him out so they can nail Caballo on his next trip north."

She updated him on Julie Campbell.

He stared at the board. "And the killer slashed her chest with a symbol, too?"

"Third in the progression."

"I don't like saying it, but that creeps me out in the extreme."

Kim stared at Marisa's pentagram. "Me, too. I'm heading over to One-PP. Please check on that license plate number and tell me if you hear anything from Phil Vitello or the others."

CHAPTER THIRTY-SIX

Swarms of protesters poured off the Brooklyn Bridge, choking the path between the subway station and One Police Plaza. Police had already closed off Centre Street, so the human river flowed south, turning onto the Park Row underpass. Kim glimpsed some signs carried by the protesters.

"Justice for Mariano Avila."

"Defund the police."

"End the police coverup."

"NYPD—the new Gestapo."

"Avenge Avila."

She showed her badge at a police checkpoint on Centre Street.

"Where you headed, Detective?" an officer asked.

"One-PP."

He shook his head. "Not the happiest place to be today, I'm afraid. Continue up Centre Street to Foley Square. There'll be another checkpoint before you can proceed across St. Andrew's Plaza, and a third at One-PP itself."

"Thanks. Take care, Officer."

"Doing my best."

Kim found Vera buried in a mountain of printouts. The only item on her desk not covered by paper was her desktop and its keyboard.

"Takes time but I'll finish soon." Vera had gone through pages and pages of printouts of e-mail lists, starting with Harwood, Conroy, Desmond, Joey Simmons and Jack Maitland, the administrator for the Defend Our Home website. "I added Maitland because he showed up on Harwood's list. On the floor, there are more lists— printouts of sites they visited for the past year." She glanced up smiling, but without humor. "That Defend Our Home site, and some other political sites, and plenty of pornography, except for Maitland." She shook her head and scoffed, "Like twelve-year-old boys."

"Thank you, Vera." Kim had gazed over the mountains of paper. "I can't believe you did all this yourself."

"Is what I do."

The top page listed the sites Maitland accessed. Kim grabbed it and began scanning the list. "These aren't ordinary political sites, Vera. Some are militia groups. They're on the FBI's watch list."

Vera didn't look up. "*Da.*"

"May I mark these up?"

"Use highlighter on the desk. And pencils."

Next came the e-mails. The bulk of the traffic was between Harwood and the other members of his foursome, and between Harwood and Maitland. The subjects were all cryptic. Several included "the bird". Had to be a reference to the Eagle Tavern.

Maitland had corresponded with many people, presumably connected with Defend Our Home. One of them, named Tony, had used "Quisling" as his subject. And he'd copied Harwood on it.

"Vera, what's this 'quisling'?"

"He was a Norwegian army officer who collaborated with Nazis during Great Patriotic War. Means traitor."

By all appearances, Maitland hadn't responded. Had Tony meant that Harwood was the traitor, or Maitland, or someone else? She needed to see the e-mail. But it was less than six months old, so to get the e-mail, she'd need a warrant. To get a warrant, she needed probable cause. To establish probable cause, she needed the e-mail.

"Shit."

"You say something?" Vera asked.

"Just thinking out loud," Kim sighed. "But thank you. I can't believe you did this all on your own. I'd asked Cord to help. What happened?"

A sad smile. "Nice boy. But is not patient. This work requires patience of a chess master." The smile evaporated. "This thing, these groups, they're hateful, a sickness this country has, like I never dreamed. For first time since I arrive from Russia, I'm afraid."

"What are you afraid of, Vera?"

She gestured at the printouts. "They are full of the sickness. They respect nobody. Think they know everything. And I think they stop at nothing, don't care who they hurt. They destroy this country if not stopped." Vera reached out and touched Kim's hand. "Afraid for you, too. You're a wonderful person." A sly grin. "But not a good matchmaker. Please be careful." Vera resumed her work.

Kim's eyes were already burning. How could Vera work on this stuff for such long hours and keep her focus? "Vera, do you have Harwood's e-mail list, there?"

"*Da*. What you need?"

"Someone named Tony copied him on that quisling e-mail sent to Maitland. Please check Harwood's list for any correspondence."

"Tomorrow morning is good for an answer? Good. Now go home to husband before he thinks you forget about him."

On her way to the subway, though, she saw a familiar figure, Joanna Dunbar, a reporter for *City News*, obviously there to cover the protest.

"Please don't turn away," the reporter said. "I need to ask you something."

"If it's about an ongoing case, you realize I can't comment on it." Kim hoped she didn't appear too brusque. She liked Joanna, who'd once helped her slip a key witness past a gaggle of press people.

"It's about something Senator Brandt said yesterday morning. Why would Internal Affairs take part in a sting conducted by SVU?"

"If we had, I couldn't tell you."

The reporter's eyes locked on hers. "If you did, Brandt shooting off his mouth must have pissed you off in the extreme. And if you didn't, DCPI should raise hell with Brandt for dragging IAB into the spotlight for no valid reason. And since Brandt's statement yesterday morning, DCPI hasn't said a word."

"Joanna…"

"This is about to get a lot worse." The reporter gestured to the passing crowd, now much heavier than before. The signs were also more aggressive.

"Abolish police."

"Kill or be killed."

"Amerika—new police state."

"Tonight's special—roast pig."

Joanna lowered her voice. "I'm doing some digging into this guy. If you're as pissed at Brandt as I think you should be, I suspect we can help each other."

"I give you something and you give me something?"

"Correct. I'll even tell you, first. And my questions, which you already know, are for background, not a specific story."

"You mean you would reveal nothing I tell you in a story, on the air or in print, without my express permission?"

Joanna laughed. "You should have been a lawyer. Yes, nothing without your express permission. Brandt is running against Sabrina Dunn in the June special election."

"That's not a headline."

"No. The headline is—or rather, should be—that he's terminated his authorized committee under the Campaign Finance Law."

The bell wasn't ringing. "All that means is that he gives up public matching funds and avoids all the filings and disclosures."

"Right. Something that billionaire candidates do. Not some C-student from Brooklyn Law School who couldn't make a living as an attorney or selling real estate. The law says that non-participating candidates can spend as much of their own money as they like, but they're still limited in what they can accept in contributions."

So, Brandt had a hidden deep pocket somewhere. "And the limit on contributions might very well violate the *Citizens United* decision."

Joanna stared at her and smirked. "No question you should have been a lawyer. Anyway, he accomplished nothing for three terms except getting re-elected, but suddenly he's a senate committee chair getting inside information from the NYPD. That sure makes my nose twitch. So, was IAB involved in the Morales bust, and if so, why?"

Deep breath. "We took part, owing to the ring's proximity to Avila's murder scene. Avila had confronted Morales about the ring. And you're right, I was furious that he mentioned it. But I don't know who informed him."

"So, IAB is investigating the Avila murder? The rumor about the killer being a cop is true?"

"An eyewitness described the killer as wearing a police uniform. We're almost certain it's an imposter."

"Brandt was right for once? Holy shit." She stared back at the protesters. "But it's playing like a coverup. No one believes him."

"And no one will until we have the actual killer in custody." Maybe she shouldn't have trusted Joanna. "You can't..."

"I know. Nothing without your express permission. Please alert me to anything that doesn't smell right in your neck of the woods. I'll advise you of anything I learn in mine." She thought a moment. "And we'd both better walk damned softly. There's sure to be a reason Brandt landed that particular committee chair."

CHAPTER THIRTY-SEVEN

Guilt mounted with each step on Kim's walk home. She glanced at her watch as she reached the top of the front steps. Ten after seven. At least Jake didn't have a game tonight. As she entered the apartment, the wine glasses were full, and two places were set for dinner.

"I figured I'd try 'take two' from last night," he said, then pulled her into a sweet embrace. After a deep kiss that didn't come close to lasting long enough, he said, "You look strung out."

"I know. It's just..."

"This case." He was grinning. "I get it. It's a homicide, and they always consume you. I'd almost forgotten what it looked like."

She sat at the table. "I'm sorry about last night."

He joined her. "No need. Unfortunate timing. So, I'll start from the top. They have offered me the position. As advertised, it's a big bump up in salary, which could come in handy if my dad ever charges me market-rate rent for our little abode, here; or even if he doesn't. A lot of analytics, reviewing video from the spatial tracking system and using what I see to augment and interpret the numbers. I'll be working from home most of the time. I won't be doing game stat collection anymore. And I'll attend league meetings and stuff like that. Attendance at games will be optional, and I won't have to feed the announcers factoids. I have to tell them by tomorrow if I'm taking it."

"You're taking it. You're dying to. And it's a significant move up. This case is a one-off. I have over a year remaining on my IAB tour. Things return to normal when my tour ends."

He grew quiet. "Kim, when I mentioned this opening, I said that if we ever changed our minds about having children, this job would make it easier for us. You interpreted that as me pushing to have them."

"Have you changed your mind?" Her heart sank when he hesitated.

"No, but I'm allowing for the possibility that we could both change our minds."

It sounded like a hedge. So much flashed through her mind at that moment: Dad cheating on Mom, their divorce, her loneliness. Dysfunctional parents raised kids who grew up to be dysfunctional parents. And the world in which Kim worked brought her face to face with the results, including teen girls being pimped and controlled.

She pulled herself back to the present. "I don't think I'll ever change my mind. But I'm afraid you might change yours."

He laughed in that simple way of his. "I like kids. But I love you more than my life. Please don't worry about that, or about the demands your job makes on you. We already had that conversation."

That they had. When she was with Manhattan South Homicide, and the demands of the job had boiled over in his resentment. Not a reassuring thought.

But that had been when he was in danger and she was trying to protect him without telling him why. Totally different. She nodded and smiled. She pushed back her fear and kissed him.

Her cell buzzed.

"Go ahead," he said with a teasing laugh. "Otherwise, you won't sleep."

It was a text from Abe. *We got something. He scouted the place out. I'm bringing the drives to One-PP in the morning to see what we can get. If it's print quality, I'll get it to you as quickly as possible.*

She texted back, *Thanks.* And then Jake pried the cell out of her hand. "You are desperate for a long, hot shower. Me, too. Let's save water."

She agreed. Maybe it would stop her from wondering what Abe had found and Vera would find.

Or if Jake meant what he'd said about children.

CHAPTER THIRTY-EIGHT

Thursday, March 22nd
"What began as a peaceful protest over the murder of community activist Mariano Avila turned violent last night after police turned protesters back from One Police Plaza. Angry mobs smashed store windows along Park Row and allegedly engaged in looting. As fears mount of further violence tonight, Mayor Dunn is urging calm while defending the right of protesters to be free of police harassment. State Senator Raymond Brandt immediately attacked the acting mayor, accusing her of undermining her own police department."

***

Kim surveyed the line of boarded-up windows where sanitation workers were still cleaning up the debris. She proceeded through the maze of police checkpoints on her way to One-PP, where Abe and Bob waited. Abe put out his cigarette and led them down to the video analysis center, where a technician already had an image up and paused on the screen. "This is from the recording on March 2nd, the first on which our friend appears." The technician hit "play". A heavyset male appeared near the edge of the right-hand screen, walking along the opposite side of the street.

Abe pointed. "What do you think?" The figure on screen crossed the street, but as he got closer, he moved off the left side of the screen. "Don't forget, they positioned the camera to pick up intruders on the sidewalk."

"Rewind to a minute before he leaves the screen," Kim said. When the tech had the figure at his closest before going off frame, she had him freeze it. She pulled out the sketch. "Looks like our guy. We have anything else?"

The tech ran through two other segments they'd found. None of the views were definitive. The sketch was the best likeness they had. "That's all we've got?"

The technician shrugged. "Sorry, Detective."

"I'm sorry we took so much of your time," she replied. "Thanks."

Her cell buzzed as they left the building. It was Vitello. "We recovered a dark blue jacket from a storm drain at the crime scene yesterday, size extra-large. The lab guys are doing a complete analysis, searching for anything yielding a DNA sample. But I caught a whiff of something I thought mighty odd: nail polish remover."

Kim stopped in her tracks. "What?"

"Nail polish remover. The lab will capture whatever traces they find. Why? Does that mean anything to you?"

"The eyewitness at the Avila murder scene smelled nail polish remover on the guy she thought was a cop. Thanks, Phil, and please keep me posted." She ended the call and repeated the news to Abe and Bob.

Abe laughed. "Maybe he works in a nail salon. Should we check those?"

"Not yet." Kim did a quick search on her cell for ingredients of nail polish remover. "The primary ingredient, the one that gives it its powerful odor, is acetone, and lots of different solvents include acetone."

Julie and Avila had been killed at opposite ends of the borough. That was a huge area to search without knowing what they were searching for. "Back to Hudson Street we go."

***

It was a quick ride on the C train, but by the time they got off, Abe's normally cheerful expression had turned to a deep scowl. "Must've been something I ate."

Kim exchanged glances with Bob. "You sure that's all it is?"

Abe waved her away. "Yeah. Indigestion, nothing more." He belched. "With a dash of heartburn."

"Lay off the chili dogs and pepperoni pizzas," Bob said.

Abe managed a wan smile.

As soon as they entered the office, Cadman approached her. "I turned up a single case from 2010..."

"The Warshak case."

"Right. It said you needed a search warrant for any e-mail. But that wasn't even our circuit."

"And...?"

He gave her a blank stare. "And, what?"

"What you should tell me is that an appeals court later threw the case out on procedural grounds, which means it doesn't apply. But since it's still out there, and since New York State often takes a more expansive view than the Supreme Court of individual rights, it's not unlikely that at some point, a crusading jurist might look to get it up the appeals chain here. So, we need to be careful when our investigations include e-mails."

Cadman shook his head. "Damn it, Kim, I'm not a lawyer."

"If you want to be an effective cop, you'd better learn to think like one. And tomorrow, you'll recite everything you can tell me about the in-plain-sight exception." She scowled when he walked away pouting.

"Anyone got an antacid in their desk?" Abe asked.

Marisa opened a desk drawer and extracted a bottle of pink liquid. "Just please don't drink directly from the bottle."

Abe took it. "Not in a million years, honey."

Cadman perked up. "What else you got in there, Marisa?"

She glared at him, said nothing, and snapped a bubble.

Well, he sure has pissed off Marisa. Kim called the team into the conference room for the latest update and turned to the map. "The murders have all been in Brooklyn and the people we've been looking at are all scattered around Queens, but close to Brooklyn." She'd made certain to mark all the locations—the murders, where the hookers had been, the church, the rectory, the factory where they got the video, the residences of the four horsemen, and the Eagle Tavern.

"We've got protection on Youth Colony," she said, "and Brooklyn SVU has assigned some of their people to watch the Blessed Mother rectory." She marked the map.

Cord spoke up. "You still sure the four horsemen figure in this, even Simmons' murder?"

"That makes little sense," Colangelo said. "Wasn't Simmons one of them?"

Kim had been struggling with that since Marisa had told her what the symbols meant. "I don't grasp how they're connected, or what the motive was for killing Simmons, but some factor links the three deaths. Also, I'm convinced there will be a fourth incident soon, followed by a fifth."

"You mean because of the symbols?" Colangelo asked in a manner that showed he thought little of them.

Kim refused to back down. "Someone has taken great care to draw the line from Simmons to Avila to Campbell. The symbols are a progression, which could be first-second-third, or it might mean something more specific."

Colangelo's scowl deepened. "We need to move this along, Kim. You should see what Park Row looks like this morning..."

"I saw."

"So did the commissioner. If this was the work of an imposter—and I hope to Christ you're right—the public needs to know that before the whole fucking city gets burned to the ground."

Deep breath. "Let me get this straight. Sabrina Dunn is ready to give looters a free pass, Ray Brandt wants to blow our case open before we can solve it, and the commissioner, who this morning issued a directive to all Members of Service to 'use great care and best judgment when engaging with the public', wants it solved yesterday. The commissioner should tell the pols to shut the fuck up."

Nolan broke in before Colangelo could snap back. "Shelton from the Brooklyn ME's Office called. Julie Campbell's killer used the same size blade, same manner of attack, same gouging, and the same work on the symbol."

That settled it. "All three by the same killer."

"Which may mean he has no link to Harwood, Desmond, and Conroy," Cord said. "They ranted about someone killing Simmons. I can't see a motive, there. But Morales saw our suspect in the area where his hookers worked. Maybe he had a problem with them."

"Simmons wasn't a patron," Kim replied. "Conroy was. And he's alive and well." She thought back on the interviews. "Harwood said he'd gotten Simmons out of a lot of jams. Maybe he resented it."

"Yeah," Cord replied. "But he bought the Coburn-Tyler version of Simmons' murder."

That rang a bell. Kim pulled up the notes on the Harwood interview. "The Coburn-Tyler version is that Ortega fled the jurisdiction. Harwood said he got away, but both Desmond and Conroy said he got deported. As did Clara Simmons. Who would've told them except Harwood?"

Abe stared at her. "You think he made it up?"

"It would be a little easier for Clara Simmons to swallow."

"But why would he tell it to Desmond and Conroy?" Bob asked.

Good question. Even if they'd heard him tell Clara Simmons, one would think he would have cleared it up later. Kim turned to Martin, who hadn't said a word. "Keep your ears open tonight, Mr..."

"Tillman," Martin said with a grin. "Steve Tillman."

CHAPTER THIRTY-NINE

It was after seven when Captain Forrest dropped in to see Colangelo. He found him in the conference room, staring at the board. "Impressive." Colangelo jumped. "Sorry, Steve, I didn't mean to startle you. How's it going?"

"We've got leads. We'll get him. Or them."

"You're sure the killings are all linked?"

Colangelo continued staring at the board but said nothing. Very unlike him.

"Is that a 'no'?"

"Let's go to my office and talk."

Colangelo was already on his way, and the captain's sole choice was to follow. He took a seat as Colangelo closed the office door. "What's wrong, Steve?"

"Yes, we're sure…" Colangelo stopped and sniffed. "You're back to smoking?"

No way he was copping to that. "Of course not. I passed a couple of people in the vestibule smoking. They damned well ought to know better."

Colangelo didn't look convinced. "The killings are all linked. Same method, same signature."

"And we believe the sketch guy is our guy?"

"Brady's certain of it."

This was like pulling teeth. "And we're certain he's not a Member of Service?"

"Yes."

This wasn't like Steve at all. "Damn it, I shouldn't have to interrogate one of my own subordinates. What gives?" He picked up a pen from a plastic Rangers cup on the desk.

"You tell me, Captain. How did a political hack like Ray Brandt discover we worked with SVU in the Morales sweep? Or that the killer in uniform is an imposter? Was it Cadman? Or is the leak further up the chain of command?"

"I told you the commissioner approved his assignment here." The dodgy reference had worked before.

"Who asked the commissioner for that approval? And who came to you? Because the commissioner's too smart to have come to you himself."

Only one play left. "I'm afraid that's above both our pay grades. I'm not any happier than you." Time to slam the door shut. "Now, we have the sketch of this cop imposter. I'm forwarding it to DCPI tonight to make it public in the morning." He waved the pen for emphasis.

"You can't be serious. He doesn't realize we have it. He believes he's operating incognito. If we publish that photo, we'll drive him underground, generate a ton of false leads, and we could get our only eyewitness killed."

But the more he thought about it, the more he liked it. "Driving him underground will give us time to get the girl into protective custody and may also disrupt whatever lunatic timeline this guy has set for himself. With this morning's pronunciamento from the commissioner regarding 'interactions with the public', he has the green light to do whatever the hell he wants. It might also cause a stir that the FBI can pick up. And it's the one chance we've got at defusing a violent mob before things get worse." Most important, it would temporarily remove a certain state senator from his neck region. "I'll also have DCPI set up an 800 number." He put the pen back in the cup, realizing too late he'd been holding it between his index finger and middle finger, like a cigarette.

But Colangelo didn't back down. "Without more evidence, it will reek of a coverup, and the violence will get worse."

CHAPTER FORTY

Entering the Eagle Tavern always made Rafer Harwood feel like he was coming home. The sight of the two flags hanging over the bar—the stars and stripes and "Don't Tread on Me"—was all the welcome he needed. The stars and bars hung over the doorway, and a banner of the 101st Airborne hung from the opposite wall. Framed front pages of various newspapers shouted headlines from the past: "Japs Surrender"; "One Small Step..."; "Mets Win!"; "Shock and Awe". A sign near the door said, "Security by Smith and Wesson". Another read, "Under every good man is a good woman."

Rafer accepted the beer that Tom, the bartender, placed in front of him. "Thanks. Anyone been in here asking about me?"

"No. Why? Expecting someone?"

Good question. "Not sure. Two detectives paid me a visit day before yesterday—a bitch and her 'minority' sidekick. What a pair. They asked for my whereabouts last Friday night."

Tom snorted. "Shit, that's easy. You were here, ripping Jack Maitland a new one."

"I told them that, minus the Maitland detail. Felt shitty about bringing the bar into it. Any cops who put up with that Sanctuary City shit, you don't need sniffing around here."

"How was the bitch?" Tom asked.

"Not bad, dressed up the right way. But she'd need a little discipline." Rafer smiled at the thought. "Bet she gets plenty from her buck."

"Mixing the races," Tom said. "That's another thing destroying this country."

"One of many." Rafer noticed a tall, lean guy at the end of the bar, near the door. He was thin, blondish, very fair. German or Polish ancestry. He was wearing a dark blue work shirt, blue Dickeys and work boots and was drinking Brooklyn Lager from the bottle.

He'd been listening and now raised the bottle. "Got that right."

"Do I know you?" Rafer asked.

He picked up his bottle and moved over. "Steve Tillman." He extended his hand.

"Rafer Harwood." Good firm handshake. "You work around here?"

"Yeah, sometimes. Here, Glendale, Ridgewood, Middle Village. Cable installations."

Installations. Lots of work with his hands. And yet his hands showed no callouses. "Must make for some interesting situations."

Tillman laughed. "Not quite. Sometimes I get women coming on to me, but they're way past their prime and usually drunk, besides. Anything else you hear is bullshit."

"At least it's a steady income," Tom said.

"Yeah, but it ain't what I wanted to do." Tillman took another gulp. "Construction. That's what I wanted."

"What stopped you?" He seemed like an okay guy. But Rafer T. Harwood didn't get where he was by falling for first impressions.

"Moved here from Pennsylvania, and it was like a whole different world. Didn't have any family connections so I couldn't get into a union, and non-union jobs pay shit money 'cause they hire illegals. Fuck that. I took the cable job." Another gulp of beer.

Tillman's bottle was empty. So was Rafer's mug. "Tom, another round on me."

The door opened, and Rafer's evening slid down the drain. Desmond. He was getting to be a major pain in the ass, and the look on his face made it clear he was about to get worse.

"We have to talk," Desmond said as he took the stool on Rafer's right.

"Evening, Jeff." He turned to Tom. "Him, too." Maybe that would cool Desmond's jets.

For a moment, Desmond looked like he might refuse it. Tom set a mug in front of him before he could decide for sure. Well, that was typical for Desmond. He drank in silence.

"Meet Steve Tillman." Rafer kept his tone friendly. "Cable guy, for real."

"Jeff Desmond." He made no move to shake hands. Tom moved down to the other end of the bar to refill empty glasses. Desmond pushed the mug away. "Fuck your beer," he said in a gloomy voice.

"Relax," Rafer said with more conviction than he felt. When Desmond drank while angry, he could be a motormouth. Tillman struck him as an excellent potential addition to the group. Best not to give a poor first impression. With a slight backward toss of his head that he hoped Desmond caught and Tillman didn't, he added, "I think Steve agrees with us."

Tillman reached across Rafer and extended a hand to Desmond. "If you've tried to get a non-union construction job, you sure as hell know where I stand."

Desmond cast a quick glance at Rafer, then shook Tillman's hand. "Entire country's being overrun. Where do you live?"

"Bayside," Tillman said. "A coworker mentioned the Eagle. I decided I'd stop in. Love the decor." Tillman gestured toward the banner of the 101st Airborne. "The Screaming Eagles. My grandfather was a member in good standing."

Desmond's eyes lit up.

"Yeah?" Rafer said. "So was Jeff's. Was he in Easy Company?"

Tillman chuckled. "Everyone asks that. No, Fox Company." He nodded to Jeff. "How about yours?"

"I never knew which company," Jeff said. "A shell fragment shattered his kneecap in Normandy. He spent the rest of the war recuperating and never walked right again. Yours?"

"Made it as far as Bastogne," Tillman said. "When they pulled out, he had a bad case of trench foot. When he returned to the line, the war in Europe was finished."

"You big on military history?" Rafer asked.

146

"Not an expert or anything, but I've read some. Other than sports, ain't much worth watching on the tube."

Rafer glanced up at the flat screen TV in the corner. Basketball. That suited him, since he needed to make sure he had Desmond smoothed down, and he had to decide about Tillman. Rafer Harwood rarely made mistakes about people. Rarely made mistakes, period.

Desmond drained his beer. Rafer slapped a twenty on the bar. "Tom, another round on me."

"What, you hit the fucking lottery or something?" Desmond stared at him in disbelief.

Yeah, the Mom lottery. "Just in a pleasant mood." Rafer drained his own.

Desmond glanced toward the back room. "Look, we need to talk. Maybe someplace a little more private."

"Oh, hey," Tillman said, putting his bottle down. "I don't want to interfere. I can grab a table over there."

If Tillman moved, he might leave. "No need for that, Steve. Jeff and I will be right back."

He steered Desmond back to the room with tables and chairs. "I haven't decided, yet, about Tillman. But if he's what he appears to be, he'd make an excellent addition to the team, don't you think?"

The question surprised Desmond, as Rafer had intended. "I suppose. But..."

Don't allow him to get rolling. "So, it's worth me spending a few extra bucks to find out, right?"

"Well, sure. But..."

"So, what's the beef? I'm buying for you, too. Relax. Enjoy. We've got a job to do—returning our country to its roots."

"Yeah. But what's this shit you been telling Conroy?"

He couldn't show a reaction. Had Conroy been running his mouth? "Nothing. He's still freaked because he lost his playground. I'd have thought you'd be enjoying his discomfort."

"Well, yeah. You know what I think of that. But then, you tolerate it."

"I tolerate a lot. The Founders weren't all choir boys, either."

Desmond hesitated. "No. Look, this Tillman guy looks okay. But Conroy said the pizza guy..."

"I'll handle him. Not your problem. You focus on what I ask you to do. That's worked for us so far, and it'll keep working if nobody fucks it up." Rafer turned back to the bar to end the conversation. Tillman was waiting, watching the basketball game. Looked interested. A discouraging sign. Real patriots watched hockey when football wasn't in season. Best to keep him at arm's length for a while.

"You sure you got the full story on Joey?" Desmond asked as they sat down.

"Jesus, Jeff, I told you. I got sources."

"Count me out for pizza," Desmond said in a gruff voice.

Rafer gestured toward the television. "Geez, Tom, ain't there anything better on than this shit?"

"Only west coast games in the NHL tonight," Tillman said.

So, he liked hockey better. Another point in his favor. "Guess this will have to do."

Desmond glared. "You hear me?"

Rafer dropped his voice to a whisper. "Yeah, along with half the damned city."

Desmond was becoming more trouble than he was worth. Best to cut him out of the next step of the plan.

CHAPTER FORTY-ONE

Friday, March 23rd

"Good morning and here are the lead stories. Violence again erupted in Manhattan last night as angry demonstrators smashed windows, set fires, and looted major retail businesses from SoHo to Herald Square. Mobs attacked three precincts in lower Manhattan, with patrol cars being overturned and burned. Police in riot gear fired tear gas to disperse the mobs and made over two hundred arrests. Mayor Dunn called for calm by demonstrators and restraint by police, while reiterating her support for diverting over ten percent of the current police department budget to social programs…"

***

Kim muted the unit's television. She'd heard it all last night, as had Jake, who'd muttered, "this city is becoming a hell of a place to raise kids."

It couldn't have been a chance comment. She'd let it go, but the question of children was going to crop up again. She could sense it. And with Easter dinner at her in-laws' only nine days away, she was certain pressure was going to mount. She also wondered whether his new job, with so much working from home, would cause him to resent the extra hours she spent on the job on a case like this.

Focus on the case.

Cord had marked the residences of Clara Simmons, Rafer Harwood, Jeff Desmond and Cliff Conroy in blue on the map, the three crime scenes in red. Kim connected the red dots with a thin red line and the blue ones with a thin blue line. The effect was fascinating, like a military diagram showing an attacking army moving from north to south, and a defending army spread from west to east. Cord had added purple spots for nail salons on either side of the Brooklyn corridor of crime scenes, and in green for other facilities that would have a use for acetone. Nothing struck her as an obvious connection.

Cord had also made a notation on one of the marker boards, under the license plate number they'd caught on video: "Rented from Star Cars at JFK by 'J. Simmons'; no video; clerk recognized sketch guy—evidence?"

Kim's cell buzzed with a text from Cord. *I'm at the Property Clerk's Office. Simmons' wallet is here; driver's license gone. Star Cars has a photocopy of the license, too faint to see the photo.*

So, this guy killed Simmons, carved a symbol in his chest, then rummaged through Simmons' wallet for his driver's license, and still had time to get away before police arrived.

Martin walked in. "Steve Tillman reporting." He recounted the details of Harwood and Desmond at the Eagle. "That's no mutual admiration society. Desmond came in pissed, and a quiet talk in the back didn't appear to help much."

"You mean you didn't hear any of it?"

"No. But when they returned, Desmond pressed Harwood on 'the story about Joey'. Had to mean Simmons. And Harwood said, 'I told you I got a source'. Has to be a leak."

Kim agreed. "And doubtless from the Seven-Four. The only question is whether he got the deportation version, or he made it up."

"Why would a cop fabricate a story of someone getting deported when they didn't?"

"Makes it look like ICE fucked it up instead of the department. Rather thin, and few people would care. But a group of white nationalists might very well care."

"Why would Harwood lie to his friends?"

She pulled out her cell again. "Good question." She pulled up Vera Koshkin's number on her contact list and hit "message". *Sending you e-mail addresses of four Members of Service. Please find their IP addresses and check to see if any of them have frequented the Defend Our Home website.*

Vera took less than a minute to respond. *Good morning, brilliant American lady detective. It's early even for you. As always, I am happy to assist.*

Vera always made her smile. *How soon can you get back to me once I send you the information?*

Only one site you need me check?

The larger the list of sites, the longer it would take. *For now, yes.*

A half hour or less.

"Which four is she checking?" Martin asked.

"The four who arrived first on the scene the night of Simmons' murder: Coburn, Tyler, Warren and Burrows." Back at her desk, she powered up her laptop, retrieved the four e-mail addresses, and sent them to Vera.

Colangelo walked in. "Captain Forrest had DCPI release the sketch of the killer."

Kim stared at him. "We can't, yet. The killer will realize Amara was our source. If he saw where she went after he pushed her away, he'll target her and the rectory."

"Sorry, Kim, but he had me send it over to DCPI last night." He held up a hand. "We've got three stiffs, two of them very public, and a city that thinks a cop did it. The longer we wait, the more it looks like a cover-up."

"Splashing this all over the media will not help solve this case," Kim said. The fear of losing control roared back. "Please tell me we didn't give out the information on the symbols."

"No, we didn't. We'd have every wacko in eight states claiming responsibility. But this guy has a distinct look. At the very least, it'll drive him underground for a while."

Kim's temper flared. "Making him harder to catch. And putting our only eyewitness at risk."

But Colangelo remained cool. "It might also slow him down on his next move. You said yourself, you think he'll strike again, even twice more."

"Lieutenant, I thought we'd agreed that we would not release the sketch until we had Amara in protective custody."

"I'm sorry, Kim. I argued that with Captain Forrest last night, but the commissioner ordered it."

Cadman walked in. "What did the commissioner order?"

"Captain Forrest released the sketch to DCPI," Kim said.

"Are we trying to get Amara killed?"

As bad as it was, she wasn't about to let Cadman make it worse. "It's done. We're not debating it." She switched gears. "I heard from the lab about the shirt CSU found in the storm drain. It tested positive for traces of acetone. They say it got there in a vaporous state. No traces of ethyl acetate or tuolene, the other two ingredients in nail polish remover, so it looks like whatever this guy was doing, he was working with pure acetone."

Colangelo nodded his appreciation. "So, scratch the nail salons. We're looking at chem plants. That should make it easier." He turned back to Martin. "Pick up anything else last night?"

Martin repeated what he'd told Kim.

Abe and Bob walked in, with Cord close behind. Kim updated them all. "Okay, Cadman, pull the LUDs of Harwood, Desmond and Conroy..."

Cadman blanched. "Pull their what?"

Geez, did this guy know anything? "Local Usage Details. Phone records. Marisa can show you how when she gets here. Get their cell numbers and check those, too. Also, contact Brooklyn SVU and make sure they've got eyes on that rectory. Cord..."

Her cell buzzed with another text from Vera. *Only get one IP address on the website. Burrows.*

He'd been lurking outside the interrogation rooms the night of the sweep. She should have grilled him on the spot. "Burrows must be the leak. Cord, please check the Master Roll Call and see when Burrows is on duty."

Marisa arrived, out of breath. "Sorry, you wouldn't believe the trains this morning. Signal trouble again."

Kim brought her up to speed. "Show Cadman how to pull LUDs, then I need you to find the meaning in the symbols, assuming the same guy killed all three. Why was Simmons 'earth', then Avila 'water', then Julie Campbell 'air'? Once we understand that, perhaps we can determine the meanings of 'fire' and 'spirit.'"

"Why does Cadman need help with something so simple?" She snapped a bubble for emphasis.

"He's never done it before. Don't take any shit from him."

Marisa cracked a hint of a smile.

Cord returned to the group. "Burrows is on eight-to-four today, off tomorrow."

"Okay," Kim said. "Lieu, I need to talk to you in private for a minute." They walked to his office. "Learn anything about Brandt's information source? I grilled Cadman, and he swears he didn't tell a soul about the sweep, and that he's never even met Brandt."

"I talked to the captain. He neither admitted nor denied that Brandt is Cadman's rabbi, and he neither admitted nor denied knowing how Brandt learned we took part in the sweep."

"Which means the answer to both is 'yes', otherwise there'd be no reason to play games." She had to struggle to keep her voice down. "We're being fucked over by our own captain?"

"I wouldn't say that. Forrest is a good man. Keep doing what you're doing. Do you believe Cadman?"

"I think so. He doesn't even live in Brandt's district. I checked. But I'm done putting him on assignments I don't believe he can handle."

Colangelo chuckled. "Fair enough. Try not to rub his nose in it."

"Cadman's or the captain's?"

"Yes." Colangelo turned serious. "One other thing. These demonstrations. They started with some immigrant advocacy group in Brooklyn. You know anyone who could explain how they morphed into anti-police rioting?"

"Several years of anti-police rhetoric from the mayor's office seems like a reasonable explanation to me."

A humorless laugh. "Could be a job in your future writing campaign copy for Ray Brandt."

"Well, Lieu, then consider this. Illegal immigrants fly under the radar, even in this city, so they're unlikely to engage in this sort of thing. But there's no dearth of folks who look for any chance to light a fuse."

"The four horsemen?"

"Or others of their ilk. Or garden variety anarchists, Marxists, whatever-ists. To answer your question, there are a couple of people who might know. I'll see what I can dig up in my spare time." She rejoined the others. "Abe, Bob, let's go. I want to lean on this bastard. Cadman, please pull Burrows' LUDs, too. Cord, please text me as soon as he does."

CHAPTER FORTY-TWO

As they pulled into the Seven-Four's parking lot, Kim's cell buzzed with a text from Cord. *Nothing on Burrows' LUDs connected with Harwood et al. Must have been up close and personal.*

She read it aloud to Abe and Bob. "Either that or he's using a burner. We'll jump off that bridge when we come to it."

Sergeant Warren was on the desk. A look of alarm crossed his face as he saw them.

"Sergeant, is Officer Burrows on duty today?" Kim asked.

A quizzical look. "He called in sick this morning."

Not the response she'd been expecting. "Did he say whether he expected to be in tomorrow?"

"I couldn't say," Warren replied. "I didn't take the call. Anything I can help you with?"

"Perhaps. Would you mind stepping outside?"

Warren followed the three detectives out into the parking lot.

"Sergeant," Kim began, "how often have you partnered with Officer Burrows in the past six months?"

"Not at all since I started regular desk duty four months ago."

"You no longer go out on patrol?"

"No, I'm on a rotation for periodic patrol duty..."

"Supervisory patrols?" Abe asked.

"The captain does those. I patrol with the regular partner of the officer he accompanies."

She needed to refocus him. "Prior to your desk assignment, how long had you partnered with Burrows?"

Warren reflected. "About six months."

"Get to know him well?" she asked.

"Not really. We talked sports, maybe news of the day. That kind of thing."

An opening, perhaps. "Did he have firm opinions?"

"Similar to most cops, I guess."

Sounded like a hedge. "How effective was he dealing with the community?"

Now he grew cautious. "Ike's a quiet guy. Kind of shy. He never took the lead in something like intervening in a street fight or making a traffic stop. He was better in a group or as backup."

"Were you aware he belongs to an anti-immigrant group called Defend Our Home?"

"No." The shock appeared to be genuine. "He never struck me as the type."

"The type for what? Racism? Intolerance?"

Warren held up a hand. "Hold on. Someone can want their country's borders respected without being racist."

Time to change it up. "Did you and Officer Burrows discuss the Simmons case during the investigation?"

Warren grew wary. "Well, yeah." Kim gestured for him to continue. "He was kind of anxious about it. Seeing Simmons like that had shaken him up. All that blood. When I said that Simmons had called in a report to ICE, Burrows got agitated."

"How did he take the news that Ortega had fled the jurisdiction?"

"He became as upset as I was."

"Determined to take action?" Kim asked.

"I didn't say that. And he never told me. By that time, we were no longer patrol partners."

Kim and Abe exchanged glances. A dead end. No choice but to interview Burrows, which meant schlepping out to his home on Staten Island.

***

Kim's visit to Evelyn Burke's office on Livingston Street would have to wait. She texted Colangelo the latest while Bob drove to St. George, where Burrows had an apartment.

There was no place to park, so Bob stayed with the car while Kim and Abe entered the building. Clean but unattractive. Kim buzzed the apartment. No answer. She waited a bit and buzzed again. Still nothing.

Abe pressed several buttons. Someone answered, "Who is it?" He replied, "Con Ed. Got a report of a gas leak." The person buzzed them in.

Kim laughed. "Mike Resnick used to pull that all the time. Burrows is in 4B."

The elevator was slow. When they got to the fourth floor, there wasn't a sound. They found 4B and knocked. The door creaked open.

Not good. She reached back and pulled out the Chief's Special that had belonged to her grandfather when he was a hero detective. It was her secondary piece. Abe pulled his Glock. They entered the apartment without making a sound.

It was a studio. The sofa bed remained unmade. A closet door hung open, as did several dresser drawers. The kitchen was tidy and the light on the dishwasher showed last night's load had finished.

"Burrows left quickly," Kim said. "I guess he's not sick."

"I don't think he's gonna be at work tomorrow, either."

Kim's cell buzzed. Colangelo. Great. He'd love this latest bit of news. "Hi, Lieu. We're at Burrows' place. He's gone AWOL."

Colangelo's response was a growl. "Never mind that. Get your asses back to East New York in one quick fucking hurry. Blessed Mother rectory. It's bad."

CHAPTER FORTY-THREE

Kim squeezed into an improvised space in the lot of the Blessed Mother Church and Rectory, already jammed with police cars, two ambulances, an Emergency Services truck, a CSU van, a van from the Brooklyn ME's office, and two news vans.

"How the hell did the media get here?" Kim almost screamed when she saw them.

Phil Vitello ran up to meet her. "Someone phoned in a tip. Come on in. But brace yourself. It's bad."

Just what Colangelo had said. She hadn't liked it then, either. Please, not Amara.

CSU had cordoned off a small area between the Sacristy entrance to the church and the rectory with crime scene tape, but there were no ground markers for evidence. She followed Vitello inside the rectory.

Fr. Lynch was sitting in the dining room in shock. A paramedic sat with him. "We tried to get him to go inside, but he won't move."

Kim followed the priest's stare into the kitchen. Red droplets spattering the gleaming white cabinets had already streaked downward. Blood remained pooled on the floor, having nowhere to drain. In the middle of it lay Ms. Westwood, flat on her back, blouse and brassiere torn open, a triangle carved in her chest with precision, apex up, no line.

"Fire," Kim said in a whisper.

"What's that?" Vitello asked. When Kim didn't answer, he added, "You need a minute? This is tough stuff."

"Where's the girl?" Kim asked.

Vitello nodded back to Fr. Lynch. "That's all he's been asking. What girl? We checked. There's no one else here."

"Fuck." She wheeled around. "Where are those assholes from SVU? He waltzed in?"

"Lieutenant Fredricks is outside," Vitello replied in a calm voice. "The intruder got in through the back door. We think he followed her in when she took out the garbage. He didn't approach from Smallwood or Livonia because one of the SVU guys would have seen him. There's an abandoned factory behind the property with an enormous gap cut in the fence. We found bloody footprints headed through the dining room, a men's size eight. Two sets of tracks out the back door, a men's eight and a woman's size six."

Amara. "He took the girl out the back way so she'd see Ms. Westwood, to terrorize her." She turned to Abe and Bob. "Check the street running by that abandoned factory for any video cameras." Back to Vitello. "Anything else?"

"We got some good footprints that show wear patterns," he said. "Won't do much to help us find him, but it may help us convict him."

"I have to find him first. I have to find the girl." She returned to the dining room. "Father, I need to talk to you. Let's go inside."

"I... shouldn't have... left..."

She kneeled in front of him. "You couldn't know. These folks need space to work, though, and we're in their way. We can talk inside." She led him into the living room with the paramedic close behind. "What happened, Father? Where did you go?"

"Church... Say Mass. Where's Amara?"

"We don't know, yet. How long were you gone?"

"Nine o'clock."

She thought a moment. "You went to say nine o'clock Mass?" He nodded. "When did you leave the rectory?"

"Ms. Westwood..."

"She's with God," Kim said in a whisper. "I'm so sorry."

"Last rites... They wouldn't let..."

"God loves her, Father. You can appreciate that. She had such a good heart."

For the first time, he focused. "She did. She really did."

"We need to establish a timeline, Father. Do you remember what time you left the rectory?"

"Not sure. Eight-forty-five, perhaps. Maybe a few minutes later. Don't remember the precise time."

She patted his hand. "That's fine, Father. How long was the Mass?"

"It's a weekday Mass. No Gloria because it's Lent. Somber time. I try to keep my homilies light, though, because there's so much..."

"Father," she said, giving his arm a squeeze, "about how long did it take? I need you to tell me."

He shook his head. "I'd say thirty minutes."

"And after that?"

"Well, perhaps five minutes to hang up my vestments, clean up. Ten minutes at most. Don't lock the church during the day anymore."

"So, you were back here by nine-forty-five?"

His expression twisted with fresh pain. "I called out to Ms. Westwood when I came in. I was hoping there was some coffee left from breakfast. She didn't answer. I thought she might be upstairs, so I checked. Amara wasn't there, so I returned downstairs to the kitchen and... Called your office number..."

"They forwarded the message. If you don't mind, I only have a few more questions. In the past week, have you noticed anything unusual, anyone lurking around?"

He shook his head. "I'd have called you if I had."

She pulled out the sketch. "Have you seen him around?"

"No. Ms. Westwood... She's in the spirit realm, now... Infinite..."

"Just a couple more, Father. Have you seen anyone else around here, in the congregation, who appeared out of place?"

His eyes locked on hers. "It's my fault. I shouldn't have insisted Amara stay here."

"It's not your fault." She pulled out the photos of Desmond and Conroy. "See either of these guys around?"

His eyes drifted away again. "She's such a sweet girl, Detective. A pious young lady, in her own way."

She pushed the photos in front of him. "Please. Have you seen either of these men?"

He focused. "No. I'm sorry, I haven't."

She patted his arm again. "Thanks, Father. I'll call you when I have some news. In the meantime, please call me the moment anyone contacts you about Amara." He nodded.

Kim stepped out into the fresh air. For a moment, she thought she might vomit, something she hadn't done since her first murder crime scene back in Brownsville, when Phil Vitello had taught her the trick of putting Vicks VapoRub under her nose to screen the smell. But several gulps of fresh air helped her settle. That's when she spotted Lieutenant Fredricks. "This was a fuck-up, Lieutenant."

"Yes, it was. Although we're not set up for witness protection, where she belongs. You want us to check the perimeter?"

"Detectives Stewart and Nolan are already checking. I'm aware of the challenges. This location should have had more people assigned to it. An abandoned factory at the rear should have been a red flag. Or did you assume it had the latest in laser fencing?"

Fredricks replied through clenched teeth. "The last time I checked, a lieutenant outranked a detective, Second Grade. You're treading dangerously close to insubordination, Detective."

"Your detail allowed the abduction of the only eyewitness we have in a serial murder case and the murder of another person. I'm entitled to a little insubordination."

Abe and Bob were back. "Other than the shuttered factory," Abe said, "it's all houses. No video anywhere. But two more news vans pulled up."

Kim turned back on Fredricks. "Not one word to the media. Not one."

"Hey," Fredricks snapped, "I'm not an idiot."

Kim saw Colangelo and strode to meet him rather than say what she was dying to say.

"What's the word, Kim?"

"It's Number Four. Fire. And they grabbed Amara. Oh, and someone tipped off the media. They're circling like a flock of vultures. No one here is talking, but you'd better give DCPI the word."

"I'd give my right arm to know where that tip came from," Colangelo said. "Dig a bit if the opportunity arises. We need a break." He stalked away.

Abe came over. "Something wrong?"

She nodded toward the media vans. "Somebody tipped them off."

"Yeah, we talked to some guys on the perimeter. *City News* and *Telemundo* were here when CSU arrived. It's possible they picked up the radio run on a scanner..."

"If they arrived ahead of CSU, they were already in the neighborhood when the radio run went out." The major local cable news provider and the major Spanish language outlet. Two perfect places to plant a story you hoped would terrorize a segment of the population.

They took a roundabout route, so it looked as though they were returning to their parked car, before slipping over to the *City News* van where Joanna Dunbar sat with her chin in her hands, looking glum.

"Guys," Kim said, "please leave us alone. She's a friend."

"Let's see if Vitello's boys have anything else," Bob said to Abe, who'd lost some color and spark.

CHAPTER FORTY-FOUR

As soon as Joanna saw Kim approaching, she shooed the rest of her crew away. "Why do I sense this is about to get worse?"

"Because these things often do."

"You already have my word, and I forgive you in advance for whatever you held back yesterday. Just please tell me, now. Same deal as before."

"Okay, but first I need your source for the tip that brought you here." If Joanna refused, there'd be no deal.

"I can't. It was anonymous."

"This wasn't a simple murder. Someone was abducted. The information I need from you may help us find the abducted person. As soon as we find her, you can report what I give you."

Joanna's eyes went wide. "Abducted? Who? Why?"

"Not until I learn your source."

She pulled out her cell and pulled up her recent calls list. "That's the number."

Kim punched it into her notes app. "What did he say?"

"Just that there was a gory story—his words, not mine—waiting for me at Blessed Mother rectory, and that it was a warning to Sanctuary cities everywhere."

"That was the entire message?" When Joanna nodded, Kim asked, "What did he sound like? White, black, accent, no accent, young, old..."

"I wasn't on FaceTime. But he sounded like a white guy, not too old. Can't tell you much else. It was a two-sentence statement."

Kim finished the note. "Okay. The abduction victim is fifteen. She saw Mariano Avila's killer, who appears to have committed this murder and that of Julie Campbell on Wednesday..."

"Can I report police have linked this murder to the other killings?"

"No. That would tell the killer what we've learned, and both DCPI and my lieutenant would flame my ass."

Joanna looked like she might burst. "I have to say something, so it doesn't sound like I'm making shit up. How about informed sources suspect links in the killings?" When Kim scowled, she added, "Hey, it's a fig leaf."

"Too small a fig leaf."

Joanna gave a heavy sigh. "I could say, 'suspect potential links to the other three killings.'"

Still revealing too much. But it suggested that the police only knew what the killer wanted them to know. "I guess that will do, although DCPI still won't like it."

"Neither will my boss. One other question: how do you know they're all linked? And please don't tell me it's a hunch because you are way too certain."

"I can tell you, but you can't report it until I give you the okay." Kim waited for an outburst, but Joanna nodded. "All three killings were identical to one back in November." Aw, hell, might as well throw her a bone. She described the stabbings and described the symbols. "We still don't know how the first ties in with the rest."

Joanna's thumbs were flying over the keypad on her phone. "Jesus." When she finished, she asked, "So, what's the terrorist angle?"

"You already know that. The reference to Sanctuary cities gave that away. This is some anti-immigrant group."

"That doesn't exactly narrow it down."

"We're not sure, ourselves."

Joanna locked eyes on her. "You have a lead. You have to."

"I'm sorry. We do, but we're working with the FBI. I can't afford any possibility of a leak on it. I trust you, but you don't work in a vacuum."

"You object if I do some digging myself?"

"Fine with me," Kim said. "I'll even tell you if you're on the right track if you keep to our agreement." They shook hands. "Anything on Brandt?"

"Not yet. Could you do some checking on your end?"

Kim's cell buzzed once. It was a text from Marisa: *Think I have it. Need to talk FTF.* "I'll see what I can do. In the meantime, have you wondered who is behind these riots?"

"I sure have. But anytime I say it aloud, my boss says it's the usual pissed off masses going 'a little too far'. Why? You have something?"

Kim sighed. "Nope. Only the stench of week-old fish."

CHAPTER FORTY-FIVE

On their way back to Hudson Street, Kim had called Cord to give him the number she'd gotten from the reporter, with instructions to get the call history and the list of towers pinged.

"Think Marisa will be there when we get back?" Abe asked from the passenger seat.

"Probably." Kim chuckled. "A little young for you, isn't she?"

But he didn't laugh. And he was still pale. "Way too young. No, I need some more of her antacid."

"Crime scene got to you?" Bob asked from the back.

"Just indigestion. And heartburn."

"Better stop putting jalapenos on your corn flakes." But Bob wasn't laughing.

Ken Taylor was waiting when they arrived. "We're setting up a sting using Epstein as bait. It's amazing what some guys will do to stay out of federal prison. I heard about what happened this morning."

"They grabbed Amara. I would appreciate anything new you can give me on Defend Our Home, including any hints of offshoots."

"My God." Taylor hesitated, stunned. "If you get even a hint that they might take her across state lines..."

"You'll be the first to know. But I'm more afraid she might already be dead. I can't figure out why they didn't kill her there."

He pondered that before answering. "With these guys, it's never just about what they say out loud. Yeah, it's about hatred and racism. But for individuals, it's often about something else."

"Like what?" She cringed, unsure she wanted to hear it.

"With this guy? I expect it's about power, getting off on the fact that he could waltz in and grab the girl and get away unseen, killing her guardian, right under the noses of a police protection detail. These guys are like ISIS or al Quaeda. They lust for power but run from responsibility."

"So, you think this is a group?"

"Has to be. The killer is one guy. But he didn't give the orders. Hence the symbols, the signature. That's him saying, 'Fuck all of you, I did this'. He didn't pick the targets, and whoever did wouldn't have picked the method."

"What about the commander, the guy picking targets?"

Taylor laughed. "Also power, but of a different kind. The killer's power is the same kind a rapist projects over his victims. But for the other guy, it's the power of command, the sense of giving an order and having it obeyed. And he uses the killer to pursue a higher order goal."

"Excuse me? Higher?"

"Not morally higher. Organizationally higher. He sees himself as heading a movement, accomplishing some long-term goal."

It almost made sense. "For example, closing the borders?"

"More likely, it's more elemental, like ridding the country of people who look different, speak unfamiliar languages, eat strange foods, listen to different music. In the term, 'illegal alien', they claim to focus on the 'illegal', but what terrifies them is the 'alien'. The guy commanding this could have lots of things scaring him shitless. Listen with care to one of them, and you hear it. I'll keep you posted."

As he left, a text from Vera interrupted her. *Defend Our Home site is down. Went offline early this morning. Many posts I never got to see.*

A moment later, a second text. *One e-mail this morning from Desmond to Harwood.*

What's in the subject line? As much as she craved knowing the text of the e-mail, she couldn't ask. She didn't have a warrant, so a judge would throw out any evidence she gleaned from it. But if the subject gave a hint…

Says, "We're done." That's all. Two words.

Shit, it was nothing but continuing their spat. Or could it be more?

Captain Forrest walked in, breaking her train of thought. "Kim, you've met Randi Mozlin, and this is ADA Rick Conti."

CHAPTER FORTY-SIX

Conti extended his hand. "I've heard a lot about you, Detective. Glad to be working with you."

"Given this newest development," Forrest said, "Ms. Mozlin and I felt it best that we bring Rick in now. This is about to become a media firestorm, which is what this group—whoever they are—wants. Any indications whether the girl is alive?"

She related what Ken Taylor had said. "I have to assume she is. No way to guess how long."

Forrest gestured to the sketch with a pen held between his fingers. "That appeared in every New York media outlet this morning. I can't believe he attacked, anyway. Are we sure it's him?"

"There's no doubt," Kim replied. "It's his signature, and it fits in the progression. We're still having trouble with how the first killing fits with the other three. Marisa texted me she might have something on that."

"Well," Colangelo snapped, "get her in here."

Marisa appeared a moment later with the bottle of antacid, which she handed to Abe. She turned to Kim. "I thought I'd brief you first..."

"No time," Kim said. "Give it to us straight."

Marisa explained the five elements and the steps from earth to spirit. "Each of the first four elements has two qualities—warm or cold and moist or dry. Each element has one quality in common with another and one quality in opposition to another. That chart on the marker board shows the progression. Warm is the male attribute, apex up, aspiring to the spiritual, and cold is the female attribute, apex down. I'm puzzled because the killer inscribed the male victims with apex-down symbols, and the female victims with apex up symbols." She pointed to a note Kim had made on the marker board about her interview with Harwood. "In those circles, femininity is weakness. Whoever killed Simmons may have thought him weak because he pursued a love affair with a Latina. The killer would have viewed Avila the same way because he was an enemy, working to help the very immigrants they despise. But I still haven't worked out why he inscribed male symbols on the female victims."

Kim saw the hole. "That would mean that he knew in advance the identity of all of his victims and the order in which he would kill them. I suppose it's possible that he might have known at the time he killed Simmons that Avila would be next, but he couldn't have known that Amara would see him leaving the scene of Avila's murder, or that Julie Campbell would be a key figure in protecting the girls after the sweep. The last two events were clearly reactive."

Marisa's shoulders slumped. "You're right. So, the symbols are likely nothing more than a progression to the ultimate event. Chalk one up for confirmation bias."

"Okay," Kim said. "Cord, what did you find out?"

"Burner phone. The call to *City News* pinged off a tower in Woodside, Queens. A second call, made a minute later to *Telemundo*, pinged off the same. An hour after the murder, that phone received a call from another burner phone, this one pinging off a tower in Long Island City, right by the expressway." He broke into a grin. "Kim, you know of anyone who lives in Woodside?"

"I can think of two." But that wasn't probable cause. It wouldn't get them a search warrant or an arrest warrant. She turned to Rick Conti. "What's the current law on Stingrays?"

"What the hell are Stingrays?" Cadman asked.

"A device for intercepting cell phone traffic and tracking cell phones to specific locations," Conti replied. He turned to Kim. "It's being challenged, but it's still okay for now."

"Captain," Kim said, "if we can get hold of two Stingrays, we can patrol two areas until we get a ping off the phones."

"And while we're playing Minesweeper," Cadman said, "what happens to Amara?"

"No worse than if we do nothing." Cadman still had put no emotional distance between himself and Amara. Could be a problem.

"I can get you the Stingrays," Forrest replied, "but it will take two or three hours. Officer Cadman has a point. Blind pinging only works if the target cell phones are on. You logged the last call this morning. Those damned phones could be in the East River by now. Woodside and Long Island City are dense places. You may struggle to even get a hit."

"I can guess where to look, at least for the Woodside caller," Kim said. "It has to be Harwood or Desmond."

"So," Colangelo said, "you're saying they had their own buddy killed?"

"Yes."

"Just for making it with a Latina?" Forrest asked.

It was all making sense. "Martin, didn't Harwood refer to his 'source' for information on Ortega?"

"Yeah," Cord said, "but that was misinformation."

"Most likely distorted by Harwood to anger the troops." Bingo. "He hated the fact that Simmons was sleeping with a Latina. Said he warned Simmons 'not to go all West Side Story on it'. Warned. And he was looking to solidify his hold over his little group. It's possible he sought to draw in others, too." She turned back to Cord. "Remember how he recalled having 'saved Simmons' ass enough times to know'?"

"Yeah, like it repulsed him."

"Simmons was weak," Kim continued. "In jail, he wasn't able to defend himself from being assaulted. Harwood considered him useless. Perhaps he made a martyr of him to force everyone to get in line. Burrows, who is now AWOL, is a member of Defend Our Home and had access to all the information on the Simmons case. He could tell Harwood that Ortega had fled the jurisdiction and Detective Grant had retired and Coburn and Tyler were fresh out of suspects. Harwood then took his time before he planned the next move."

Nods of agreement all around.

She turned to Cord. "Did you by any chance pull the LUDs on the tipster's phone?"

Cord walked to one of the marker boards. "It's only ever called two other numbers." He wrote the tipster's number and circled it, then drew black lines to the two other numbers. "The tipster also received one call from a third number." Cord drew a red line connecting the two.

"Any activity among the three remotes?" Kim asked. "No? Then let's call the first number Hub One, the red line phone Hub Two, and the others Remotes One and Two."

"Wait for the Stingrays," Colangelo said. "Use the interim to develop a search plan."

"Finding Amara should take priority," Cadman said in a loud voice.

Kim regarded him with concern. "The problem is that when we find her, Harwood will hear about it and flee."

"Aren't you going to question him?" Cadman asked.

"No. All he'd do is deny everything, and we'll have tipped our hand." But there was another way. "Martin, didn't you say there was tension between Desmond and Harwood that night at the Eagle?"

"Big time. Why?"

"Of the three of them, Desmond struck me as the most genuine in his anger about Simmons' death. Let's talk to him before we try Harwood."

Cadman pounded the table with his fist. "And suppose Harwood takes off while you're doing all this talking? I thought time was of the essence."

Decision time. "It is. But unless somebody tells us the exact location where she's being held, we don't have a prayer of finding her without the Stingrays. So, I want you to keep eyes on Harwood for as long as it takes. If he goes anywhere, tail him, and keep us informed. You are not under any circumstances to approach him, question him, detain him, or engage him without personal authorization from me or Lieutenant Colangelo."

They were about to leave when Captain Forrest pulled her aside. He should have been jumping for joy at this lead, but he looked like he had a major problem. "I understand you got this cell number from a reporter."

Shit. The only ones who knew were Abe and Bob, and they wouldn't have complained about it. Who else could have told him?

"Is that true, Detective?"

"Considering that the killer called in the tip, I'd say that was obvious. Why?"

"A political reporter?"

Strange question. "What difference does that make?"

"Someone saw you talking with a reporter at the scene of a crime…"

"From whom I received the best lead we've gotten so far. I'd love to hear why you think this is a problem, Captain."

"What did you trade for her lead?"

"The promise of future information."

"I'm sure Joanna Dunbar had a much higher price than that."

He knew. This grew more intriguing each passing minute. "She didn't, and I'm waiting for your explanation of the problem. We make deals for information all the time."

"She's a political reporter responding to a tip from a criminal. I need to know if we've left any back doors open."

"I've already told you I haven't. Now, how did you hear this?"

Captain Forrest stiffened. "That's none of your concern. And I believe your team is waiting for you." He gestured with a pen, which he was holding like a cigarette.

CHAPTER FORTY-SEVEN

The last thing Amara remembered was the prick of a needle in her arm following the horror of stepping through the lake of blood—poor Ms. Westwood's blood—as the man she'd described to the nice lady detective and the police artist dragged her through the rectory kitchen with his arm clamped around her neck.

Now she was lying in a huge, dark, frigid room reeking of nail polish remover. Her head throbbed and her shoulder joints hurt. She was naked, lying on a mattress, her hands tied and pulled back so she couldn't move her arms at all, her ankles tied and splayed far apart. She tried lifting her head to look around, but large piles of boxes blocked her view.

Voices.

An argument. She strained to hear.

"Listen, you moron," It was the man who'd taken her. "You don't kidnap witnesses, you kill them. Alive, she's a threat to all of us. I can't believe the general agreed to this."

"He needed my help." The voice was familiar, but she couldn't place it. "He didn't want her killed at the rectory because it might take too long and you might get caught. You couldn't get her out of the rectory undetected except through the back. You couldn't do that unless you knocked her out, and you needed someone to give her a shot of something and help you carry her, and that was me. At last, my affliction of being diabetic becomes a strength."

"Good for you."

"Oh, it is. You have any idea how much shit I've taken because of it? Even when I was in school. 'Hey, it's the pin-cushion.' Now, you needed me, and my price was that I get her."

Amara's head continued to throb. Where had she heard that voice?

"You can't hold her forever. And as soon as she breaks free, she'll tell the cops everything."

The familiar voice laughed. "Then, you'll have to trust me to keep her happy and quiet. She was my price to help you."

He had to be an old john.

CHAPTER FORTY-EIGHT

Rafer T. Harwood allowed himself a smug smile as he locked up the house. The local news station was already blaring the story of the horror found at a rectory in Brooklyn. Of course, they only hinted at the carnage found there, but even the communist news outlets couldn't sugar-coat the damage inflicted by Sanctuary cities.

A soft breeze blew, and only a light scattering of clouds dotted the sky. He unlocked the car door and pulled it open.

Delightful day.

An arm reached from behind him and slammed the door shut. "Mr. Harwood, I presume? Police." A badge flashed inches from his face. "Officer David Cadman."

"What's the meaning...?"

"Lock the car."

Cadman was two or three inches taller than Rafer, glaring at him like he knew something. A quick glance around. No one.

"Lock it now," the cop said in a low growl.

"You got a warrant?" It was worth a try.

The cop laughed. "This is the new America. None of that ACLU snowflake bullshit." He nodded to the door. "Inside."

"I don't have to..."

The cop brought his knee up in a sudden motion and delivered a searing blow to Rafer's groin. Pain and nausea engulfed him. "Yes, you do. Now. Or the next one will be worse."

"You fucking..." But Rafer never had time to finish as the knee slammed home again. Much worse the second time.

"You have two choices, Harwood. Either we step inside, now, or I take you in my car somewhere more private, and we continue our conversation there. Either way, you will answer my questions."

A quick calculation. He had a better chance of someone overhearing at the house than wherever this fucking maniac might drag him. "Okay."

He unlocked the front door and let the cop in. He slammed it behind them hoping Mom would hear upstairs.

The cop drew a semi-automatic from inside his jacket. "Don't try anything like that again, Harwood."

"Sorry. I'm nervous. My apartment is behind the garage."

The thrumming of the washing machine in its spin cycle penetrated a door as they passed. The cop stopped. "What's in there?"

"Laundry room."

"Your load or someone else's?"

"My mother's. She lives upstairs. I do it for her..." Rafer stopped. Too late.

"Because she can't manage the stairs on her own?" the cop asked, grinning. "Perfect." He gestured with the weapon toward the laundry room door and Rafer let them in. "Lock it."

With great reluctance, Rafer turned the lock on the knob.

"Sink doesn't drain too well, does it?"

"No, it..."

"Lint comes out of the drain hose from the machine and gets caught in the trap." The cop glanced around. The sink was full of soapy water, draining at an imperceptible rate. "You should have someone come and snake it out. Then, buy little screens that roll over the drain hose, like a condom." He broke into a sick grin.

Rafer wasn't sure what to do, so he allowed himself a slight grin as well.

The cop held the grin. "But they catch the lint and that keeps your drain clear."

"Thanks."

"Don't mention it. Can your hands reach the ceiling?"

"Only if I stretch."

"Show me."

Rafer brushed the wood planked ceiling with his fingers.

Sharp pain as something hard slammed into his back near his right kidney. Rafer collapsed to the floor.

"You see? I've struck you three times in ways that will leave no marks. If you complain of police brutality, you'll have no proof."

He hadn't finished. The blows would continue.

The cop pulled him off the floor and over to the slop sink, which was still full, grabbed a tuft of his hair and pushed his face into the water. Rafer snatched a breath of air before he went under and tried to close his eyes, but not quite in time and they burned from the detergent. He was powerless to force his way up against the cop's strength, His lungs burned with desperation to take a breath. He couldn't hold much longer.

The cop pulled him out. Rafer was panting so hard he sucked in droplets of soapy water. He retched at the taste of detergent and fabric softener.

"You have limited aerobic capacity. Disadvantageous when you're being waterboarded."

"What do you want?" Rafer asked.

"Ready to give up so soon? That's not what I expected from the great Rafer Harwood, patriot, self-styled leader of men." Without warning, he shoved Rafer's head back in the water.

Rafer caught his breath and shut his eyes. But the traces of detergent already in them burned, and his lungs felt close to bursting. This time, when the cop pulled him out of the water, he breathed in with such desperation that more water came in, causing him to cough and gag.

"Where's the girl?"

"What girl?" But when his head hurtled back toward the water, Rafer screamed, "No!"

"Then tell me. I know you know. You can't bullshit your way out of this one." Another knee to the groin.

The pain was worse than ever. Rafer vomited into the soapy water.

"Where's the girl?" Cadman's voice was now demanding. "Tell me now, or you'll drown in your own soapy puke."

Rafer held up a hand. In such ways were noble revolutions crushed by repressive regimes. "All right. All right. I'll tell you."

CHAPTER FORTY-NINE

It was almost noon when technicians delivered two early model Stingrays to Hudson Street. Kim drew up the plan. "Cord and I will be in Car One, Martin and Bob in Car Two; Abe and Marisa will stay here to monitor the phone numbers we have as close to real time as possible. Marisa, you'll also keep in touch with Vera Koshkin and relay any fresh developments. Our first stop will be Desmond's and we will only split up if necessary."

"What if Desmond doesn't help us?" Cord asked.

"I'm sure he will, when we tell him what we have," Kim replied. "Martin, please come in with me to question him."

Martin blinked, stunned. "And blow my cover?"

"Yes. I want the shock value. We won't need you at the Eagle Tavern after this."

"What about Harwood?" Colangelo asked.

"Cadman's monitoring him," Kim said. "Marisa, please text him and ask for an update to be sure."

Kim settled in behind the wheel of Car One while Cord cradled the Stingray in his lap in the passenger's seat.

As they emerged from the Midtown Tunnel, Kim's cell buzzed. It was a text from Marisa. *I've texted Cadman three times, no response. I called and left a message to call back.*

She'd try reaching him herself once they finished questioning Desmond.

Another text, this one from Vera. *IP address from the Tony e-mail is in Camden, New Jersey. Likely a cellphone-based account. Sorry.* A dead end.

They found Desmond at his family's ramshackle house next to the Long Island Railroad tracks in Woodside. When he saw Martin standing on his doorstep with Kim, he shook his head. "So, Tillman, you're a cop?"

Martin showed his badge. "Stransky's the name."

"And I suppose the story about your grandfather being in the 101st was bullshit, too?" Desmond spat the words.

"I never lie about my grandfather. He was a Bastard of Bastogne."

Desmond turned to Kim. "You still 'investigating' Joey Simmons' murder?"

She tried disarming him with a smile. "May we come in, Mr. Desmond? It'll be more comfortable for you and us."

"I can't tell you any more about Joey than I already have."

"We don't have questions about Joey," Kim replied. "We have answers. Can you shed light on three other deaths and an abduction?"

He blanched. "I didn't commit any murders or abductions."

"I believe you." When his jaw dropped, she gestured to the door. "May we?"

He waved them into the cramped living room, stuffed with old furniture and old photos. "My folks work."

Kim sat next to Martin on a dusty old sofa. "Eduardo Ortega did not kill Joey Simmons."

"Yeah, he did. A friend of mine got it from someone in the police department."

"Either your friend's source lied, or your friend did. Ortega had an ironclad alibi supported by sworn statements given by several people who were with him, and a deli owner who sold him beer that night. Furthermore, ICE didn't deport Ortega. He fled the jurisdiction because he feared being framed. ICE received a report but hadn't begun its investigation. And they would not deport someone wanted for a felony in the United States. If you don't believe me, I can provide a sworn statement from an FBI agent."

"It was a lie?"

Kim nodded. "Joey Simmons was killed by the same man who killed Mariano Avila, Julie Campbell and, this morning, a woman named Jamelia Westwood. He also abducted a young woman who gave us the description for the sketch you may have seen in newspapers or on television. We know this because he left a distinctive signature carved in the chests of his victims, including Joey."

Desmond leaped from the recliner. "That fucking bastard. He played Joey and then got him killed."

"Who?" Kim asked.

Desmond froze.

"If you want justice done," Kim said, "you must act with justice."

Martin spoke up. "At the Eagle, I suspected a problem between you and Harwood."

"Harwood," Desmond snorted. "That piece of shit. He lords it over all of us because he has his fucking college degree. Loves telling stories about outsmarting his professors. Thinks he's a brilliant leader. Said he would 'put some fire' into Defend Our Home. But Jack Maitland…"

"The founder?" Kim asked.

"Yeah. Maitland had started it to pressure the government to enforce the immigration laws. He and Harwood argued all the time. Harwood wanted fucking Lexington and Concord. He never got it. Most guys enjoyed drinking beer at the Eagle and talking tough. So, he formed a militia—the Militia of Light, he called it, shining a light on the fucking world. Signed up me, Joey, and Cliff Conroy as founders. Kept telling Joey about these illegals stealing construction jobs in East New York and how we should do something about it. You know how that went. But Joey came out of jail desperate for a woman, any woman, and he chased a girl he'd met while working. Around the same time, Cliff Conroy started with the ninth-grade hookers, and Harwood freaked out. Said we were all going soft."

"Was there anyone else in this militia?" Kim asked.

"Three others, two guys I don't know, and an Italian guy named Tony. Don't know his last name."

"Hence the pizza references in the Eagle Tavern," Martin said. Desmond nodded.

Kim pulled out the sketch. "Is this him?"

"Yeah. He had a major problem with Joey. Hated him. Cliff, too. When that sketch appeared in the paper, I realized Tony had offed Avila." He flopped back down, holding his head in his hands. "Poor Joey. He finally found a girl who liked him, and Harwood made him prove his loyalty to the cause by ratting out this other guy. Joey felt guilty as hell that he'd done it. Told us he was going over that night to beg her forgiveness."

"Did you ever hear Tony talk about symbols like these?" Kim showed him a sketch of the five elements.

Desmond stared at it. "Yeah. At the Eagle, Tony would doodle, drawing these triangles on cocktail napkins. Why?"

She pointed to the first one. "Joey's killer carved that in his chest." She pointed to the second symbol. "Avila's killer carved that in Avila's chest."

Desmond's jaw dropped. "Holy shit. I thought he was bullshitting. We were at the Eagle when we got news of Joey's death. Harwood went nuts. 'War, a fight to the death'. The following night Tony started waving his napkin with the symbols and mumbling some shit about 'the time is nigh' and a progression."

Whoa. "He said 'progression'? Did he ever say what the progression was?"

"Eliminate the weak first, then the collaborators and temptresses. Then strike the mighty blow."

It all fit. All that remained was the mighty blow.

Desmond nodded toward Martin. "The night before you came to the Eagle, I walked in on Harwood, Tony and Cliff talking in the back room and heard Tony say the girl at the rectory was a temptress and we had to kill her. Cliff realized who she was and had a fit. Said he'd tell the cops everything. So, Tony agreed to kidnap her instead if Cliff kept her quiet."

"Where are they holding her?" Kim asked.

"Some empty warehouse building in East Williamsburg. Don't have the actual address, but it's practically under the Koscuiuszko Bridge, close to the water. Tony's been using it to plan for his 'mighty blow', but only Harwood knows what that is."

"To your knowledge, has Tony had any involvement with these violent protests?"

Desmond looked stunned. "Helping Latino immigrants? You kidding me?"

She shook her head. "Not to help, to escalate the violence and turn public opinion against them."

"Not a chance. He's perennially pissed at the cops for not clamping down sooner, but he hates illegals. No way he'd ever lift a finger to help these guys."

It had been worth a shot. "Thank you. One last thing. Can you tell us anything about any prepaid cell phones Harwood and the others might have?"

Desmond reached into his pocket and pulled one out. "This is mine. Keep it." He fished a slip of paper out of the same pocket. "The numbers for Harwood and Cliff."

CHAPTER FIFTY

Kim pulled into the Staples parking lot on Queens Boulevard and 58th Street with the other car right behind her. Cord laid his iPad on the hood of her car with Google Maps open. Kim repeated Desmond's description. "Under the Koscuiuszko Bridge, close to the water. Newtown Creek."

"So, we need to head over to the BQE," Cord said.

Kim shook her head. "We'll need to hook up with ESU, first. Besides, at this time of day, the Brooklyn-bound BQE is a parking lot."

Cord was still studying the map. "Based on the description, that warehouse is probably either on Thomas Street or Scott Avenue. We can take 58th Street down to Maspeth Avenue. From there, it's a quick hop to the Grand Street Bridge."

"Right." Kim called Marisa. "Anything on the LUDs? And anything from Cadman?"

"Nothing from Dave. Harwood's LUDs show mostly ordinary traffic except for heavier traffic with Desmond and Conroy. But Harwood had one call from a burner phone a few minutes before the Avila murder. Afterward, reduced traffic. So, I pulled the records for the one burner phone. It shows repeated calls to one phone and a couple of recent calls to two others. I'll text you all four in a moment."

Kim read the four numbers out as the others all made notes on their apps. "The one that registered on Harwood's phone is the hub phone. Probably Tony's."

"Harwood isn't the hub?" Cord asked.

"No," she replied. "Tony is, The second phone with heavy traffic has to be Harwood's. The other two could be Conroy and someone who Tony recruited to the militia. No matter, once we're in the neighborhood, we'll need to scan for all four. Cord and Martin will split the load. Switch from one to the other every couple of minutes. We'll keep in contact by radio and..."

Her cell rang. It was Cadman at last. "I know where Amara is."

"How is that possible? Your instructions were to monitor Harwood's..."

He cut her off, excited. "Yeah, yeah, yeah, but he came outside and saw me, so I didn't have a choice."

Her blood was boiling. "You were out in the open?"

"I... Look, I had a chance, so I took it. All that matters is rescuing Amara. You said yourself the chances were slim. So, now, they're not so slim. She's at..."

"You interrogated him? After I gave you a direct order not to?"

"I took my chance. It was for her sake. Amara's all that matters..."

Kim lowered her voice to a growl, so she wouldn't scream at him. "Amara is not all that matters. We have a terrorist on the loose who has already killed four people and may kill more." Deep breath. "All right. How did you get this information?"

He chuckled. "Oh, I have my ways."

A shiver ran down her spine. "Was it coerced?"

"Nah, I pushed him a little."

This was getting worse by the minute. "Did you get physical?"

"Hey, Kim, you know how it is..."

She raised her voice. "Did you get physical? Answer me straight."

"Well, if you put it that way, I guess a little. But it was..."

"Stop. Now. Do not tell me a single thing he told you. Not a fucking participle." This entire case was about to crater. He'd beaten information out of Harwood. How to recover? How to organize? "Where are you now? And no bullshit."

"I'm in my car, in front of Harwood's house."

"Stay there. In the car. Do not get out unless someone points a weapon at you. Wait until Abe gets there, then return to Hudson Street and report to Lieutenant Colangelo."

"But what about where they're holding Amara?"

"I already know that, asshole. I got it through normal legal procedure. Now, thanks to you, we may very well not be able to nail Harwood, and we can't use anything he gave you. Shut the fuck up and stay in your vehicle until your relieved, or I swear to Christ I'll arrest you as a fellow conspirator."

She ended the call. They'd all heard, which was unfortunate. She called Abe and had him drop everything to arrest Harwood based on Desmond's statement, bring him to Brooklyn North and send Cadman back to Hudson Street. "Mirandize Harwood but do not question him. Get him medical attention but do not take down anything he says until we get the okay from Rick Conti."

She called Colangelo and asked to have an Emergency Services Unit detail meet them in East Williamsburg.

CHAPTER FIFTY-ONE

The man who was lying on top of her, spent, was Cliff. She was still naked and tied up.

He raised his head, so his eyes met hers. "You probably hate me. Please don't hate me. I've been in love with you since I first saw you on the street."

She would die, and soon. The fat man wanted her dead. "You kidnapped me because you love me?"

"In a way. I convinced them not to kill you. I will protect you."

She nodded toward the ropes. "By tying me up and...?"

He slobbered a kiss on her neck. "No." A sloppy kiss on her mouth.

She didn't return it. "If you love me, untie me. My shoulders hurt."

He raised himself to his knees. "I'm sorry about that. He made me do that. He was afraid you'd run away. But if you agree to come with me, I'll untie you and give you your clothes back and we can run away together."

It had to be a trap. She would go with him, and he would take her some place to kill her. "When?"

"Right now. I..."

He answered his ringing cell. "No... I told you I'd be responsible for her... No, I won't." He reached for her clothes.

"See, they want you to kill me," she said.

"He'd like that, but I won't let that happen if you agree to come with me and be with me." He held out her clothes to her, but the ropes still immobilized her arms.

She could still see Ms. Westwood in a pool of her own blood. "Did you kill Fr. Lynch, too?"

"I didn't kill anyone, didn't even go inside. When he brought you out, I took care of you, protected you. But, no, he didn't kill the priest. He waited until the priest left." He dropped her clothes in a pile on her stomach. "Please say you'll come with me."

When she said nothing, he pulled his clothes on. Fully dressed, he walked to a nearby door. "The outside world is waiting for us."

He turned the knob.

Nothing happened.

"Shit." He ran to the far end of the building. Metallic rattling sounds.

Again, nothing.

When he returned, he'd turned a deathly pale. "I think he wants to kill us both."

CHAPTER FIFTY-TWO

Kim stopped at the light at Grand Avenue. Cord was scanning for Conroy's cell with the Stingray. The shrill ring of her cell through the car's speakers made Cord jump.

"Brady."

"It's Marisa. LUDs on the hub phone registered a call to Conroy's phone about ten minutes ago, off a tower in your search area. The originating tower's in Greenpoint. LUDs only show that call and the one made to Harwood."

"Should Bob and Martin break off and go search?" Cord asked Kim.

"Not yet. We can't tell what we'll find when we locate Amara. And whoever this Tony guy is, he may well come to us."

After crossing the Grand Street Bridge, Kim pulled over behind a large Emergency Services Unit truck and got out of the car. A lieutenant in uniform approached and greeted her. "You must be Brady. I'm Zimmerman."

She took his hand. "Nice to meet you, Lieutenant." She brought him up to speed. "We'll continue on Grand, right on Vandervoort, right on Lombardy until we make contact."

Zimmerman nodded. "My men are ready to break in and give any emergency medical care or anything you need. We even have an explosives specialist attached. If you don't mind, I'd like to ride with you.

That way, if you need to make a quick decision, you don't have to relay it to me over the radio."

"Glad to have you with us." She introduced Cord.

They followed the route Kim had described and were heading up Thomas Street when Cord said, "Conroy's live. GPS pegs his phone at the corner of Thomas and Scott."

Kim hit the siren and grille lights. Bob and the Emergency Services truck did, too. As they made the sharp right onto Thomas, Cord said, "He's trying to make a call."

Twenty seconds passed. "He's trying again."

"He's spooked about something," Kim said. She pulled up next to a ramshackle old brick building with boarded-up windows. A steel door faced the street. Shrubs, saplings, and weeds grew sparingly around the outside.

Several members from ESU deployed with riot gear while two paramedics stood by.

"Kill the Stingray. I'll see what he wants." Kim took out Desmond's burner phone and punched up Conroy's cell number. ESU members deployed to scout the building.

Conroy answered after the first ring. "Rafe, what the fuck is going on? Why didn't you answer?"

"Mr. Conroy, this is Detective Kim Brady of the NYPD. We spoke on Tuesday. Do you have the girl with you?"

"How did...? What's going...?"

"We're right outside but I need your help if we're to help you. Is the girl with you?"

"Yes. She's okay."

Relief. "That's good. Now..."

"He wants to kill us. I don't know how." Conroy was deep into panic.

Kim kept her voice soft. "Will you let us in?"

"I can't. The two doors are double-locked."

"Is anyone else in the building?"

"No. Just us."

Lieutenant Zimmerman returned from speaking with an ESU sergeant. "Both doors are new, steel-reinforced. But there's a skylight. Looks like our best bet."

Back to the cell. "Mr. Conroy, are you anywhere near the skylight?"

"No. It's over the center of the room and we're back against one wall."

"Any booby traps he knows of?" Zimmerman asked.

Conroy replied before Kim could repeat it. "Don't think so, no."

"Keep away from the skylight," Kim said.

ESU members scurried up ladders as they propped them against the building. Two smaller ESU trucks pulled up with extra men. A crew began drilling the side door lock.

Zimmerman's radio squawked. "The skylight is chicken-wire glass, reinforced by an iron frame."

"Okay, fuck the skylight. Stick with the door."

"Cliff," Kim said into the phone, "was it Tony who called you?"

A pause. "Yeah, how did you…?"

"What did he threaten you with?"

"He said if I didn't kill the girl, and soon, we'd both be ash."

She checked her watch. Three-forty-five. "What else is around you?"

"Just old junk. Some old crates and boxes and…" He coughed several times. "Some lumber and shit."

"Are you okay? I heard the cough."

"Yeah, something stinks in here. Smells like…" His voice dropped in volume. Possibly turning away from the phone? "What did you say?" Then, louder, "She says it's like nail polish remover."

She turned to the lieutenant. "When the girl saw Avila's killer, she smelled acetone. A shirt recovered from Campbell's crime scene contained traces of acetone. Now they're coughing because of it. There must be a supply in there."

Zimmerman clicked his radio. "Fire Team, deploy with suits. Hazardous materials."

Conroy started screaming. "Get us out of here."

"Please stay calm, Cliff. We're getting a rescue team to you as soon as possible. Do you see any full chemical containers?"

"Yeah, fifteen of them. Plastic containers. Looks like about five gallons each."

"I'm putting a lieutenant from the Emergency Services Unit on the phone, Cliff. Answer his questions the best you can." She switched the cell to speaker mode.

"Okay, son," Zimmerman said, his voice soothing and paternal. "Are the containers covered or open?"

"Covered. Most of them have regular caps on them, but five of them have these metal things sticking out the top."

The radio squawked. "We're in." Zimmerman thrust the phone back into Kim's hand. "Okay, fire team in first, with shields."

"I'm coming." Before he could argue, Kim added, "this is my case and I take full responsibility. He's holding a teen kidnap victim. I'm getting her out." She raised the cell. "Cliff, stay calm. We're coming in."

The rest of her group were right behind her as she caught up to the cluster of fireproof-clad figures, extinguishers at the ready, clustered around the door with the drilled lock. She pulled her Glock from her shoulder holster.

It took a moment to adjust to the poor light and the choking fumes of the acetone. Beyond the barrier of piled crates was a vast open area. A semi-circle of clusters of 5-gallon jugs stood at one end of it. Each cluster had one jug with a slim cylinder protruding out of the top. Beyond them, Cliff Conroy was sinking to his knees next to Amara.

She was naked and bound by her hands and feet with heavy rope.

Kim reached for the rope binding Amara's left wrist.

An explosive specialist placed his hand on hers. "Not yet, Detective. We need to make sure it's not booby-trapped."

Amara was shivering, but Kim couldn't waste time on niceties.

Three other explosives experts joined them. Each pronounced, "Clear." Cord joined her as the explosives team turned to the clusters of acetone jugs. He cut Amara loose.

Kim helped her into her clothes.

The first explosives expert examined first one, then another of the jugs with the silver cylinders. "Detonators. Connected to cell phones. No other leads."

He gave a gentle tug at the detonator, and it gave way. He moved with agonizing slowness, extracting it from the jug, dripping with acetone. "Go ahead, guys. Pull them out, nice and easy."

Together, the team carried the five detonators, and the phones, outside and placed them on the ground. The wail of sirens hailed the approach of the Fire Department. Phil Vitello's CSU team arrived as well.

"They'll get the acetone out of here, safely," Zimmerman said to Kim, who now led Amara outside while Cord cuffed Conroy and read him his rights.

The first fire truck pulled up with the hazmat truck close behind. As the crew of the first truck unlimbered hoses and connected them to a hydrant, the hazmat team conferred with ESU.

"No other devices inside?" Kim asked Zimmerman.

CHAPTER FIFTY-THREE

Kim swung around as someone shouted a warning. A detonator sent up a small plume of flame as the residue of acetone ignited, then burned out. A moment later, a second detonator ignited its bit of acetone. The others followed in short order.

"I hope to God that's all of them," Cord said as the hazmat team poured into the building.

Espada pulled up. "Colangelo called. I have two cars with me. Is Amara all right?"

A hell of a question. "She's alive. He had her tied up and naked. And there are clear signs of rape." She nodded toward the building. "The main perpetrator remains at large. I need to find him."

"A woman from my unit will accompany Amara to the emergency room," Espada said. "My partner and I will take this piece of shit in for processing."

The leader of the hazmat team approached. "Detective, we'll wait for CSU to finish and then we'll take care of the acetone. We found multiple traces from spills. We discovered an enormous pile of empty containers piled up in another room, a hell of a fire hazard. And there were scorch marks on the floor, I'd guess from testing various types of detonating systems. Whoever did this has deadly plans."

The circle above the pentagram. "Thanks. Anything else?"

"We also found scraps of wire from old detonators."

Lieutenant Zimmerman was inside, studying some scraps of wire. "Ever hear the phrase about a little knowledge being dangerous? This guy is lucky he didn't blow himself to Saturn."

"He's killed four people as it is."

"He was planning on two more. If we hadn't gotten here when we did, those seventy-five gallons of acetone would've gone up in a flash."

But this was out of the progression. It wasn't the usual MO. "Hazmat said there were empty acetone jugs."

"Shit, yeah." He led her to an adjacent room. Empty containers of various sizes lay piled to the ceiling, several rows deep.

"Oh, my God." There had to be more than a hundred containers.

"He experimented with various types of bombs. Detonators, too. It appears he's settled on cell phones as activating devices. It means he can call from anywhere, set off an explosion, and have any alibi he wants."

The progression suggested there was one event left. He could have meant this as an event. But those empty containers suggested something on a massive scale.

"Does he strike you as an amateur, Lieutenant?"

"He knows detonators and explosive systems. We found what we think are traces of C-4, a common plastic explosive. If he has a knowledge gap, it's with acetone. And I'm not sure it's still a gap."

Kim texted Marisa. *I need you to pull the most recent LUDs on Tony's phone, anything after the call to Conroy. I want times and numbers for any calls. Thanks.*

Outside, Amara was sitting in the small ESU truck. Kim took both her hands. "Amara, they're taking you for medical attention. I'll call Fr. Lynch and tell him you're okay."

"I won't be able to go back, will I?"

In Kim's pocket was a new deck of cards she'd bought to have handy. But no time for Conquian here. "I'm afraid not. Youth Colony will be more secure, and you'll be with some girls you're own age. I'll check in on you once you get settled in."

Amara jumped into Kim's arms and hugged her. Stunned at first, Kim held her for several moments until the woman from SVU said, "We're going, now."

Kim watched as they drove off, blinking back unexpected tears, staring until the car disappeared from view.

***

Espada was still babysitting Conroy, who was sitting sideways in the back seat of the unmarked car, handcuffed, with his feet on the ground, sobbing.

She squatted down in front of him, as if talking to a child. "Cliff, do you understand you're under arrest for kidnapping, rape, and accessory to murder?" He nodded. "Did Detective Espada read you your rights?"

Another nod. "But I was trying to save her. I love her."

"We don't have time for that. We can talk later about what happened and why. Where is Tony hiding? What's his next target? I need you to tell me, now, and if you do, I can tell the district attorney how helpful you've been."

Conroy stared at her with pleading eyes. "Tony never told me because he didn't trust me. He and his friends didn't like us."

"What friends? How many?"

"I'm not sure. I think there were two. They didn't come to the Eagle much. Rafer thought they were great and said they'd add muscle to our Militia of Light. Rafer said we would avenge Joey's death."

She couldn't waste time. "Cliff, can you tell me any names? What about Tony's last name?"

Conroy sobbed again. "They never told us." Then he brightened. "No, wait. One of them called the other Bart once. But that's all."

"Where is Tony, now?" She needed something, anything. "What does he do for a living?"

"Auto body work. But I don't know where."

"Did he mention anything at all to you about his plans?" There had to have been something. This guy would have needed to brag to somebody. Who better but a dim bulb sidekick for whom he had no respect?

Conroy stopped crying and focused. "He talked about how hell was real, and some people needed to see it here on Earth. He ranted on about how Hispanics were inferior, and we never should have let them into the country, and he'd make them pay."

"How did he plan to do that?"

"He didn't say. He only said that he'd make God judge them regardless of whether he was ready. And then they'd be like so much incense. He told me to enjoy what I had now because my time would come, too."

It was obvious he had nothing else for them. "Book him," she said to Espada.

Next step: what had happened with Harwood?

Text from Marisa. *LUDs from Tony's phone show calls to five different burner phones, all off the same East Williamsburg tower. The call originated off the same tower in Greenpoint as the earlier call to Conroy. And call the lieu. Forrest freaked about Cadman.*

Sorry, Lieu. No time.

CHAPTER FIFTY-FOUR

Through the haze of pain in his groin, his lower back, and the horrific stomach cramps that no amount of puking seemed to ease, Rafer Harwood was vaguely aware of knocking at his apartment door.

"Mr. Harwood?"

Shit. He'd left the door open. The goon was back for more.

"Mr. Harwood, are you here?"

Not the goon. An unfamiliar voice. A different torture routine? Rafer tried to lift his head. He was lying on the bathroom floor, in a small puddle of puke because he hadn't been able to raise himself to the bowl the last time. Still couldn't, and an involuntary groan accompanied the effort.

"Mr. Harwood, are you all right?"

The voice was coming closer, older than the goon.

The bathroom door opened. A guy in his late forties stood over him. "I'm Detective Stewart of the NYPD. I saw your apartment door ajar and heard you groaning. Are you going to be sick, again?"

Rafer's voice croaked when he answered. "Don't think so."

"Can you stand up?"

He shook his head.

"Okay," the detective said. "You'll be more comfortable if you lie on your back." He helped Rafer shift position. And he was correct, as lying on his back eased the pain. "Would you like a glass of water? It will help."

"How?"

"Hydration. At least, that's what they told us in first aid class at the Academy."

Rafer wasn't taking anything from this guy. "Where's the…" He made a vague gesture toward the door. "Your partner."

"He's not my partner." He took a plastic cup from the shelf and filled it with tap water. "You should drink this. It'll help with the cramps."

As if on cue, another spasm wrenched his abdomen. Either the water would help, or he'd puke it back up. Right at the cop? He took the cup and sipped from it. His stomach still felt like shit, but drinking the water eased the pain. He drained the cup in a series of small sips. "Well, one of your fellow storm troopers worked me over. Kneed me in the balls a few times and tried to fucking drown me."

"That's what made you sick?" The detective refilled the cup with water.

Rafer took it and drained it as he had the first. "Swift, aren't you?"

"Thorough." The detective tore off a piece of paper towel, wiped the rim of the toilet, and dropped it into an evidence bag he'd extracted from his pocket. "Did the officer identify himself?"

"Flashed a badge. Tall guy, over six feet. Young. Brown hair. Dark blue jacket, gray pants, red tie." Then he remembered. "Cadman. He said his name was Cadman.

"So, you could identify him if you saw him again?"

"Afraid so. You can forget your blue wall." His voice grew stronger.

"The 'blue wall' is more myth than reality. Most cops, like me, get pissed off at dirty cops and cops that cross the line." He punched up a number on his cell, identified himself and gave the address. "Need a wagon and police officers as escorts."

"You need a paddy wagon for me?" Rafer's laugh turned in to a fit of coughing. "Shit, that hurt."

"Easy," the detective said. "Wagon is police slang for an ambulance. You need medical attention."

"No, thanks."

"You don't have a choice, Mr. Harwood. I'm placing you under arrest for your role in the murder of Jamelia Westwood and the abduction of Amara Delgado. The EMTs will take you in custody to the emergency room for treatment of your injuries, and you'll have the chance to make a full statement regarding the man who injured you. You have the right to remain silent; we can use anything you say against you in court. You have the right to an attorney; if you can't afford one, the state will provide one. Do you understand these rights as I've described them to you?"

"Yeah. I can remain silent until another goon beats me."

"I'm not basing my arrest of you on anything you may have told the officer this morning, since he never revealed what that was."

"What about my mother? She's old and sick; lives upstairs."

"I'll contact the Department for the Aging and get someone in for her. Mr. Conroy is in custody and the girl is safe. A team of technicians have disarmed the explosive devices your Italian friend left at the warehouse. But he's constructed many more, and he intends to strike again. You can help yourself a great deal, here, by telling us who he is, where he is, and when and where he plans to strike."

Rafer broke into a sneer. "And if I don't, you'll bring back the goon?"

"No. But if you tell me, the DA will go a lot easier on you."

Rafer T. Harwood, slowly and painfully, pulled himself to his feet. "See, that's what you defenders of this rotten Status Quo don't get. You think we're petty criminals, that we'll sell out anybody to save our own skins. But we're patriots. We're willing to pay whatever price we need to pay to cauterize the wounds in our country. And you can't stop it."

Because he now had them by the balls, these lefty snowflakes whose hearts bled for the rights of the accused. Rafer T. Harwood was now one of those accused, and he would shove it right up their collective asses.

The bell rang. The detective let in two officers from the local precinct and a team of paramedics. They examined Rafer before cutting away his vomit-soiled shirt and putting him on a stretcher. The detective took the shirt and slipped it into another evidence bag.

"That ain't gonna prove I did anything."

But Detective Stewart didn't appear bothered. "Nope. But it will help prove what someone else did to you. There's a reason we blindfold Lady Justice." He lit a cigarette and asked a paramedic, "Where are you taking him?"

"Elmhurst Hospital."

As they loaded Rafer into the ambulance, he heard the detective on his cell again. "He's not talking. I'll ask the lieu to notify CSU. Please contact the Department of the Aging for his mother on the second floor and get some uniforms on him at the hospital. I'll head back to process the arrest." After a pause, the detective added, "I bet his computer will have some interesting stuff on it."

CHAPTER FIFTY-FIVE

It was after seven by the time Kim returned to Hudson Street. Marisa was still there. "I don't think what we stopped today was 'spirit'."

"I agree," Kim said. "But it's part of the progression. Could it be that the four 'earthly' elements are finite, but spirit is not? And, therefore, can be multiple events?"

"I believe so. Is Martin okay?"

"He's fine. He should be back in a few minutes."

Colangelo waved her into his office and closed the door. "Where the hell have you been? I've placed Cadman on Administrative Leave pending our investigation. The captain is furious. We assigned you to him as his mentor. What the hell happened?"

"Cadman disobeyed a direct order. I told him not to even approach Harwood without getting permission from either you or me first. He was to shadow him. Period. I was specific."

"You left him on his own..."

"Goddamn it, Lieutenant, he's a graduate of the Academy and a member of this department. That should be enough. And if it isn't, then he's got no fucking business being here. And I don't give a shit who his rabbi is."

"Don't go there, Kim."

"Okay, how about this? Anything new on who leaked our involvement in the Morales sting to Senator Brandt?"

Colangelo sank back down in his seat. "No. We're lucky no one from the press has tried to check that out."

"You mean, as far as we know. You think they're going to call up DCPI and ask? I'm betting there are lots of busy beavers scratching away right now. And when one of them hits pay dirt—and they will, you can count on it—there won't be anywhere to hide."

"Forrest is still pissed at you for talking to that reporter."

Now, that was funny. "Is he pissed that we located Amara by legal means and rescued her? How will he explain IAB accepting a mediocre cadet with only nine months experience in a soft precinct, no respect for the law, and a hot temper? Because Cadman's name will soon enter the news cycle."

"You'd better cool it, Kim. You're out of your league, here."

He was right. But she wasn't the only one. "If our case against Harwood tanks because of Cadman's fuck-up, we might all end up in the Housing Bureau."

"You've got probable cause based on Desmond's statement..."

"And you realize, as I do, that to get it in, we must prove we had it before Cadman coerced Harwood's statement. That will be difficult since Cadman called me before we located the warehouse. Harwood could get the entire case against him tossed, and he's the ringleader. He also isn't giving up the killer who is now also a potential bomber. I'm sorry if it embarrasses Captain Forrest, but those are the facts."

"Okay, okay. We'll deal with Cadman. Anything new from Ken Taylor?"

The change of subject amounted to a retreat. "Not yet. I'll call him when we're done here. Martin and Nolan scanned all Greenpoint, block by block, and came up empty. This Tony guy knows how to stay off the radar. I'm waiting for CSU to deliver Harwood's computer. I want Vera Koshkin to give it a good going-over as soon..." She stopped. "If we draw the wrong judge, Harwood's computer could get tossed, too."

Colangelo stared at his desk. "Shit."

There had to be something. They'd already been looking at Harwood. And Desmond had given him up before they knew Cadman had stepped in. "We could request a search warrant, now, for the computer."

"Post-seizure? That's tantamount to admitting we didn't have probable cause."

No question, it was a risk. "In front of the right judge, it's belt-and-suspenders due diligence. I'll tell Vera to hold off. Can you please talk to Rick Conti and get his opinion? I still need to track down Burrows. His timing smells like week-old fish."

"It's possible he wanted out. Anyone else you can talk to?"

"This Jack Maitland guy, the head of Defend Our Home. He and Harwood had a falling out—Martin heard the bartender at the Eagle say that Harwood was there 'ripping Maitland a new one' the night of the Avila murder."

"Your Mr. Harwood doesn't work and play well with others." Colangelo allowed himself a grin.

"No. Also, the Defend Our Home website went down this morning and hasn't come back up. My gut tells me that's an important fact. What about Conti?"

He sat back, looking ten years older. "I'm in an awkward spot, here. I don't think I should ask an ADA to ask a judge to cut one of my detectives a little slack because another of my people did something they shouldn't have done."

"You think it's any better if I ask?"

He didn't answer for several moments. "You need to talk to Ken Taylor and see what they've found."

There wasn't enough air in his office. He wouldn't ask Conti. She would have to do it. And if it all went south, she'd be left holding the bag.

CHAPTER FIFTY-SIX

"No, Captain, I don't understand. It makes no sense at all. You assured me you had your best detective working with the boy to make certain this was a success. Now, you're telling me he's being subjected to some disciplinary rigamarole?" The voice on the other end of the phone was Senator Brandt's, and he was fuming.

No promotion was worth this. "He disobeyed a direct order, violated a suspect's rights, fucked up a major case, and left the city wide open for a major lawsuit. I'm sorry, Senator, but there's no play, here. If…"

"Rights? We're worried about a criminal's rights? What about…"

"Enough, Senator. Your protégé's police career has crashed. There's an official complaint. The department will investigate…"

"Your unit?" The senator's voice brightened. "That's fine…"

The man couldn't be that dim. "Not my unit. He's in my unit. We can't involve ourselves in this investigation. When I was in school, they called that conflict of interest."

"You can speak to whoever's in charge of it, can't you? Write a recommendation for leniency? I'm sure you're permitted to do that, at least."

He thought back on their first conversation about David Cadman. He'd known then he should have nothing to do with it. But the deputy commissioner for Internal Affairs and the commissioner were both already on board. And then he'd waved the promise of a promotion in his face.

But he now understood where it was going. "Permitted, yes. Willing, no."

A momentary silence. "I think you should reconsider your position."

"No. Cadman doesn't belong on the NYPD, let alone in Internal Affairs. If he survives this, he'll be lucky if they let him move to School Safety."

"That would be... unfortunate. He's a..."

"He's a lousy cop, and today he showed he's a dangerous one. Sorry, Senator, no sale. This goes where it goes. And I'm happy retiring at the rank of captain."

For once, the mayor-wannabe remained silent.

"Good night, Senator."

Captain Forrest hadn't thought about retiring, but it occurred to him, now. Not while the Cadman matter was still open. Too obvious. But once the department finished with him, after a brief interlude, it might be his best option. Find fresh worlds and all that. He needed a cigarette.

"Captain? You busy?" It was Colangelo.

"No, Steve, I was getting ready to leave. What's up?" He gestured to a visitor's chair.

Colangelo took it. "We all figure someone's been looking out for Cadman. No way he'd be here, otherwise. You need to tell me who it is."

"You and who else?"

Colangelo laughed without humor. "The entire unit's curious, some members more than others."

"Who?"

"Kim Brady thinks it's this guy, Brandt, because he knew we were in on the Morales bust. Cadman denied knowing anything about help from above. She believes him. And you weren't very forthcoming when we talked yesterday. Kim also thinks Cadman's actions could make it impossible to convict Harwood or to use any piece of evidence connected to him. And I can't argue. 'Fruit of the poisonous tree' and all that."

Brady. A bulldog, like her father was. And as likely to go off on her own if she got angry enough. "Is she doing any digging on her own?"

Colangelo sat back wearing a what-do-you-think expression. "She didn't say."

He almost asked his lieutenant to warn her off, but then he'd have to explain everything.

"Answer me straight, Captain. Who leaked to Brandt that we were in on the Morales bust?"

"I don't know." He hated lying to Colangelo, but he needed time to control events. "And this topic is closed."

CHAPTER FIFTY-SEVEN

Ken Taylor had expressed sympathy for her situation, but hadn't been able to give her anything new, except Jack Maitland's IP address and that he lived in the St. George section of Staten Island. "Defend Our Home hadn't been on our radar until recently, when the more radical posts appeared."

Cord had checked the Department of Motor Vehicles database and tracked it down to Westervelt Avenue.

It was a narrow Queen Anne house on a steep hill near the water. Maitland lived there with his wife and two daughters, but he was home alone when Kim and Cord got there.

"Movie night," he said with a scowl.

"You don't approve?" Kim asked.

Maitland cast a wary eye at Cord. "No. Hasn't been a decent film made in years. What do you want?"

"May we come in?" Kim asked. "We need to ask you about your website."

Maitland didn't budge. "I don't discuss my website with law enforcement unless you have a warrant."

"I don't have a warrant, but we also are not interested in the site's content. We're investigating several connected murders, one of which took place this morning along with a kidnapping. I don't believe that you would approve of these acts, and we need your help in bringing those responsible to justice. You took your website down early this morning. Why?"

Maitland still held his ground. "It didn't involve criminal activity."

"We disagree," Cord said.

Maitland snarled at Cord, so Kim intervened. "We think it could be criminal activity beyond your control."

"I'm sorry, Detective. I cannot divulge any information about Defend Our Home. If I did, no one would ever trust me, again."

Kim pulled out the morgue photo of Joey Simmons. "Were you acquainted with Joey?"

"An illegal immigrant killed him," Maitland said.

"Did Ike Burrows tell you that?" Kim asked.

Maitland drew back, uncomfortable. "Yes. And he's a cop. He'd have access to police records."

Kim pulled out the second photo, showing the triangle carved in Simmons' chest. "Did he mention that?"

Maitland blinked. "What the hell is that?"

"A pagan symbol," Kim replied. She pulled out the photo of Avila. "Similar to this." She pulled out a photo of Julie. "And this." Finally, Ms. Westwood. "Let's not forget this." When Maitland only stared, she said, "We have solid evidence Eduardo Ortega didn't kill Joey Simmons, and he was long gone by the time the other three died."

"All killed by the same person." Maitland's eyes met Kim's. "A serial killer?"

"A terrorist. We understand you argued with Rafer Harwood at the Eagle Tavern last Friday night. What about?" Maitland lost his combative stance and leaned back against the door frame, silent. Kim pressed him. "Was it a disagreement over actions a splinter group of Defend Our Home was planning, a group that calls itself the Militia of Light?"

Maitland showed them inside, to a living room with Early American furniture that was threadbare but tidy. Kim and Cord sat on the couch while Maitland flopped into an easy chair showing severe wear at the armrests. "Harwood has been growing increasingly militant over the past year. He was impossible even before Joey's murder, and downright maniacal since. Last week at the Eagle Tavern, I told him that Defend Our Home stood for the law, and if we violated one law to uphold another, we'd gain nothing. He got the group pretty riled up after that, saying they'd take action regardless of what I said. They'd run me out of Defend Our Home and take it over." He shook his head. "It sounded like the Beer Hall Putsch. So, I left. When I saw the headlines the next day about that lawyer, I got a sick feeling in the pit of my stomach. Because there'd been one member of Harwood's group who hadn't been there."

"Was the missing member named Tony?" Kim asked.

Maitland stared at her. "Yeah. Never gave his last name. I didn't like that. He hooked up with Harwood seven or eight months ago, around the same time Harwood turned hard-core."

Kim showed him the sketch. "Is this Tony?"

"Yes." After a moment, he added, "I've seen that in the papers and on TV. He's the one who killed the lawyer?"

"And the social worker, the housekeeper at the Blessed Mother rectory, and Joey Simmons," Kim replied. "Did he ever bring anyone else to the Eagle?"

"A guy named Nick. Much taller, approximately six-two. Muscular, black hair, brown eyes. Cleft in his chin. And once, there was another guy named Bart. I remember little about him. Quiet guy, as I recall."

"Any tats?" Cord asked.

Maitland had to think about it. "I think they both had the same snake tat on their necks that Tony had. Harwood claimed he had one on his chest, but I never saw it."

"What does Tony do for a living?" Kim asked.

"He claimed he had an auto body shop, but never said where. I think Nick works for an oil heating company. He always has oil stains on his hands and smells of it."

Since he was now cooperating, it was time to push her luck. "One last thing. Please tell us why you took the website offline this morning."

"How is that connected with your investigation?"

Time to show her cards. "Both the FBI and the NYPD have been watching your site. You took down several posts before we could capture them. Did you take the site offline to prevent additional posts?"

That shook up Maitland. "The FBI is watching us? What in God's name...?"

Enough stalling. "We're trying to apprehend a home-grown terrorist who has been hiding out in your group. Do you have copies of the posts and the IP addresses from which they came? Your website is a public forum. There is no right to privacy there."

Maitland pushed himself up from the chair and ambled to the desk across the room, upon which sat a desktop computer. He opened a file drawer and pulled out a folder with several sheets of paper and handed them to Kim. She scanned each one.

"The one true militia will strike yet again, and woe to the wicked."

"Illegals burn and die, along with anyone who helps them."

"We don't need a wall; we'll burn them here."

"Fire will purify those who worship at the altar of the damned."

Kim gave the sheets to Cord. "Three references to fire. It fits." She turned back to Maitland. "Is there any chance that Harwood or Tony might have any involvement with these protests, the violence?"

Maitland gave it a little thought. Good. "I can't see that, and I've never heard any of them suggest anything like that. While I'm sure that they're thrilled to see proponents of illegals clashing with police, none of them is Machiavellian enough to come up with a plan to make it happen. Maybe, instead of having the FBI monitor us, work with them to find out who is really behind these riots."

"I'll see what we can do." She extended her hand to Maitland. "Thank you. This is helpful."

He took her hand with reluctance. "You realize this will spell the end of my group."

"Perhaps you can come up with a better name, one that focuses on upholding the law while seeking genuine reform. I'm told that was your goal when you started." She stopped at the door. "What details did Ike Burrows reveal to you about the Simmons case?"

The question took Maitland by surprise. "Just that an illegal immigrant had killed him and had gotten away before they could arrest him."

"Did he say the feds had deported Ortega or that he fled?"

"He said Ortega had gotten away. Didn't give any details. Harwood later said they had deported him, so I figured Burrows had given him more detail than me. Which was..." Maitland stopped.

"Which was strange because in reality he was your friend and not Harwood's?" Kim glared at him. "Where is he, Mr. Maitland? I think you can tell me, and it's important we locate him. At the very least, he could lose his job." She handed him her card. "Can you at least get a message to him? Have him call me? I'm from Internal Affairs and I can help him out of the jam he's in, but I need his help to do it."

CHAPTER FIFTY-EIGHT

"Why," Kim asked as she drove across the Verrazano-Narrows Bridge, "do I feel like everything in this case is unwinding like an old-fashioned watch spring?"

Cord, staring out the window, declined to answer. She didn't have to ask why. They could have squeezed Maitland a little harder and might have gotten what she needed to find Burrows. But she hadn't, because she sensed she'd pushed him as far as she could without him getting defensive. She also could have taken him into custody as a material witness, but why spook someone who's showing signs of coming around and cooperating on his own?

Cord's cell buzzed. "A text. From your little Russian pal. She's got Harwood's computer and is ready whenever you say to go."

Kim's phone had buzzed when they were questioning Maitland. It must have been Vera, who hated not getting an immediate response to a text. "I have to ask, Cord. What did she do to put you off?"

"Doesn't matter."

"If you're still angry, it matters."

"Who says I'm angry?"

"Those nails you're spitting are a good clue."

He stared across the Narrows at the Brooklyn skyline.

"Strikes me as strange," she said. "You had such a thing for her. And then..." The shrill ring of her phone coming through the car speaker interrupted her. "Brady."

"Hi, Kim. Ken Taylor. One of our teams bagged Caballo's truck on I-95 north of Philly. Caballo's hiding out near the Louisiana-Mississippi border. Wanted to let you know."

"Any chance of locating Amara's parents?" Kim asked.

"Too early to tell. Our priority is bagging Caballo. I'll keep you posted." The call ended.

"A little pleasant news," Cord said.

Kim entered the Hugh Carey Tunnel. "Don't change the subject. I like and respect you, and I like and respect Vera. So, something's off."

It wasn't until they were halfway through the tunnel that Cord said, "She's racist."

"Vera? I doubt she's even conscious of race. And I'm certain she found you attractive."

"Yeah? How?"

Kim thought back to her conversation with Vera. "She told me she thought you're a nice..." She stopped at the light at West Street.

"Yes?" Cord's voice was like acid. "A nice... what?"

So that was it. "Boy. But she's Russian and has no context for that, Cord. She often refers to men as boys." Like when she described Desmond and Conroy as acting like twelve-year-old boys. Best not to mention that one. "She means it as a term of endearment."

"I'll bet."

She drove the rest of the way to Hudson Street in silence. As she pulled into a vacant spot, her cell pinged with a text.

It was from Officer Isaac Burrows.

CHAPTER FIFTY-NINE

Kim groaned. "Breezy Point. Why did it have to be Breezy Point?"

Cord laughed. "Don't they call that the Irish Riviera? Suitable place for him to hide out."

"The name Burrows isn't Irish, it's English."

"Close enough for me."

She lapsed into silence, focusing on the heavy traffic on the eastbound Belt Parkway. It was easing when she reached the Flatbush Avenue exit.

"We can all guess why I'm not thrilled about Breezy Point," he said. "What's up with you?"

"Memories." She turned onto Flatbush Avenue. "My grandfather's friends on the force introduced him to the place in the forties when he married my grandmother. They loved it. He bought a little five-room summer-only bungalow and then bought into the co-op as one of the founding members two years before he died in the line of duty."

"Wasn't that, like, way before your time? What memories?"

"My gram held on to the place for years, and we'd visit her there every summer. She doted on me." Kim couldn't help the smile.

Cord snickered. "Sounds awful."

She turned serious. "I wish I'd known her better. She died when I was six, and my dad inherited the bungalow. We spent four summers at the Point. The last two years, they fought constantly, and the houses were so close together, all the neighbors could hear everything. The other kids looked at me funny. I swore I'd never go back."

"Never say never." He heaved a deep sigh. They were approaching the Gil Hodges Bridge. "But, since you feel that way, why not call Burrows?"

"This needs to be face-to-face. Burrows is a buddy of Maitland's, and he's Harwood's 'source'. He's one of those mousy little guys no one notices, but who notices everything and everyone. Never takes the lead, no accountability, does what he pleases. I want to squeeze him, to flush him out where he knows he can't hide."

She came off the bridge and turned onto Rockaway Point Boulevard. After several minutes, she passed a sign that said, "Drive like your kids live here". She reached a checkpoint, and they showed their badges to the guard on duty. He checked their badges and shone his flashlight on Cord's face, where he held it for several seconds.

"Hey," Cord said. "You mind?"

"We're here on official police business to see a guest of one of your residents," Kim said.

With grave reluctance, the guard nodded and waved her on. After she'd driven further down the road, she said, "There's a local police officer here, paid by the cooperative. It won't surprise me if he's waiting for us when we come out."

"You know where we're going?"

"Oh, yeah." She drove until they reached a parking lot on the left. A large, recently built house stood on the corner across from the lot.

"Where the hell are the side streets?" Cord asked.

"Most houses here aren't on streets. They're on narrow paths called walks." She stopped in her tracks. "What the hell happened? Where did these enormous houses come from?"

"There weren't houses here in your golden youth?"

"There were, but they were five-room bungalows like ours, most of them seasonal." Then she laughed. "Right. Superstorm Sandy back in 2012. Much of Breezy Point burned to the ground. I'd read that they'd rebuilt in record time. Look at all those two- and three-story houses. No more little bungalows."

She led the way down a narrow path lit only by floodlights mounted on the fronts or sides of houses. Burrows' address was near the end of the walk, close to the beach.

"Think he's hiding militia in there with him?" Cord asked.

"I doubt it." She strode up to the front door and knocked. Burrows answered in faded jeans, dirty socks, and a stained Jets sweatshirt. Kim held up her badge and introduced herself and Cord.

Burrows waved them inside. "This belongs to my cousin."

"Are you here alone?" Cord asked. Burrows nodded.

"Taking a brief vacation?" Kim asked.

"Something like that." Burrows' voice was only a whisper.

"Except you called out sick," Kim said.

"I had some accumulated sick leave, and our lieu doesn't like last-minute call-outs. Is that why you're here?"

"You know why we're here," she said. "One guy has murdered four people and kidnapped another."

Burrows drew back. "I had nothing to do with that."

"Really." Kim took a step closer. "You mean, you never passed on false information about Joey Simmons to Rafer Harwood?"

Burrows blinked. "What false...? Look, when Joey was killed, Harwood was furious. The day Coburn said Ortega had fled the jurisdiction, I told Harwood. He went postal."

"What specifics did you relay to Harwood?" Kim asked.

"That Ortega had taken off. I agreed it was frustrating, but Grant had never liked Ortega for the murder, anyway. Harwood didn't want to hear it. Made a big speech at the Eagle, said it was time for war. Everybody cheered him on, drank their beers, and returned home and forgot about it. Harwood talked about forming an intelligence network, and I was his eyes and ears inside the NYPD. I didn't know what to do..."

"My first choice would have been reporting it to a superior," she said.

It pulled him up short. "Well, yeah, I guess. But I didn't realize where it would lead. I asked Jack..."

"Maitland?" Kim asked.

"Yeah. And he said to give Harwood enough information to gain his trust and report back everything Harwood told me."

"So, what did you tell him?"

"Not much until Avila started making a stink about the hookers, demanding we clean them out. The precinct commander was considering it, so since one of Harwood's boys was a regular, I gave him a heads-up. A few nights later, Avila was killed. Harwood asked me to keep him posted. When you guys stung Blade Morales, I suspected a connection to the Avila murder."

"Which is why you were loitering outside the interrogation rooms that night." It was all coming together.

"I heard all of them lawyer up and I passed that on to Harwood."

"What else?" she asked. "Tell me everything you passed on."

Burrows paled.

"You be fucked either way, Bro," Cord said. "The more you give us, the more petroleum jelly we can give you."

"I heard the girl who'd seen Avila's killer was staying at the rectory, and a social worker named Campbell would bring the other girls to Youth Colony. After end of tour, I drove to Harwood's place."

"Was anyone with him when you got there?" Kim asked.

"Just this guy named Tony. Rarely comes around the Eagle but hangs out with Harwood when he does. Maitland hates him. Says he and his sidekick, a goon named Nick, are dangerous."

Kim was making entries in her Notes App. "What's Tony's last name?"

"Rizzo, though he don't tell nobody. I saw his driver's license, once. Never learned Nick's last name."

"Ever hear Rizzo mention anyone else who could be working with him?"

"I've heard him mention some guy named Bart a few times."

For the first time, she softened. "Okay, Burrows, pack a bag. You're coming with us."

"You're arresting me?"

"Protective custody," Kim said.

"You're gonna need it," Cord added.

The Breezy Point police officer was waiting at the checkpoint, but with no roadblock, Kim sailed past.

CHAPTER SIXTY

Saturday, March 24th

"Good morning, here are the lead stories. The wave of unrest continued to sweep across the city last night as violence struck several areas, including an attack on the Seventy-Fourth police precinct in Brooklyn. Police in riot gear retaliated, injuring several protesters and one police officer. Acting Mayor Dunn called for an end to the violence while urging the police to respect people's right to protest peacefully."

***

The television outside woke Kim. It was five after seven in the morning. She'd grabbed a couple hours of sleep on the sofa in Captain Forrest's office, the first time since she'd transferred to IAB that she hadn't gone home.

Jake hadn't been happy about it. "Totally digging into the case, I see. Try to call or text when you get a chance."

Getting resentful because her work time was back off the charts again while his was about to become his own. She was sure of it.

Or he wanted children more than he was admitting, and the resentment was seeping out at last.

She scanned her new notes on the board. Still no way to know what to protect. One large target meant a lot of time unloading in one place, making it easier to catch them in the act. Many small ones meant multiple brief stops, a greater possibility of being caught on surveillance cameras but harder to apprehend.

She needed coffee.

She left the building and crossed Spring Street to the Sprout Deli and Grocery. She was suddenly hungry and ordered an egg sandwich to go with her coffee.

As she waited for change, Joanna Dunbar sidled up beside her. "I was hoping you'd come in here. Can we talk?"

Kim glanced around. No one from the department was there, but that could change. "Not here."

Outside, the temperature struggled to reach forty. But then, her cold breakfast would be the least of her worries.

"What's wrong?" Joanna asked. "You look awful."

Kim nodded to the Hudson Street building. "Spent the night." She started walking down Hudson. "Also, I got scorched by my captain for talking to you at the rectory."

"Didn't the cell number help?"

"Yes, it did." A quick glance to make certain they weren't being followed.

Joanna snickered. "Since when did you become paranoid?"

"Since my captain discovered I had spoken to 'a political reporter' without me telling him."

"He meant me?"

"He later referred to you by name." She picked up the pace until they reached Freeman Plaza, where she took a seat at one of the neon yellow tables and opened her sandwich. "Want half?"

"No, thanks." Joanna was now stewing. "Shit."

Kim pulled the top off her coffee cup and gulped. It was hotter than expected. "What?"

"The only person I know who regards me as a political reporter is Ray Brandt. I thought I glimpsed one of his lackeys at the church, but I had more important things on my mind."

"Does he bird-dog you often?"

"He never has, and I don't think he was on Thursday. I think he was tailing you guys. Brandt has a police scanner, and he keeps an ear out for anything he thinks might be in his interest. This happened right across the street from the Avila murder and Morales' bust."

The coffee was already getting cold. "Lucky me."

"But why would he tell your captain? What's going on here, Kim? Something relevant to what I told you about Brandt?"

"Possibly." She told Joanna about Cadman being assigned to IAB and getting the red-carpet treatment.

"So, you think Brandt greased the skids for this kid?"

"I would, except Cadman swore up and down that he's never even met the man." Time to bring out everything churning inside her. "Besides, if Brandt is as much of a hack as we assume, how does he have the juice to get the commissioner to override established procedures, not once but twice? Even as chair of a committee, he's based in Albany, and this is New York City. So, it's possible he's a mere front man for whoever is now funding his campaign. In which case, why would his benefactor give a shit about Cadman?"

"Perhaps he doesn't, but he might care about someone who does."

Kim drained the last of the coffee. "A miniscule group. He only has an older sister who…" She froze. Cadman introducing her to Loretta flashed through her mind—the exquisite clothes and shoes, the perfect nails…

"Who… what?"

"Who works as an administrative assistant at Emory Equities and was wearing an outfit way above what a typical admin could afford when I met her. A workday."

"Name?" Joanna was already into her Notes app.

"Loretta Cadman."

"I'll tell you anything I find. Watch yourself."

***

Kim had returned to the board, but she added nothing about her chat with Joanna Dunbar. That was Joanna's case, not Kim's.

"Good morning."

She jumped at the voice. "Hi."

It was Colangelo. He closed the door and nodded back toward the TV, which was showing Sabrina Dunn spouting platitudes. "You believe that shit? Peaceful protests? We're lucky we didn't lose that guy from the Seven-Four last night. A bunch of them knocked him down and beat the crap out of him. No one we know in case you were wondering."

"I was. Did we collar any of them?"

"Yeah. And they'll all be out, no bail, by this afternoon, free to attack another precinct or maybe loot some more stores." He nodded in the general direction of the TV, where the image had changed to Senator Brandt holding forth. "He says he wouldn't blame the PBA if they staged a 'sick-out' tonight."

"Nothing like pouring gasoline on the fire."

"Tell that to Madam Mayor."

"Madam Acting Mayor." Kim smiled without humor. "As my gram used to say, two wrongs don't make a right."

It pulled him up short. "You didn't go home last night. I can't say I approve."

Good, he could keep Jake company. She pointed to her fresh notes. "We're close. Rizzo uses his body shop as a legitimate business front, but apparently has no signage on it. Martin and Bob must have driven right by it yesterday, but he either wasn't there or had his cell powered off, except for when he triggered the detonators. Whatever he has planned, he's got to be moving soon. But if he knows we've grabbed Harwood, he'll stay off the phone."

Colangelo remained lost in thought for a few moments. "Kim, do you think there's any tie-in between the violence we're seeing and Harwood's group?"

"I asked Desmond yesterday and Maitland last night, and they both said no way. Their arguments made total sense to me, so I shot Ken Taylor an e-mail asking if they know who might be instigating. As soon as he gets back to me, I'll let you know."

"We could question Harwood about what he knows of Rizzo's plan." But he said it with little conviction.

"Isn't anything he says, now, tainted because of the coercion?"

"No. I believe the sole tainted information is what he told Cadman. But if Harwood set everything in motion..."

She got it. "The last thing he'd do now is to help us stop it." An additional concern. "What's the deal with Cadman?"

"Indefinite Administrative Leave. Harwood gave Abe a full statement, a copy of which I've already given to the captain."

"Who is, no doubt, hard at work finding a discreet assignment for him as we speak." Kim allowed the barest hint of a humorless smile. She might face a rough future, depending on who Cadman's protector was.

Colangelo remained serious. "It's out of his hands. They've already assigned Cadman's case to another section of IAB. Don't get sidetracked, Kim." He gestured to the board. "What do we know about Rizzo?"

She pointed to the facts Ken Taylor had already unearthed.

Colangelo caught it. "And he's using his demolition training. Any hints about his entry into auto body work?"

Cord walked in. "See?" he said to Marisa, who was right behind him. "I predicted we'd find this a happening place early in the morning." He turned to Colangelo. "Morning, Lieu. Kim giving you the latest?"

"How late were you here last night?" Colangelo asked.

"I begged off about two-thirty. But I should've stayed."

Marisa laid a basket filled with little egg-shaped chocolates wrapped in colored foil, festooned with ribbons. "Tomorrow's Palm Sunday, so I thought this would set the mood for Easter Week."

The mention of Easter reminded Kim of the upcoming dinner with Jake's parents, Mr. and Ms. When-are-we-getting-grandchildren. She banished the thought. "Lovely idea, Marisa."

Abe Stewart entered and draped his windbreaker over the back of a chair at the conference table. "Great, a working breakfast. Anyone order bagels and coffee?"

"Think your stomach can handle it?" Marisa asked.

"I'm fine, thanks."

"Morning, Abe." Kim gestured to Rizzo's name on the board. "I'd love to know where he got the money for the chop shop..."

"Most likely by doing lots of work in someone else's." Cord popped open his laptop and started searching while Martin took breakfast orders and called the Sprout.

"Just coffee for me," Kim said.

Cord soon had useful information. "It's a sole proprietorship, which cuts down on the paperwork. First filings were early last year. He's doing business as Minutemen Auto Body..."

"Cute," Colangelo said.

Cord went on, "The address listed is 505 N. Henry Street."

"Puts him right in the middle of Newtown Creek," Abe said.

They needed a plan. "Okay, guys. Ken Taylor is continuing his thorough analysis on Rizzo. Vera is checking out the IP address Maitland gave us last night, the one that generated the posts he took down. Marisa, start combing Motor Vehicle records for Tony or Anthony Rizzo in Brooklyn and Queens. The bastard must have a driver's license. It'll be an extensive list, so tell me if you need help. Get dates of birth so we can cross-reference with Rizzo's army records. And please monitor Rizzo's cell phone activity."

Bob Nolan sauntered in. "Whoa, and I thought I was early."

Kim gave him the summary. "I'd appreciate it if you and Cord could see what you can find out about this chop shop. See if you can triangulate Rizzo's known records to locate him. In the meantime, Abe, as soon as Martin gets here, you two should head over to Greenpoint."

The IP address Maitland had given her differed from the one Vera had identified as Rizzo's. But she still needed to figure out what other help Rizzo was getting. "This Nick guy sounds like pure muscle. Rizzo likely isn't as smart as he appears. I'm thinking he's got at least one associate who's there for brains, not brawn. Could be this mysterious Bart that Maitland, Conroy, and Burrows all mentioned. He'll be the toughest to find."

CHAPTER SIXTY-ONE

"I know it's a lot to ask for," Kim said, standing in Ken Taylor's office, "but I need to run this bastard to ground, fast. I need intel on how big a group I'm chasing. I know Maitland isn't involved."

He gestured for her to relax. "I heard your message around seven this morning," he replied. "Did his basic training at Fort Benning, qualified for demolition training. He punched out a second lieutenant and served six months in Leavenworth before being handed a dishonorable discharge."

"What triggered the assault?" Kim asked.

"We'll need the court martial transcript for that. Might take time. You want it?"

"How much time?"

"Longer than you'd like."

"Were there any co-defendants?"

"None. I've got a list of everyone who went through basic with him, and everyone in demolition training with him. Three Nicks in the first group, one of whom was Nick Kotsonis, hometown Perth Amboy, New Jersey."

"Okay, forget the trial transcript for now. Did anyone from his basic training company go to demolition training with him?"

"No. And no one named Bart in either."

"Can you please send both lists to my e-mail?" she asked.

He turned back to his desktop. "Doing it now. Text me any leads on this guy. We'll help you bag him. We've now classified him as an imminent risk."

"Will do. And can you please check back with the army to see if anyone else in either group was dishonorably discharged, and if so, when?"

"Is that all?"

She couldn't suppress a snicker. "Well, no. A lead on who's behind these riots would be a big help."

"I'm sure. But that's definitely not in your jurisdiction."

Not an argument she expected to hear. "It is if Rizzo's involved."

"I doubt he is. We suspect it's a militant left wing group, possibly several, but we don't know for sure. We doubt it's the group that first organized the vigil for Mr. Avila."

"The Coalition for Immigration Justice? Impossible. That's Evelyn Burke's group. But I tell you what. I've been meaning to drop by her office for a chat. I'll let you know what I learn."

***

Colangelo was waiting for her when she got back. "Marisa located Rizzo's address on the DMV database before she left. Monitor Street, right off the BQE. Think that's legit?"

"It's a place where he can be sure to get his mail," Kim replied. "If it isn't his, it's family or a friend." She texted Cord with the address.

Ken's e-mail was at the top of her in-box. Names, serial numbers, and state of residence, only. They had to check them all, one by one, with the National Crime Information Center's database.

She searched for Nick Kotsonis. No hits, no record. Unusual for dumb muscle. If that's what he was. She worked her way through the rest of the list. A few names appeared on the NCIC database, most of them assault or drug offenses, scattered across the country, but nothing that looked related to this case.

Cord called. "The Monitor Street address is his mother's apartment. She's elderly. Very elderly. Says he's in the army, hasn't been by in years.

I asked for his current address, and she lapsed into a thousand-yard stare."

"An act?" If so, she'd likely tip off Rizzo.

"Given the overwhelming odor of kitty litter and the piles of old newspapers everywhere, I'd say probably not. My guess is he sleeps at his chop shop wherever that is."

The resounding boom of Colangelo's fist hitting his desk made her jump. "Okay, thanks. Keep probing with the Stingray." She ran into Colangelo's office. "What's wrong?"

He was shaking, his eyes flaming. "Rick Conti called. Judge Vickers, old Let 'em run Ron, released Rafer Harwood on his own recognizance, saying that with only accomplice testimony and a coerced confession to go on, anything more was unconscionable."

"But Desmond wasn't an accomplice. He was against this from the start. Can't we..."

"He's already out. Get eyes on him as fast as you can. If he so much as jaywalks, I want him back in the can. And talk to Conti about that search warrant on Harwood's computer."

CHAPTER SIXTY-TWO

He was still uncomfortable walking, and his back was still sore, but Rafer T. Harwood was strong enough to push on. Eight hours rest on the city's dime helped, and the hours of enforced solitude had allowed him to analyze major issues.

He'd made a huge error, granting Cliff's plea to spare the little whore's life, even for an hour. Rizzo should have killed her. The whole point of the attack was to eliminate the one person who could identify the chief weapon in Rafer's personal army. But with the cops watching the rectory, Rizzo needed a lookout, and with Desmond no longer trustworthy, that left Cliff and his plea.

Rizzo also bore some responsibility. Rather than torching the old warehouse immediately, he'd drawn things out to terrify Cliff, giving the police time to locate it, save their witness and pick up another. He held no illusions about Conroy's ability to stand up to police questioning, let alone what he, the great Rafer T. Harwood, had endured.

His men, his chosen militia, had all let him down. First, Joey had lost his soul to the siren song of Latina pussy. He'd wanted to forgive Joey after what they'd done to him in jail, but once he started talking about wanting to marry the Mexican, or whatever the hell she was, Joey was lost for good. Then, Cliff started. Rafer realized now his failure to halt Cliff's adventures at the start resulted in lost authority with Desmond, the only one of the three with the potential fortitude to hang in. But *et tu*, Desmond.

All that remained of the militia was Rizzo and company.

The light at the corner of Smith and Schermerhorn Streets was red, a chance to stop walking for a minute. It was only four blocks from the court building to the Jay Street-MetroTech subway stop, where he'd take the R to Sixty-Fifth Street, but it felt more like four miles. Fucking cops.

They wouldn't let him stay on his own for long. Cliff and Desmond knew enough to alert the cops something big was afoot. If he and Rizzo weren't careful, they'd all be grabbing their ankles at Rikers.

Wait. Going home was the worst thing he could do. It would be the first place they looked. The "don't walk" sign was flashing. He struggled to cross Smith Street before the traffic light changed. The Hoyt-Schermerhorn stop on the G line was closer and offered the hope of a much better option than doing nothing but waiting.

CHAPTER SIXTY-THREE

"Geez, Kim, I don't know." Rick Conti rubbed his temples with both hands. "That's a hell of a reach."

She recounted everything Vera Koshkin had found. "Plus, we have Desmond's statement. Doesn't that add up to probable cause?"

He raised his head and met her gaze. "Yes, and if you'd presented that to a judge before grabbing the computer, you'd have gotten your search warrant."

She had to think fast. "My team only grabbed it because we were afraid the location had been compromised. We haven't analyzed it, yet, and we've kept it secured. And since our expectation was that Mr. Harwood, as a suspected terrorist, would remain in custody, it's not as if we were denying him access."

Conti cracked a smile. "You should have gone to law school."

"That's what my dad wanted. I'm confident Judge Castellano would accept the argument."

Conti's smile vanished. "He's in Manhattan. All four homicides and the kidnapping occurred in Brooklyn."

"But the conspiracy…"

"Took place in Queens."

She sat back. "I was about to say that it's city wide, as is IAB, whose case this is."

"Nice try, Kim. But all actual criminal activity took place in Brooklyn. My boss disapproves of judge-shopping, and he won't stand for judge-shopping out-of-borough. What's worse, the police have already assaulted the defendant and coerced a confession, and that puts me behind the eight-ball. We have to play this one by the rules."

"And my boss disapproves of incinerating the populace, which is what will happen if we don't find these guys. I need whatever is on Harwood's hard drive to find them."

Conti held up a hand. "I'm on your side, Kim. Let me work on it and I'll get back to you."

She wrote a phone number on a card. "That's where you can reach Judge Castellano."

CHAPTER SIXTY-FOUR

The walk from the Greenpoint Avenue subway stop to Rizzo's unmarked rented garage on Calyers Avenue was only about half a mile, but Rafer was gasping for breath and soaked with sweat by the time he got there. He paused at the corner to catch his breath and to mop the sweat and rain from his forehead and face. The rain, which had started as he climbed the subway stairs, developed into a downpour, causing his teeth to chatter. Re-establishing his authority after what had happened would be difficult, but it was necessary. They were too near the finish.

Kotsonis answered the coded knock—three quick knuckle raps followed by a slam of the fist. "V" for victory. "What the hell do you want?"

"Is he here?" A silly question. Rizzo left no one alone in his shop.

After hesitating, Kotsonis let him in. A serviceman for the Saturn Oil and Heating Company, he remained on call for the weekend. He'd parked his van, with its distinctive orange ringed-planet logo painted on the side, over the work bay.

Rizzo was sitting in a worn-to-a-frazzle recliner he kept in the garage's corner, draining the last of a bottle of beer. "You look like shit."

"You would, too, if they'd waterboarded you."

Rizzo put the empty bottle down. "Is that your excuse for turning traitor on us? You squealed about the location. Cops got there before I could detonate it. Got the girl, got Conroy."

"Not my doing. Desmond ratted us out, as I discovered at my arraignment. Some ACLU judge called it 'accomplice testimony' and let me go with no bail. Fucking snowflakes make it easy for us."

Rizzo shifted in his seat. "So, you're telling me that your two buddies turned quisling on us, and that makes you okay?"

"I'm telling you I stood up to police torture and I'm still here. I came direct from the courthouse so we could decide on next steps."

Rizzo scoffed. "What the fuck you mean, 'we'? In case you ain't heard, you ain't no leader no more, not a lieutenant, not even a fucking foot soldier."

"And who decided that? You?" A voice in his head told him to stay cool, because he had damned few cards left to play.

A familiar voice came from the office, shrouded in shadows. "No. I did." The man who called himself 'the general' among close associates. "You didn't even stop to think your sudden release might have been something other than the stupidity of a snowflake judge. They might have something up their sleeves. The cops must be fucking desperate to locate this place, and it wouldn't surprise me at all if they've followed you. Coming here was rank stupidity on your part."

Rafer T. Harwood had taken enough. "I'm not the one who got carried away carving voodoo symbols on victims' chests, handing the cops a fucking roadmap. And, no, I didn't tell them anything about that, but they asked me if I recognized Asshole's stupid triangles. I said I didn't. But catch this. They also asked about the circle."

"Excellent," Rizzo said.

Rafer strained his neck, but he couldn't make eye contact with the general, still standing in the shadows. "You don't think it's so excellent, do you? Because you're smarter than that."

The general remained silent.

"Didn't think so," Rafer said. "You're also smart enough to realize your desired target is too big and would take way more men than we've got to set the explosives." He turned to Rizzo. "Even you know that."

The general's voice became a snarl. "You suggesting we give up?"

"If I wanted that, I wouldn't have risked coming here. See, in your brilliant analysis, you overlooked one slight detail. The judge released me on my own recognizance. It's the same as being on bail, only there's no

234

bail. But if I'm found to be violating the rules of bail—like, for example, consorting with terrorists—they can throw my ass right back in jail." He nodded toward Rizzo. "Even he realizes if I risked that, it had to be for a reason."

"Go on."

"I said nothing other than my complaint about police brutality—and how ironic is that—but I listened a lot. The goon who damned near drowned me was from Internal Affairs. So was the bitch detective who questioned me, Desmond, and Conroy. They knew Maitland had taken the Defend Our Home website down yesterday morning, which means they'd been monitoring it, which also means the FBI could be on the case."

"They told you all this?" The general was now interested.

"No, I overheard."

"But why would Internal Affairs be…"

"Because Numb-nuts, here, wore his police costume the night he offed Avila." And what a joy it was to say it.

A lengthy silence followed before the general spoke. "What is your recommendation, Rafer?"

CHAPTER SIXTY-FIVE

Kim fidgeted as she waited in the visitors' lounge for Amara to join her. Her visit with Evelyn Burke had been brief, and the lawyer had been frank, voicing her frustration at militant elements infiltrating the Coalition for Immigration Justice and remaining well-hidden. The CIJ would release a public statement later that afternoon condemning the violence and pledging peaceful cooperation with the police to root out those inciting it.

The police presence outside Youth Colony remained low key. Presumably, there were plenty of undercovers around.

Amara appeared in the doorway. Dressed in black leggings and a teal sweatshirt, she looked like any other teen girl. Except for her eyes, which had the same hunted look as the first time Kim had met her. The girl nodded a silent greeting.

"How are you?" Kim asked.

Amara shrugged but said nothing.

"I'm afraid Amara hasn't been talking much since her arrival," the social worker accompanying her said. "Just a few whispered phrases."

Kim didn't take her eyes off Amara's. "May I visit for a while?"

Amara nodded.

"She's had a tough time of it," the social worker said. "I hope you're not here to interrogate her."

Kim took Amara's hand, who clasped hers in return. "No, nothing like that." But the girl's hand squeezed tight, and Kim fought down the lump rising in her throat. "Just a friendly visit."

"I'll leave you two to your visit, then." The social worker cast a meaningful glance at the video camera mounted overhead.

"Thanks." Kim gestured to the chair next to hers and Amara sat in it. "I wanted to check how you're doing. How are you feeling?"

Amara shrugged.

Kim pulled the deck of cards from her pocket. "Want to play some Conquian?" When Amara brightened a little and nodded, Kim dealt the cards, and they played a hand.

Amara won.

"Talk to me," Kim said. "Your eyelid doesn't twitch anymore."

"*Si.*" She held out her right hand. "No shaking, either."

"Are they taking care of you here?" Kim had already learned that they were proceeding with detox.

"It's nice. Most of the other girls from—you know—have gone, but one is still here, and we talk sometimes. Is Father all right?"

"I'll see him later today. When I do, I'll tell him you were asking for him. That'll make him smile."

Amara lapsed back into silence. Her eyes reflected nothing but loneliness and pain.

Kim felt a sudden urge to say something to give her hope, but also realized she had nothing to offer with any certainty.

Amara must have sensed it, seen something in Kim's eyes. "Have you heard anything of my family?"

No choice. "The FBI found the truck they used to bring you here. They're following leads in each place the truck has stopped. I've asked them to look for your parents. They've promised they would and that they'd do their best to protect them."

"If they're still alive." A tear tracked down Amara's cheek.

Kim reached across the chair and took both Amara's hands in hers. "You told me how strong they are. I'm sure they're all right."

Amara squeezed Kim's hands. "I almost died. They could, too. Then, I'd be alone."

How long before whoever was watching on video sent someone in to intervene?

Fifteen. Alone. Bereft of hope. "You'll never be alone. I'll make certain of it." The words were out before Kim could stop them.

Amara gazed at her through tear-filled eyes. "How?"

"We'll try to find your family. But if we can't, I'll…" Amara flew into her arms. Kim held her as tightly as the girl held her until the social worker appeared and asked if everything was all right.

CHAPTER SIXTY-SIX

Command was once again within Rafer's reach. "Rizzo, your original plan was to hit one of the massive churches in Brooklyn on Easter Sunday during one of the Spanish masses. Even though neither Desmond nor Conroy knew anything about it, the plan is no longer viable, if it ever was."

"What's wrong with it?" Rizzo asked.

"It requires placing too many clusters of jugs in locations that might be inaccessible. An unfortunate by-product of yesterday's disaster was that the police now know you are using containers of flammable liquid. Any trace of it will set off alarms."

"You mean your disaster." Rizzo shouted the words. "You went along with Conroy taking the girl prisoner."

"But I opposed bringing them to the warehouse to kill them both. We've lost our staging area, which we'd kept off the police radar."

Rizzo gestured to the garage. "We have this, unless they followed you here."

"No one followed me, but that doesn't mean they won't find this place."

The general's voice was calm. "If you oppose the original plan, Rafer, what do you want to do?"

"Am I in command?" Best to clarify this now.

"Convince me you should be."

One shot. Better make it good. "We clear out of here. Bart's place in Bushwick is best. It's private, convenient, off the cops' radar, and he has a garage which is vacant now."

Rizzo stirred. "You hope it's off the cops' radar." His voice dripped with resentment.

The general took command. "Quiet, Rizzo. He's right. You guys get to Bart's on the double. Take the van and park it in the garage. That's the idea, isn't it, Rafer?"

"It is. And since the garage faces a community driveway behind the house, pulling in won't attract attention. I doubt anyone will even see it. Once we're there, we can plan the operation."

"Tell me what your idea is." He'd caught the general's interest. "I won't be going to Bart's with you. If I like it, I'll leave it to you to work out the details."

"We hit the Blessed Mother church…"

Rizzo exploded. "You're fucked. Cops are watching the place, asshole."

Rafer remained calm. "But you've already hit it, and you've never hit the same place twice. They're watching the rectory, not the church, and they expect nothing. Nick, you said the church is a Saturn Oil client. When was your last service call there?"

"A month ago. The heating plant, like the rest of the place, is falling apart. Why?"

"This afternoon strikes me as a wonderful time to check if everything is satisfactory, since the weather is unseasonably cold."

"You want to blow it, now?" Nick asked.

"No." Don't roast him. Show him patience. Rafer turned to Rizzo. "Unlike the bigger churches, Blessed Mother is all wood, correct?"

"Yeah."

"And the plume of a firebomb rises, correct?"

Rizzo raised his head, his interest caught. "Yeah."

"And the odor from acetone in the cellar wouldn't be detectable in the church above it, correct?"

"Not at first," Rizzo said. "And if it was, people would simply wonder who spilled the nail polish remover."

"When do you want to attack?" the general asked.

"Seven o'clock, the first mass tomorrow morning," Rafer replied. "It's Palm Sunday. The place will be packed to the rafters."

The general considered it. "Rafer, I approve your operation. You have go/no-go authority. Rizzo, you'll take care of the details. The three of you, plus Bart, must work together. I want no screw-ups this time. None. Now, get over to Bart's."

Almost done. "We'll need a diversion, first. Rizzo, before we leave, get out your cop costume."

CHAPTER SIXTY-SEVEN

"Let me get this straight." Judge Ronald C. Vickers leaned forward and alternated his glare from Kim to Rick Conti. "You're asking me to sign a search warrant for a computer that the police already seized without a warrant?"

It was an hour since Kim had gotten the frantic phone call from the ADA telling her that Vickers was the only judge available and that he had no choice but to go to him. He'd asked her to join him.

"I suppose that's one way to put it, your honor, but..."

"Oh? How would you put it, Counselor?" As Rick searched for the right words, the judge turned on Kim. "What about you, Detective?"

She'd been preparing herself for this question since the phone call. "Your honor, we have evidence of extensive e-mail traffic within a ring of terrorists..."

"Suspected terrorists," the judge said.

"With all due respect, your honor, these 'suspected terrorists' have already murdered four people and abducted another. We see powerful indications of a plan for a much larger terrorist act, and..."

"'Indications'. An interesting word choice, Detective. In my experience, it often leads to a ruling of prior restraint."

She would not back down. "When an unexpected attack can kill hundreds, that's sometimes all the police have to work with to keep the

242

populace safe. Your honor, what if we had come to you with this affidavit before the police took custody of the computer..."

"You mean before police seized it without a warrant?"

Fine. "Yes. Would you have issued the warrant?"

He glanced down at the affidavit on his desk. "Probably yes."

"Then I don't see the problem. The computer has remained under lock and key, untouched, unexamined, since we acquired it..."

"Seized. Without a warrant. And meeting none of the criteria for exigent circumstances. I know your record, Detective Brady. And even if you don't want to admit it, I'm certain you see the problem. We can only guess what might have happened if Detective Stewart hadn't taken the computer, but I'm also bound to consider what might have happened if Officer Cadman hadn't tortured Mr. Harwood, if he had obeyed orders and remained in his car. I can't pretend that none of that happened."

"You also can't pretend that your decision has no consequences," she replied.

"Don't you presume to lecture me, Detective. There is no tougher balance to maintain than personal liberty against communal security. And the current fear of terrorism makes many willing to sacrifice the former for the latter. But the law is the law. And if I sign your warrant, I open the door to police covering up civil liberties violations with warrants issued after the fact. No, thank you."

"Your honor, there's one other thing..." Rick said.

"If you're about to argue inevitable discovery," the judge replied, "don't. This is blatant bootstrapping. I'm denying your request for a search warrant and ordering the police to return the computer to Mr. Harwood with all deliberate speed."

CHAPTER SIXTY-EIGHT

On her way back to Hudson Street, Kim stopped in to see Yvette Driscoll, the Manhattan ADA with whom she had worked in the Cove Shooting case, asking her if it was possible to go to Judge Castellano to get the search warrant.

"I'm sorry, Kim," Yvette replied, "but my boss would charbroil me if I tried to overstep an ADA from another borough to overrule a judge from another borough. Besides, even Castellano would have trouble with this one."

Still nothing from Cord and Bob or Martin and Abe.

Marisa grabbed her as soon as she entered the office. "Glad you're back. Check this out."

Kim peered at Marisa's monitor. Three calls from Rizzo's cell to previously unlogged numbers, one right after the other, none lasting more than a few seconds, within the last forty minutes.

"Think they all went directly to voice-mail?" Marisa asked.

Kim thought back to the cell phones connected to detonators at the warehouse. "Too short. Looks more like testing the circuitry. Check the towers pinged by his cell on the calls."

"Only one tower for all three calls. In Bushwick."

"Have you located the tower?"

Marisa checked the screen. "Evergreen Avenue and Chauncey Street."

Nowhere near Greenpoint, which is why the guys didn't pick it up on the Stingrays. Bushwick must be home to either Bart or Kotsonis.

She updated Colangelo.

"So, they're planning their 'spirit' move today?" he asked.

"Or for tomorrow. There were three cell tests, suggesting three detonators. That could be three separate incidents or one big one. Also, Judge Vickers ordered us to return Harwood's computer immediately."

"He'll get it when we're good and goddamned ready. I…" His phone rang, and he snatched it up on the second ring. "What!" As he listened, color drained from his face. "We're on it." He slammed the phone down. "That was the lieutenant from Brooklyn North Homicide. They got a dead cop by Broadway Junction in East New York. Williams Place, between Herkimer and Fulton. He thinks it's connected to our case. Another stab in the neck and something carved in the victim's chest. You drive. I'm coming with you."

***

The knocking on the study door broke Fr. Lynch's concentration. "Yes?" He still hadn't written a word of his Palm Sunday homily.

The door opened. Domenica Soto, a parishioner who'd organized the cleanup after the police had gone, had arrived this morning, offering her services as housekeeper. "Sorry to disturb you, Father, but there are two men here from the heating company."

"I didn't call them," he said, searching his memory.

"One of them mentioned a servicing follow-up. They're waiting at the front door."

He followed her out. They were waiting in the vestibule, both in oil-stained work clothes.

One extended his hand. "Hello, Father. We sent a man over about a month ago to service your boiler…"

He remembered. "The one in the church?"

"That's right. According to our records, it's over thirty years old. We thought it would be wise to check it out and make sure everything is still okay. It's been a chilly spring and the heavy rain makes that worse."

"Thank you." He reached into his pocket for the keys to the church. "There's a separate cellar entrance. I'll show you where…"

"No need for that, Father. I know where it is. We'll take care of it. Okay if we pull our van up to the other side of the church by the basement entrance?"

"Sure. But please be careful not to trample the flower bed. It's marked. I have perennial tiger lilies there, and they're sprouting." He handed over the keys. "It's this one."

"Don't worry, Father, we'll be careful. Wouldn't want to ruin your flower garden."

He returned to his study. Even the smallest gesture of kindness could help soften the pain of tragedy. He'd have to remember to call Saturn Oil and thank them for their thoughtful service.

CHAPTER SIXTY-NINE

Kim spent the first leg of the trip—from Hudson Street to the Williamsburg Bridge—arguing with Colangelo to pull out the two units scanning Greenpoint. The testing calls had come from Bushwick, not Greenpoint, so whatever purpose Rizzo's chop shop had served no longer was holding him there. And this most recent attack had occurred less than a mile from the cell tower the test calls had pinged.

Colangelo conceded the point. "Then, unless you have a better idea, I think they should all join us at the scene. I'd like to have everyone's input."

She couldn't argue with that, but doubt tugged at the pit of her stomach as Colangelo made the calls. She was missing something. "Please also call Marisa and have her do a phone records search for anyone named Bart or Bartholomew within the operating radius of that cell tower. Have her locate Nick Kotsonis' address, too. If she finds someone, she should relay that information to Ken Taylor over at the FBI."

"Yes, ma'am."

Traffic slowed coming off the bridge, so she hit the siren and grille lights. At her first opportunity, she cut over from Broadway to Bushwick Avenue, which was wider and less congested.

Phil Vitello from CSU greeted her as they got out of the car at the scene. "You ain't gonna like it."

One look was all she needed. It was Sergeant Warren.

Kim kneeled next to the body, careful to avoid the pool of blood on his left side. Same gouging of the neck. Two concentric circles formed an exact copy of the circle Marisa had drawn.

"So, this is it?" Colangelo stared in disbelief. "This is 'spirit'?"

"Not by itself. Unlike the other events, this one may not be a single occurrence." She turned to Vitello. "Where's his partner?"

"Warren was working the desk today and took his lunch break alone, by all appearances headed to the diner on Fulton. That fellow across the street is the only witness."

A homeless man was cowering under an enormous cardboard box that he had cut open to form a tent. The pouring rain had saturated the box, which was for a sixty-five-inch Smart-TV.

"Sergeant," she said to Vitello, "can one of your men please go into the diner and get him a cup of coffee and something to eat?" She fished a ten-dollar bill out of her purse.

He fixed a warm smile on her. "Sure."

She approached the homeless man. "Sir, can I talk to you for a moment?"

He grinned at her from under his soaked, stained hoodie through cracked lips. His hair and beard were both long, gray, and filthy. There were sores on his face. "I ain't going to no shelter."

"I won't force you to go anywhere you don't want to go. An officer is getting you a nice hot cup of coffee and something to eat."

His eyes brightened at the mention of food. "Yeah?" But then they turned hard. "What you want? I ain't leaving here."

She smiled and squatted down next to him. He smelled little better than a dead body. She tried not to let it show. "No one will force you to leave. Did you see that police officer get killed?" She pointed toward Warren's body.

"Didn't see it happen. That car was in the way." He pointed at a patrol car parked right in front of them with "74th Pct" in blue on the quarter panel.

"Was the police sergeant driving that?"

"There was two sergeants." He held up two filthy fingers.

"Did they arrive together?"

"Nope. Can I change that coffee to something stronger?"

She grinned back at him. "I'm afraid not. Was the other one waiting when he parked here?"

The homeless man furrowed his brow. "Yeah. Saw him walking around the corner. Then pacing. Wondered why a cop would pace in the rain like that."

"You're sure he was a cop?"

"He was in uniform. Except his shoes. He was wearing sneakers. What kinda cop wears sneakers?"

She knew full well what kind. She pulled out the sketch. "Do you recognize this man?"

His laugh turned into a fit of coughing until he spat out a massive glob of yellow phlegm. "Sorry. That's the guy who was pacing on the corner. He ain't no real cop, is he?"

"No, he isn't. Did you see anything that happened after the sergeant left his car?"

"Some. He walked to the corner, crossed the street, then walked back down on the other side. That's when I lost sight of him."

"Did you hear any voices? An argument or someone calling out?"

He shook his head. "Can't hear with trains passing overhead. That's a wonderful sound, though."

One of Vitello's men approached with a large paper coffee cup and a wrapped sandwich.

The homeless man's eyes lit up, and he stumbled to his feet. "Thanks, lady. Thanks."

She returned to where Colangelo was now standing with Cord, Martin, Abe, and Bob. "It was Rizzo."

Her cell buzzed. Not a number she recognized. She let it go to voicemail.

"It doesn't make sense," Cord said. "DCPI publicized the sketch. He knows we know he dressed as a cop when he killed Avila, so why use it again?"

Kim was still thinking it through. "Not only did he use it, while he was waiting, he walked right past the homeless guy. He knew we'd find out. Ergo, he wanted us to find out."

"And ergo…?" Bob asked.

"This was a diversion." It was the only conceivable reason.

Her cell buzzed with a text from the same number as the call. She checked it. *Kim, this is Joanna. Loretta C isn't an ordinary admin. She's Kyle Emory's secretary. He's the CEO, and a big donor to conservative PACs. I'm digging further. Will advise what I find.*

Kim texted an answer. *Thanks. Can't deal with that right now. Murdered cop at B'way Junction.*

She knew she shouldn't have, but she owed Joanna a lot. She was putting her cell away when it buzzed again, this time with a text from Marisa. *Found a Bart Lamonica, address on Piling Street, off Bushwick. Taylor checking him out. Also found a Nicholas Kotsonis nearby in Highland Park.*

Kim responded. *Pull Lamonica's LUDs. Kotsonis', too.*

Colangelo was still waiting. "Diversion for what?"

"For whatever they're planning." She studied the area, and who had responded: Crime Scene Unit, Medical Examiner's Office, Brooklyn North Homicide... And a large contingent of the Seven-Four, including its captain.

The captain bore down on her. "Well, detective, you got one of my officers killed. Congratulations."

"Someday," she replied, "you and I can discuss how you came to that conclusion, captain, but right now I need to know whatever you can tell me about how Sergeant Warren came to be here while on duty, alone."

"It was his designated mealtime. He was at lunch, and he likes this diner." The captain turned to Abe for confirmation.

Abe nodded.

Kim's cell buzzed with another text from Marisa. *A call originated from Lamonica's number at 12:05 to the number we have listed on the board as Sgt. Warren's cell.*

"Do you know if he received a call on his cell before he left?" Kim asked the captain.

"No idea."

But it fit. "A call placed to Sergeant Warren's cell as he was leaving for lunch lured him here." She showed him the text.

The captain checked his watch. "That would have been about ten minutes after he left the precinct."

She turned to Abe and Bob. "Check the security video for the Broadway Junction station. All of them. If he didn't walk, he came from the stop before this one."

"Chauncey Street?" Abe asked.

"That's on the line for the J and Z trains. More likely Bushwick-Aberdeen on the L. But I also want to know where he went afterward. Call or text the minute you have anything."

The three detectives scattered. She turned back to the captain. "There's a sizeable group here from the Seven-Four…"

"They all heard the 'officer down' call. If you consider the location, it had to be one of ours."

"What 'officer down' call? Warren was alone." She turned to Vitello. "Who notified you?"

"A call came in from the 911 center reporting an attack on a police officer," Vitello replied. "ME's office got the same call."

"I'll get the specifics." Colangelo punched up a number on his cell and walked away.

"Just what are you implying, Detective?" the captain asked.

She ignored him. Rizzo had done everything but take out a full-page ad in the *New York Times*. "Everything we're doing now he expects us to do. Wants us to do."

"Because it keeps us from catching up to him," Cord said.

The captain spluttered. "That's the craziest thing I…"

Kim adopted her most bored, officious tone. "We won't be needing you, here, Captain. You may return to your duties. Please get your people back to theirs." She turned away before he could answer.

Colangelo returned as the captain strode away. "Kim, where's that phone number you had for Lamonica?" She showed him. "That's it. That's the number the call to 911 came from. At 12:25. They're sending me a recording of the call."

CHAPTER SEVENTY

"Got him on video," Abe said. "No question it's the same guy as in the sketch. Cameras on the eastbound platform caught him getting off an L train at 12:10 in his cop costume. No sign of him leaving in either direction."

"Shit." Kim's sense of being played was intensifying. "Lieutenant, we have Lamonica's address. If Rizzo's on foot, it's the logical place for him to have gone. We've got probable cause."

"But without a warrant," Colangelo replied, "you can only question Lamonica at the door. You can't get inside without his permission."

"We got another problem," Cord said. "The batteries on both Stingrays are flat. No power at all. We've got to bring them back to Hudson Street to recharge them. Takes a few hours."

"Plus, there's travel time each way." Could this get any worse? "All right. Cord. You and Martin take both units back and recharge them. Get them back out to us as soon as possible. Abe and Bob, you two stake out Lamonica's residence. Note anyone who enters and grab anyone who leaves."

"Why don't I ride back with Cord and leave Martin out here with you?" Colangelo asked.

Deep breath. "I need a favor. I need an arrest warrant for Rizzo and a search warrant for Lamonica's residence. Please contact Yvette Driscoll and have her get them, even if it means going to Judge Castellano. Since we're not dealing with Harwood yet, we can ignore Judge Vickers. Have someone bring it out to me as soon as you've got it."

Colangelo didn't quite suppress a grin. "And Cord will babysit the Stingrays. I guess that works."

"Not exactly." She turned to face Martin. "I need you to go back into the Eagle Tavern tonight. Desmond's in protective custody, so he can't give you away. I still don't see who's drawing up the set plays here, but I suspect the Eagle is where the huddles take place."

"Kim," Colangelo said, "for all we know, Desmond could have tipped off someone about Martin, and they could have passed it on."

Martin spoke up. "Not a chance. He was boiling about the killings and the abduction, with no letup in sight. He wanted nothing to do with it."

But Colangelo held firm. "Not pissed enough to notify us. You had to confront him."

"We're running out of time, Lieu," Kim said. "No choice but to press."

Colangelo reflected for a moment. "All right. But he wears a wire, and I'm having Ken Taylor provide an FBI surveillance team outside. First sign of trouble, they get him out."

She couldn't argue with that. "Okay."

"And what will you be doing while we're all busy bees?" Cord asked her.

"Checking with the protection details at Youth Colony and Blessed Mother to make sure there has been nothing amiss this afternoon. Because Rizzo took extreme care to gather us here. Like a magician who makes sure you're looking at something other than what he's doing."

CHAPTER SEVENTY-ONE

It hadn't been difficult. The remaining cops had paid no attention to the van with the friendly logo. Too busy listening to their radios for the latest update on their poor, slain comrade. Two of the patrol cars had already left when they'd pulled into the parking lot by the rectory.

Rafer took no insignificant amount of pride at the extent to which his plan had worked, even if it hadn't been his idea in total. If he wasn't quite the commanding general, he was the officer in tactical command. The general had ordered him to develop a diversion. Rizzo had been stupid enough to serve as the decoy. Ike Burrows, wherever the fuck he was now, had been good enough to provide Warren's cell number back in November in case Harwood needed it.

Rafer T. Harwood never forgot a detail.

After making certain they'd placed the clusters as Rizzo had suggested, so that either of two clusters when detonated would be certain to ignite the other, he'd wired each of the two detonators to burner phones.

"Here's a special bonus," Nick said. "This oil tank is corroding at the bottom, and fuel oil is already seeping out. When the jugs ignite, the tank ignites, too. I doubt we'll even need the third cluster."

But Rafer wasn't taking any chances. He'd already placed the third cluster of jugs at the top of the stairway, inside a door to the vestibule of the church at its main entrance. When it went up, the blast would create a wall of fire trapping everyone inside. He wired the detonator to the third phone.

Burner phones. Good name for them.

CHAPTER SEVENTY-TWO

Kim arrived at Youth Colony shortly after three. Marisa had located Rizzo's garage through Con Edison's records and Colangelo had added it to the search warrant affidavit.

Special Victims Unit was still handling the protection detail, but it surprised her to see Detective Espada in the lobby.

"I blame you," he said with a laugh. "You sure fried Lieutenant Fredricks' ass after Blessed Mother, so we're taking no chances."

Kim told him the latest.

Espada's humor evaporated. "These guys are serious. What am I looking for? Besides the guy in the sketch, I mean."

"You may not see him. We think he'll be using a cell phone signal to detonate his device; he can do that from anywhere. But he's egotistical enough to want to see the fruits of his labors. Look for anyone who carries containers that smell like nail-polish remover."

"Okay, I'll alert the team."

"Thanks, Julio. I..." She froze. Joanna Dunbar was on the TV screen in the waiting area, and the crime scene at Broadway Junction was in the background.

"The victim, a police officer, died by stabbing. Police are searching for the killer, whom they suspect was also responsible for the stabbing death of community activist Mariano Avila a week ago, and two other stabbing deaths this past week, all in North Brooklyn. One officer, who asked to remain nameless, suggested that the killer may still be in this vicinity."

An image of the sketch flashed up on the screen. "Anyone with any information on this tragedy should call the Crime Stoppers Hotline. This is Joanna Dunbar reporting."

As soon as she got to the car, she called Joanna's cell.

"I'm sorry, Kim. I had no choice. He said it. I couldn't refuse to use it."

"Who said what?"

"One officer at the scene. He told me about the stabbing in the neck and that you were sure it was the same guy who killed Avila. Then he begged me not to use his name. I guess he figured he'd let his mouth get away from him."

"Uniform or plain clothes?" Kim held her breath.

"Uniform. A captain."

Exhale. The precinct captain, whose distress would have prompted him to say more than he should.

"I'm sorry if this makes things worse for you," Joanna said. "But if I didn't get it, someone else would have. Besides, it allowed us to ignore an anonymous call we got from someone who claimed responsibility on behalf of the CIJ. I also got some additional information on your boy's sister. She's more than Emory's secretary. He's got accounts at about a dozen upscale retailers, with all deliveries going to her. And in the past year he's taken her to Bermuda, Nice, and Positano. I'm checking now for any evidence of direct links between Kyle Emory and Senator Brandt. I'll inform you when I find them."

"Thanks, but what did the caller say?"

"Just that he was from the CIJ, and they were fighting fire with fire. He also said, 'We tremble with indignation at every injustice.' Sounded convincing to my editor until I got the quote from the pissed off captain."

"Okay, thanks." Kim immediately texted Ken Taylor about this new twist, adding a comment about Evelyn Burke being convinced someone with a violent purpose had infiltrated the CIJ protests.

Taylor's response was immediate. *Holy shit. Keep this quiet while I check on something.*

CHAPTER SEVENTY-THREE

The lieu went to talk to Driscoll. Stingrays taking a long time to charge. Nothing further from Marisa. Anything else you need from me? The text from Cord made her smile. She could picture him pacing, sweating it out.

Kim was sitting in her car in the parking lot at Blessed Mother. Sunset was approaching. Her sense of being played grew stronger. *Please send me a photo of the map with the site of Warren's murder marked and all the previous crime scenes.*

In the meantime, she strode to the front door of the rectory. A woman in her late thirties answered. Kim showed her ID. "I need to talk to Father Lynch."

"He's resting. It's been difficult for him…"

"I know. I'm the lead detective on the case."

The priest appeared behind the woman. "Thank you, Ms. Soto. It's all right. Please come in, Detective."

They sat in the living room. The news of yet another killing hit him hard. "This has to stop."

"We believe this isn't the end, that today's murder is a prelude to something bigger, possibly as early as tomorrow." Her cell buzzed. Cord's response. "Excuse me, Father. This could be important."

"By all means."

She opened the text and tapped on the link to the photo. The crime scene on Williams Place sat near the center. Blessed Mother was southeast of that, and the Elton playground, the site of Joey Simmons' murder, was southeast of Blessed Mother. An arrow pointed off the map to the left labeled "Youth Colony" and another to the upper left-hand corner labeled "chop shop and warehouse".

So, Rizzo could have chosen Broadway Junction because of its proximity to Bart Lamonica's residence. Except that he had arrived by subway.

"Detective? Are you all right?"

She held up a hand. Rizzo had known to avoid surveillance cameras the night of the Avila murder and the morning of Julie Campbell's murder. So, his appearance on the subway cameras had to be intentional.

She peered again at the photo. No one from Clinton Hill had diverted to Broadway Junction. "Father, did you notice if anyone left the protection detail this afternoon?"

"I'm sorry, but I wasn't paying attention."

She couldn't blame him for that. It wasn't his job to keep tabs on the cops. "Did you notice anything out of the ordinary today? See anyone around who didn't belong?"

"No, it's been quiet. Ms. Soto has kept it that way. The only visitors I had were from Saturn Oil, the company that services our heating systems. They were checking up on work they did about a month ago. They're quite good that way." He frowned. "Do you really think something could happen tomorrow?"

Sudden thought. "Would you excuse me a moment?"

She checked with the sergeant in charge of the protection detail. "Has everyone remained in place all day?"

"Two units responded to the 'officer down' call this afternoon. I had everyone else keep a sharp eye out until they got back."

"How long were they gone?"

He considered it. "About an hour, or it could have been a little more."

"What positions did they leave open?"

"One here in the lot and one on Livonia. I kept an eye out until they returned. Saw nothing unusual, Detective. It's been quiet."

His explanation didn't reassure her, but she could do nothing else. She returned to Fr. Lynch. "Please let me know if you see anything out of the ordinary."

"Thank you for your concern, Detective. I hope you're wrong about tomorrow, though. It's Palm Sunday."

CHAPTER SEVENTY-FOUR

"Brilliant American lady detective is not here?"

Cord snapped out of his concentrated study of the board in the war room, unnerved at the sudden appearance of Vera Koshkin. "No, she's in the field."

"It's a hard case, yes?"

"You could say that." For the first time, he noticed her bloodshot eyes, the way her long blond hair hung limp and stringy, and the two coffee stains on her wrinkled top. "You look like you could use some sleep."

A tired smile. "Impossible for me until I finish work." She nodded at the Stingrays sitting on the conference room table. "Problem with them?"

"Just recharging the batteries." He pointed to the file folder under her arm. "Is that for Kim?"

"*Da.* Is information I find on IP address she gave me, the one I traced to the posts that forced the Defend Our Home website to shut down. It's in Bushwick. But no street address appears in our databases."

Cord took the file and studied her printouts. "Looks like you did a lot of digging, Vera. Thanks."

"Is nothing. I worry for this country." She broke into a tired smile. "But I meet honorable people like you and Kim, who fight so hard; I think we overcome the sickness."

"I hope so. May I keep this? I'm thinking Ken Taylor over at the FBI might find it useful."

"*Da.* Is why I bring." She examined the Stingrays, peering at the power meters. After a moment, she frowned. "How long have these been recharging?"

Colangelo walked in. "Got the warrants. Took a lot longer to convince Driscoll than it took for her to get Judge Castellano to sign them."

"Thanks, Lieu." He turned back to Vera. "About three hours. Why?"

"Battery meters read 'zero'," she said. "How much power they have when you start?"

"Zero. Both were flat."

"These are old units. When rechargeable batteries get old, they discharge with increasing speed and sometimes don't recharge."

"You're familiar with Stingrays, Vera?" Colangelo asked.

"*Nyet.* But I'm familiar with rechargeable batteries. Had one in a laptop die on me earlier this week."

Cord was trying not to panic. "These won't recharge?"

"Not even in a hundred years."

Colangelo tossed the warrants on the table. "Why the hell didn't they warn us about the batteries when they signed these out to us?"

"Can't we get replacements?" Cord asked.

"Tomorrow morning at the earliest," Colangelo replied. "Shit, no, tomorrow's Sunday. So not until Monday."

"Whatever these fuckers are targeting will be ash by then."

Colangelo gathered up the warrants. "Forget the Stingrays. Deliver these to Kim in the field and have her begin the searches."

"Perhaps is something I can do?" Vera asked.

"Yes," Cord said before Colangelo could respond. "Marisa has been tracking LUDs and tower pings all day. She's exhausted and can use whatever help you can provide."

"You look rather tired yourself," Colangelo said.

Vera waved it away. "I am fine. Glad to help."

Colangelo shrugged. "Okay. Thanks. Cord, you'd better get moving. Time is short." He walked out.

As Cord turned to go, Vera grabbed his hand. "*Dasvidanya.*"

***

Captain Forrest switched on the television in his office while he debated with himself whether to stay or go home. But he froze when the set came on. Senator Brandt appeared to be haranguing a group of reporters.

"Our community will not sit by, passive, watching the slaughtering of their fellow citizens and the devastation of their property while the police remain hamstrung. This city needs the acting mayor to step up and take charge, not sitting in judgment and casting aspersions on honest police officers without whom we can't survive. Why isn't every able-bodied officer working on this case, protecting us from further carnage? What is the acting mayor hiding?"

One reporter's voice carried above the gaggle. "Senator, what makes you think the police aren't committing their full available resources?"

Brandt drew himself up into a dignified stance. "I'm not prepared to discuss such matters in public. But the administration's undermining of the police is a matter of public record."

The reporter persisted. "What specific resources should the police be committing that they aren't, already? And do you have direct proof that it's because of Mayor Dunn's interference?"

"Acting mayor. She hasn't been elected. No comment."

"Senator," another reporter called out, "you attack the mayor for criticizing the police, but aren't you doing the same thing?"

"That's absurd."

"We all heard you claim the police are doing nothing."

Cries of assent.

Brandt's face reddened. "I said the police are hamstrung. The administration continues to tie their hands. Don't you twist my words. If you're carrying Sabrina Dunn's water, be honest and disclose it in your stories. Otherwise, tell the complete story. For example, how the officer who was hurt in the attack on the Seventy-Fourth Precinct the other night remains hospitalized in critical condition while every arrested looter is already out without having to post bail, ready to riot again. Or how the organization behind these so-called protests has said nothing about the violence."

For a moment, the group fell silent.

"Senator Brandt." Joanna Dunbar's voice rang out loud and clear. Brandt tried looking in the opposite direction, but she added, "Right over here, Senator. It appears you're privy to an impressive amount of information on this case, including the level of resources committed. How is it you have such detailed knowledge?"

Brandt again drew himself up. "Ms. Dunbar, as a political reporter, you know I chair an important senate committee on crime and law enforcement. I have a natural interest in these matters."

"So, you admit you are being provided inside information."

"I said no such thing."

She grinned without humor. "I think you did, and we all heard it. Who is your source?"

"You have abused my generous nature. This press conference is over." Brandt stormed off.

Forrest snapped off the set and his stomach churned. The senator was a loose cannon. And eventually he'd do actual damage.

He needed a smoke. But when he reached for the pack, it was empty.

That was fast.

CHAPTER SEVENTY-FIVE

Rafer approached the house with caution. After setting the devices, Nick had dropped him off at the Broadway stop on the G line. At Court Square, he'd changed to the E, which, thank the MTA, was making all local stops in Queens. It allowed him to take it all the way home without changing trains. At least the rain had finally stopped.

Although he was certain he was under police surveillance, he saw no sign of cops around. His plan had worked perfectly, or else they'd have grabbed him by now. When Rizzo detonated the bombs tomorrow morning roasting all those illegals, he'd be here, home sweet home. When they came to question him, he could give them his best innocence act.

A moment of doubt assailed him as he unlocked the front door, but he pushed past it. As soon as he closed it behind him, he felt relief. He looked in on his mother, who was dozing in front of the TV, which had an old "Andy Griffith" episode on. A half-eaten dinner sat on a TV tray in front of her.

She started. "Home already?"

"Yes, and I need a shower. I'll be back upstairs later to help you into bed."

"Thank you, dear."

Time to assess the damage. The laundry room was first. Someone had cleaned it up and disinfected. Nice how cops cleaned up after they tortured a patriot. He tried the apartment door and found it locked.

Another plus. Once inside, the apartment was in perfect order, and the bathroom smelled only of disinfectant.

Back in the living room, the blank spot on his desk caught his eye. He recalled the detective saying something on the phone about his computer. He wracked his brain. How much had he saved on the hard drive?

The doorbell rang. When he peered out the peephole, there were two cops standing there. He couldn't make out any details in the fading light. He'd locked the storm door on the way in, so he opened the main door.

"Mr. Harwood?" one cop asked.

"Yeah."

The second one hefted a box. "This computer belongs to you. Someone took it without a warrant, and a judge has ordered us to return it to you."

"I guess that means you've already analyzed it, invading my privacy."

"No, they delivered it to our computer lab, but no one touched it." The cop with the box waited. "Mr. Harwood, will you open the door?"

"Leave it on the top step. I'll take it when you go."

He shrugged. "Fine with us. Have a good evening, sir."

Rafer waited until they drove away before retrieving the computer. After setting it up, logging in, and finding nothing amiss, he took a long, hot shower. The cops had been telling the truth. If they'd examined it, the shit would've hit the fan by now.

Stupid fucking cops.

CHAPTER SEVENTY-SIX

"What do you mean, they're dead?" Kim tried not to shout.

"Dead," Cord replied. "Lifeless. We can't revive them. The Lazarus factor is zero. And the lieu doesn't think we can get replacement units until Monday. The good news is…"

"There's good news in this scenario?"

"Yeah. Judge Castellano signed the warrants. The IP address of the source of those posts prior to Defend Our Home shutting down was right here in Bushwick. Vera couldn't locate an exact address, but…" He cast a meaningful glance at Lamonica's house.

Kim didn't crack a smile. "Let's get moving."

"You want to split into two teams?" Abe asked. "Get to the chop shop faster?"

"No. The FBI has placed a surveillance team on the chop shop. Let's go."

Bart Lamonica lived in the first-floor apartment and had sole access to the basement. He answered the door with a stunned expression. "Yes?"

Kim flashed her badge. "We have a search warrant for your premises." She held it in front of his face. "Please stand aside while we conduct our search. Is there a laundry room in the basement?"

He followed her downstairs.

The odor of air freshener hung heavy. "Did you have some kind of accident, Mr. Lamonica?"

"No. Why?"

Nolan sniffed. "It smells like you emptied a case of Lysol in here."

"It gets musty down here in the spring. I hate that."

"Kim," Cord said from the laundry room. "Check this out." He pointed to three scorch marks on the cement floor.

They were the same as the marks she'd seen on the floor of the warehouse where they'd found Amara. "Been playing with detonators, Mr. Lamonica?"

"I don't know what you're talking about."

"Kim," Abe called from the top of the stairs. "Are we grabbing the computer?"

There wouldn't be time for Vera to check it out before whatever would happen tomorrow, but at least it would take it out of the network. "Yes."

Lamonica lost his cool. "You can't take my…"

Kim again held up the warrant. "Read it. The judge says we can. We'll get it back as fast as possible. Now, you can answer some questions for me and save some time. Do you know a Tony Rizzo?"

"No."

Cord pulled out the sketch. "This guy."

Lamonica shook his head.

"You sure?" Kim asked. "Because he killed a police officer this afternoon. Stabbed him in the neck and let him bleed to death."

Bob rushed down the stairs holding a fistful of papers. "I found these in the desk."

Kim looked them over. "You don't like immigrants much, I see."

"Only the ones who break the law."

"Right. Always obey the law, Mr. Lamonica?"

"Yes."

"Even when the law protects illegal immigrants?"

He gave her a quizzical look.

She responded with a humorless smile. "You wouldn't approve of murdering illegal immigrants?"

"No."

She pointed to the scorch marks. "What caused these?"

"I don't recall."

She gasped in mock shock. "Don't recall? Let's see if we can jog your memory. A flash of ignition taking place on the floor could have caused them, perhaps from testing detonators wired to cell phones." She used her phone to photograph them.

Lamonica mumbled. "I don't know…"

She showed him the photo she'd taken. Then, she showed him the photo she'd taken of the marks at the warehouse. "If we hadn't arrived when we did, several firebombs inside the warehouse would have ignited, incinerating the two people trapped inside." She brought up a photo of the clusters of acetone containers. "Ever see anything like that?"

"No." But his eyes said something different.

She got in his face. "Oh, yes, you have. I don't like it when people lie to me, Mr. Lamonica. And you're lying to me right now. Ever hear of a group called Defend Our Home?"

"No, I haven't."

The lying bastard. "Let's go. Back upstairs." Once in the living room, she turned to Abe, who was ready to disconnect the computer. "Hold it. Cord, you have that IP address handy?"

He pulled up his notes app. "Right here."

"What's that?" Lamonica was now panicking.

"We have the IP address that was the source of some very inflammatory posts on the Defend Our Home website. So inflammatory that the administrator of that site shut it down. My detectives are going to take a quick peek to see if your IP address matches that IP address."

Lamonica swallowed hard. "I want a lawyer."

"That's without question your right. Call her."

"Who?"

"Your attorney. We'll wait."

"I don't… I mean, I can't…"

"You can't afford one. You want a public defender."

"Yeah."

"Cord, check the computer."

They moved to the apartment itself. Cord powered up the desktop but stopped at the login screen. "What's the password, bro?"

Lamonica said nothing.

"Hey, man," Cord said, "you can tell me, or we can let our techies get in without it."

"I'm not saying anything without an attorney present."

"Cord, check the desk. It's covered by the warrant." Decision time. They would arrest Lamonica, but where to hold him? Hudson Street meant working with Yvette Driscoll, but also losing time shuttling between Manhattan and Brooklyn. Holding him at the Castle eliminated the shuttle problem, but also meant working with Rick Conti, with the potential of running afoul of Let 'em run Ron.

Cord rifled through unkempt bundles of loose pages. "Found a password list." He tapped out a password. "We're in."

"Fucking commies," Lamonica muttered.

"Hear that, Kim?" Bob guffawed. "He thinks you want to seize the means of production."

"Bingo," Cord sang out. "Kim, meet the man who posted, 'Fire will purify those who worship at the altar of the damned.'"

She read him his rights. Once outside, she had Cord put him in the car. "I'll be with you in a minute."

She called Conti. "We've bagged a member of Rizzo's group. He's already lawyered up. How fast can you get him counsel? I need to interrogate him immediately if not sooner."

"It's Saturday night, Kim. Let me make some calls."

Shit. More wasted time. "I'll remind you they may well strike sometime tomorrow."

"I'll get right back to you."

After twenty minutes, nothing from Conti. She called Yvette Driscoll with the same request.

"You know Brooklyn will want the case, Kim. As it is, I'm likely in for some serious shit about the warrants I got you."

"I don't care about that. I only care about getting information as quickly as I can get it. Can you get me a public defender tonight?"

"I can't guarantee it, but I'll try."

Cord nudged her shoulder. "Remember, Vera's at our shop helping Marisa."

Decision made. "Okay, Yvette. Do your best. We're heading for Hudson Street."

CHAPTER SEVENTY-SEVEN

Martin sat on the same stool he'd occupied his initial visit to the Eagle. The Dallas Stars were playing the Los Angeles Kings on the wide-screen TV at the end of the bar.

The bartender greeted him. "Hey, I remember you. The cable guy. Nice to see you back so soon."

"Steve Tillman. Nice to see you, Mister..."

"Quinn. But everyone calls me Tom. Beer, right?"

"A bottle of Brooklyn Lager." He glanced around. A raucous crowd jammed the Eagle, a contrast to Thursday night. Harwood wasn't among them.

Tom placed a bottle in front of him. Martin laid a twenty on the bar. "No sign of Rafer or Jeff?"

Tom shrugged. "They had something of a falling out. Not for the first time."

"That's a shame. Both seem like agreeable guys."

"Rafer's got his good points and bad. Desmond?" Tom shook his head. "Not the guy you want next to you in the foxhole."

"I hear that. Too bad. You want to rely on a guy, you know? Even if it's not life-and-death."

Tom's face clouded over. "Yeah. And even more when it is."

Martin took a sip of beer. "Sounds like there's a story behind that. Is Rafer okay?"

"I'm sure he is, although he hasn't been here since Thursday evening."

"Yeah. He seemed preoccupied. I was hoping we could chat more. Sounded like we agree on a lot."

Tom stepped away to fill glasses. Dallas had scored a goal. "Most of these guys agree on stuff. Makes for a comfortable fit. Thing about Rafer is that he's not satisfied sitting around talking."

Martin grinned. "Man of action, huh?"

The bartender shook his head. "Don't know about that."

Martin knew better than to push. He drained his beer.

"Another?" Tom asked.

He would have to pace himself. "Sure."

CHAPTER SEVENTY-EIGHT

Kim sent Abe and Bob to the chop shop, figuring the FBI surveillance team there could act as backup, while she and Cord took Lamonica to Hudson Street.

"No activity on any of the cell numbers we have," Marisa said as soon as they placed Lamonica in an interrogation room.

"*Da*," Vera added. "Is silent."

"Thanks for helping, Vera," Kim said.

"Is my pleasure." But she gazed at Cord when she said it.

And it registered because Cord immediately replied, "We bagged this guy's PC, Vera. I have his password list. Could you check it out?"

Vera sauntered over to him. "If you be so kind as to hook up to monitor, keyboard and mouse, and get me energy drink, I'll be happy to look."

"Um, sure." He started toward the door, then stopped and turned for a cubicle.

Kim choked down a laugh. "Cord, first please connect Lamonica's unit to the spare keyboard, mouse and monitor. Then, power up the unit, and then please get Vera her drink."

"Right."

Colangelo waved her into his office and closed the door, breaking the mood. "Rick Conti called me. He's pissed because he thinks you're giving this case to Manhattan instead of Brooklyn. I can explain the warrant request as exigent circumstances, but you're wading into inter-borough politics, here."

Kim explained the reason for her action and added, "Also exigent circumstances."

Captain Forrest entered without knocking and closed the door.

It was clear the interruption displeased Colangelo, but he pushed on. "Yes, and no. It's unlikely anyone outside of our unit will understand why you were in such a sweat to get that guy a free lawyer."

"Because he refuses to talk without one. If we don't find out where Rizzo placed those firebombs before they go off tomorrow, we'll have a lot more to explain than stepping on some toes in Brooklyn."

He held up a hand. "Okay, first, you're not stepping on toes, we have serious political issues. Second, you're only guessing an attack is coming tomorrow."

"Warren's murder was a deliberate act to divert us."

"Is that what you told Joanna Dunbar?" Forrest asked. "How did she manage to be the first media type at the scene?"

"I didn't tell her anything about Warren's death. The captain from the Seven-Four spoke to her."

Forrest was sneering. "Seems that she's told you quite a lot. You two must be quite chummy. And what did you give her?"

"Details of the killings, on the condition that she not use them until I say so."

"Which she broke this afternoon," Forrest said.

"She only repeated what the captain from the Seven-Four told her, and she said nothing about the symbols. Also, she told me the station received an anonymous call claiming responsibility for the killing by the CIJ, but because of what I'd told her, she knew to believe the captain. Also, our dialogue started when Brandt blabbed to the press that we were in on the Morales bust. She asked me if we were and, if so, why. She's digging deep to find Brandt's source of money and power, because some pissant state senator wouldn't normally have access to that kind of info."

Colangelo broke in. "Kim, I told you, stay out of the politics."

"The politics already found us, Lieu, when Cadman was shoved down our throats. We've got no choice."

Colangelo paused and turned to Forrest. "She's right there, Captain. Did you see Brandt's tussle with the press a short while ago?"

"He's suggesting the CIJ is behind the riots," Kim added. "Imagine if Dunbar had believed the anonymous caller."

"How do you know they're not?" Forrest asked.

"Because Evelyn Burke is frantic to find out who is. I've already given what Joanna told me to Ken Taylor at the FBI."

"Does Dunbar have a suspected source?" He appeared anxious. It was possible he didn't know.

"She hasn't found a money trail, yet." What the hell, why not be big about it? No hard feelings? "But Cadman's older sister, his only surviving family, is Kyle Emory's secretary, the twenty-four-hour, seven day, all-kinds-of-personal-services variety. Lots of vacations to exotic places together."

Colangelo guffawed. "Emory? Isn't he in his seventies?"

"And twice divorced," Kim replied. "He's made billions and has contributed to several PACs. Brandt has some strong money behind him, and he's opted out of the city's campaign finance program. Strikes me as enough for reasonable suspicion."

"That fuck." Forrest was shaking and holding a pen between his fingers. Not the reaction she'd been expecting.

"Kim, have you determined the likely target?" Colangelo asked. "No? Didn't think so. Abe Stewart called in. Rizzo's got his chop shop locked up tight. No one in sight. Neighbors report there's been no activity there in days."

"Right. And he can set off his firebomb—or bombs—with a simple phone call." She had to make sure she didn't lose her footing, no matter who she pissed off. "When can we get replacement Stingrays?"

"Noon tomorrow at the earliest. Why?"

"I keep coming back to tomorrow being Palm Sunday. Sounds like a day someone might want to 'purify by fire' 'those who worship at the altar of the damned.'"

CHAPTER SEVENTY-NINE

Sunday, March 25th

It was a few minutes after midnight and Martin was on his fourth beer—still within the range of what he could handle, but beyond the limit recommended for Members of Service engaged in undercover work. He hoped Lieutenant Colangelo would arrange for some hot coffee. Or the FBI detail would.

Shit. Keep focused.

The Stars were leading the Kings, 3-2. The noise level in the crowded bar was drowning out the announcers calling the game.

Tom, the bartender, was waxing poetic about the good old days in between refilling drinks. "You know, the two worst things that ever happened to this country were birth control and household appliances. Gave women too much time to think."

Martin laughed, imagining how Kim Brady might react to that. Or Marisa. He scanned the bar for signs of Rafer Harwood but noticed a guy in oil-stained coveralls approaching the bar.

Tom greeted the newcomer with a jovial, "Hey, Nick." But his expression was anything but. "Been out for pizza?"

Nick took the stool next to Martin. "No decent places open around here. Haven't seen any all day."

Tom appeared relieved. "Off duty, now?"

"I'm on call, so I can't have too much. No telling when some poor old lady's boiler will break down."

"No assistant with you," Tom said.

"Um… no. Dropped him off at the subway after we made our last delivery."

Tom gestured to Martin. "This is Steve. Cable guy. He and Rafer met here Thursday evening. They seemed to hit it off."

The newcomer held out a hand. "Nick Kotsonis. Nice to meet you, Steve."

Martin tried not to let his gaze linger on the Saturn Oil logo on the oil man's breast pocket. "Pleasure. On-call repair guy for oil burners in early spring. Sounds like an easy gig."

"Yeah, well, it makes up for having to rush out in the middle of the night in January when it's snowing up to your ass. That's when it's rough. This time of year, I take advantage of having the company van to drive around when I'm on call." He put a twenty on the bar.

"You can use a company van for personal stuff? Cool."

"Yeah. If I respond to a call, I have whatever parts I'd need handy. As for personal stuff, who's gonna know?" He took a large gulp of beer. "So, you're a friend of Rafer's?"

"Just met the man the other night. Seemed like a friendly guy. Talked a lot of good sense. Thought I might see him here."

"Did he talk to you about…"

"We all had a pleasant chat about things." Tom slid the twenty back to Kotsonis.

Kotsonis hesitated, then picked up the bill. "Yeah, well, I'll be right back." He headed for the men's room.

Twenty minutes passed, and Kotsonis still hadn't returned. Martin waited until Tom's attention was elsewhere and moseyed back to the bathroom. As soon as he walked in, frosty night air chilled his face.

The window was wide open.

CHAPTER EIGHTY

"In the most violent protests yet over the death of attorney and community leader Mariano Avila, angry mobs looted stores, overturned vehicles, and set fires along Brooklyn's stylish Fulton Avenue. Several vehicles were spray-painted with the letters 'CIJ'. Evelyn Burke, speaking for the Coalition for Immigration Justice, vehemently denounced the violence and stated the CIJ seeks a just immigration policy through community involvement and nonviolent protest. When asked about State Senator Raymond Brandt's statement asking, 'If the CIJ is so concerned about violence, why do they do nothing about it?' she replied, 'We are not the police. We report all acts of violence to them.' Senator Brandt's office declined to comment further."

***

Legal Aid arrived a little after two in the morning. "I understand my client is under arrest, but you have not yet charged him."

"Correct." Kim recounted what they had found on his computer and the floor of his laundry room. "Our team has identified the cell tower a block away from his home as the one pinged in testing detonators. Your client is a member of a small group that is planning a large-scale attack on immigrants, possibly later today. We're prepared to believe he is a minor participant if he tells us where his group has planted any explosive or incendiary devices, allowing us to prevent a mass terror event, and the location of the man who conducted the tests on the detonators in his basement yesterday morning and murdered a New York City police officer in the afternoon."

"And this alleged cop killer's name?"

"Tony Rizzo. We have him on video at the Broadway Junction subway station minutes before the murder on Williams Place. An eyewitness has identified him as the perpetrator of another murder and his method in this one is consistent with that prior attack."

"It sounds like you have a hell of a case against Mr. Rizzo," the attorney said.

"And, since he conducted his detonator test in your client's laundry room, we have a hell of a case against your client, too."

Two knocks on the door. Colangelo poked his head in. "Martin's back. He has some news you'll want to hear."

"In a minute." Kim closed the door. "If I get the information I need from another source, we will book your client as an accessory and fellow conspirator. My colleague, who is waiting for me outside, may very well have that information."

"Shit," the attorney muttered under his breath.

"Sorry, Counselor. Every minute ticking off that clock is one less I have available to prevent a terror attack. I have no time for fucking niceties. If he gives me Rizzo's current location, when and where the firebombs will go off, and the names and locations of the individuals who placed them after Rizzo killed the police sergeant, I will assure the DA that he has been most cooperative and was, at worst, a naïve dupe."

"I need assurances the DA will agree…"

A fist slammed against the door. "Kim!" Colangelo's voice.

She checked her watch. "Fifteen seconds, Counselor."

The attorney turned to Lamonica. "Tell her whatever you can."

Kim opened the door. "In a minute." She closed it. "Now, Mr. Lamonica."

"I don't know everything you want."

She leaned over him. "Give me everything you have, now."

The attorney nodded. "Do it."

"Okay, okay. Yes, Rizzo tested the detonators in my laundry room. He placed all three in the caps to five-gallon containers filled with acetone. The fumes made me sick. I don't know where Rizzo is hiding. He mentioned 'going underground' after a job, but he didn't mention the job itself. I only knew him through a friend of mine, Nick Kotsonis. He and I discussed immigration and taking action against all these illegals, and he claimed Tony had joined some militia. Sounded good, so…"

Enough rambling. "Did Nick Kotsonis set the firebombs?"

"Yeah."

"Did he have help?"

"Yeah, one guy. But I didn't see him. He stayed in the van with the rest of the jugs."

"What van?"

"Nick works for some heating oil company. I don't remember the name. He had one of their vans because he's on call this weekend."

"Did you see it?"

"Sorry, no. He didn't say where they were going when they left, only that we had to move fast because Rizzo was setting up a diversion."

It was still too fuzzy. "Did you post the messages on Defend Our Home that caused its administrator to shut it down?"

"Yeah. But the one about being purified by fire wasn't my idea. Nick said the general wanted it posted, word for word."

"What general? Rizzo? Harwood?"

Lamonica shook his head. "No. The guy they took orders from. I never met him, don't know who he is, but they know him from the Eagle Tavern. I don't know Harwood very well, but Rizzo's pissed at him. Kept referring to him as 'Quisling.'" His face brightened. "He may have been the other guy in the van. The last thing Nick said before he left my place was, 'Quisling's waiting.'"

The attorney glared at Kim. "Deal?"

It wasn't even half of what she needed. But she'd gotten a line on Harwood and a hint at where they might find the leader of the ring. "Yes. We'll keep your client here in protective custody for the time being."

Her cell buzzed. It was a text from Ken Taylor. *We have a lead on the group claiming responsibility for the cop killing for CIJ. A radical left group called Come Home Ernesto. They adapted the comment at the end of their message from a quote from Che Guevara: 'If you tremble with indignation at every injustice, then you are a comrade of mine.' I'm interrogating some rioters arrested tonight. Will let you know if I find anything.*

CHAPTER EIGHTY-ONE

"So, you're telling me he made you?" Kim couldn't believe it.

"Not him. Tom Quinn, the bartender. I think he was being cautious because I was a newcomer and Kotsonis liked to talk a lot. He asked Kotsonis about pizza, and Desmond said Thursday night he wasn't interested in pizza. I think 'pizza' is their code word for Rizzo or whatever Rizzo does."

There was only one plausible conclusion. "Quinn's the leader. The 'delivery' was placing the firebombs."

"Here, drink this." Marisa poured him another cup of coffee and kept her hand resting on his shoulder.

He drained it. "When I got outside, there was no oil company van, either. The FBI guys said they hadn't been watching it and had only noticed when it had already gone."

"So, you never saw it, either. Never saw the name of the company."

"Oh, I saw that on his shirt. Saturn Oil and Heating."

"The company Fr. Lynch said was at the church today." Kim checked her watch. It was already after four-thirty.

She dashed into Colangelo's office. "The target is Blessed Mother church."

"I thought you said…"

"Fuck what I said. That's it. Martin will explain. I need an ESU unit with a bomb expert and an FDNY hazardous materials unit to meet me there in…" Shit. How much time did they have? "Marisa, see if there's a Sunday Mass schedule for Blessed Mother parish online."

She checked. "There isn't."

Kim remembered a church bulletin she'd picked up on her first visit to the rectory and pulled it out of her desk. "It's at seven. Cord, take Abe and pick up Harwood. Martin, go with Bob and pick up Kotsonis. See what you can find out about Rizzo's location."

"Should I try calling his cell?" Marisa asked.

"No, any sign that we know about that number could make him switch phones, flee the jurisdiction, and set off the bomb early. As soon as we've secured the bomb, we'll turn to tracking him down. In the meantime, you're with me. Vera, can you monitor the LUDs of that phone?"

"*Da.* It's easy, now I know how."

Kim turned to Abe. "Make sure you guys have backup."

"I'll call the One-Oh-Eight."

"Cord." It was Vera. "You buy me breakfast, later?"

"Um… sure. Glad to."

"Let's move, people," Kim said, trying not to smirk.

"Go," Colangelo said. "I'll make the necessary calls."

CHAPTER EIGHTY-TWO

The pounding was persistent. Not the main door upstairs, but the side door that functioned as the private entrance to Rafer's apartment. He figured it was that asshole, Kotsonis. Bad enough the fumes from the acetone had made him feel shitty all day, now he couldn't get his sleep.

"Mr. Harwood, police."

Oh, fuck. There'd been cops there when they loaded the shit into the church. No one had said anything because they hadn't seen anything. Had the priest checked their work? No, Kotsonis had said he'd swallowed the story and even expressed his thanks.

"Open up, Mr. Harwood, or we'll break down the door."

Familiar voice. The detective who'd found him after the goon had left him for dead. The one who'd taken his statement. Pretended that justice would be done. Yeah, right.

"Last chance, Mr. Harwood. We have your house surrounded. This ain't gonna be pretty."

Another familiar voice. The black detective who'd come with the bitch. She might be out there, too.

He dragged himself out of bed. Turned on a lamp. Pulled on a pair of work pants.

He hesitated before opening the door. In such ways were noble rebellions snuffed out by repressive regimes.

"Mr. Harwood," the older one said, "you're under arrest for conspiracy to commit a terrorist act and accessory to murder. You know your rights, correct?"

He sure did. "Yeah. I'm allowed to get dressed before you drag me from my home." They let him pull on a sweatshirt, socks, and shoes before cuffing him. "What's this gonna accomplish for you? The judge already said you got nothing on me."

"You can wait for your attorney," the older guy said. "Or you can help yourself in a big way right now by telling us when those firebombs you planted yesterday are going to go off."

"Yeah," the black guy said. "The jugs of acetone." He looked Rafer up and down. "And Bro, you look downright peaked. You know breathing that shit can make you real sick? Why you think the bartender stuck you with moving it?"

The bartender. Tom. How could they know that? Only Rizzo and Kotsonis knew. One of them must've talked. Or did Tom? Was Rafer T. Harwood the only true patriot left?

At any rate, he was the only one with a case against the NYPD for police brutality. "You guys gonna try drowning me again? Seems to me, any case you try to make against me is gonna be fucked from the start because of that most egregious violation of my civil rights. Right, Bro?"

"You won't have a half-assed judge to set your ass free this time. See, you done violated your bail. You ain't going nowhere, except Rikers."

"Answer my question, Harwood," the older guy said. "Or tell us where Rizzo is."

So, Rizzo wasn't the rat. That was at least something. This could still go down if the cops remained ignorant of the target.

"First Mass at Blessed Mother church this morning," the older guy said. "Right?"

Now, they were fucked.

CHAPTER EIGHTY-THREE

The call came in from Cord as Kim was navigating around a flipped SUV on Eastern Parkway. They had Harwood, and he wasn't talking. No surprise there. No word on Kotsonis. He could be hiding with Tom, the Eagle's bartender. The FBI was checking him out.

It was already getting light when they pulled into the lot next to the rectory. The ESU and FDNY units had not yet arrived.

Ms. Soto answered the door on Kim's third ring. "Do you know what time it is?"

"Later than you think," Kim said, flashing her badge. "I need to see Fr. Lynch at once. It's urgent."

"He's getting dressed. I don't think…"

Kim pushed past the stunned housekeeper. "Upstairs, right?" She started up. "Father Lynch? I need to talk to you right now."

He appeared at the head of the stairs wearing his bathrobe. "If you can give me a moment, Detective…"

"When is your first mass today, Father?" Never assume.

"Seven o'clock. Why?"

"Then I have less than an hour to assure your parishioners' safety. I need the key to the cellar of the church. Now, please."

The priest appeared stunned. "Well, I…"

"There's no time, Father. Now."

"Yes, of course." He dashed back into his room and hurried down the stairs a few moments later, holding a ring of keys. "It's this one. A cellar entrance on the opposite side of the church. You'll see the steps leading down and…"

"Thank you, Father."

He called after her. "Detective, my parishioners are going to be arriving soon for Mass. Is it all right if I open the doors?"

"No. Please keep them locked and keep far away from the church building. Say Mass in the parking lot if you must, but please don't let them inside, and don't go in there, yourself."

The engine was still running. The tires screeched as she made a quick U-turn out of the lot. She stopped at the patrol car on the corner. "Secure the perimeter of the church. No one goes in except ESU and FDNY."

"With what? It's just two of us."

"Then call for backup and secure the fucking perimeter." She sped away, knowing they couldn't possibly have backup in time, and made the sharp turn onto Livonia and another up onto the grass at the far side of the church. The tracks of the oil van were still visible.

It was twenty after six. Kim reached the cellar door and froze.

"Aren't you going in?" Marisa asked.

"We need to wait for ESU. Rizzo took demolition training in the army. It's possible the door is booby-trapped."

CHAPTER EIGHTY-FOUR

The FBI surveillance team that had backed up Martin at the Eagle Tavern now deployed around Nick Kotsonis' residence in Highland Park, the narrow strip of Queens that lay sandwiched between the Jackie Robinson Parkway and East New York. The Saturn Oil van in the driveway made it easy to see which was the right house.

Martin lurked in the shadows while Bob Nolan banged on the front door, rang the doorbell, and shouted, "Open up. Police." Kotsonis would try to sneak his way out, as he'd done at the Eagle. Martin was certain of it.

The heads that momentarily appeared in windows from behind drawn curtains in neighboring houses left no doubt that anyone inside Kotsonis' residence could hear Bob's bellowing. Excellent idea, Bob.

But Martin was listening for something else—the squeak of a window, the click of a lock, or footsteps on the driveway gravel.

Crunch.

From his right, as Martin crouched in the hedges. He drew his piece.

The soft crunching came closer.

Martin pushed through and leveled his piece at Kotsonis' head. "Hey, Nick. What's happening? How about I buy this round?"

CHAPTER EIGHTY-FIVE

The sun was already peaking over the buildings to the east of the church when ESU and the FDNY both arrived. Six-forty-three.

"Sorry for the delay." It was Lieutenant Zimmerman. "We meet again."

She briefed him on the situation. "We only have about fifteen minutes." She gave him the key.

And then she heard it.

Organ music from inside the church. "I asked him to keep everyone out. Marisa, please go investigate."

The ESU bomb expert unlocked the door with a slowness that was almost painful. "Spotlight." Another ESU officer placed a powerful light next to him.

He pushed the door in a couple of inches. "You were right, Detective. There appears to be a trip wire attached to the doorknob. If I push further, I might very well set off a secondary device."

"Can you cut it?"

He studied it. "It's thin, so, yes, I can. But I need to know what kind of triggering mechanism they've used. Chances are, it's a simple trip wire— push the door open, and the cord pulls on a triggering device. But it could also be a device where opening the door sets the triggering mechanism and losing tension from cutting the cord sets off the device. My guys can cut through the door, but…"

No time. Kim speed-dialed Abe.

"Hey, Kim. You're on speaker."

Perfect. "You have Harwood in custody?"

"Yeah, they have me," Harwood called out. "Don't you guys realize that judge is only gonna spring me as soon as he finds out? What's that phrase? Fruit of the poisonous tree?"

Don't fuck with me. "I don't have time to instruct you on the finer points of Constitutional Law, Harwood. We have Mr. Kotsonis in custody. And his van, which our lab people are sweeping as we speak." Not quite true—the crime lab wouldn't get to work on it until tomorrow morning at the earliest, but he didn't need to know that. "I'm outside the basement door of Blessed Mother church, and there are clusters of firebombs with three cell-phone detonators inside. We have proof Tony Rizzo tested those detonators yesterday in Bart Lamonica's laundry room—we have Lamonica in custody as well—and that Rizzo will trigger them by cell phone, possibly within the next fifteen minutes. I have bomb experts here and we have unlocked the door."

Six forty-eight. The organist was playing "All Glory, Laud and Honor."

Harwood had a fit of heavy coughing. "So, what do you need me for?"

"Rizzo didn't tell you what a bitch it is working with acetone, did he? All those hours working with the containers yesterday fucked you up." She let that sink in. "You've already dug yourself a deep hole, Harwood. And because we've never relied on anything you told Officer Cadman his misconduct won't help you very much. If those bombs go off, you will officially become a terrorist, subject to both New York and federal prosecution. But if you tell me what I need to know to prevent that— whether the rope tied to the inside doorknob is a simple tripwire or a loss-of-tension triggering device—the DA will go a lot easier on you."

Thirty seconds passed. No answer.

Lieutenant Zimmerman pointed at his watch.

"Mr. Harwood, do you understand?"

"I understand. You're offering me a deal to sell out a noble revolution."

"There is no revolution. All your fellow conspirators, except two, are already in custody and cooperating. And we should have Tom Quinn and Tony Rizzo in custody by nightfall. Even Defend Our Home has disowned you. There's nothing noble in a mass killing. It's time to save what you can."

Another minute of silence.

Marisa returned with her face twisted in desperation. Kim placed her finger to her lips. Whatever Marisa had learned, it was too late to do anything about it.

Six fifty-two.

"I know you're not ISIS, or al Quaeda," she said at last. "But you've fallen into the same trap they did. Don't make it any worse for yourself than you already have. Is it a simple trip wire, or a loss-of-tension mechanism?"

Six fifty-three.

"Mr. Harwood, I refuse to believe you're a terrorist."

More heavy coughing. And then in a voice so soft she strained to hear, "It's a loss-of-tension mechanism. If you cut the cord, it will detonate. Open the door slowly and maintain the tension."

It could be the truth. Or it could be a lie. The seconds ticking away were almost audible, almost physical.

Six fifty-five.

The bomb specialist from the ESU was staring at her.

Rizzo hadn't set the explosives, Harwood had.

All glory, laud, and honor
To you, Redeemer, King
To whom the lips of children
Made sweet hosannas ring...

This was Rafer Harwood. A man consumed by hate and self-pity. He saw himself as a martyr.

Thou art the King of Israel
Thou David's royal Son
Who in the Lord's name comest
The King and Blessed One.

She turned to the bomb specialist. "It's a simple trip wire. Cut it."

CHAPTER EIGHTY-SIX

"Kim!"

Abe and Cord shouted it together.

And waited for the blast.

But there was only silence.

And then a gaggle of voices.

"Get those detonators out of there."

"There's a third one here someplace, find it."

"We need the Hazmat guys."

"Who's got evidence bags?"

"Got the third device, up here by the door."

"All three devices cleared."

"Let's get these jugs secured."

"Kim, are you okay?" Marisa's `voice.

A cell phone ring tone.

A moment later, a second. Then a third.

"Kim," Cord yelled. "Are you all right?"

Her voice was steady. "Sorry, Cord. It's a little busy here. I'm fine. Take the terrorist to Central Booking on Centre Street. We'll let the DAs fight over his sorry ass."

CHAPTER EIGHTY-SEVEN

By the time they had all the evidence secured and tagged and the FDNY's Hazmat team had cleaned up the traces of acetone in the boiler room, the first mass of this Palm Sunday at Blessed Mother Church was over. Fr. Lynch came out, still wearing his vestments. "I'm so sorry. Our sexton opened the church before I could warn him, and people streamed in. At that point, I was afraid if I said anything, it might cause a general panic. So, I trusted in God and in you wonderful people."

Kim couldn't believe it. "You said Mass?"

"Thanks to you, Detective. I will write to the Commissioner to express my deepest appreciation for your zeal and courage in preventing what could have been unimaginable carnage here. And I haven't forgotten that you got Blade Morales off the street."

"Thank you, Father. It means a great deal. I wish we could have saved Ms. Westwood, Mr. Avila and Julie Campbell, too."

He patted her shoulder. "I was still a seminarian when I learned you can't save everyone."

"Detective?" It was the sergeant from the protection detail. "With this wrapped up, I take it we can return to our normal duties?"

"Not yet. Two members of the group are still at-large and we can't yet rule out another attempt against the church or Father Lynch. I'll have Captain Forrest make the official request." She turned to Marisa. "Let's go. We still have to track down Quinn and Rizzo."

CHAPTER EIGHTY-EIGHT

"Bomb experts from the NYPD's Emergency Services Unit defused the devices before anyone could detonate them, and Palm Sunday masses proceeded as normal here at Blessed Mother Church. Police confirm a tiny domestic terrorist ring is responsible for this morning's attempt, and most members of that ring are already in custody. One of the two remaining at large, a man identified as Tony Rizzo, is also the prime suspect in five murders in North Brooklyn, including yesterday's killing of NYPD Sergeant Peter Warren. This is Joanna Dunbar reporting."

"Thank you, Joanna. In other news, the FBI now confirms the Coalition for Immigration Justice is not behind the recent wave of street violence, but they are not ready to say who is."

***

Twenty minutes after the piece ended, Captain Forrest's doorbell rang. A moment later, his wife appeared in the den. "You have a visitor."

Senator Brandt barged in right behind her.

Forrest thanked his wife and waited until she left the room. "Good morning, Senator. Early for a social call on a Sunday, isn't it?"

"That bitch detective of yours sold information to that political reporter again, didn't she?"

Forrest took a sip of coffee. "Can I have my wife get you a cup?"

Brandt was seething. "No. DCPI would never release such detailed information so soon after a police action."

"Have you spoken to the deputy commissioner? Did he tell you that?"

Brandt grumbled. "I haven't been able to reach him."

"Well, I have. He granted permission to Lieutenant Zimmerman to give out that information."

That cooled Brandt's jets a bit. "Well… never mind. It's a shame Officer Cadman missed out on this. When will you people clear him so he can return to his duties?"

Not again. "I already explained the matter is out of my hands. He's not fit to be a New York City police officer and our most appropriate action would be immediate termination as a Member of Service. And you have my permission to repeat that to your benefactor."

A lengthy silence. "I see."

"Also, considering the FBI's statement this morning about the CIJ not being responsible for the violence, I suggest you stop beating that drum. Makes you sound like an anti-immigrant conspiracy theorist."

"Well, thank you, *Captain* Forrest." Brandt stormed out.

Captain Forrest sipped from his coffee mug, and for the first time in ten days, the flavor was exquisite.

CHAPTER EIGHTY-NINE

"You should take the rest of the day off, Kim."

It was the first thing Colangelo said when she walked into the office at Hudson Street shortly after noon. But Rizzo and Quinn remained at large. "I'm fine, Lieu. Thanks."

"You're not even within shouting distance of 'fine'. This morning gave Abe chest pains, and he wasn't even there."

"Being dramatic, aren't you?" She tried a grin.

But Colangelo remained serious. "No, he had chest pains. Cord's taken Harwood to Central Booking. He dropped Abe off at New York-Presby on Beekman on his way to Centre Street."

"Then we're down a man. I think I'll stick around." She walked over to the conference room, stunned to see Vera with her head down on the table, surrounded by piles of printouts, asleep. Kim updated the board, keeping as quiet as possible.

The first time her marker squeaked, Vera popped awake. "Ah. It's the brilliant American lady detective."

"Been sleeping like that for long?"

Vera brushed unruly strands of blond hair from her eyes. "*Da.* Every time I wake up, I check on cell phone number. Three calls at seven o'clock this morning, then nothing. As if he went to Siberia."

"Did you check to see what cell towers his phone pinged?" Although she was asking a lot.

"*Da.* I thought you might ask." She pointed to the map. "I marked on map with red x."

"Elmhurst, Queens."

Colangelo entered. "What's in Elmhurst?"

"The cell tower Rizzo pinged this morning when he tried to set off the bombs," Kim said.

Cord joined them. "Any word on Abe?"

Colangelo turned grave. "He's had a heart attack. He's in the CCU. I'm heading over there, now. Kim, they should deliver two brand new Stingrays within the hour. Batteries are one hundred percent charged, and I've received assurances these are new units. They also have phone-tapping capabilities. As soon as Martin and Nolan get back, I'll deploy them with the other one."

"Both deployed to Queens?" What if something popped in Brooklyn?

He considered it. "Yes. Kotsonis gave up Quinn's cell number, and I've given that to the FBI. They're taking over the search for Quinn. They think he lives close to the Eagle, which we've already shut down. Meanwhile, I've got Vera here on loan and she and Marisa can keep track of LUDs and e-mail traffic."

"Hi, Vera," Cord said, then looked sheepish when he saw Kim and the lieu.

"Good afternoon, Detective." Vera was being coy, stringy hair and puffy eyes notwithstanding.

"Yes," Kim said. "Good afternoon, Detective."

Cord turned serious. "Hi, Kim. I can't believe you did that this morning. Gutsiest thing I've ever…"

"Thanks, Cord. But I don't want to talk about it." Not going there. Not thinking about what would have happened if she'd been wrong.

Before Cord could answer, Colangelo said, "Kim, if Vera can check one of those new Stingrays and make sure it's functioning, I'd appreciate it if you and Cord could get out to Elmhurst as soon as possible. Vera will contact you with any new information she gets." He retreated to his office.

Kim grinned at Vera and Cord. "I guess you two will need a little time to… um… check out the equipment." She smirked seeing Vera blush.

CHAPTER NINETY

They rode in silence until she was entering the Midtown Tunnel. "I take it the Stingray checked out all right?"

"Fine. Battery at one hundred percent."

"Yours or the machine's?"

"This is the latest model, much better than the last ones we had."

"Make a date, yet? Or stuck at the flirting stage?" But he said nothing, staring out the car window at the passing tiles and lights. She waited until they were out of the tunnel, speeding eastward. "I have to give her credit. A girl has something if she's an effective flirt after two straight all-nighters." She turned serious. "I'm glad you were able to get past it."

"She's funny," he said at last. "She says what she thinks, like there's no filter."

"Some would call that socially inappropriate."

"No doubt. Getting off at Queens Boulevard?"

"No, Woodhaven. The cell tower he pinged is a short distance west of the Queens Center Mall."

The shrill ring of her own cell reverberated from the car speakers. It was Vera. "He called Harwood's cell two minutes ago. Same tower. Bob and Martin are on the way."

"Thanks, Vera."

Cord already had the Stingray on and had entered Rizzo's cell number. "So, his phone will think this is a cell tower and link to it. And if he makes a call, this will pass it through to the nearest real cell tower. And we'll hear it?"

"Yes, and with the wiretap warrant Judge Castellano was good enough to provide, along with everything else, we'll be able to use anything we hear."

Three blocks east of the mall, Cord said, "Got him."

"Radio the address to Nolan and get an ETA."

A moment later, Martin's voice crackled on the speaker. "Be there in ten to fifteen minutes. Over."

Kim took the mic. "We'll wait as long as we can, but if he moves, we'll have to take him ourselves. Hope you're both wearing vests. Over."

"That's affirm. Out."

They pulled up to a rundown motel.

"This is it." Cord was still staring at the screen. "He's making another call." A pause. "Holy shit. He's calling Quinn's cell."

"Call Marisa. And set to record."

Quinn picked up on the second ring. "What the fuck went wrong? The news says they prevented the bombing and arrested members of the ring."

"I don't know," Rizzo replied. "I can't reach Harwood, Kotsonis or Lamonica."

"That means they're all in the can, asshole. This is a fuckup of biblical proportions. Where are you, now?"

"In the motel, like we planned. You still at your place?"

"They've shut down the Eagle. I'm crashing at my sister's, over by the Met Oval. I'll swing by to pick you up in half an hour, and we'll get out of the city for a while. Lie low until you hear from me."

The call ended.

The odds of collaring these two motherfuckers were improving by the minute. "Pass the info on to Marisa and have her pass it on to the FBI."

"Do we wait for Quinn's arrival and grab them both?"

"No way. It's 'every man for himself' time. Quinn has no intention of coming for Rizzo. He's going to run as soon as he can pack."

Bob and Martin pulled up. "Fast enough for you?"

"Perfect." She gave them the update. "You two cover the fire exits. Cord and I will take him."

She and Cord entered the lobby. The desk clerk was fiddling with his cell phone while a housekeeper vacuumed the waiting area. Kim flashed her badge at the housekeeper who turned off the vacuum cleaner and shrank back, then at the desk clerk, who dropped his phone.

Kim pulled out the sketch. "This man is staying here. He's here, now. What room?"

The clerk was trembling. "I... I don't know if I can..."

"Tell me now, or I arrest you as an accessory to all the murders he's committed."

"Two sixteen.

Not on the ground floor. One less escape route available. "Stay off the phone. You tell nobody. Is there a stairway?"

He pointed to her right.

"Man," Cord whispered as they climbed. "You are one tough..."

"Watch yourself."

"...accomplished female detective."

The floor was quiet. A housekeeping cart sat halfway down the hall and the smell of disinfectant hung heavy. A "privacy, please" tag hung on the doorknob of two-sixteen. Sorry, Rizzo, but there won't be any privacy where you're going.

She knocked on the door. "Good morning. Housekeeping."

"Later," Rizzo called through the door.

"Your toilet's leaking into the room downstairs, sir. I gotta get in now."

The door lock clicked, and Rizzo opened it a crack. Kim and Cord both pushed hard, catching Rizzo off balance and knocking him to the floor.

She kept her feet and leveled her Glock at him. "Freeze."

He gestured his surrender.

"Stand and keep your hands visible."

Cord pulled him up, a little rougher than necessary, and cuffed him.

"Anthony Rizzo," she said, "you are under arrest for the murders of Joey Simmons, Mariano Avila, Julie Campbell, Jamelia Westwood, and Police Sergeant Peter Warren; the abduction and unlawful imprisonment of Amara Delgado; the attempted murders of Amara Delgado and Cliff Conroy; attempted arson; and for conspiracy to commit a terrorist act." She recited his Miranda rights.

301

"Look what I found." Cord, already wearing latex gloves, picked up an assisted-opening knife. "We been looking for this, Pizza Man." He dropped it into an evidence bag.

"Let's go, Rizzo," Kim said. Once they were back outside, she handed Rizzo's keys over to Bob. "We'll process the arrest. You go conduct the search."

CHAPTER NINETY-ONE

"I have to say, Rizzo, you haven't left me much room to trade up." Kim parked at the Hudson Street office. "About all you have left to give me is Tom Quinn, and we're on his tail, now. As I already explained, you don't have to say anything, and you can wait until they assign a lawyer to you before you do. But once we collar Quinn, I lose any incentive to talk to you. If you tell us exactly where he is and where he's going, and who else he's connected to, I can ask the DA to go easy on you."

"How easy?"

He was aware of how fucked he was. Good. She waited until they were in an interrogation room to answer him. "You'll be charged with five murders, second degree, each of which carries a twenty-five-to-life term. Those can either be consecutive, meaning you serve each one in turn, or concurrent, meaning one sentence for all five. Makes a sizeable difference in total years you serve."

"What about the other charges?"

"That would be up to the DA. But I can vouch for you, explaining you helped us out when we needed it."

"You done some nasty shit, Pizza Man," Cord said.

"Stop calling me that, mud..."

Cord jumped up to his full six-four height and leaned over the table. "Whatchoo say, Pizza Man?"

Rizzo swallowed hard. "Sorry."

"You know, Rizzo," Kim said, "on second thought, I don't really need you for anything."

Colangelo walked in a moment after Cord returned to his seat. "Martin called. They're still at Rizzo's chop shop. At least a dozen more jugs of acetone, a bunch of detonators, and a lot of shit about pagan symbols. They're waiting for CSU. Also, Ken Taylor called. The FBI collared Quinn. They thank you for the intel on his location."

Rizzo's face fell.

"There goes your bargaining chip, Bro."

"Cord," she said, "please take him to Central Booking and…"

"No," Colangelo said. "Take him to Brooklyn North Homicide. They'll handle processing him in Brooklyn. Kim, I need to talk to you."

CHAPTER NINETY-TWO

Colangelo closed the door to his office as Kim took a seat. "We're through playing Musical Prosecutors."

"I don't understand."

"Yes, you do. You're trying to end-run Let 'em run Ron. I don't blame you, but I heard from Yvette Driscoll. It seems the Brooklyn DA's office has taken umbrage at your sudden change of boroughs and threatened to go to court to mandate assignment of these cases to them. The Manhattan DA's office has already assured them that won't be necessary."

"I figured that might happen."

"Then you shouldn't have pushed it. I realize you meant well, but this entire case has engendered significant ill-will from the Brooklyn political establishment toward the department, and the commissioner is not pleased."

"What ill will? Because we caught a serial killer and kept one of their churches from being firebombed?"

"Because we appear to have cut corners to do it. Harwood's attorney has already moved to dismiss all charges. In Brooklyn. The hearing is tomorrow morning."

"If you tell me Vickers is presiding…"

"Not likely. But call Rick Conti, now, and advise him you'll be there." As she rose to leave, he added, "Take some leave. You've earned it."

"Thanks. I'll stop by to see Abe on my way home."

CHAPTER NINETY-THREE

Kim found Abe awake and alert. The constant beeping from the monitors was only somewhat distracting. "The FBI got Quinn. We got Rizzo."

"And Harwood and the rest. Plus, the church didn't blow up. That's a damned fine week's work, Detective. Glad I got to work with you before I drop my papers."

"You're retiring?"

"Turns out the heartburn, indigestion, and nausea were warnings. This is a louder warning. Maybe my last one. Suppose I'd been the one at the church this morning instead of on the phone?" He shook his head. "Doesn't bear thinking about. I've already got thirty years in. That's enough."

"Any chance they'll offer you a soft assignment to stay on?"

"In your dad's day, that was possible. But today, they'll be glad to pension me off. Replace me with someone younger. And cheaper."

She had to admit he was right.

"You okay, Kim? You don't look so good."

"Wear and tear, combined with possible pending political bullshit." She told him about the latest on the case.

"See," he said, "that's another reason I'll be glad to retire. The political establishment of this city has already forgotten everything we learned in the nineties about policing and law enforcement. Watch yourself at that hearing tomorrow. Don't let them trap you or finagle you into second-guessing yourself on this case. And don't let them try to blame you for Cadman's fuckup."

"How could they do that? They violated regulations by even assigning Cadman to IAB." It made her angry every time she thought about it.

"Right. So, we know there is someone highly placed who stands to lose a lot if the dirty details come out. And whoever that is will do everything possible to make it appear like you screwed the pooch."

"Then I guess I'll have to make sure I have all my facts in order. I'm sure as hell not backing down."

As she was leaving the hospital, her cell buzzed with a text from Joanna Dunbar. *Got confirmation that Kyle Emory is the sole source of funding for the Law and Order PAC, which is supporting Brandt for mayor. Emory is Brandt's deep pocket.*

CHAPTER NINETY-FOUR

Monday, March 26th

Rick Conti had met her outside the courtroom. His demeanor was nothing like the friendly camaraderie they'd enjoyed when he was first assigned to the case. "We're in an odd situation, here. We need to make sure Harwood doesn't win his motion to dismiss, but to do that, I'll have to be judicious about my protection of you. I may not object every time you think I should."

Now, she was on the stand, Harwood's attorney having called her as a witness. He asked for permission to treat her as a hostile witness before he'd asked a single question. The judge, who at least was someone other than Vickers, granted permission.

"Detective Brady, you say that you assigned Detective Cadman for the sole purpose of observing my client's movements while you allegedly questioned a certain Jeff Desmond, correct?"

"First, David Cadman is not a detective, he is a police officer. Second, I did not 'allegedly' question Mr. Desmond, I did question him, along with Detective Martin Stransky, and Mr. Desmond signed the statement he gave us. As to your question, yes, Officer Cadman's instructions were to observe Mr. Harwood's movements and report them to me. I…"

"Thank you, Detect…"

Not so fast, Counselor. "I instructed him not to take any other action without my prior approval. I was specific on that point."

"And why was that?"

She'd thought long and hard planning this. It was the only way. "Because Officer Cadman had precious little experience before being assigned to Internal Affairs. And part of my job was to complete his training."

"Hadn't he graduated from the Police Academy?"

"Yes."

"And yet you thought he hadn't been adequately trained?"

"Not to my satisfaction, no."

"Your satisfaction?"

"That's right. Some of Officer Cadman's comments indicated a less-than-complete understanding of the law and proper procedure."

The attorney took a step closer. "Can you please be specific? In what ways was Officer Cadman lacking, and what did you do about it?"

She stared at Conti, who turned away. Put me on a spit and spoon on the sauce? I don't think so. She said nothing.

"Detective?"

Not yet.

"Your honor," the attorney said, "please instruct the witness to answer."

The judge turned to her. "Detective Brady, please answer the question."

"I'm waiting for the District Attorney to object to the question as irrelevant, since the issue is whether the statement illegally obtained by Officer Cadman played any part in any subsequent police action."

"Does the District Attorney wish to object?" the judge asked.

"Not at this time, your honor."

The judge turned back to Kim. "Then I must instruct you to answer the question, Detective."

Here goes. "Very well. In several instances, he demonstrated a lack of understanding of and appreciation for certain constitutional protections and the procedures we are required to follow to assure those protections. I used some of our time together to quiz him on the law and procedure."

"And you believe yourself to be qualified in that area, Detective?"

"Yes, I do. I excelled in it at John Jay College and later at the Academy. You have my permission to request my academic records."

"But your informal education was quite different, wasn't it?"

She caught the scent in the wind. "If you're referring to my practical education once I began working, Counselor, no, it did not contradict what I learned at the Academy. And if you check the record, you will see I earned commendations both in the Seven-Three and at Manhattan South Homicide…"

"That is not what I meant, Detective."

Make him say it. "Then I don't know what you meant."

"Wasn't your father also a New York City detective?"

"Yes, he was. So was my grandfather, who was killed in the line of duty."

"But your father was not. Nor was he as pure about the law as you claim to be, correct?"

She glared at Conti. He still wouldn't meet her gaze. Well, Rick, you can go fuck yourself. "My father is dead, Counselor. He has zero relevance to this case."

"But the example he set for his daughter, who has followed in his footsteps, is quite relevant. And that example is far from pristine, isn't it?"

"He taught me to always be true to the law and to myself."

"I asked about his example. You're a member of the Internal Affairs Division. In that capacity, would you judge all his actions as 'true to the law'?"

Still nothing from Conti. She leaned forward in the witness box. "What do you think, Mr. District Attorney? Doesn't that call for speculation? Shouldn't you be objecting?"

Harwood's attorney flared. "Request to strike as nonresponsive."

The judge banged his gavel once. "Strike both the question and answer. Move on, counselor."

The attorney shrugged. "Detective, didn't your father commit suicide?"

"Yes."

"Isn't it safe to assume guilt was the reason?"

"I don't know what the reason was, Counselor. He never told me he was going to do it. And I refuse to answer any more questions about my father, who has no connection with this case."

"Very well. What was your reaction when my client was released on his own recognizance?"

"I thought it was wrong. The reasoning was that we had arrested him on accomplice information, when in fact Mr. Desmond was not and had never been part of the plot of which Mr. Harwood stands accused."

"And that's why you had my client shadowed?"

"Yes."

"Is that also why you suddenly requested search warrants and arrest warrants through the Manhattan DA's office from a Manhattan judge? To avoid dealing with a judge who disagreed with your unprofessional interpretation of the law?"

"This was an IAB case because someone impersonating a police officer had committed the murder of Mariano Avila. IAB is based in Manhattan. Our working relationships are in Manhattan. The conspiracy of which this was a part spanned multiple boroughs. But the most important factor was speed. We needed to expedite those warrants because we knew a major terrorist event was in the offing."

"And Judge Vickers never entered your calculations? Even after he denied your request for a warrant to search my client's computer? You vehemently disagreed with his decision, didn't you?"

"Yes, I disagreed with it."

"With vehemence?"

"I argued with him about it. I still believe I was correct."

The attorney leaned forward. "And that entered your decision to seek a friendlier judge in another borough."

Another glance at Conti. Nothing. "Are you asking me or telling me?"

"My apologies. Did it?"

"I've already testified that my concern was speed. I also knew that whoever signed off on the warrants, the case would be tried wherever it was appropriate to try it, and that wasn't my decision."

CHAPTER NINETY-FIVE

Rick Conti caught up with Kim as she was leaving the courthouse. "You've got one hell of a nerve, Detective. I look like an ass, thanks to you."

"Oh, no, all credit for that is yours alone, with your desperation to appear objective. Even a first-year law student would have known what Harwood's lawyer was pulling. And she would've done far better protecting her witness than you did."

"You weren't my witness."

"Yeah? And what do you expect me to do at Harwood's trial, assuming the judge doesn't agree to dismiss the charges? Or do you plan on pleading him out with a wrist-slap to avoid looking worse than you already do?"

"The reason we look bad is that your cowboy cop tortured him. And his lawyer's going to claim the bomb plot was a reaction to being tortured."

"We have ironclad evidence Harwood and Quinn devised the plot months before that happened. Not that you'll look at it. But don't worry. Just put me on the stand, let his lawyer bring up my father, and trust everything will turn out all right." She started down the steps.

He called after her. "It's not over about Cadman."

She froze. "What do you mean?"

"I heard this morning. Cadman comes off Administrative Leave next Monday. You didn't do yourself any good with what you said on the stand. I guess I owe you a heads-up."

"You owe me a lot more than that."

CHAPTER NINETY-SIX

Thursday, March 29th

"The FBI today announced the arrest in Louisiana of one Juan Caballo, charging him with running a human trafficking ring targeting undocumented immigrants. The ring is allegedly a link in a chain that provided teenaged girls for the prostitution operation recently shut down in East New York. In other news, the FBI arrested two individuals charged with inciting the recent riots across the city following their release from custody by the New York City Department of Corrections. The Southern District of New York intends to file charges against them in federal court, where New York State's new liberal bail rules will not apply. The two individuals now in FBI custody are part of a radical Marxist group called Come Home Ernesto. Police officials are cautiously optimistic that the recent wave of violence is at an end."

***

Jake had echoed Colangelo's suggestion for Kim to take some leave and cool down. At first, she'd resisted, but it turned out to be what she needed, especially after being interviewed by another unit in IAB on Tuesday about Cadman. She'd told them everything she knew but did not speculate about a rabbi, saying only, "From the beginning, it baffled me how someone with nine months on the job could have qualified for Internal Affairs." She felt tremendous satisfaction placing it in the record.

Ken Taylor called. "Have you seen the news about Caballo? We've shut down his whole sick operation."

"Yes, and I also saw your other news about Come Home Ernesto."

"They're now in federal custody. And they're not so dedicated that they won't talk. Not sure we'll be able to shut them down completely, but we've got a handle on them. Thanks for the tip, Kim. We'd never have known to look at them, otherwise."

"Glad we could help each other. Anything on Amara Delgado's parents?"

"Yes. We learned they were working in a sweatshop in the Bronx with a bunch of other undocumented immigrants bamboozled the same way. A city agency somehow discovered it and arrived before us, so ICE remained unaware and uninvolved."

"You're a good man, Ken."

He sighed. "We do what we can. It would be nice if we could have a rational discussion and arrive at a sane and reasonable immigration policy and end this nonsense."

"Amen to that, Agent Taylor." As she ended the call, she sank into an easy chair. Amara would soon be with her parents.

She wouldn't need Kim to make good on her promise.

She stared out the window at the magnolia, now in bloom, and took several deep breaths. It was best for Amara.

But the memory of that desperate, clutching embrace at Youth Colony wouldn't go away.

CHAPTER NINETY-SEVEN

Friday, March 30th

Colangelo was waiting for her as she entered the office on Hudson Street. "Got a minute, Kim?"

She followed him down the hall to Captain Forrest's office and braced herself. Sometimes, you could sense shit waiting to fall on you.

"Glad to see you, Kim," Forrest said. He nodded to Colangelo, who left, closing the door behind him. "Coffee?"

"No, thanks." When in doubt, press. "Is it true that Cadman is being returned to active duty on Monday?"

He shifted in his seat. "If you don't already know, the judge ruled that your arrest of Conroy and all evidence from subsequent warrants was not fruit of the poisonous tree and therefore was admissible. The Brooklyn DA decided not to turn the case over to the feds. They'll all be prosecuted in Brooklyn."

"Okay, but…"

"I want to say that you have handled yourself with complete professionalism. I do wish you had informed us how unprepared Cadman was, though. We might have been able to move him."

"I voiced my concerns at the beginning, and Lieutenant Colangelo knew I was quizzing him on the law, and his other shortcomings. And I'd think assigning someone with his lack of experience and training to IAB would have been a warning to anybody."

"Yes, well, to answer your question, Cadman is not being reassigned. He's being discharged from the department. Both IAB and the commissioner found your statements convincing."

"Not to mention that returning him to active duty with no disciplinary action would only bolster Harwood's civil suit against the city."

"I would think that a convicted terrorist would likely have difficulty prevailing in such a suit." He looked drained. "That's rather cynical of both of us. It's hard not to be if you have experience in police work. And I've probably been in it for too long, which is why I'm retiring soon."

Kim couldn't hide her surprise. "I heard a rumor about you making deputy inspector."

A sad smile. "No." It looked like he had more to say about it, but he shifted gears. "Coburn and Tyler have been demoted from detective back to police officer and assigned to precincts in different boroughs. The captain of the Seven-Four has been relieved for ignoring Morales' prostitution ring, which was clearly common knowledge in the precinct. Burrows has been reassigned to the Property Clerk's office."

She had to admit, that was an excellent result considering the cards she'd been dealt.

Forrest cleared his throat. "Anyway, there is the matter of your position."

"What about it?"

"You still have thirteen months left on your tour of duty with us, but this case shows where your true talents lie. You are, hands down, the best homicide investigator I've ever seen, so…"

"Wait a minute. You're transferring me out of Internal Affairs a year early and then retiring? How do you think that's going to look, especially since the public already links my name to Cadman's? It'll look like a complete housecleaning."

"Anyone knowing all the facts understands that's not true."

"And that's what? Eight people? Ten? Jesus, maybe we should've let them firebomb the damned church."

"No one will forget the brilliant work you did, Kim. Under other circumstances, you'd have gotten another Meritorious Duty citation."

"You mean, if I hadn't been saddled with an asshole like Cadman."

Forrest gave a heavy sigh and sat back. "I'm sorry, Kim. This wasn't my decision. It's out of my hands. God's truth."

"So, whose decision was it?"

"The Chief of Detectives. He implied the commissioner insisted, but that may have been smoke. And he approved of my decision to retire. Between us, I think he's glad to have all of us—you, me, and Cadman—out of IAB."

"A purge." Kim couldn't hide her disgust.

"I doubt that. More like scrubbing the institutional memory and allowing IAB to move on."

There was no point in battling with Forrest any further. "Okay, Captain, let's get it over with. Which command and when do I report?"

"Brooklyn North Homicide, and you report Monday morning. At least you won't have a heavy commute."

She almost gagged. "Brooklyn?"

"North. Abe Stewart is retiring. Health reasons. They have a need, and you'll fill it well."

"Oh, that's peachy. And the first time I need a search warrant, I get to ask Rick Conti, who we last saw leaving me twisting in the wind on the witness stand."

"You handled yourself with perfect aplomb, Kim."

"Well enough to get my ass transferred out of IAB." She stood. "Thanks, but unless you have anything else official to tell me, I think I'll leave before I totally lose it."

"Sorry, Kim."

She stopped at the door. "Joanna Dunbar found a direct link between Kyle Emory and Ray Brandt. Emory is funding Brandt's campaign outside of the constraints of the campaign finance law, and Loretta Cadman is

Emory's secretary and vacation companion. In case you were interested."

"She gave you that for free?"

"Because I needed the information. And she alerted me to the fact that a radical group had infiltrated the CIJ, a tip I passed on to Ken Taylor with excellent result."

CHAPTER NINETY-EIGHT

Cord greeted her when she returned to her desk. "Sorry, Kim."

She liked that about him. No bullshit or pretending he didn't know. "Thanks. Had a date with Vera, yet?"

He broke into a sheepish grin. "Yeah. I stayed at her place last night."

She wanted to ask more, but Colangelo called her into his office and closed the door. "I fought him on it, Kim. You must realize that. I also recommended you for a citation. He nixed it. But I believe it's out of his hands."

"Yeah, I figured."

"An awful lot of the history people carry with them in this department is unofficial."

"I've heard that. I can imagine what my history might look like."

He broke into a grin. "It won't be that you fucked up with Cadman. It'll be that he caused you to be fucked over."

"Thanks, Lieu. In the meantime, who'll square things between me and Rick Conti?"

His grin turned to a laugh. "You and he will square them. Because you'll each need the other's cooperation. You're both excellent at your jobs. Sometimes, there's an invisible hand working."

"I've been at this too long to fall for romantic mysticism. You know me better than that."

"I know you better than you realize. You're so much like your dad was, but without the missteps that caused the guilt. You have your own way of doing things, an independence that those without a political agenda in the department love and admire, and those with a political agenda loathe and despise. Whatever you do, you leave your own special footprint."

He was trying to tell her something, but she wasn't thinking clearly enough to decipher it. "Thanks. Can you at least tell me if Forrest wanted me out? Because I'd totally like some part of this day to be straight talk."

"Understandable. Okay. It wasn't his idea, but he didn't fight it. It came from the Chief of Detectives, but I'm certain it wasn't his idea, either. That leaves the commissioner. In which case no amount of fighting would have changed things. Forrest probably figured, fuck it."

So, it had to be to appease Emory. She wondered for a moment if Emory had sent Loretta Cadman packing, too. That might mean she'd have to go back to buying her clothes at discount stores. "What about the decision to send me to Brooklyn North Homicide?"

"That was within IAB."

Colangelo. He knew Abe was dropping his papers, so no one would veto it. And he'd predicted that she and Conti would work out their differences. With complete confidence.

But Ray Brandt's base was in Brooklyn, and Kyle Emory gave him enough juice to get Forrest promoted to Deputy Inspector in return for a favor, if only his protégé hadn't fucked up at the worst imaginable time. It gave some credence to Colangelo's notion of an invisible hand.

Or hands.

"I can't tell you anything else, Kim." It was as if Colangelo was reading her mind. "I may have already said too much."

She reached out and shook his hand. She was going to miss him a lot. "You said just the right amount."

***

Kim packed a box of her belongings from the office. A small box—she had accumulated little in a single year at IAB. Cord, Martin, and Marisa had taken her to lunch. Bob Nolan called to tell her that, while politics sucked, he was looking forward to working with her. Word was spreading fast. Life in the NYPD. Rick Conti probably already knew.

Ken Taylor texted. A good ally to have. *Amara and her parents will settle in Corona, Queens. Call me if you ever need my help. The FBI has your back.* A good ally, indeed.

She said her goodbyes and was out the door. Never look back.

Joanna Dunbar intercepted her on Hudson Street, having waited inside the Sprout Deli. "They kicked you out? Well, I guess it fits. I was all set to report on Brandt's money from Emory and his access to the NYPD hierarchy, but the station killed it. Said they didn't want to drag Emory into it without knowing all the facts."

"Sorry to hear it, Joanna. I know you've done a lot of work on this, and I appreciate you passing on your intel to me. I have my own issues." She told her about her transfer.

"Another addition to my growing list of things that suck. Catch this: far from sending Loretta Cadman packing, Emory has hired her brother for some as-yet-undefined position."

Kim smirked. "She must have some skill set."

"Yeah," Joanna replied with a laugh. "No wonder I'm turning into a cynic. And thanks for the intel you passed on to me. I can't use it, now, but there's no telling when or how I might use it in the future." She paused for a moment. "They're sending you into Brandt territory. This could get interesting."

"I guess."

"He's already backtracking on the terrible things he said about the CIJ, affirming his unwavering support for a healthy immigration policy." Joanna grinned. "We make a rather striking team, a cynical cop and a cynical reporter."

Another wonderful ally to have. Maybe Colangelo had known what he was doing.

CHAPTER NINETY-NINE

She'd called ahead to Jake to tell him, so he was watching for her when the cab pulled up and she stepped out.

He welcomed her home with a hug. Already settling into his new position, he insisted they dine out that evening, with reservations at the River Café, in the shadow of the Brooklyn Bridge.

She decided on a dress and heels—a special effort to not look like a cop. As she got ready, she couldn't push away all her thoughts of Amara. It was wonderful that they had reunited her with her family. And yet, Kim kept coming back to the last time she'd seen Amara, when she'd promised her that if they couldn't find her parents, Kim would always look out for her.

Amara had clung to her.

Kim hadn't wanted to let go. It was an emotion she'd never experienced before.

"You ready?" Jake's voice startled her.

"Sure."

It was a quick cab ride to the restaurant. Throughout dinner, Jake talked about his recent promotion, how involved he was in the decision-making, and how it wouldn't be long before the Nets were a legitimate NBA contender. She made what she thought were the appropriate appreciative comments.

"Okay," he said over dessert. "What's the deal? You've been quieter tonight than any time since we first met. I know you're bummed about your gig in IAB ending early, but I think Homicide is where you belong."

"It's not that."

He took both her hands in his. "Then what is it?"

She'd been so adamant. And it had been settled.

Except it really wasn't, not for Jake.

She told him about the last time she'd seen Amara.

And about the hug.

"So, what are you saying?" He looked like he was holding his breath.

"I'm uncertain," she said at last, "but I'm thinking that maybe, after you've settled into your new position and I've settled in at Brooklyn North, a child wouldn't be such a terrible idea. Perhaps a foster child, someone like Amara who needs our help. Or maybe one of our own."

A huge grin broke out despite his obvious effort to suppress it, and he squeezed her hands. "We'll figure it out."

Yes, they would.

ACKNOWLEDGEMENTS

It's sometimes said that writing the second novel is harder than writing the first. I didn't find it that way. And it helped that Reagan Rothe of Black Rose Writing extended an invitation to submit the manuscript even while I was still polishing it. Many thanks, also, to the other folks at Black Rose who do such a great job: David King for his cover design, Chris Martin for publicity, Justin Weeks in sales, and Minna Rothe in marketing.

I must thank my intrepid beta readers for their support and advice: Jan Foley, Ray Lodato, and Sydney Young. My wife of 45 years, Cindy, was a beta reader but also a constant support and faithful critic, pointing out the latest features on the Investigative Discovery channel and waking to the sound of my clattering keyboard every morning

ABOUT THE AUTHOR

Edward J. Leahy was a finalist for the 2018 Freddie Award for Excellence. He is a member of Mystery Writers of America and International Thriller Writers and has been published by *New York Teacher Magazine*. He's a retired International Issue Specialist for the IRS with investigative experience and holds a B. A. and M. A. from St. John's University in Government & Politics. He serves on the Board of Directors of AHRC-NYC.

NOTE FROM THE AUTHOR

Word-of-mouth is crucial for any author to succeed. If you enjoyed *Deceived by Ornament*, please leave a review online—anywhere you are able. Even if it's just a sentence or two. It would make all the difference and would be very much appreciated.

Thanks!
Edward J. Leahy

NOTE FROM THE AUTHOR

Word of mouth is crucial for any author to succeed. If you enjoyed [this book], please leave a review online — even if it's just a sentence or two. It would make all the difference and would be very much appreciated.

Thanks!
Edward Lewis

We hope you enjoyed reading this title from:

BLACK❦ROSE
writing™

www.blackrosewriting.com

Subscribe to our mailing list – *The Rosevine* – and receive **FREE** books, daily deals, and stay current with news about upcoming releases and our hottest authors.
Scan the QR code below to sign up.

Already a subscriber? Please accept a sincere thank you for being a fan of Black Rose Writing authors.

View other Black Rose Writing titles at
www.blackrosewriting.com/books and use promo code
PRINT to receive a **20% discount** when purchasing.

www.ingramcontent.com/pod-product-compliance
Lightning Source LLC
Chambersburg PA
CBHW010727100726
47899CB00009B/2955

* 9 7 8 1 6 8 4 3 3 9 0 7 5 *